# Murder at the Maple Festival

# MURDER AT THE MAPLE FESTIVAL

Paul A. Newman

# MURDER AT THE MAPLE FESTIVAL

*iUniverse books may be ordered through booksellers or by contacting:*

*iUniverse*
*1663 Liberty Drive*
*Bloomington, IN 47403*
*www.iuniverse.com*
*1-800-Authors (1-800-288-4677)*

*Because of the dynamic nature of the Internet, any web addresses or links contained in this book may have changed since publication and may no longer be valid. The views expressed in this work are solely those of the author and do not necessarily reflect the views of the publisher, and the publisher hereby disclaims any responsibility for them.*

*Any people depicted in stock imagery provided by Thinkstock are models, and such images are being used for illustrative purposes only. Certain stock imagery © Thinkstock.*

*ISBN: 978-1-4917-5246-3 (sc)*
*ISBN: 978-1-4917-5245-6 (e)*

*Library of Congress Control Number: 2014919626*

*Printed in the United States of America.*

*iUniverse rev. date: 10/30/2014*

# CHAPTER 1

S pring does not arrive in Chardon, Ohio until the close of the Maple
Festival, held annually the first week following Easter. This year was
no exception to the general rule; the snow descended in swirling gusts. The
weather wanted to be warm, but it was in conflict with Old Man Winter,
who wouldn't let go. Consequently, the raw winter wind blew heavy, wet
snow that stuck to clothing, skin, and eyeglasses.

Tim Snyder, twirling his mustache that is too long, Burton police
sergeant on temporary loan to the Maple Festival for security, exited the
tent covering the entire 250 feet of Short Court Street in front of the
courthouse. In five more minutes, it would be 7:30 a.m., and he would be
relieved of duty protecting the vendors' wares from thieves, vandals, and
miscreants. He could only remember one instance, three years ago, when
a vendor complained of property missing.

Tim looked at the courthouse through the blowing snow, a typical
Maple Festival Friday. Built in 1869, its Victorian architecture made a
stately appearance. The activity at the courthouse would begin soon; it
opened for business at 8:00 a.m. Tim watched Linda, the second-floor
magistrate's secretary, rush out of the courthouse, look around wildly, spot
him—he was hard to miss, he knew; his height and handlebar mustache
made him easy to spot—and rush down the steps, almost falling. She
caught herself on the rail, jumped the last three steps, and rushed toward
him. He hadn't moved.

"The judge has been killed!" she wailed, tears blotching her eye
makeup.

"Where?"

"Second-floor bathroom. Ohhh!"

Tim glanced at his watch: 7:28.

"Linda, don't let anybody in the courthouse. I'm going to check it out. I'll call the station. No one comes in, okay?"

"Okay ... ohh!"

Tim rushed up the steps past Linda, ripped open the massive outer door, the second door past the security desk, and headed through the magnetic security arch, down the black-and-white checkerboard-squared marble hall floor, to the second-floor steps. The elevator, a remnant of the 1950s, was too slow. Up the steps, turn right, up the steps, turn left toward the bailiff's office, down the hall, past the secretary's office, up three more steps. He kicked the partially open bathroom door all the way open.

Earl William Kuhmer, or EW, as the judge was known, was bent over the toilet, his head immersed in the water, the left side of his face showing. His hands and arms were slack as if he were embracing the bowl. His pants were lowered. A small baseball bat, the kind received from Jacobs Field for kids' night, was sticking out of Earl William's butt. And a huge butt it was. EW must have weighed 310 pounds.

"God save Ireland," muttered Tim, as he bent to his old Irish slang.

Tim put his hand on EW's hip, pushed slightly, no movement at all, rigor mortis, stiff. Clearly he was dead, but he knew that already by looking at him. Time of murder ran through his mind.

Tim bent over and peered closely into the toilet at EW, whose face was tilted slightly. He saw a large welt on EW's forehead: something had hit him. The toilet was to the left of the entrance. Facing to the right was a sink with a paper towel dispenser on its left. Tim touched nothing.

He pressed his radio, called Dispatch, but guarded his commentary, because he knew many people listened to the police scanner to keep up on community activity.

"Dispatch, Snyder here. I'm at the courthouse, EW's floor. Need Lieutenant McKenna here ASAP. And need a forensic team."

"Dispatch. Say again, Snyder."

Tim repeated his message.

"Dispatch. Care to elaborate, Snyder?"

"Snyder. No, but please move quickly. Out."

Tim took his Minolta DiMAGE-Xi from his pocket. He always carried a small camera just for these incidents. He shot four angles in the bathroom, EW from the top, and reached his arm so he could get the backside too.

He took photos of the hallway leading to the bathroom, walked to the judge's chambers, edged the door open without touching anything, and photographed the walls, the desk, and the floor. He looked toward the magistrate's and court reporter's rooms: the doors were shut. The clerk of court's office was shut. He heard commotion coming up the steps.

He put the camera back into his pocket as Lt. Mike McKenna bounded up the steps.

"What and where?"

"EW has been killed. In the bathroom, down the hall. Might not want too many people up here just yet."

"Okay, seal it off. I'll go see."

Tim Snyder stood by the steps to prevent anyone else from entering the second floor.

Several minutes passed before the lieutenant came back.

"Yup, he's dead all right. Now what the hell are we gonna do? I'll call it in. We don't have the people to do this. Let's keep everyone out of the building. You stand at the desk. No one comes to the second floor. Keep the building empty until the scientifics make their exam."

Tim went downstairs to the front entrance. Linda was sitting at the sheriff deputy's station, shaking, still crying.

"I'll take over, Linda. Why don't you go sit in the hallway there?"

Linda stood like a zombie, walked down the hall, and sat on the long, wooden bench.

Tim kept everyone out of the courthouse, turning them away without telling them the reason. "A safety issue. Go get a cup of coffee, maybe later. Sorry, can't let you in. Well, it's an emergency, really. Just can't let you in. Sorry."

The deputy arrived at 7:45—he was supposed to be on the job by 7:30.

"Howdy, Tim, what are you doing here?"

"Got a problem, Greg. Can't let anybody into the courthouse." He told three clerks they couldn't enter; they started to argue.

"Joan," Tim asserted sternly, "you may as well get some coffee somewhere else; no one is coming in, got it?"

After they left, grumbling, Tim told Greg that EW had been found dead. "Lieutenant McKenna is upstairs. He says no one comes in."

"Jesus! Okay, I got it. Heart attack?"

"No, I think he was killed. It's going to be interesting."

"Killed, like in murdered?"

Tim nodded his assent.

"Okay," Greg said slowly, shaking his head in disbelief. "No one except the proper people, of course. I'll take over."

Tim ascended to the second floor. McKenna was standing at the top of the steps.

"Who's watching the door?"

"Greg—sheriff's deputy. It's his job there. I told him no one but cops."

"Chief's on his way over. Says don't do anything until he arrives. I told him we need forensics; he said he'd make that decision." The lieutenant raised his eyebrows, rolled his eyes.

Tim compressed his lips, said nothing, and nodded his head in agreement.

After a minute, Mike said, "Well, maybe forensics would rather examine later than earlier anyway."

"God save Ireland."

# CHAPTER 2

"Watch it, here he comes," the lieutenant whispered as they heard the clunking up the steps.

Chief of Police David Jenkins, a portly five-foot-ten and red as a beet, breathed deeply trying to catch his breath. "Where?" he demanded.

McKenna pointed down the hall. "Bathroom."

The chief rushed down the hall, up the three steps. Tim and McKenna followed. The chief bent over to touch something, when Snyder said, "Chief, you might not want to touch anything—crime scene and all that."

He knew it was the wrong thing to say, but he also knew the chief was so excited that he was going to screw up the crime scene if he didn't say something. Jenkins immediately realized that he was about to commit the number-one offense in police work and alter something. He was embarrassed, but he wasn't going to show it. He intensely disliked Tim Snyder, and he especially disliked being upstaged by a subordinate.

Jenkins stood up, bent over to check the corners of the bathroom. Make up some time so he wouldn't appear to be too embarrassed after having his finger in the cookie jar.

After a moment, he turned to the lieutenant. "McKenna, clear the scene. Snyder, you're dismissed. You're only here for the Maple Festival anyway, not for anything else. And don't tell anybody what you saw here. You understand that, Snyder?" Chief Jenkins, recovering from his embarrassment, had turned on the attack.

"Yeah, sure, Chief. I'm out of here, just like you want," Tim said as he walked away. "God save Ireland from SOBs."

# CHAPTER 3

Fred wanted a pancake breakfast in the tent at the festival, but Joe Parker was in the parking lot at work, obviously waiting for him. Breakfast of pancakes and sausage would have to be postponed.

"Fred, got a minute? I need to see you on a very important matter."

"Yeah, sure, Joe, come on in."

Fred was the first to arrive at the law office, a parsonage built in 1837 on the northeast corner of the square in Chardon at East Park and North Hambden Streets. The building appeared angelic, with arched windows on the second floor. Directly across the street was the courthouse. People had approached Fred over the years and told him they had been married in his office when it was still the parsonage for the Methodist church. Fred liked to think that the present-day law office also had an angelic presence, but with the practice of the law, he knew better.

Joe Parker was six feet in height, slightly balding, a lawyer *and* client of Fred's on several previous occasions. His distinguishing feature was a glass eye. Given the disastrous result of the last case, Joe might not want Fred representing him in front of Judge Kuhmer anymore.

Fred climbed the five steps to the porch, unlocked the office door, and entered. He switched on the lights to the foyer, main reception area, and then his office. "Come on in, Joe, take off your coat. Let me get a few things turned on first."

Fred rebooted the computer, turned on the coffee machine, and unlocked the fireproof file cabinets. Three cabinets in a row weighed, without the files, 2,700 pounds. Fred had put six metal posts in the basement under the support beams—cherry logs that still had bark on them 160 years after they were installed.

The secretaries, Judy and Ginny, arrived together. Fred said his good mornings, shut his office doors, sat down, and looked at Joe.

"Okay, what's so pressing this early in the morning?"

"I need to hire you for another matter."

"Okay. You sure? I didn't do much good for you on that last one in front of Earl William."

Joe reached into his sports-coat pocket, extracted an envelope, opened it, and took out a pile of bills.

"You know what I think of Earl William! Five thousand dollars." He placed the bills on the desk. "Now you're my attorney."

"That's it? Five thousand dollars and I'm your attorney. I don't think so; want to tell me what I am representing you for, or on, or whatever?"

"I can't tell you yet. There may not be a case, but if there is, I want you to be my attorney."

Joe was serious, too serious.

"You sure this is the way you want to do it? Not tell me what it is, but give me a bundle?" Fred watched. Joe was very nervous. His fingers squeezed the chair. Fred observed him closely. Joe's tie was loosened at his neck, top button unbuttoned. The left collar of the Ivy League shirt was also unbuttoned. Joe did not look good.

"Yes, I am absolutely positive. Something strange came up and I believe I am going to need an attorney—and I want to protect myself in advance."

"Okay, Joe, what's it about?"

"Fred, really, I can't tell you yet. When the time comes, you'll know why I need representation. Then I want you to act on my behalf and represent me to the best of your ability."

Fred watched him. Joe was in some great distress, but it was difficult to assess. Joe's one eye, blinded in a youthful dispute, never seemed to focus. It was unable to focus at all, but the musculature had been somehow manipulated so that the eye could move in sync with the right eye, albeit somewhat delayed or askew. It was that delay of movement that was disconcerting to the observer.

"What did you do, kill someone? Come on. Why all the secrecy?"

Joe scrunched his eyebrows together, jerked his head back quickly but slightly. A sudden look of surprise, concern.

Joe quickly recovered, then continued. "It just isn't time to tell you yet, Fred. I hope it never comes to it, but I wanted to make sure I have the attorney I want when I need one. I may call you at any time on it, but I wanted to secure the relationship. It's a touchy kind of thing that I'd rather not go into now."

Fred's intercom buzzed.

"I'm with a client."

The speakerphone blared: "I think you might want to take this call. It's Larry Morrow; he wants to be the parade marshal."

"Okay, I'll take it." Fred put a finger up and looked at his visitor, before taking the call. "Sit right there, Joe; won't be but a minute.... Hello."

"Fred? Fred Newman?"

"Yes."

"Fred Newman, president of the Geauga County Maple Festival?"

"Yes."

"Fred, this is Larry Morrow from WN104.3 radio. You're live on the air. How are you today, Fred?"

"Well, Mr. Morrow, if I were any better, there would be two of me."

"Ha-ha, Fred. Good one, Fred. Fred, I am reading *The Plain Dealer*. An article by Barry Kawa says you can't find anyone for parade marshal. Is that correct, Fred?"

"Yes, it is correct. Been looking for one but have been unable to find one."

"Who have you asked, Fred?"

"I wrote to Al Gore, no response. John Glenn, denied. Dick Feagler broke his leg and is unable, but he wanted to do it. President Bush, no reply. I'm looking for someone big, a VIP."

"Well, Fred, I think I have your answer. I'll be your parade marshal. How's that?"

"That would be great, Mr. Morrow."

"Larry, please."

"That would be great, Larry Please."

"Okay, Fred, fantastic. Folks, I am talking to Fred Newman, president of the Geauga County Maple Festival. And Fred has just invited me to be the parade marshal for the festival. And, get this, folks, I have accepted!

That's wonderful. Thank you, Fred. Okay, Fred, I've got to go, but I'll have my staff call you for the details. Have a nice day, Fred!"

"You too, Larry Please, and thanks."

Fred put the receiver down. Smiled at Joe.

"Pretty neat, huh? Couldn't get anyone to be parade marshal for the last three months, then I get an article written, and there it is. Now we have a parade marshal. I've heard his name, but I can't even remember what radio station he works for. Pretty nice of him to do that. Good PR for him and the festival, too. Okay, Joe, back to your thing here. Five thousand bucks for unknown representation, for something in the future. It sounds very serious. Nonrefundable? Is this criminal or civil?"

"Not sure yet. Could be either or both."

Fred looked at the $5,000. Joe was being deadly coy. Something was in the works. He either got his hand in the escrow account or he was going to be sued for malpractice or something. The office needed the money, as it always did. Weekly overhead was at least $3,500. This would cover a week. He wasn't going to get much work done this week, anyway. As president of the Board of Directors of the Geauga County Maple Festival, he was going to be very busy indeed. He didn't need long to think it over.

"Well, client, keep your nose clean. Let's hope you never call." Fred scooped up the money.

# CHAPTER 4

The walk from Fred's office to the pancake tent was less than four hundred feet, but the falling snow, so heavy and quick, made the walk longer. Snow lightly covered everything. Snow, yes, snow, what a wonderful and expected natural event for the Maple Festival. Last week was beautiful weather, and next week would be beautiful as well, but for the festival, snow. Fred noticed four police cars at the courthouse parked askew. Two Chardon cars and one sheriff's deputy vehicle, in addition to the usual deputy car. He walked by them, moved the flap to the main tent that covered the entire Short Court Street and cut the park in half, and walked through. Inside, several vendors had removed the plastic covering from their wares, getting ready for the opening of the big event. Fred watched his step over wires and around boxes toward the pancake tent halfway to the sugar house. He shoved aside the flap and entered the smaller area.

"How are the pancakes today, Walt?" Fred asked.

"Best ever. How many do you want?" said Walt Beech, a short five-foot-six, with a gray bushy mustache and matching hair. Walt had been in charge of the pancake tent for three years, ever since the board of directors had decided that the festival needed to get back to its roots. *Pancakes and maple syrup, that's what this festival is about, and by golly, we need to make and sell pancakes. Walt, it's your job, okay?* Walt accepted and ran the program with gusto. His son, Scott, his main worker, slave, go-to man, towered above him at the grill, flipping pancakes.

Scott used his spatula to salute Fred. "Mr. Newman."

"Hey, Scott, don't burn them."

Not more than fifteen people sat in the tent. The pancakes were cooked in a trailer provided *gratis* by Artie Pritt. Artie owned a number of trailers out of which he sold multiple items at fairs and festivals across Ohio. He also had the concession contract at the Geauga County Fairgrounds to be the food vendor for all events throughout the year. And, since he wasn't using the trailer during the Maple Festival, he just thought he'd donate its use for the occasion. Such generosity made Fred buy his junk food at the fair from Artie's trailers.

Some special items had to be provided to comply with the Board of Health, such as running hot and cold water, ventilation, double sinks, and the like. Walt arranged for the supplies. Most were purchased from Heinen's grocery store, which also gave a donation in excess of $3,000. That donation alone more than purchased the required supplies. This donation inspired Fred to eat lunch at Heinen's Café at least twice a week. Such charity deserved support.

The pancake trailer end opened into the twenty-four by forty-foot pancake tent, which was squeezed into the area north of the sugar house located at the south end of the park. Squeezing all of the rides, trailers, concessions, tents, and free-standing units in the park was a feat annually accomplished by Gene Adams and Gary Dysert. Arranging all of the units in the park was an art.

The park itself was hallowed ground, or at least so considered by the current residents of Chardon. However, one J. O. Converse had compiled a history of its origins way back in 1880 that still held sway in the present day.

> In 1808, Chardon township was unpopulated, for it was an unbroken wilderness. Within the existing limits of Geauga County, there were, at that time, several settlements, the oldest and most important being in Burton and Bondstown (now Hambden). The seat of justice for Geauga County was established in 1808. Peter Chardon Brooks of Boston, a man of considerable wealth and liberality, was the original proprietor of the land, and, evidently, wishing to make his middle name immortal, proposed to the commissioners appointed to locate the county seat, to give them the use of the land now embraced in the town plat of Chardon, if they would call it by that name. Samuel W. Phelps was appointed

director of Chardon town plat. It was nearly four years after this gift was made by Mr. Brooks before anyone took up residence here. In 1811, Captain Edward Paine, then of Painesville, with the aid of Samuel W. Phelps, succeeded in getting most, or all, the timber chopped on the public square. Gomer Bradley, a longtime a resident of Claridon, and Curtis Wilmot of Burton did most of the axe work. An opening was made in the heavy timber, the sunlight let in to warm the soil and hasten the ripening of the farmers' crops, and the forests gradually disappeared to give place to grain, and meadow, and pasture.[1]

And so, the park area had been donated by Peter Chardon Brooks for the formation of a town to be named Chardon after him. It was, and the town got its square. A small impediment that seemed to cause problems throughout time was that a deed restriction for the square required no structure to be located on the park area that interfered with the view from South Street to North Street. Consequently, the subsequent erection of the courthouse had to be offset from North Street so the vision endured unimpaired. A further restriction only permitted public structures, such as schools or meetinghouses on the square, which was to remain a commons for the town of Chardon.

The commons, at one time, was fenced for the containment of livestock when farmers brought their animals for sale; over time and with the growth of the town, it was converted to a public park. Benches were set throughout. A gazebo was erected in the middle of the south park. The park was divided in half by Short Court Street. The current courthouse, built in 1869 after a big fire gutted the King Courthouse on the west side of the square, took up the north end of the park, while the south end was used by the general public. Concerts held weekly in the summer of string quartets or brass bands in the gazebo had been bringing crowds with blankets and chairs for over a hundred years. A log cabin—or a reasonable 1950s' facsimile thereof—was built on the east side of the park

---

[1]     1798 *Pioneer and General History of Geauga County, with Sketches of Some of the Pioneers and Prominent Men.* Published by The Historical Society of Geauga County, 1880; Chardon, by J. O. Converse.

for a meetinghouse. Much discussion about creating a permanent sugar house in place of the log cabin for a meetinghouse and educational center had circulated for years.

After Fred got his plate of three pancakes and two sausages, which Scott topped off with three more pancakes for good measure, he set his plate on the table and went back for plastic utensils and orange juice. Tim Snyder entered the tent as Fred sat.

"Hey, Tim, what's the commotion at the courthouse? Three extra cop cars? What's going on?"

"Wish I could tell you. It's bad, that's for sure. I've been told by the chief that I can't say anything." Tim inhaled deeply.

"Oh!" said Fred.

Tim looked at the pancakes on Fred's plate. "Looks good. Think I'll join you."

Tim sat with his plate of six piled pancakes, no sausage. He applied a pat of butter between each pancake and drenched the mountain in pure maple syrup. He then proceeded to cut the entire stack with the plastic knife and fork into smaller pieces before he took a single bite.

"Carbo-loading for the Sap Run?" asked Fred.

"Nah! Just hungry. I had tent duty last night. This is my dinner."

"So, really, you're not going to tell me what's happening at the courthouse?"

"Can't. Chief's being an—ah, well, you know."

"Don't I? Speak of the devil, here he comes."

Chief Jenkins, with Lieutenant McKenna trailing behind, came into the tent and walked right up to Fred and Tim. The chief put his hands on his hips, looked down at Tim accusingly, then directed his attention to Fred. He stood too close.

"You were in the law library last night from 10:30 p.m. to 1:00 a.m. this morning." It was a statement, not a question.

"Okay, I was, so what?" Fred answered slowly. He had to stretch his neck to make eye contact. There was no mutual approval or friendliness between the two. It was clearly obvious to all around that these two men did not like each other.

"So what do you know about Judge Kuhmer?"

"Earl William. I know a lot. Someone ought to shove a baseball bat up his ass!" Fred didn't miss noticing all three cops stiffen.

Tim's eyes opened wide, a forkful of pancake halted two inches from his mouth.

McKenna's mouth formed a silent "Ohhh!"

"What did you say?" the chief demanded.

"What, you hard of hearing, Chief?" Fred spoke very slowly for the benefit of the chief, who bent closer to Fred. "I know you must be having a hard time hearing, but I said, someone ought to shove a baseball bat up his ass. That's what I said. Did you hear it?"

Before he could finish, the chief had grabbed him by the arm and jerked him up.

Fred pulled away, but Jenkins wouldn't let go. "What's your problem?"

"You're under arrest. Cuff him, Lieutenant."

"What for?"

"You damn well know what for! I said cuff him, Lieutenant. Now!"

McKenna reached for Fred's right arm, "Sorry, Fred," he whispered, and placed the cuffs on Fred behind his back.

Fred said, "Tim, let Brice know, will you?"

The chief interjected, "Patrolman, you'll do no such thing. You'll tell no one, you understand me? Take him away, Lieutenant. Now!"

Walt yelled to Fred from behind the pancake grill, "I'll tell him, Fred!"

After they rushed Fred from the tent into the blizzard, Tim stood, told Walt breakfast was just fine but that he didn't have time to finish it. He'd tell Tom Brice, regardless of what the chief said, and he walked through the storm to Newman & Brice Law Firm.

# CHAPTER 5

The police station was less than five hundred feet away. Tim had placed Fred's coat over the man's shoulders, but his hands were already cuffed, so he got cold. Fred's large-brimmed hat kept the snow off his glasses, but even the adrenaline couldn't keep him warm. He was shaking with cold and maybe some fear by the time they arrived at the police station. Few people were about, but those who were stared at the two police officers dragging the trial lawyer along.

Fortunately for Fred, he wore rubbers. The police officers didn't. They slipped several times on the slick snow, now almost two inches deep. The snow was heavy and wet and fell fast and furious. Fred didn't have time to think how the storm was going to affect the attendance at the festival.

As soon as the chief appeared in the window, the dispatcher opened the door. Lieutenant McKenna directed Fred to a room with three desks and told him to sit in a chair facing one of the desks. Fred sat, his coat draped over his shoulders, involuntarily shaking. Slowly the warmth crept into him.

"Okay, Newman," the chief said. Fred didn't even warrant a Mr. Newman, or a Fred, now it was just *Newman*. "Tell me the details."

"How about you telling me what I am arrested for, chief of police of Chardon." Fred spoke slowly with a slightly nasty lilt at the end.

"Don't play coy, Newman."

"Don't play stupid, chief of police of Chardon."

Still standing, Jenkins, without a windup, slapped Fred with his left hand. Jolted, Fred was jerked off the chair, hit the desk with his shoulder, and landed on the floor with a thud. He just sat there, his back leaning against the desk, his face glowing red with pain. Not moving.

"Get up, you asshole. Get up." The chief grabbed him by the jacket, which lifted off Fred like a blanket. He threw the jacket on the floor, grabbed Fred's shirt, which ripped at the arm, pulled him up, and shoved him back into the chair.

McKenna hurried over. "That's enough, Chief!" The lieutenant moved between Fred and Chief Jenkins. "That's enough." Then with a mutter to the chief, "What are you doing, buying a lawsuit? Stop. I'll handle this."

Jenkins glared at Fred, red-faced, turned abruptly without a word, and walked out of the room.

"Sorry, Fred."

"That's the second time you have said that this morning. Want to tell me why I am here?"

"You don't know?"

"No!"

"Really?" The lieutenant looked surprised.

"Really. What am I doing here? I guess that … whatever you want to call him, still hates my guts, doesn't he?"

"I'd guess so. You cost him money, remember?"

Fred did remember. Only five years ago, and the chief still held a grudge.

Out of the blue, the chief had written a letter to the board of directors of the Maple Festival, with a carbon copy to each member of city council and the law director, Milt Psenicka, complaining about an alleged statement Fred had made. The letter accused Fred of circulating rumors that the chief was double-dipping—which Jenkins vociferously asserted was untrue. The chief had heard the rumor and contested it. Apparently, Fred had circulated the rumor at the Chamber of Commerce Christmas party where all of the local businesses were invited for free hors d'oeuvres and punch at the Eging House, the second-oldest building on the square and the offices of the chamber and the Maple Festival. The Eging House was owned by the Geauga County Public Library, located immediately to the north of the library on the east side of the square and leased for one dollar per year.

The chief's letter stated that he was entitled to be paid for the work he performed for the festival and that he was not, as Fred's rumor had indicated, a double-dipper. The festival paid directly to as many as sixty police officers sums of money for the security for the festival. The festival had no direct control over the officers, or the hours they worked, but they were required to pay them. The contract with Chardon Village stated that the Chardon police had exclusive control over security for the village and that they would direct the police officers, even if they were paid by the festival. Security cost the festival in excess of $7,500 for that year alone. The chief's bill was for $445.

Although Fred knew he did not start the rumor, he had heard it. One of the previous festival presidents complained to the council mayor that the chief was double-dipping and that security was very expensive for the festival—and that it shouldn't be so. All the cops worked in twos and threes. Why did they have to send so many out together? There was no alcohol at the festival; so those problems associated with drunks were nonexistent. Why was the chief greedily draining the festival? Everyone knew that he didn't like the festival, but to milk it, well, it just wasn't right.

After Fred got the letter, saw that it was copied to everyone in the world and that it seemed to be the chief's justification for lashing out at the festival, Fred went to work. He discovered that the chief's contract with the village required him to be on-call twenty-four hours a day, seven days a week, for the salary that he was paid. Fred also discovered that Jenkins had retired from an adjoining community police department after twenty years and was collecting retirement benefits from the Police and Fire Retirement System of Ohio. Fred also discovered that the festival paid Jenkins for the time he spent on the job in the Village of Chardon for the festival. Fred figured the chief received three sources of income from the public: his salary, his retirement, and his extra money from the festival.

Fred didn't like the concept that the chief was retired but still working, because someone who was not retired could sure use the job; however, he grudgingly accepted the fact that the chief was legally entitled to be retired from one place and to continue to work somewhere else at the same time. After all, he was earning his money. It would not be such a difficult concept if it were anyone other than Jenkins.

However, Fred believed that since the chief was compensated by the village, to which Fred paid taxes, to be on-call *all the time*, that the chief was not entitled to extra compensation from the festival for work he performed under his contract with the village. Fred thought he was being paid twice for the same work. He was compelled to work during the festival, because he was on-call twenty-four hours a day. There was no time for him to do private security in the Village of Chardon, ever. In fact, Fred thought he *was* double-dipping.

But Fred had not wanted to alienate the chief from the festival any more than he already was, so he had called him to speak with him. The dispatcher refused to put him through. Finally, after the third call, Fred was informed that Jenkins had been advised by legal counsel to not speak with Fred.

Fred was incensed—advised by legal counsel over something so trivial as a rumor? What's this world coming to? No wonder the courts are so clogged with lawsuits when the people in power won't even sit down and discuss their issues. So Fred called the legal counsel, Milt Psenicka. Milt was tersely peremptory.

"The chief has made his point. He won't talk to you about it. You're an attorney—when do you let your clients talk to the other attorney?"

"Milt, this is the Maple Festival, not a federal case. Do we want to resolve the problem or just make it bigger?"

"You pissed him off; you're wrong, and he is not going to talk to you." Milt hung up the phone.

Fred was angry, puzzled, and then he laughed. What a stupid situation! The chief sends a nasty letter out that is wrong, by the way, and he won't talk about it. And the law director hangs up on me. Fred laughed out loud. The absurdity of it.

In response, Fred drafted a letter. He set forth his efforts to ameliorate the matter by calling the chief, who wouldn't take his call, and the law director, who had hung up on him. He then got to the issue. Fred outlined that the chief was on the town's dime twenty-four-seven and was not legally entitled to pull any private security positions in the Village of Chardon; that any security details he pulled in Chardon were as a consequence of his being the chief of police, not hired by anyone else; that the retirement funds, while not looked upon favorably by everyone, constituted additional income. That, in fact, the chief *was* double-dipping, because he was paid to participate in the parade and other miscellaneous festival activities by the village, and then again, by the festival; that it was illegal and constituted *de facto* double-dipping. Fred stressed the double-dipping language because it sounded so ... so greedy and selfish. Like someone taking advantage—which was exactly what the chief was doing.

Fred copied his letter to all the same people to whom Jenkins had directed his: all council members, the law director, and the Maple Festival directors.

Then Fred heard nothing, absolutely nothing. Six months later, he learned that the village administrator had had a word with the chief and that no further double-dipping would occur, that he was not permitted to work private security in the village so long as he was chief and on-call twenty-four-seven.

The lines were drawn. If the chief had disliked the festival before the incident, he now hated it, and especially Fred, who represented the event. Fred had embarrassed Jenkins, and that inflamed his hatred. Although Fred was justified, or so he thought, the fact that he had embarrassed the chief caused Fred a mortal enemy in town.

Jenkins didn't work the festival for three years thereafter, wouldn't even be in the parade with the chief's car. Fred wasn't happy about the situation, but he also thought the chief was taking advantage and that he shouldn't be such a selfish baby about the whole thing. All of these people involved with the festival donated their time for free, and the chief wants to double-dip even when he is getting a triple income with retirement? Yes, Fred thought, how to contribute to your community—it's a good thing.

"So, what am I doing here?"

"You're under arrest for the murder of Judge Kuhmer."

"He's murdered?"

"Yes, he was. And you were the only other person in the courthouse last night. Your key card to the law library shows up at the police station when you enter and leave. It showed you going into the courthouse at 10:34 p.m. and leaving at 1:19 a.m. The only other person in the courthouse was the judge. *Opportunity.* You two were the only ones there. And then when you said you thought someone should stick a baseball bat up his ass, that did it. *Motive.*"

"Why would that mean anything? He deserved a baseball bat. He could be one mean judge. What does that have to do with it?"

"I shouldn't tell you this." The lieutenant hesitated, looked around. "The judge had a baseball shoved up his ass when he was found dead."

"Oh my God!" Fred drawled slowly, his eyes opened wide.

# CHAPTER 6

Tim Snyder watched the chief hustle Fred into the snow. He had been astonished when Fred mentioned the baseball bat—he wouldn't have said that if he had known, Tim thought. *What coincidence!* "God save Ireland," he muttered. As he walked up the five steps to Fred's office, he thought it was the prettiest building on the square. It had a holy look.

Tim was always invited to the Maple Festival porch party that Fred held for the parade on Saturday and Sunday at 3:00 p.m., but instead of going, he traditionally gathered with his family at the south corner of the square by Farinacci Auto Repair. With this snow, he wondered what the parade would be like this year: *Not good. Maybe the family should stand on the porch for the parade.*

Tim entered the office foyer; Fred Newman's law partner would know what to do. To the right was the reception area. Photos taken by Fred hung on the walls, a huge photo of the courthouse, resplendent with fall colors, the Assembly of God church silhouetted in the setting sun, and several landscape shots. Tim leaned on the counter that separated the secretaries from the sitting area.

"I wonder if I might see Tom. It's a matter of some urgency."

Judy, the secretary, pressed a button on the phone. "Tim Snyder wants to see you; says it's an emergency." A pause. "Yeah, he's covered in snow … in uniform." She put the receiver down. "Go on up, Tim."

Tom's office was on the second floor, and he greeted Tim at the door. "Come on in, Tim. Have a seat."

Tim surveyed his surroundings; he had never been in Tom's office. Baseball paraphernalia was everywhere. Photos of Tom with his state-champion high-school team, Latin High School. Framed newspaper clippings showed the state championship team. Signed baseballs on pedestals, little bats—like the one used on the judge—framed prints showing little kids at play with baseballs. Either the theme of the office was quite overdone or Tom was a fanatic about baseball, which he was.

"Fred's been arrested for the murder of Judge Earl William. Just been taken to the jail."

"Earl William's been murdered? Fred? How the hell … Explain, please."

Tim related what he knew so far, including what Fred had blurted out in the interrogation. He showed Tom the photos he had taken, but swore him to secrecy that he had taken them, at least until he really needed them.

Tom said, "I knew he had that brief due, and I knew he had to do some law-library research, but kill Earl William? No way. There's got to be some mistake."

"I couldn't believe he said that about the baseball bat! It was electric. Only the three of us standing there knew about the baseball bat, and then he says it." Tim shook his head in bewilderment.

"But that's it, why would he say it if he knew about it? It doesn't make sense."

"Fred seemed to indicate that you would know what to do. What can you do? He hasn't been charged yet. They can hold him for a day or two before they even charge him."

"They can, but they're not going to get the chance. The chief hates Fred's guts; he'll do whatever he can to cause Fred trouble. He's got the Maple Festival stuff to do. He's a nut for that Maple Festival." Tom reached for the phone.

"Kinda like you're a nut about baseball? Maybe."

Tom raised a single finger in response. Tim smiled.

"Could I speak with Judge Albert, please? Yes, this is Tom Brice. Yes, it is a matter of great importance. No, really, I need to speak with him now. It is really urgent. Thanks."

Tom waited a full five minutes before Judge Albert got on the phone.

"Tom, what's so important?" asked the judge. Judge Craig Albert presided over the Chardon Municipal Court, which exercised jurisdiction throughout Geauga County. He handled felony bond settings, preliminary hearings, and civil cases where the dispute did not exceed fifteen thousand dollars. Tom knew that he would be able to facilitate the bond-setting for Fred.

"Judge, got a big problem. Did you know that Earl William was murdered last night … or this morning, in his office?"

"What! Murdered? Earl William, you say? You're bullshitting me, Tom."

"No, Your Honor. I'm not. Earl William got killed by someone. Big to-do at the courthouse right now. But I got a bigger problem. The chief arrested Fred for the murder."

"Wait a minute. This is too much. Earl William gets murdered. And they arrest Fred. I don't believe it."

"They just arrested him at the pancake tent. This is Maple Festival weekend. He's the president. And he didn't do it. Even you know he wouldn't do it."

"*Wouldn't*, yeah, but *couldn't*, no. Okay, what do you want from me?"

Tom explained that since this was Maple Festival weekend and Fred needed to be available as president of the festival. That he had to be bonded out today—now, not next Monday. That the chief had it in for Fred and this was just another little thing he could use to punish him. That if the judge left it to the chief, he'd keep him in jail until Monday when the courts were open—just for punishment against Fred. There was no discussion about the ethical propriety of an attorney talking to the judge about a case without the opposing attorney privy to the conversation. The necessity for action and expedience overrode the ethical considerations of the fine points of legal procedure.

"Yeah but, Tom, they don't arrest someone without some evidence. What have they got?

Tom related the conversation about the baseball bat.

"He said that?" Craig laughed. "Holy shit, he said that! But if he did it, he wouldn't have said that." He paused. "Okay, if I get him over here for bond-setting, are you available?"

"Yes, Judge."

"Plan on eleven o'clock. Be here."

\* \* \* \* \* \*

"Judge Albert here," he said to the dispatcher. "Get me the chief." As Craig waited, he could hear the dispatcher talking to the chief—*He must be in the next room.*

"Yes, Judge."

"Chief, I hear you arrested Fred Newman for the murder of Judge Earl William."

"Yes, Judge, we did. We think he did it, and his statements confirm our suspicions."

"What statements?"

"He said, when we confronted him, that Earl William should have a baseball bat shoved up his ass. That is exactly how Earl William died. Who else would know it?"

"Chief, why in the hell would Fred say that if he knew a baseball bat had been shoved up Earl William's ass? Tell me that. It just doesn't make any sense, does it?"

"Makes sense to me, Judge. He's wily enough to cover his tracks."

"Chief, no way. Get him over here for a bond-setting. I want him here at 10:45 today."

"Judge, we haven't charged him yet. We can hold him for two days."

"Bullshit, Chief. You arrested him for murder, so he's charged. I want him here. I'm not going to let you keep him for two days while the festival is going on. You got that, Chief? Don't give me any shit."

"I'll check with the law director, Your Honor."

"Yeah, you check with Milt, but you better get Fred over here when I say to get him over here." Craig slammed the phone in its cradle.

\* \* \* \* \* \*

Milt Psenicka had been Chardon's law director ever since Wally King retired. It seemed like forever. Initially, Milt had been police prosecutor. At that time, he hired Craig Albert right out of law school for his assistant. Having been the tool that hired Craig into the county, Milt exercised a certain control, or attempt at control, over Craig, now judge of the same court in which Milt had practiced.

"Milt, I don't give a shit whether you think you can keep him for two days. What for? You think he's going to run away? He's president of the

23

damn Maple Festival. Milt, you used to be on the board of directors of the Maple Festival. You know how much work is involved. This is the week of the Maple Festival. Instead of being a toady for the chief, I want you over here with Fred at 10:45, today. Milt, I said don't give me any of your shit. I said today, now! In about fifteen minutes. Don't forget, you're only the damn law director; I'm the judge!" Craig screamed into the phone. "Just get your skinny ass, the chief's fat ass, and Fred's no-doubt-loose ass over here at 10:45. We're going to hold a bond-setting, and I'm not going to put up with the chief's bullshit holding Fred for two days during the Maple Festival. He's full of shit about Fred, and you're full of shit about Jenkins. Get him over here now, or I'll put you in jail for contempt. And don't think I won't.

# CHAPTER 7

Judge Albert peered over the bench as the chief nudged Fred into the courtroom. Fred was handcuffed behind his back. His face was bright red on one side of his face.

"Chief, you can uncuff him right now. You know there is no reason to cuff Fred. What are you doing?"

"This is a murder suspect, Your Honor. We follow policy, and policy is to secure the prisoner with handcuffs." The chief of police motioned Fred to a chair and unlocked his handcuffs. Fred rubbed his wrists.

"Why is your face so red, Fred?"

Fred rubbed the side of his face, felt the warm glow. "Must have been a bee sting, Judge."

"Yeah, a bee sting. Five inches of snow out there. I'm sure the bees are just buzzing all around at the jail." Fred glanced at the chief, saw him reddening as he looked away from and past the judge.

"Tom, you ready?"

"Yes, Your Honor."

"Nick Gorsh, put the tape on. Geesh, this is the damnedest thing." All eyes turned toward the bailiff as he fiddled with the recorder that would provide an audio and video display of all the activities. Nick wore a black turtleneck with a black jacket that matched his jet black hair. At six-foot-four, a competitive weightlifter, Nick was huge, but he smiled genially. "Okay, Judge, we're ready."

"Milt, you ready?"

"I object to these proceedings, Your Honor. They are very irregular. The police are entitled to have the suspect in custody for up to twenty-four hours before bringing him to a magistrate or releasing him. Your Honor—"

Judge Albert cut him off. "Milt, just shut the hell up, will you? You know that the only reason you're keeping Fred is so that the chief can screw him up with the festival. That's the only reason, so don't give me your shit. You got that?"

"Your Honor, I object." Milt stood and waved his right arm with his index finger extended.

"Milt, did you hear me? Shut the hell up until I ask you for something."

All was quiet, ten seconds, twenty seconds, then Judge Albert said, "Okay, Milt, tell me about the charge. Keep it orderly."

"Your Honor, the suspect, Fred Newman, is accused of murder in the first degree, with or without death specifications. The investigation is only in the beginning stages, so the officers have been unable to complete the full charge."

"Who was murdered, and when?"

"Your Honor, the deceased was Judge Earl William Kuhmer on Thursday night or Friday morning. Judge Kuhmer was a well-respected jurist—"

Judge Albert interrupted him. "Milt, you don't have to do your opening argument for a trial; just give me the facts."

Without missing a beat, Milt continued. "We don't yet have the exact time of death. The coroner's office is determining that as we speak; suffice it to say that it was within the twenty-four-hour period I have stated.

"In the evening hours, there is only one method of ingress to the courthouse for attorneys. That method is to use a key card in the basement back door. When the attorneys use the key card, it registers at the police station. When the key cards are issued by the law librarian, the name of the issuee is forwarded to the Chardon police. So whenever there is an entry, the police know the name of the person entering."

"You're assuming no one stole a card."

"Yes, Your Honor, we are. Mr. Newman still had his card in his wallet; it was not stolen." Milt flamboyantly waved toward Fred, patted his left rear cheek indicating where the wallet was stored. Milt paused, looked at his notes, bent over to whisper to the chief, nodded his head and continued. "Your Honor, Judge Kuhmer's key showed entrance to the courthouse at 10:00 p.m. on Thursday evening. Mr. Newman's key card showed entrance at 10:34 p.m. on the same night.

Mr. Newman's key card then shows exit at 1:19 p.m., Friday morning."

"Fred," asked Judge Albert, "what the hell were you doing in the law library at one o'clock in the morning?"

"I was writing a brief due in Judge Kuhmer's court, Your Honor."

"Holy balls. I didn't even know you could get into the courthouse after hours."

"May I continue, Your Honor?" Milt was, while not overly concerned, somewhat disconcerted by the camaraderie between Fred and Craig.

"Yeah, Milt, continue."

"This morning, at about 7:00 a.m., Linda, the magistrate's secretary on the second floor, discovered the body of Judge Kuhmer in the second-floor bathroom, dead."

"No other key card showed entrance or exit; well ..." Milt paused, "the evidence shows that access was only had by Fred and Judge Kuhmer."

"Wait a minute, Milt. What do you mean, 'access'? What about exits? Did other cards show exits?"

"The twist here, Your Honor, is that Judge Kuhmer's card showed an exit at 11:00 p.m. We have been unable to locate that card so far. The police believe it was a ruse, Your Honor. That Fred took the judge's card, swiped it across the reader, opened the door, and then went back to the law library."

"Why, Milt?"

"We don't know that yet, Your Honor, but it is obvious that he can then blame someone else."

"Milt, it doesn't make sense." Judge Albert looked over at Fred sitting next to Tom Brice. "Fred, did you kill Earl William?"

"No, Judge, not a bit of it."

"Okay, Milt, what else do you have connecting Fred? Anything?

"Well, Your Honor, Mr. Newman apparently had certain information about the crime scene that no one else is privy to."

"What is it?"

"Your Honor, I see the press is here. I would prefer not to have to disclose these facts so that they are splashed all over the front page of the paper."

"Milt, no matter what happens, they are going to be splashed all over the paper. Out with it. I need to know the connection of Fred to the crime so I can set an appropriate bond. Is the evidence strong, weak, anything more than research in the law library at one o'clock in the morning. Come on, out with it."

Milt paced before the prosecutor's table, back and forth, three times jerking his arms up, then down, then up and down again.

"Milt, today! Okay?"

"Yes, Your Honor. The crime scene showed Judge Kuhmer in the second-floor bathroom of the courthouse; his head was shoved into the toilet."

"Oh, Jesus!"

"And his pants were lowered. And inserted into his anus was a mini-sized Louisville Slugger baseball bat."

"Oh, Jesus! Fred?"

"Not me, Judge."

"What else, Milt?"

"When the defendant was approached in the pancake tent at the Maple Festival, he was asked what he knew of Judge Kuhmer. He stated he knew that a baseball bat was shoved up his ass."

"Fred?"

"Not quite, Your Honor. What I said was in response to a question by the chief. The question was: 'What do you know about Judge Kuhmer?' My response was: 'I know someone ought to shove a baseball bat up his ass.' That was all, Your Honor."

"Pretty timely."

"Unfortunately, yes, as it turns out."

"Your Honor," said Milt, "we believe that Fred Newman, being in the same building at the same time and having intimate knowledge of the crime scene, is the number-one suspect in this case. And we are securing evidence that Newman had a grudge against Judge Kuhmer."

"A baseball bat up his ass. Holy balls. Unbelievable. A baseball bat. Someone sure didn't like him, did he?"

"We believe it was Fred Newman, the defendant, Your Honor."

"Okay, Milt, enough of that crap," Craig shook his head, "what are you looking for, for bond?"

"We ask that no bond be set because of the potential death specifications, Your Honor. The risk of flight on a death case is great. No bond. Some other factors are that this man was in the army and he was in combat. He was a US Army Airborne Ranger. In fact, the rumor is that he has killed while in the army, so killing is no stranger to him. Certainly he has the capacity to kill."

"Come on, Milt, be reasonable. This is Fred. You've known him for years. Is that what you want, Chief?"

"The risk is great, Your Honor."

"So, chief, why is Fred's face so red? Somebody smack him?"

"No, Your Honor, must have been a bee sting." Jenkins flushed again.

"Yeah, bee sting. Okay, Tom, what do you want to say about bond? Wait a minute. Fred, you're an attorney; you know I have to give you all your rights and stuff. You already know them; do you waive all those things I have to tell you in these situations?"

"Yes, Judge."

"Thanks. Okay, Tom, proceed."

"Your Honor, Fred has been a member of this community for over thirty years. He is an attorney licensed by the Ohio Supreme Court. He has taken an oath to support the law in Ohio.

"Fred Newman has a family, a wife, two daughters, horses, cows, dogs, etc., that require his presence in this state. He has an active law practice.

"Fred is president of the Geauga County Maple Festival, on the Geauga County Public Library Board, and a member of several other civic groups. The risk of his flight is nonexistent.

"The connection of Fred to this heinous crime is minimal at best. Any intelligent person would not have told the police chief what the chief told this court that Fred had said.

"Your Honor, I ask that personal recognizance bond be granted."

Milt leaped from his chair. "No way, Judge. This man is a killer. He must be put in jail."

"Sit down, Milt. You're full of shit and you know it. Fred isn't going anywhere. And I doubt he did it. I don't know what Chief Jenkins has against him, but it isn't working. Fred could have killed a thousand enemy soldiers in Vietnam, but he didn't kill Earl William. You know it, and I know it. Fred Newman will be released on his personal recognizance.

"This case will be set for preliminary hearing; get the dates from Virginia in the clerk's office. We are adjourned. Fred, don't make me a liar." The judge hesitated, then added, "Why is your face so red on one side, Fred?"

Fred looked at the chief, whose fear and embarrassment were reflected in his eyes.

"It's those damn bees in the police station in April, Judge."

\* \* \* \* \* \*

Fred remained unshackled as he was processed out of the police station. The chief looked at him sullenly.

"You're going down for this, Newman."

"Yeah sure, Chief. You going to give me another bee sting before I leave?"

Jenkins stared, a mean down-turned smile on his face. Fred walked out of the police station.

# CHAPTER 8

As Fred left the station, snow covered the tops of his overshoes, soaking his socks. *Time to switch to boots,* he thought. *The festival will be a disaster today. No one will go on the rides in the snow.*

He crossed Water Street by the Geauga Theatre, then Main Street to walk the middle of the square. Heavy, wet snow, already five inches deep, covered everything. Although the ride operators did not expect much business, they were brushing snow off the equipment in preparation for opening.

Fred pondered his arrest coincidental to Joe Parker's visit early this morning. Is that the connection? Was Joe involved? There certainly was bad blood between Joe and EW. Has Joe compromised him by getting Fred to be his attorney so he could not implicate him? But now *Fred* was implicated, charged in fact, with the murder of Earl William. Earl William deserved a baseball bat up his butt, but not to die. And that was only a figure of speech anyway.

Fred's relationship with Earl William had always been collegial, and insulting. Earl William had been an assistant prosecutor before ascending to the bench. His race for the judgeship against Joe Parker was one of the meanest local campaigns ever. Earl William had been in practice only two years longer than Fred. He had been a handsome man before the accumulation of fatty tissue overwhelmed his frame. Since the election two years ago, Earl William had put on a tremendous amount of weight. At five-eight, he weighed in excess of three hundred pounds. His father, an immigrant from Germany, had come to the US shortly after World War II. Earl William still had a slight German accent, but you had to listen closely to discern it. However, the weight of his body did not affect his head. His head was still perfectly proportioned, full of wavy hair. Of course, it looked out of kilter on the huge body, but his engaging smile disarmed and made those he addressed comfortable.

Their relationship was insulting, because before Earl William was elected to the bench, both Fred and EW could trade professional barbs without infringing on the personality of the other. They enjoyed the insults. After EW's ascension to the bench, their relationship became formal.

Earl William was a local boy from Middlefield. He had attended the Cardinal Local School District. As an assistant prosecutor, he had represented townships and school boards. Both he and Joe Parker were eminently well-respected in the legal field; both would have been good judges, or so Fred thought.

Fred, a Democrat, had given money to Joe Parker's campaign, because Joe ran on the Democratic ticket. Fred thought Earl William and Joe were equally qualified and he could live with either one as judge. But after Earl William got on the bench, he changed. He began to belittle attorneys in the courtroom in front of their clients. Fred had escaped this behavior until recently. The judge appeared to feel a threat to his absolute authority, and he went out of his way to exercise it, to impose it, and to let those upon whom he was imposing it, know it.

For Fred, the conflict had happened a mere two months ago. He'd had a divorce case against Pat Bowers, an attorney from Willoughby. The trial was set for a week ahead, but there were multiple pieces of farm equipment that Pat still wanted their clients to have appraised. Fred also didn't think the parties were ready to try the case, because of the real property appraisal and the great number of cows. The dairy herd was appraised too highly for the current price of milk at seventeen cents a gallon. Farms were closing all over northeastern Ohio. Fred thought the city-boy appraiser had no real idea what a farm was worth. He wanted another evaluation by a farm appraiser.

Pat was having problems with her client. The client wanted the divorce over with—no matter what. The client did not know that the judge would completely dismiss the case if the evidence did not document all the assets of the marriage. Her client would be on the short stick if Pat did not get the personal property appraised. So Pat asked Fred to make a motion for continuance, because her client would not consent to it. Fred acquiesced. Why not? He also wanted a continuance, no big deal.

It did turn out to be a big deal. Fred made the motion to continue the case scheduled for the following Monday. The judge outright denied it; his bailiff, Joanne, called to notify Fred. Fred then walked over to the courthouse and talked to Joanne. He didn't exactly whine, but he cajoled her into speaking to the judge to turn the trial into a pretrial. He explained about the necessity of obtaining appraisals and other documentation. Finally, Joanne called and said Earl William would convert it to a pretrial, but that the clients had to be in attendance. Okay, that was normal. Fred suspected nothing other than that he had obtained a continuance, the parties would negotiate, maybe settle the case, or at least get closer to resolution. It was better to resolve these cases than try them.

Fred appeared with his client, Marty. Pat appeared with her client, Michaelean. They went into the jury room after checking in with the bailiff and began negotiations. One of the greatest difficulties with domestic-relations negotiations is that the parties have loved one another so greatly, presuming that is the reason they married, and now that great love pendulum has swung so far to the other extreme. They now hate each other with that same degree of passion turned topsy-turvy. The emotional relationship interfered with their ability to think rationally about almost everything. They argued over possession of a single spoon that had some significance to them before, during, or after their relationship. Pet ownership was worse. My dog, your cat. No, my dog, your cat. At that point, Fred would suggest euthanizing both of them and both clients would look daggers at him.

Joanne knocked on the door, peered in, and told the attorneys that the judge wanted to see the attorneys and clients together. She wore a look of somber apprehension. Fred assumed the pretrial hearing would be extremely formal if the clients were to be present: it was a rare occurrence. Fred wasn't concerned, after all, he had gotten the continuance.

Earl William was stiffly formal. Introductions were made. The attorneys' table was ninety degrees perpendicular to the judge's desk. Several prints hung on the walls. One of a fence line in the snow. One wall held family photos. A luxurious walnut-based pen holder with the name *Judge Earl William Kuhmer* sat on his desk facing the attorneys. Fred sat across from Pat, both equally close to the desk. The clients sat next to their respective attorneys.

Once ensconced behind his desk, the judge started in. He began with the current history of how cases are conducted in his court in an orderly fashion. How he issues his pretrial procedure orders, sets discovery deadlines, sets expert-report deadlines, and on and on. Fred's mind wandered. Why was EW boring everyone to death? This was obviously for the benefit of the clients, because it was not advancing the case on the docket in any manner whatsoever.

Then EW switched his attention to Fred. Fred perked up and listened. EW focused on why attorneys didn't get their jobs done. Why certain attorneys asked for continuances only one week before trial. Obviously, Fred thought, the judge had forgotten that he practiced law at one time, a short two years previously. EW explained, in a very nasty and malicious tone, that certain attorneys who did ask for continuances were a pain in the backsides of the legal system. He complimented Pat: she had not asked for a continuance. She was prepared. She said nothing, didn't even glance at Fred. Without the attorneys saying a single word, he then dismissed all of them.

Outside the chambers, Marty smiled broadly. "He sure cleaned your clock, didn't he?"

"He sure did." Fred did not say what he really thought.

The parties and attorneys went back to the jury room to further negotiate.

Pat was gentle. "I guess he was not happy with the continuance."

"Guess not," said Fred, looking at her, waiting for some reaction, some apology, because he had done what she had requested on the continuance and gotten scorched.

The bailiff came in and said the judge wanted to see the attorneys only.

"You're in for some shit now," said Marty gleefully.

"What's he going to yell at us for now?" said Pat.

"For existing. For having the gall to think we might know our own cases. For helping out fellow attorneys who won't even come to the aid of those yelled at."

The judge instructed them to sit. Not sit down, please. Just "Sit." The Judge was seated. He didn't stand, only moved his tightly compressed lips to issue, "Sit."

They took the same seats. The judge began, once again. He emphasized how this was his court and he would set the schedules. How attorneys were not going to be controlling his court. That his timelines were reasonable and designed to comply with the Supreme Court rules on disposition of cases. That it was a reflection on him if he did not dispose of cases in a timely fashion. That this case could have been tried this week, the issues were not that difficult. That the attorneys had not done their jobs correctly or efficiently. That the problem was arrogance. He stared directly at Fred.

"Arrogance, that's what it is. Just pure arrogance."

Fred, never one to be a whipping boy, looked directly at Earl William and said, slowly and quizzically, "Mine, or yours?"

In that instant, the atmosphere turned frigid. Fred could almost see the icicles forming cartoonishly along the perimeter of the judge's ceiling. Earl William was pissed and stunned. Fred was pissed at Earl William for acting like such a spoiled baby, and he was pissed at Pat for not jumping in and apologizing. Earl William was momentarily at a loss for words. He stared, unable to comprehend. Fifteen seconds of silence ensued. Someone had actually refused to sit there and be tongue-lashed by the judge.

Pat said nothing. She looked incredulously at Fred—eyes wide, mouth slightly open and askew. The judge began to talk, small talk, no one listened to it. Earl William was going to ignore the comment; it was too hostile to deal with. However, the icicles were beginning to drip. Fred rolled his eyes, bored. Pat looked down at her legal pad.

Finally, EW wound up his dissertation: "You're dismissed." The attorneys stood. The judge did not rise. He was red in the face. He didn't even glance at the attorneys. His anger was palpable. The lines of hostility were drawn.

Fred and Pat walked toward the jury room past the bailiff's office. As they passed the open door, Fred said loudly, "Screw him!" The bailiff looked up sharply. They walked on.

Pat hurried forward; discussion of anything in front of the bailiff would only bring further recriminations. There was not much to be gained by additional negotiation.

Fred thought Earl William would get over it quickly enough, but he didn't. Two weeks later, at a pancake breakfast at Berkshire High School put on by the Burton-Middlefield Rotary Club, Fred, who was in charge of the kitchen, came out to check on the dining room. Earl William and his wife were in line for pancakes. Fred, ebullient, thinking the earlier incident was just a professional bleep on the radar of the field of the practice of law, went up to Earl William, stuck out his hand for a handshake, and was surprised and astonished that Earl William looked away, then turned aside. Earl William's wife, Mabel, said, "Hi, Fred," ignoring the judge's rudeness.

Fred was concerned; it was obvious Earl William was still angry from the confrontation. Fred had thought it was just one of those legal tiffs that occur … but you get over it. Apparently not. To Fred, it looked like he was going to have some problems with Earl William in the future. Maybe even a grudge.

\* \* \* \* \* \*

Fred walked past the activity of the sugar house. Walt Beech pushed a pole on the underside of the pancake tent to cause the snow to slide off the tent and prevent its collapse. He jiggled the pole and a large chunk of wet snow slid off the roof into a pile on the side of the tent. The snow was now deeper than Fred's galoshes; his feet were cold and wet. Fred glanced toward the courthouse through the gazebo. Snow was everywhere. The vendors were moving slowly to open their trailers. Walt saw Fred.

"You okay? That was pretty scary."

"Yeah, don't worry. It's all a mistake … I hope."

"The judge was murdered?"

"That's what they tell me. They think I did it, but I didn't."

"I don't think the chief likes you too much. He was his usual nasty self, but that went way beyond. Let me know if there is anything I can do."

"No problem, Walt, and thanks."

Fred continued along the slushy, snow-covered walk. Vendors scraped the trailers, lifted the awnings to open, hooked them. The wet snow dropped heavily, steadily, ponderously. Fred saw the continuation of a bad festival day. This day was not moving forward in a fashion he liked.

He walked by the Buffalo Burgers, Elephant Ears, Chinese on a Stick, Kettle Corn, around the gazebo that was fenced completely with a wooden, snow fence, toward the main tent. Fred heard the rip and knew immediately, before he saw it, that the big tent was collapsing. He looked as the snow gradually slid through the huge rip on the west end of the tent. As the snow moved through the hole, causing the weight to be lifted off the left side, the entire tent shifted to the right and careened slowly, so slowly, coming down in slow motion. People shouted and screamed and poured from the tent at all exits.

Fred chuckled. "It can't get much worse, can it?" Three-quarters of the tent had collapsed entirely; poles stuck through the canvas; snow piled on the downed tent; vendors frantically tried to protect their wares. Fred heard loud swearing. That was understandable, for sure. Fred watched. He hoped no one was hurt; it appeared that there were no casualties. Fred immediately took photos.

Gene Adams emerged from the tent, what had been the tent. He smiled at Fred, turned, and went back into it. A few moments later, he came out again and approached Fred.

"Don't think anyone's hurt. That's good." He paused, then said, "Heard you got arrested? Trouble?"

"Yeah, sure, it's trouble. But I sure as hell didn't do it. The chief thinks I did, but then, that's the chief."

"Yes, he is a ... hm-mm. What do you want to do here?" Gene pointed to the collapsed tent.

"Get everyone out; let me take some photos. I'll call the tent company, see what they want to do."

"We're going to have to disassemble the entire structure inside."

"Mike will have fun with that." Fred shot more photos with his pocket Minolta. He went around the entire tent snapping shots. He went inside and took photos looking out through the rips. Then he went across Main Street to Bob Prusynski's Photographic Studio on the second floor to get an overall view of Short Court Street. The tent was flattened on the west end; poles stuck out askew; snow piled in heaps.

It stopped snowing.

Fred thought about it for a single second. The snow had stopped. The first good thing to happen today: the snow had stopped. Bob helped Fred open the window to get clean shots of the devastation. Vendors had parked at both entrances to the tent and were carrying out their wares and placing them in vans, trucks, and cars. Fred thanked Bob and walked back to his office. He'd call the tent company, then the insurance company. He had to rush to the Maple Hall of Fame Luncheon at the Patterson Center in Burton. No time, no time.

* * * * * *

Fred located Gene Adams and Gary Dysert. Gary was shouting at a vendor to walk under the bracing, not around it.

"Stupid shit. You tell them and tell them, and they act like a bunch of kids and do whatever they want. Hey, Fred, you still doing okay? Talk about shit, looks like you got your own pile of it. And then this."

"Yeah, thanks. The tent company is on its way out. They want to see if they can salvage it. They will replace it immediately. Can you guys get the framing out?"

"Mike thinks it will take about an hour after we get these stupid, and I mean *stupid*, vendors out of here."

"All right. I called the insurance company and talked to the tent company. They don't insure their tents at this time of the year; it is our cost because of the variable weather. They said the contract requires us to insure it. Then I called the insurance company; they say they are reviewing the policy. They aren't sure if rented items are covered. Won't that be great? No insurance coverage. We'll see…. I'm going to the Hall of Fame Luncheon if you need me." He looked at the tent, shook his head slowly.

"It's a great day so far. Let's see what else we can do," said Gary. He turned and stalked off into the tent, waving his arms and yelling at a vendor.

# CHAPTER 9

F red checked in with his secretary, told her where he would be. Then he went upstairs to check with Tom Brice. Thanked him for his services and said he would talk later.

Fred slogged through the slush to his car. The sky was blue, scattered clouds wisped across the sky. It was not snowing. A clear day finally.

He exited the parking lot onto North Hambden Street and drove to the Patterson Center located at the northern edge of the Great Geauga County Fairgrounds—eight-point-four miles from his office. With the parking lot full, Fred drove further into the fairgrounds and parked along the grandstand bearing the logo "The Great Geauga County Fair."

As he drove, he tried to assimilate and understand the morning's activities. Joe Parker greeted him first thing and wanted representation for a mysterious matter. What was his connection to Fred's charge of murder? There had to be something. There was no love between Earl William and Joe—that was a certainty. Fred had observed Earl William's cold, dispassionate temperament toward Joe during the last trial. And he had observed that same temperament toward Fred at the last pretrial.

Fred had represented Joe in a case against an Amish man, Adam Mose Gingerich. Joe had owned a lot along Swine Creek Road for years. The property adjoining Joe's property, which was subject to an ingress and egress easement for Joe to have access to his property, had been sold to Gingerich. Swine Creek traversed the frontage of both properties, but there was a small bridge crossing into the Gingerich property. Once across the bridge, there was a defined trail, road, or track that traversed into the property several hundred feet, then cut to the left toward Joe's property.

Joe had owned the property for ten years and had had no problems with ingress and egress until Gingerich purchased it. First, Gingerich put his house directly on the path where Joe turned toward his property. Joe, in the spirit of neighborliness, then started driving past and around the house and was still able to access his property with only a slight increase in difficulty. Then, without any notice or conversation with Joe, Gingerich started to construct a barn to house his two horses directly on the new path. It was as if he were trying to block all access to the property.

Joe confronted Gingerich. Gingerich denied there was an easement at all, because the real-estate broker had not told him about it. Gingerich stated he only let Joe go to his property because he was being Christian about it. Joe left and came back two days later and showed him the copy of the Gingerich deed, which reserved an easement of ingress and egress to Joe's property. Gingerich pointed out that Joe could travel the creek bed to his property.

Joe looked at him. Ludicrous. In the springtime, the creek bed was swollen with rushing water—there was no traveling along it at all. When he asked Gingerich how he expected Joe to travel when the creek was flooded, Gingerich said it wasn't his problem: he was allowed to build on his own property where he wanted.

Gingerich then turned sullen and wouldn't talk at all. Whenever Joe asked him a question or made a statement, Gingerich told him to get off his property.

Joe then went to Fred. Fred had looked at the deeds and the topographical map and sent Gingerich a certified letter of demand of ingress and egress. Gingerich got a brand-spanking new attorney from Cleveland Heights to represent him. Tim Slovik had been an attorney for two months and was so excited to have a client that he did whatever was asked of him. He had absolutely no client control. Instead, the client had attorney control. Gingerich told him he did not want Parker traveling across his land. Slovik's position was that the easement be extinguished altogether. So the case went to issue.

Joe had not told Fred that he had lost the past six cases he'd had in front of Earl William. Nor that he shouldn't have lost at least half of those. Joe also did not tell Fred of the latent animosity between the judge and himself. Fred was aware that Joe ran against Earl William for the position of judge and that the campaign had been a nasty affair, but he thought nothing of it. Most attorneys can put those grievances aside, and when the attorney assumes the judgeship, he or she is still supposed to look only at the facts of the case in the pursuit of truth and justice. Lofty goals, and in general, genuinely pursued by judges and attorneys, regardless of the common view that attorneys are only seeking filthy lucre or to win at all costs.

Fred had given money to Joe when he ran for office. Although judicial races are supposed to be nonpartisan, they are, in reality, extremely partisan. Democratic candidates do not fare well in Geauga County; historically, they fail 80 percent of the time. The Democratic candidate may be the best qualified, have the best name recognition, and run the best campaign, but that candidate will lose because of his or her Democratic affiliation, outnumbered two to one by Republicans. The math is clear.

Fred thought both Joe and Earl William would be good judges. They had an equal amount of time in the practice, both knew the county, and both were experienced. The Geauga County Bar Association thought so also. The Bar poll conducted among the members showed them equally qualified. The Bar poll itself was a matter of heated debate. Some members thought it was merely a popularity contest. Others thought it was their duty to inculcate the voting populace with the attorneys' opinion of the judicial candidates, that the attorneys see the candidates in action, and that they, therefore, are best qualified to tell the voters who would be a good judge.

However, the voting public paid no attention to the Bar poll and oftentimes voted specifically against its recommendations. In some instances, the public voted in line with the Bar poll. In other cases, the public voted the most *unqualified*—at least, unqualified according to the Bar poll—into office. One candidate used the unqualified label attributed to him by the Bar poll as leverage with the public, claiming "that it was clear to him and the public that he was not there to serve avaricious attorneys, but he was there to serve the public." He was elected. He also never joined the Bar Association thereafter.

After a hotly contested race, Earl William became the judge. Only within the last several months did Fred have reason to doubt his ethics and veracity. EW's judicial blow-up over the "arrogance" assertion and the case with Joe were still fresh in his mind.

Fred had tried Joe's case in front of Earl William against the wet-behind-the-ears attorney who did not know how to ask a question that was not a leading question. Fred wrote an excellent brief detailing the exhibits, facts, and the legal precedent showing he was entitled to the easement, which had been in existence for ten years and which was expressly reserved in the Gingerich deed. The cross-examination of Mr. and Mrs. Gingerich showed clearly that they told untruths. For one thing, they said Joe had never used the easement during their ownership. Photos of the land showed the trail clearly used with tire tracks traversing to Joe's property. Joe testified he used the easement about five times a year and that he had discussions with the Gingeriches en route to his property along the easement.

Joe lost. Earl William's written decision found Joe's testimony not credible, found the Gingeriches' testimony credible, and designated the location of the easement along the side of the creek bed. With the facts and the law on his side, Joe still lost. Earl William couched the opinion so as to focus all of the attention on the credibility of the witnesses.

Fred advised Joe that appealing the matter to the court of appeals was a dead issue. Credibility of witnesses is in the sole province of the judge and will not be overturned on appeal. Earl William had struck Joe a direct blow.

Fred greatly resented losing to an inexperienced attorney who did not know how to ask a question on direct examination and who wrote a terrible brief. Only then did Joe tell Fred about the prior six contested cases he had lost in front of Earl William. Some he deserved to lose, some he did not. But to lose consistently was telling. Either the judge held a grudge against Joe, or Joe made very poor presentations. Fred thought it must be the former. Now the judge was dead, and Joe had paid him five thousand dollars for a case about which he wouldn't tell Fred any facts, and now Fred was charged with murder.

\* \* \* \* \* \*

The snow melted quickly; slush squirted with each step. Fred entered the Patterson Center ten minutes late. On the right as he entered were the offices of Geauga Soil and Water, on the left was the Ohio State Extension Service, which coordinated all the 4-H clubs in the county. Fred took the steps to the basement where a large room for gatherings and food service was located. Loretta Holmes, the grand dame of the American Cancer Society, sat behind the reception table distributing name tags and taking money for lunch. She held out a name tag for Fred as he bundled up his coat and threw it on top of the coat rack and tossed his hat on top.

Loretta was slight with silver-gray hair neatly coiffed, and she wore a red dress with a corsage of purple orchids. In charge of the Old Timers Luncheon, which was always held on the Saturday of the festival, Loretta had been on the festival board of trustees longer than Fred's twenty years as president.

"You're late, Fred."

"Yes, Loretta, nice to see you, too." He smiled at her. "We had some trouble at the festival."

"Nothing bad, I hope."

"Oh, not too bad. The tent fell down with the weight of the snow. We had to clear out all the concessionaires, and now we have to take down the inside structure, put up a new tent, and keep going."

"Oh my! I hope no one got hurt."

"Not as far as I know."

The room was crowded with farmers. Plaid shirt was the apparel of the day—unless you were Amish; then a white or blue shirt with black or blue suspenders was the outfit. Jim Patterson, along with Nancy Kothera and Jan Haskins, all syrup producers, were the initiating forces behind the Hall of Fame Luncheon. Each year, one or two families were selected for their continuing contribution to syrup production in Geauga County. Sometimes the award was posthumous. The entire family was invited, from parents to siblings to nieces and nephews. A pen-and-ink drawing was created of the nominees by Helen Gaughler and unveiled during the presentation. It was a great honor in this small circle of syrup producers.

Geauga County was known worldwide for its syrup production. Vermont may have a greater quantity, but if you asked anyone in northeastern Ohio who made the best quality syrup, the unanimous answer would be Geauga County. With 203 maple-syrup producers, the syrup contest has multiple divisions: large syrup producers with a minimum of 201 taps, novices with 200 taps or fewer, and the dozen or so out-of-county producers.

The candy category formed into small maple leaves or what is referred to in the sugaring business as twelve maple sugar cakes. In addition, there are categories for maple spread, with the creamy consistency of peanut butter. The one-pound-block category emphasizes sugar, not cream. This is a challenge for the judges, because the cream blocks melt on the palate and appeal to the taste, but the graininess of the sugar blocks is the mark of high quality. Sometimes they confuse what they like with the criteria of the category.

There is also the maple swirl, a one-pound cream. But the most creative is the theme category. In keeping with the theme for that year's festival, participants use candy, block, cream, or any combination of maple syrup they desire to create a novel design. The entries weigh up to forty pounds with all the sugar in them. This year, the theme was "Support Our Troops." Harris-Parker won with a wonderful design: a slab of maple sugar eighteen inches by fifteen inches with an American flag as the background. The stars and stripes were depicted with cream frosting delicately applied. A disc five inches in diameter represented each branch of military service, with cream frosting finely portraying the insignia of each in rich detail.

Fred located a seat at the back next to Hans and Paula Geiss. Paula was forever in competition against Agnes Sojka Sperry for the candy competition. Hans worked for the Geauga Park District and produced syrup in his home evaporator.

Hans was an immigrant from Germany. Fred had attended his naturalization party and presented him with a poster of three bathing beauties in flag swimsuits that revealed most of what they had from the backside: a beautiful poster that had to be relegated to the syrup house because Paula was not going to permit pornography in her home. What a welcome gift, Hans grinned in receipt.

Jim Patterson motioned to Fred to sit at the head table. As president of the festival, he would have to say a few words. Fred moved through the rows of people, saying hello, nodding, and sat next to the festival queen on his left and Jim Patterson on his right. Jim sat next to his wife, Nancy. Also at the head table were Debbie Richards, who would announce all the syrup winners; Mayor John Park of Chardon, who sat next to the first-- and second-runners-up in the queen's contest. It was apparent that no one in this room knew Fred was charged with murder.

Fred gauged there were 175 people in the room, which had a capacity for two hundred. The head table faced rows of tables perpendicular to it. Behind the head table were pen-and-ink drawings of all the past Hall of Fame nominees. Drawings initially were rendered by Tim Struna, but when he left the area for Cape Cod, the duty fell to Helen Gaugler, whose drawings were precise, accurate, and in great detail. To the right of the dais were the pen-and-ink drawings of the winning sugar houses originally created by Tim Struna. However, since that time, about fifteen years ago when Tim left, Fred had photographed, in color, the sugar-house winners. The photos were larger than the pen-ink drawings and, being in color, contrasted sharply with the black-and-white drawings. They added a color enhancement and complemented the otherwise drab room.

Fred's most-recent photograph was on an easel in the corner for all to see. Dan Byler's sugar house, located along Burton-Windsor Road in Middlefield Township, showed bright red with scudding clouds through a deep-blue sky. In the foreground, close up, Fred had captured barbed-wire fencing and posts that enhanced the red sugar house. The photo was taken only two weeks previously. He had waited until he saw steam rising from the sugar house, so he could get a photo with maple syrup being produced. However, when he saw no steam for weeks and the season for syrup making had almost passed, he stopped in to talk to Dan Byler. Dan was not making syrup this year. He had a problem with his equipment. He had leased his sugar bush to a neighbor. Fred then took photographs. He came back on three separate occasions when the light was different and finally got the photograph he liked. And there it stood in the corner. Fred admired it, one of his better sugar-house photos.

Fred made a large, 13 x 19-inch print for Dan Byler, laminated it, and presented it to him at his house a week before the festival. In general, the Amish do not hang artwork in their homes, but Dan said he was going to have it framed.

Opposite the head table at the far wall was a display of various syrups, with light shining behind it to depict the different coloration. Next to it was a series of clear bottles of maple syrup identified by numbers one through six. A box of plastic spoons was available for anyone to taste the winning syrups. Fred had tried it in former years; the tastes were distinctive. The display was set up for the producers' luncheon so the producers could determine for themselves the difficulty of judging the various syrups. In addition to taste, which was the final arbiter, they measured specific gravity at a given temperature with another device, a *refractometer*, which measured the amount of light passing through the syrup, and whether the syrup had colloidal suspension of particles as a result of faulty filtering. Each of these factors received points from the judges, which were tallied at the end to determine the winner. The judges did not know who the producers were, because the clear bottles of syrup were numbered only. As the judges gave their results, Jan Haskins, JR Blanchard, and Nancy Kothera wrote the tallies.

There had been complaints for several years in a row that the same judges, Frank and Virginia Goodell of Goodell Farms in Portage County, only liked the same syrups from the same producers year after year. A review of the winning syrups disproved that theory, but the rumor persisted. To avoid a potential scandal, local producers were selectively invited to assist in the judging. They participated in the organization, collation, and presentation. Their personal input was only given at the taste-test portion of the judging. They were amazed at the process, the length of time necessary for judging, and their own agreement with the judge's decision. The local participation went a long way toward creating a friendly relationship among the winners, the losers, and the judging committee. The producers no longer thought they were being cheated.

Jim Patterson opened the event with a welcome and a prayer. Syrup producers were primarily farmers, and as such, the impetus of secular seclusion had not permeated this aspect of Geauga County: prayers were in order, accepted, and appreciated. Jim conducted introductions of the head table, and dinner was served. Roast beef, chicken, mashed potatoes, green beans, stuffing, the standard luncheon. Dessert was always a special treat of two scoops of ice cream covered with maple syrup.

Festivities commenced after the tables were cleared. Jim reintroduced Mayor Park, who welcomed everyone to Chardon for the annual festival. John said nothing about the status of Judge Kuhmer. Fred was next, as president of the festival, to welcome everyone.

Fred made sure he had installed his Canon 10–22mm wide-angle lens. As he approached the podium, he changed the white-balance dial to fluorescent light and the ISO to 1600. He took two photographs, one to the left, one to the right, encompassing the entire group, and he received a round of applause.

"So far, and let's hope it ends now, this festival has been a disaster."

A muttering of approval rose and fell.

"You have all seen the great amount of snow we have received this morning. It has been so great that it caused the main tent covering Short Court Street to collapse." A sudden murmur of voices drowned Fred out. He waited a moment for the noise to subside.

"However, the matter is being handled as we speak. Mike Tvergyak, Gene Adams, and Gary Dysert, none of whom are here because they are working up at the festival, are facilitating the removal of all of the concessionaires and their goods from inside the tent. It will be taken down. The entire interior superstructure must be disassembled and removed. The tent company will be out this afternoon to remove the destroyed, shredded mess of a tent and replace it with an identical tent.

"Then, Mike and his crew can reassemble the entire interior framing, and we can start over." Fred paused.

"That's the good news," the assembly grumbled.

"What's the bad news?" was shouted.

"The bad news, and I am sorry to have to be the one to inform you, is that Judge Kuhmer, the Common Pleas judge, was found dead this morning, in the courthouse. They think he was murdered." The cacophony was too great for Fred to speak. He held up his right arm, palm spread, for silence.

It took a full minute before silence was restored.

"This is a highly unusual and terrible event. An event that has never happened before in Geauga County. There will be wild, rampant rumors circulating about this event. I only ask that before anyone speculates about this tragedy, that he or she considers the source of the rumors, and lets the facts filter out before coming to any conclusions. This will be a trying time for the festival, the people involved, and all participants. The courthouse will be roped off, so all the teenagers won't be congregating on the steps—which is a good thing."

Once again, the noise exceeded Fred's ability to be heard. He waited.

"I don't have any of the details, but I am sure they will come out before long. I hear they are ugly details. What with the tent collapsing, the snow, and the situation with the judge, this is going to be an interesting and very stressful festival. Let's hope we survive it."

Fred decided on the spot not to inform them of his alleged involvement with the crime. The less they knew at this time, the less they would point an accusatory finger.

"And so, I welcome you to the Geauga County Maple Festival. I thank you for all your participation in the syrup-making process, and congratulate the syrup winners. It will be one tough year.

"This festival has been in existence since 1926. I thought I would run through all of the presidents of the festival from the start. Okay, okay, it won't take long. There have been many important and influential persons as president.

"1926-31, Art Carlson. He's related to the present Dale and Cliff Wedge family. One of the principal starters of the Maple Festival.

"1932, Philip Ward.

"1933, Art Carlson, again.

"1934, Archie Stone.

"1935, Art, again. He's like a bad penny, he keeps coming back.

"1936-39, Ernie Mauer.

"1940–41, Archie Stone, again.

"1942, Art, again.

"1943, 44, and 45, there was no festival because of the big one, WWII. I am sure many of you remember WWII.

"1946-49, Clifton Rossiter.

"1950, Carl Brinkman. Some of you here remember him. He's related to Warren Jevnikar and Dave Jevnikar, the guy who operates GTV, your local TV station.

"1951, Tom White. He's related to Lillian Swank.

"1952-53, Charlie Hall. He used to be an attorney around here. I actually tried my very first case against Charlie in Chardon Municipal Court. But that's another story. He has two local daughters and several sons in the area. Daughters are Peggy Brown and Kathy Gillette.

"1954-55, Art Carlson again. Keep in mind, from 1926 to 1955, that's twenty-nine years of involvement with the festival. What a guy! Or, they couldn't get rid of him. I think the former. And, that is ten years of being president of the festival. That's a lot of work, folks.

"1956-58, Ture Johnson. Boy, talk about a character! He's related to Curt Johnson down in Burton, and Joanne Hiscox.

"1959, Robert Smith.

"1960–62, Lloyd Carlson. Yes, you guessed it, issue of Art Carlson. Maple syrup runs in the blood in some families. In 1961, John F. Kennedy came to the Maple Festival while he was campaigning for president of the United States. In retrospect, that was quite a parade. There are many photos of him mixing with the local gentry.

"1963, Dorothy Wedge. Again, from the Carlson family, mother of Dale and Cliff Wedge. If this building fell down from the snow load, Dale, who heads the Emergency Management Services for Geauga County, would be here to help us dig out. Maybe give us a space blanket to keep warm."

Fred watched the crowd. They weren't getting bored—yet. A couple of smiles at his jokes. He'd better accelerate the litany.

"1964–65, Ture Johnson again.

"1966–67, Wayne Trask, related to Carol Brcak (Breechak).

"1968, Leland Schuler.

"1969–71, back to Wayne Trask.

"1972–73, Richard Taylor.

"1974, Beverly Carver. I know all of you remember her radiant red hair. And she was recently a councilwoman for Chardon Village.

"1975, Charles Reiss.

"1976, Bill Broadbent. Bill has been the concession manager at the county fair for years. I think we trained him to move up.

"1977–78, John Reid, former mayor of Chardon and the director of the festival for about eleven years.

"1979, Paul Richards, who all of you know is famous for Richards Maple Products, and who takes a lot of our syrup to sell across the country.

"1980–81, Doris Cook, intrepid reporter for the *Geauga Times Leader*, and when that went defunct, for some other equally impressive rag. She also, incidentally, got me involved in the festival. Wanted me to be in charge of the Sap Run, which I did for years.

"1982, Dale Schier.

"1983, Paul Newman, local attorney, still involved, etc., etc.

"1984, Bob Adams, cousin of Gene Adams working up at the festival as I speak.

"1985, Connie Burns. She shook up the festival. Tried to put it more on a business level, and it worked. She was the one who started the battle of the bands at the high school, which was a tremendous success. Now there's a sight if you want to see one. All these high school kids—the way they dress. Unbelievable. Just like in my generation … and yours.

"1986, Bob Eldridge, past mayor of Chardon Village.

"1987–88, Karen Dufur.

"1989–90, Alberta Maresh.

"1991, Bob Eldridge, again. It's interesting how these guys keep repeating themselves.

"1992–93, Debbie Richards, Paul's daughter who now operates Richards Maple Products.

"1994, yes, yours truly, and probably the worst we've seen yet.

"Thank you, Jim, it's all yours."

A round of applause, gentle, not overwhelming, settled on Fred.

Jim Patterson stood and thanked Fred and then called for a moment of silence for Judge Kuhmer. Heads bowed.

Jim introduced the past Hall of Fame recipients who were present in the hall.

"I'm handing out a list of the past Maple Syrup Hall of Fame inductees. I won't read them to you like Fred has." Slight applause and laughter.

The backside of the handout read as follows:

## Maple Syrup Hall of Fame

1984

A. B. Carlson

Elmer and Esther Franks

Ture Johnson

Anson and Ella Rhodes

Will and Rena Richards

Cliff Rossiter

## 1985

Glenn and Elsie Degroft
Otto F. And Emmy Hering
Paul McNish
Howard Messenger
Leland Schuler
Howard Taylor

## 1986

Howard McNish
N. C. Mabel Patterson
Paul and Clara Jean Richards
Kenneth and Dorothea Sperry

## 1987

Paul A. Adams
George and Catharine Binnig
Ignatius Cavanaugh
Dick and Ruth Timmons
George and Claire Timmons

## 1988

Lynn H. Hosford
Thomas L White

## 1989

Hilton Farley
Ralph Grosvenor

## 1990

Arthur Carelton Beales Carelton or Carleton?
Jim Patterson
Edward Soubousta

1992
Lloyd and Marjorie Frohring
Frank Marous

1993
Lawrence and Mattie Battles
Harry Modroo

1994
Audre and Evelyn Blair
Charles A. Haas

"But I do want to read to you about this year's inductee."

Jim, with his one arm, the result of a farm accident that has prevented him from using it for any farming ventures since, fumbled with the flyer. "Debbie Richards was born and raised in Chardon. Debbie *lived* the maple syrup business her parents, Clara Jean and Paul Richards, operated. Richards Maple Products began in the early 1900s with Debbie's grandparents, Will and Rena Richards, at the helm.

"Debbie moved to California shortly after graduation from high school. Here she met her husband, Dave Rennie. They married in July 1973 and returned to Ohio in January 1974. She became involved and learned the business that she purchased in 1997.

"Over those years, Debbie attended maple meetings in Vermont, New Hampshire, New York, and Canada and has become active in those associations. Involved in the Ohio Maple Producers Association, she represented Ohio at the International Maple Syrup Institute and now is serving as vice president of IMSI.

"Debbie's association with the Geauga County Maple Festival began upon her return to Ohio in 1974. She is currently a director on the board and served as president in 1992 and 1993, one of a very few within the maple industry to do so. Her amazing ability to organize and attend to detail served her well as she led the board those two years. While Debbie works behind the scenes, she is very capable of effectively representing the industry and leading organizations. She holds a wealth of knowledge.

"Like her parents before her, Debbie hosts the maple syrup judging team for the contest right in the kitchen of her home/business. Just as everyone begins to feel hungry, a pizza appears, compliments of Debbie. Her quiet and dedicated attention to detail has brought added consistency, thoroughness, and respect to the process of selecting the annual winner of the Best Syrup Producer each year. She has kept records that make it possible to look back into the history of these winners, the quality of syrup over the years, and the changes of selection of that winner. Her tireless work has made the Maple Syrup Hall of Fame Luncheon, held during the annual Maple Festival, an event looked forward to by *producers* because of the statistics she provides. Debbie is a person of few words yet knows everything that is going on, working quietly and unobtrusively behind the scenes. Because of that, syrup producers always know they will receive a score sheet that tells who bought their syrup at the auction for the 'A' syrup and how much it brought. They will have their scores and a list of the winners.

"What you might not know is that Debbie's favorite *off*-the-job activity is riding roller coasters! She has been all over the country following this hobby.

"A last word on Debbie from those who have received one of her many cards, notes, letters, and poems—Debbie is truly one caring person. And the maple industry is a true beneficiary. It is obvious to all who know her that it isn't blood that runs through her veins; it is maple syrup!

"Debbie, if you will come up here …"

Debbie approached the front dais where Jim uncovered the pen-and-ink drawing of her, by Helen Gaugler. Applause continued for several minutes. Debbie moved to the microphone.

"This is a great honor. I thought I was too young to be included in this group, but I am thankful. Jim was not aware, but there is another inductee this year. We kept the information from Jim, because he is related to the newest inductee. We did not include the biography of the person because we wanted it to be a surprise.

"My husband, Dave, will hand out the additional flyer to insert in your program. Let me read to you about the other inductee, Nancy Patterson.

"When Nancy Wilson married Jim Patterson, little did she know she was in for a lifetime of maple. There were a few glimpses, however. When

Jim first went down to Circleville to meet Nancy's parents, he brought with him a quart of Geauga Gold. Nancy, however, was sure it was too sweet and cut it in half with corn syrup. Needless to say, Jim was horrified.

"Forward a few years, we now have Nancy with maple syrup running in *her* veins. Canning, cleaning—whatever needs to be done, Nancy is there.

"One of her favorite things is giving sugar-bush tours to young children. She greets the children, gives them a tour of the sugar house, then takes them back into the woods for a firsthand look at the buckets and *spiles*. The highlight is when the kids see the sap dripping from the tree. Later, back at the sugar house, the kids get three silver-dollar pancakes with which to sample the maple syrup, many of them for the first time.

"Maple is a family affair, and Nancy and Jim sure share their love of syrup with their family. Sue, Bill and Mindy, Dave and Pam, and now the next generation with John. The boys, Dave and Bill, know one of the best things is the hot lunch Nancy has prepared, waiting for them at the sugar house after a day of gathering.

"Those associated with the producers' lunch know that it is Nancy who arranges the meal, gets everything organized, sends out the letter, and does her best to make sure that all of us producers have a great time socializing and discussing past times.

"I give you Nancy." A standing ovation greeted Nancy, who stood and moved to the dais. Blushing, Nancy spoke into the microphone. "Thank you all! It has been a wonderful run of syrup all these years with my wonderful husband. I thank you all."

Debbie unwrapped the pen-and-ink drawing and held it for all to see.

Jim approached the microphone smiling too greatly. "Next on the agenda is the announcement of the 2004 Maple Syrup Awards. We once again thank the *News Herald* for sponsoring these awards. They have been great supporters of the maple industry for many, many years. We also appreciate the help of Western Reserve Farm Co-op. They help to finance this luncheon and many other events for us.

"I will turn this next portion over to Debbie, although it seems she has stolen my thunder on the last portion."

Debbie rose and presented the congregation with the winners of the Hobby Taps of 200 taps or less. There were thirty-two entries in this category.

| | | |
|---|---|---|
| 1. Ken Hrabak | Hambden | 24 taps |
| 2. Mike Angelucci | Concord | 18 taps |
| 3. Gary & Beth Tabaj | Claridon | 36 taps |
| 4. Roger Roseum | Chester | 168 taps |
| 5. Brian & Mike Hasman | Newbury | 44 taps |
| 6. Jonathan White | Newbury | 24 taps |
| 7. Hershey Montessori | Huntsburg | 120 taps |

Each person rose and accepted the award and the money that accompanied it. A general applause was held.

Next were the out-of-county awards with thirteen entries in the category. They were as follows:

| | | |
|---|---|---|
| 1. Dick & Tim Sutton | Kinsman | 6000 taps |
| 2. Ken & Francie Bushee | Danby, VT | 4600 taps |
| 3. Dave & Dennis Livingston | South Shenengo, PA | 2,800 taps |
| 4. Holden Arboretum (tapped by Eli D.L. Miller) | Kirtland | 2,025 taps |
| 5. Jeff Cline | Kingsville | 450 taps |
| 6. Wade Fox | Marlboro | 500 taps |
| 7. Jeff Pochedly | Hiram | 1,500 taps |

"Jeff Pochedly was the person who served syrup to the Burton-Middlefield Rotary breakfast at the Burton High School for the entire month of March, approximately 120 gallons of syrup. Goes to show what a good syrup they serve."

Next, Debbie dealt with the candy entries. "Anyone can enter the candy contest. It does not need to be a syrup producer. One gallon of syrup will make seven and a half to eight pounds of candy. The grade-A light amber (also called Fancy of First Run) is best to use. The maker will need a candy thermometer, with which they must be sure to check the thermometer in boiling water. Water is supposed to boil at 212F, but it can vary. Candy temperatures should be adjusted up or down depending on the boiling point of water at different locations.

"The candy branches included Spread, One-Pound Brick Sugar, One-Pound Maple Cream Swirl, Granulated Sugar, Twelve-Sugar Cakes, and Novel Design. Luckily, the candy entries were included in one category. The winners were:

1. Paul Harris and Nancy Parker
2. James Miller
3. Jen Barham and Ken Freeman
4. Aggie Sojka Sperry
5. Paula Geiss
6. James and Elaine Freeman
7. Fred Dietz"

Debbie then went into the 2004 Blue-Ribbon Syrup Auction. "These comprise the one-half-gallon entries the Geauga County syrup producers enter. There were over thirty entries in this class. This was the most prestigious class, and the entries had their syrup auctioned at the festival on Sunday. The winners were:

1. Daniel N. Byler          Middlefield
2. Jim Freeman             Middlefield (FMF Sugarbush)
3. James Miller            Middlefield (Sugar Valley Maple)
4. Bob Haskins            Bainbridge
5. JR Blanchard           Chardon
6. Geauga Maple Co.       Burton
7. Rhodes Sisters         Huntsburg"

The winner, Daniel N. Byler, was Amish, so there was no picture-taking of the event. The *News Herald* newspaper gave out a shining silver plate to commemorate it. Dan was enraptured in the moment. He gave thanks for all those who helped him. It was his second win, so he knew he would be in next year's flyer like the one that Mr. Newman handed out previously.

The flyer read as follows:

## GEAUGA COUNTY MAPLE FESTIVAL
### BEST SYRUP PRODUCERS

1926 Paul McNish
1927 Erwin H. Maltby
1928 Harry Osborn
1929 R.J. Patch
1930 James Ziegler
1931 R.J. Patch
1932 George W. Painter
1933 A.C. Beales
1934 Harry L. Osborn
1935 A.C. Beales
1936 W.M. Scoville
1937 Lillian Eldredge
1938 Lillian Eldredge
1939 H.B. Hosmer
1940 Harry L. Osborn
1941 George Fahnstock
1942 Chris J. Bogaske
1947 Dewey & Harold Fahnstock
1948 Lyle Battle
1949 Glenn Beardsley
1950 John Geil
1951 Roderick Timmons
1952 Charles H. Post
1953 Vernon & Claude Howard
1954 Fahnstock Brothers
1955 Charles H. Post
1956 Frank Marous
1957 Frank C. Marous
1958 Anson Rhodes

1959 Charles H. Post
1960 Anson Rhodes
1961 Tom White
1962 Harold & Clifford Fahnstock
1963 Frank C. Marous
1964 Fred Lindow
1965 Charles Vanac
1966 Burton Armstrong, Sr.
1967 J. Wilbur Patterson
1968 Anson Rhodes
1969 Ed Soubusta
1970 Anson Rhodes
1971 Robert Haskings
1972 Burton Chamber of Commerce–Otto Hering
1973 Anson Rhodes
1974 Ed Soubusta
1975 Sterling Timmons
1976 Mike Cavanagh
1977 Rhodes Sisters
1978 James & Samuel Patterson
1979 Jim Cervenka
1980 Cavanagh Farms
1981 Dick & George Timmons
1982 Sterling Timmons
1983 Timmons Farm
1984 Daniel N. Byler
1985 Robert Haskins
1986 Ed Soubusta
1987 Charles Lusin
1988 Franks Farm
1989 Burton Armstrong, Jr.
1990 Ed Soubusta
1992 Richard Barnes Family
1992 Brian Davis
1993 Daniel N.

# CHAPTER 10

By two o'clock Fred was driving back to his office fretting, worrying, and thinking beyond the Maple Festival again. Wait until all those people attending the Hall of Fame Luncheon learn that he was the one arrested for the murder of the judge. *Won't they be surprised? Yeah,* he thought, wasn't he surprised when he was arrested? What a stunner. Fred kept trying to analyze the relationship of Parker with Earl William, but he couldn't put his finger on it. And would that relationship lead to murder? Why the mysterious hire this morning? Was it for the murder? Who would murder EW? *And a baseball bat: how weird is that? What a day this has been!*

He walked toward the collapsed tent. The sky was bright, clear blue, sunny, the snow was melting fast, the ground was muddy, and people milled around the festival. The rides blared their raucous music and metal screeched against metal. Attendance was light. The vendors in the park area were open for business, but there wasn't much.

The tent people had not arrived. All of the vendors had vacated the tent and Mike Tvergyak and friends were halfway completed with the removal of the structure that divides the vendors' booths. The wooden two-by-fours were piled next to the Dumpsters at both ends of the tent. The west side of the tent, which had collapsed completely, was being held up with long two-by-fours held by four police officers so Mike's workers could maneuver and disassemble the structure. They moved the posts to maintain an avenue of traffic to the exterior. The mood was jovial. The police jibed the workers, the workers insulted the police in reciprocally cordial fashion.

Fred took photos of the tent, the structures being disassembled, the cops holding up the posts, and Mike Tvergyak. "Hey, Mike, you seem to be moving along here."

"Hey, Fred. Yeah, it's not as bad as we thought. Look—we finally found a use for the police! This is the most work they have done in a month!" He pointed to the uniformed cops laughing at one of the workers.

"Looks like they like their jobs."

"They should. They are finally being useful."

"We should be done in about an hour. The tent people are supposed to be here at three o'clock. We'll have it up by five, I think. Only lose one day. I don't know what Gary and Gene are going to do about rebates. I've had several vendors ask me about that. They feel they lost a whole day of sales and that it wasn't their fault."

"We'll see. It wasn't our fault either, so why should we bear the brunt of the vagaries of the weather. I know it's covered in the contract anyway: there are no rebates for weather. We'd strangle ourselves with that one. A little snow and we give back money? Fat chance."

Mike moved a little closer. He spoke in a lower tone. "So, Fred. How are you doing? You getting by? I heard you had a rough time."

"Rough time? Not so much. Craig Albert got me through quickly enough. But that chief. What a …"

"He doesn't like anybody. Not just you."

"Yeah, except I'm the one he's focused on here. Can you believe it, arrested for murder!"

"No, I can't. I can't believe he was murdered at all. And to be murdered here in the courthouse just before the festival? I can't believe it. I heard he was not the nicest guy around, but to murder a judge … And in Chardon, Ohio … We don't get murders here; this is a sleepy little town."

"We got one now, and they are looking at me."

"You need to get a good attorney." He laughed. "You can't hire yourself."

"And if I did, I would have a fool for a client. Yes, I will have to get an attorney, unless they find out who did it before that."

"Who's looking?"

"Good question. I better find out. Keep those cops busy."

Fred walked to the craft show being held in the Park Elementary School auditorium on the east side of East Park Street.

\* \* \* \* \* \*

Friday was Senior Day at the festival. Groups of seniors were bused in from different organizations, churches, the Department on Aging, and local clubs. The Department on Aging held a Senior Queen contest. The winner this year was Ruth Armstrong, mother of Burton Armstrong, sugar-maker. The Armstrong family had a long tradition of syrup making. Burton had won the grand prize on three separate occasions. Their farm was located in Claridon Township along both sides of Route 608 a half mile north of Mayfield Road.

The seniors are provided a pancake breakfast at the Pilgrim Christian Church and then treated to entertainment. One of the highlights for the seniors is to mosey down East Park Street to Park Elementary auditorium for the craft show. With the slush all over the sidewalk, few seniors would be moseying that way. A white sign with green lettering announced the entrance to the exhibit. As Fred entered, his first sight was of the American Business Women's Association bake sale. He took a photo; one lady was looking to the left, the other was moving a bake-sale item. Not a good photo.

Carol Thornton was in charge of the craft show and had been for over thirty years; she allowed the ABWA (American Business Women Association) to conduct their bake sale in return for their staffing her ticket booth. The charge to enter was fifty cents.

Fred nodded to the ticket takers, snapped their photo with flash. Much better this time; the ladies were smiling. Attendance was low. The seniors did not want to walk or were not able to walk through the slush to Park Auditorium. Fred found Carol, made some small talk, and then had her escort him while he photographed each booth. Crafters are extremely proprietary. They get upset if people take photos of their handiwork and start challenging why the photo was taken, creating a scene. Fred had experienced such objections years before.

The crafters think someone is going to steal their ideas and modes of making a particular item. However, Fred thought that, instead, they should feel complimented. But artists are like that, proprietary. Fred had an artist client who wanted to sell his art on the Internet. The art was good at best, and the client was obsessed with preventing theft of his art on the Web. He had paid great sums of money to a website creator to put watermarks on his art, made sure the dots-per-inch ratio (dpi) was sufficient to duplicate a major piece of art, and was otherwise concerned.

Fred had told him succinctly, "Glenn, you are full of shit. If someone wants to copy an Internet photo to print and display in their home, you should be proud. It is obvious that particular person would never pay the going price for one of your *truly amazing pieces of art*. So for that person to print a sloppy photo of your oil painting and display it in his home or office, or even to send it to other Internet sites, is a boon to you. It is a compliment to your art. Your art is getting out there and circulating. If you start selling for hundreds of thousands of dollars, then you might want to think about copyright infringement. However, at this point, you should be downright proud if someone wants to infringe on your copyright. Get your work out there and quit worrying about someone stealing something that they don't even think is valuable enough to purchase at this point. Let them help you make it valuable."

A light had turned on in Glenn's mind. A thought had twisted upside down, and he reluctantly agreed. Now he *wanted* his works stolen: the more people who saw his fledgling art, the more who would want it, the more it would be in demand.

But the *crafters* didn't think like that, and Fred wasn't going to explain the concept to each of them. They were not his clients. So, if he took Carol along with him and she introduced him to each crafter as the photographer for the festival, well, then that was okay. Some of them even posed for the photo, big grins on their faces. Fred photographed small wooden toys in the shape of trains and drag-along dragons.

# CHAPTER 11

Tim Snyder awoke with a start at the buzz of the alarm. He quickly moved out of bed and pressed the alarm button to make it stop. Slowly he remembered the day's events. The judge murdered; Fred Newman arrested; the chief dismissing him because, he said, it was not his case. Glancing at his watch, he saw it was 3:30 p.m. He needed more sleep—five and a half hours was not enough.

Tim descended the steps to the kitchen with the sole thought of a cup of coffee. He rubbed his long, disheveled handlebar mustache into place as he poured himself a cup and stood in the kitchen looking out the window at the melting snow. Carolyn was at work. *Can't hear the kids.* Hank, a tenth grader at Berkshire High School, and Ron in the twelfth. *No TV noises, that's good. What a sloppy mess that snow is. I bet the Maple Festival is a mess.*

He anticipated the night would be a long one again, ambling through the Maple Festival tent, protecting a bunch of junk. That's what it was: sausage sandwiches, beef, bison, and goat jerky, trinkets, Chamber of Commerce literature, T-shirts, jewelry, maple syrup, and stuff. Just junk, really. Not something he was interested in. Now a sausage sandwich with onions and peppers and cheese on top, well, that was something else. Tim made sure he got one of those every day.

And Fred? The chief was out to hang him. Jenkins clearly had troubles with Fred—that was evident yesterday. Tim had heard rumors but never got the story firsthand. Fred had accused the chief of double-dipping or something. But the chief still had his job, so it couldn't have been too bad. The same couldn't be said for Tim.

Tim didn't have a job with the Chardon Police. He blamed the chief. Fifteen years ago, he did have a job with the Chardon police, as a sergeant.

He started as a patrolman and, after three years, he was promoted. He always felt an unease with the chief, but he attributed it to his height. At six-five, it was hard not to intimidate people. He worked diligently and effectively for the Chardon Police Department; however, politics defeated him. Hard work alone doesn't get you ahead in this world.

Tim had attended Berkshire High School. He played basketball when the team went to the Districts and took third place. He didn't get a scholarship, but he went out for the Ohio State basketball team. He did not survive the very last cut. Only players with scholarships survived the cuts. Not a single walk-on player made the team that year, although Tim thought he should have made it. He loved basketball, but he wasn't keen on the Ohio State team … that year. Their record was mediocre and that pleased him *that year*. He still played basketball every Tuesday and Thursday at 6:30 a.m. at Berkshire High School with an old man's team. That's what the kids call it, but the old man's team beat the high-school team every year. It was great exercise, and it kept him young.

After college, with a degree in criminal justice, Tim attended law school at Ohio State. He never wanted to be a lawyer, really, but he thought the education would be invaluable to a career in law enforcement. Law school was tedious. There were too many courses in which he had no interest. Contracts, torts, arbitration, conflict of laws, real property, surety—topics that would have no relevance to a police officer. No doubt, the courses gave him an awareness of the great body of law out there, but they didn't sufficiently hone in on *criminal* law for him. He loved criminal law, constitutional law, and the criminal-procedure courses. He aced them because he liked them. He was ahead of his professors on those topics.

During law school, he worked at Able Security. He had some interesting part-time jobs in Columbus. The culture there was entirely different from Geauga County. He chose to live in Geauga County primarily because of that cultural difference. He wanted his children to be raised in a safe, clean environment without the threat of being beaten and robbed on the street just for being in the wrong place at the wrong time, or wearing the wrong clothes in the wrong neighborhood, or having the wrong color of skin, or saying the wrong thing at the wrong time—like Fred had. Tim laughed out loud in his kitchen to himself. He jerked so violently, the coffee spilled. He quickly set down his cup.

"Someone ought to shove a baseball bat up his ass!" Tim said aloud to no one.

What a statement! The look of shock on everyone's face. Total bewilderment. It was too funny. What coincidence. Tim recovered, wiped the coffee with a paper towel, and continued to sip as he stared at the melting mush.

It certainly was the wrong thing to say at precisely the wrong time. It got Fred arrested on the spot. The chief was looking for anything against Fred anyway. What an opportunity was that—speaking out to the chief like that. The chief did that whenever he didn't like someone, and that included anyone more intelligent than he was.

Tim reflected on his own disagreement with the chief of the Chardon Police Department. He had been promoted to sergeant when Mike McKenna was the lieutenant. There were two sergeants, and he had been quite proud of his accomplishment. He could see himself as chief someday. A forgotten dream now, but a great vision then.

A series of burglaries had been occurring in Chardon Village and the surrounding areas. Chief Jenkins had handled several of the investigations himself, mostly when it involved wealthier citizens. Nothing was solved. The break-ins had been occurring regularly for eight months. At the same time, Tim had started getting bad vibes from the chief. A look askew, a strange look, a distrustful look, as if he knew Tim wanted his job someday. Well, he did, but Tim was working hard for the chief. Jenkins just didn't know how to appreciate it or utilize it to the fullest extent.

Finally, the chief dumped the burglary cases on Tim. To the chief, they were dead, bang losers. What better way to embarrass Tim than to have him fail?

"Here, you take a look at this stuff. You went to law school; you should be able to figure out the criminal mind." Tim thought the manner of delivery of the cases was somewhat nasty, but he relished the challenge. It was clear the chief was jealous of his education. There was no reason for it that Tim was aware of, but that was Jenkins.

Tim looked through the cases. There was a clear continuity to the burglaries. Quite obviously conducted by the same group of people. Back windows were broken and then opened. The back door was unlatched, a vehicle drove to the back door, and items stolen from the houses were put into the vehicle, which then left. It appeared to be a three-person job. There were no fingerprints at the scenes: they must have worn gloves. The shoes left footprints at several of the homes, but they weren't the same every time. Several were the same, but there weren't sufficiently identifiable footprints.

They stole laptop computers, electronic equipment, silver in any form, money, handfuls of jewelry, mostly portable items. Tim looked for patterns. He checked the local pawn shops, found a couple of items, but only in Lake County. He checked those traders, but the transfers were third- or fourth-level, and remembering who each of them had gotten the items from seemed to dim with each transfer.

Tim mapped out a timeline looking for a pattern. He mapped out the route in conjunction with the timeline, and there it was. A pattern. He predetermined six houses he thought the thieves would hit next, within the next two weekends. And bingo, they did. Tim was ready for them, along with four concealed patrolmen. They watched the lead man amble up the drive, slowly case out the houses one at a time, break the window, and enter the premises. Then a van drove into the drive directly to the back of the house as if it belonged there. They even turned on the lights in the house but drew the drapes. A normal house in the evening.

A woman drove the van, which she turned around to head out of the drive. She shut the motor off but stayed put.

Tim maneuvered the officers into a closer position. The first thing to do was secure the driver and then apprehend the burglars as they came out. Officer Jordan stepped out of the bushes with his gun drawn and told the driver to remain still and not say a f***ing word or she would be shot. The other two in the house came out less than ten seconds later with booty in their hands. Two officers were on either side of the van, watching as they deposited the items, and then both officers stepped out at the same time. It was a clean arrest. The burglars gave no trouble.

After the prisoners were Mirandized, they spilled, all separately. It had been the three of them for months on a spree. They thought they'd been pretty good at it, and it kept them in money.

The newspapers and television jumped all over it. Tim got great publicity. Too much publicity for the chief. Chardon Village Council gave him a special citation of thanks. The chief was livid, maybe more embarrassed than livid. He didn't show it, but Tim knew it was there. Tim could tell how his attitude had changed. He had become a threat to his employer and the chief's power. Tim had to go.

Six months later he was out of there. "So sorry, Tim, but we don't have enough money in the budget for two sergeants, and Kline has more time in grade. It's been great working with you. I will give you a glowing letter of recommendation."

And that was that. Tim's career as a police officer–on-the-go got up and went. Now he was a sergeant for the Burton police. Burton, a sleepy little village, twelve miles to the south of Chardon. Very little crime. DUIs were the greatest offenses, repeat DUIs even greater, and an occasional domestic dispute. Tim liked it, but he wanted to have a little more action, a little more ability to hone his investigative skills, and a lot more challenge. But, thanks to Chief Jenkins, Tim knew he would not get that chance … unless …

Unless he could help Fred by finding the real murderer of the judge. He couldn't believe that Fred Newman would kill Earl William, no matter how much he might have disliked him. Tim didn't even know if Fred *did* dislike him, except for the statement, the now-famous statement. "Someone ought to shove a baseball bat up his ass!" Tim laughed again.

The snow was melting as Tim watched. The sun was shining, the sky a bright, light blue with puffy clouds. What a beautiful day and a mess for the festival.

Could Fred have done it? Maybe, but not likely. If he did, would he have so glibly made the statement? Tim didn't think so. Fred had been a ranger in the army in Vietnam. Tim thought he certainly had the capacity and the ability to kill someone. But to commit murder? Tim thought not. Fred was too community-oriented. This was his community. He was too involved. Not that it would keep anyone in particular from killing someone, but it just didn't seem to be in accord with his personality and his activities. He would rather help folks work out the problem than completely alienate them. No, Tim thought, he would have to go on the premise that Fred did not do it and move forward from there.

*So what about Fred?* Tim thought. Tim was going to have to help him in this situation. Obviously, the chief was not going to investigate anyone else. He would focus all his attention on convicting Fred rather than opening his eyes to finding the real murderer.

Tim held his coffee cup in salute to the sky. "Fred, here's to helping you and shoving the proverbial baseball bat up the chief's ass. And may God save Ireland."

# CHAPTER 12

D enise Kaminski, clerk of courts, took Tim Snyder's call.
"Denise, this is Tim Snyder. I'm sure you're aware that Fred Newman was charged this morning with the murder of Earl William?"

"Yes, I can't believe it. It's not like him. It's so horrible. The courthouse has been in complete chaos today."

"I *don't* believe it, and I'm going to do something about it. I wonder if you could find some time for me to look at the records in the clerk's office. I want to see what kind of people Earl William had been dealing with. Who would want to kill him? I think maybe I can get some information from the court files."

"Well, they *are* public records. When are you thinking?"

"I just woke up. I have police duty at the festival tonight in the tent, so my time is limited. How about now?"

"We close in about twenty minutes."

"If I get up there in about fifteen minutes, can I spend a couple of hours going through them?"

"I'll have to stay here with you. I am the custodian, and this is a difficult time," she hesitated. "Sure, Tim, come on up. That way I can get a gyro sandwich before I go home. I'll read a book or something. I'll be here."

"Thanks, Denise, I'm on my way."

\* \* \* \* \* \*

The trip from Burton took ten minutes at a good speed. Tim parked in Fred's office lot across the street, strode up the steps to the second floor, and went directly to Linda's office. She wasn't there.

"Where's Linda?" he asked Anita, the court reporter.

Anita looked up, flashed her big, beautiful dark eyes, smiled her big grin. "She left for the day early. She was too shaken up by what she saw."

"I bet. Had to be a shock for her. When you see her, let her know I was looking for her. I'd like to talk to her when she has time."

"Sure, Tim, no problem."

"Let me ask you …" Tim leaned against the doorjamb, began to twirl his mustache, "Did Earl William have anybody who was so pissed at him that they wanted to kill him?"

"The police are already asking us those questions. They told us not to talk to anyone about it."

"I *am* the police." Tim pointed to his uniform. "I don't think the local police are going to work very hard to find the real murderer now that they've arrested Fred."

"I don't think so either." Anita put her index finger over the side of her mouth in a slight pout. "Oh what the hell. Fred didn't do it. He's too nice of a guy. He and the judge argued, but that was just argument. Like all attorneys, they argue and then smile and shake hands."

"Yeah, but who else? Who should I look at?"

"I hate to cast aspersions, you know. I don't like to point fingers. But," she smiled coyly, "you might want to talk to Mark Wellman maybe. The judge filed a grievance against him. Or Joe Parker! That campaign was nasty. They put on a good face when they are in the same room, but they don't like each other. But not murder. I'm just giving you these names of attorneys who didn't get along with EW. People I have seen in tense situations with him." She frowned. "Don't tell anyone I gave you any names … promise?"

"Sure, no problem. Anyone else?"

"That's all that come to mind for attorneys. There are lots of defendants, of course. Who knows what they would do? But I didn't even give those names to the police. I didn't think of them earlier. Make sure you don't tell them I said anything."

"Anita, I'm just looking into this thing because I don't believe Fred would do this, and I don't believe the police are going to make any attempt to look for anyone else who did do this."

"I understand." She smiled her big grin, showing clean, white, straight teeth—a perfect smile. "Don't forget, any of those defendants he put in jail might be suspects."

"Anyone in particular?"

"Armstrong *threatened* to kill the judge. He was on a drug charge. Said he was going to get him wiped out. The deputies had to restrain him. I think he was whacked out on drugs at the time. That was a nasty one...."

"Then there was, I forget his name. He was found to be a sexual predator ... the balding guy—short, fat, real puffy red face with a mole right under his lip. He gave me the creeps. He looked at the judge a real long time. Just stared at him. Creepy." She shook her shoulders in a tremor of fear, her perfectly coiffed hair shimmering with the movement. "That's about all I can think of."

"Thanks, Anita, that gets me started. It's time for you to go home." Tim glanced at the clock on the wall: 4:30 p.m.

\* \* \* \* \* \*

Tim almost collided with his sister, Judy, descending the stairs from the third floor where the probate court was located. The probate court, presently located in what used to be the balcony area for the second-floor courtroom, had been Judy's employer for the last ten years.

When the courthouse was rebuilt a year after the fire of 1868—which burned all of the buildings on Main Street, including the previous King Courthouse—an elaborate new courthouse had been constructed.

To quote the *Geauga Democrat* of August 24, 1870, which gave a description of the courthouse in detail:

> *The new Court-House for Geauga County, Ohio, at Chardon, is, in most respects, a fire-proof building of the first class, being constructed with brick and stone walls and partitions, and the several floors consisting of series of brick arches turned between rolled iron girders. The order of architecture employed is the Tuscan, with modifications and without many of the enrichments pertaining to the order. The objects sought to be attained, namely, a solid,*

substantial and convenient Court-House, and moderately ornamental withal, have been accomplished, and the result is an edifice that will stand through "generations yet unborn." A fitting Temple of Justice, and creditable to the enterprise of its projectors.

The dimensions of the building are, briefly, sixty-one foot wide and eighty-five feet long, exclusive of the tower projection of seven feet on the south front. The top of the balustrade is fifty feet above the ground, and the vane on the tower is at an altitude of one hundred and twelve feet.

The basement is used for the hot air furnaces by which the building is warmed throughout, and for storage of fuel, etc.

The first story, thirteen feet high, entered by broad flights of stone steps at north and south fronts and through massive wrought-iron doors, contains, on the west side of the Central Hall, which is twelve feet wide, and paved with marble tiles, the offices of the Recorder, Probate Judge, Sheriff and Surveyor. The Auditor's, Treasurer's and Clerk's offices are on the east side of the hall. The main staircase, entirely of iron-work, occupies a space of about fifteen feet square on the west side of the hall. A fire and burglar—proof vault or strong-room opens from the Treasurer's Office, and is the work of Itall's Safe and Lock Co., of Cincinnati.

The second story contains the Court-Room, forty-two by fifty-eight feet, and twenty-two feet high, at the north end of the building, and a Witness and Jury Room on either side of the hall, extending from the Court-Room to the south front, where access is had to an iron balcony in front of the tower.

The Witness and Jury Rooms and hall are twelve feet high, and admit of a third story nine feet high over them; the ceiling of the latter being in line with that of the Court-Room.

The rooms in the third story are, as yet, unappropriated to any definite use, but will be convenient for numerous purposes, such as the storage of valuable public papers, and for committee meetings, etc.

*The tower, above the main roof, is octagonal in form, and contains the belfry, which is surmounted by a dome roof, with dormer windows, terminating with ball and vane at the top.*

*The work was commenced in August 1869, and the corner-stone was laid with appropriate ceremonies, on the 10th of September following.*

*The contract was originally awarded to the late L. J. Randall, of this place, for $70,000, but, after his death, was transferred to Messrs. Carpenter & Mathews, of Meadville, Pa., who were at the time in charge of the work. It has been executed in a manner worthy of the high reputation sustained by these gentlemen as master builders.*

*Mr. Joseph Ireland, of Cleveland, was the Architect, and it is but justice to him to say that the plan was admirably conceived, and the finished work will ever be regarded by all beholders as a most beautiful and fitting monument of his skill and taste. But few changes have been made in the original specifications, and those such only as to add to the beauty and durability of the work, without materially modifying the general plan, as, for instance, hardwood has been substituted for soft in the inside finishing.*

*The above cut, skillfully executed by Mr. George W. Tibbitts, the well-known Cleveland engraver, is an excellent and exact representation of the building, except that, as stated, the tower terminates with a ball and vane, instead of being surmounted by a statue. The latter was deemed most appropriate, but was omitted by the commissioners, on account of the extra expense required to procure it. The North Park, on which the building is located, is being graded and suitably paved, and it is to be surrounded by an iron fence, as represented above.*

*The following official table, furnished us by Auditor Tilden, shows the entire cost of the*

| Court-House, and everything connected therewith: | |
|---|---|
| Original Contract for constructing building | $70,000.00 |
| Change inside finish from soft to hard wood, tiling hall with marble, etc. | $4,348.00 |
| Furniture for Court-Room and offices | $5,665.00 |
| Iron fence, flagging, grading, etc. | $7,196.70 |
| Bell for Court-House and fixtures | $880.00 |
| Transportation on same | $10.55 |
| Carpet and mats for Court-Room, etc. | $200.00 |
| *Chandelier for Court-Room, etc., say | $75.00 |
| Plans, drawing, specifications, etc. | $1000.00 |
| Total | $88,863.35 |
| *Chandelier not yet purchased, but estimated. | |

*At a special meeting of the Commissioners on Saturday, last, the work was thoroughly inspected and duly accepted. The County Officers have taken possession of their respective offices, and the Court of Common Pleas is now in session in the Court-Room, his Honor, Judge Conant, on the Bench.*

*In justice to the Commissioners, we must say that, from first to last, they have endeavored to discharge their delicate and important duty with equal regard to the proper construction of the building, and to the interests of the people, at whose expense it has been erected, and whose temple it is.*

However, the present courthouse, after extensive renovation, is a discombobulated assemblage of rooms with an attempt at, but obvious failure of, organization. The courtroom on the second floor, which originally had a balcony and ceiling twenty-two feet in height, was modified in the 1960s to remove the balcony, lower the ceiling, and relocate the probate court on the third floor. The aesthetic integrity of the courtroom was lost forever. Probate was combined with the juvenile court; a single judge presided over both jurisdictions. Probate and juvenile cases are not necessarily compatible studies of law, but at the time the juvenile court was created, it was believed that probate could handle the caseload. And it has.

Tim's sister worked as an investigator for the juvenile court. Her duties included interviewing all persons connected with any child-abuse case. Tim was repulsed by some of the stories Judy told him. Some of the child abusers even lived in Burton. Such horrible things they did to their own kids or others'. Tim wouldn't want her job for the whole world. At least in his job, he experienced some variety, not the same unseemly clientele repeatedly.

Judy smiled. "Hey, Tim."

"Hey, Judy. Got a minute? I want to talk to you."

"Sure."

"Come over here. Let's sit by the attorneys." Tim pointed to the photo of the current Geauga County Bar Association. Of the 165 members, about a hundred had shown up for the photo composite. Their headshots are displayed above one of two benches facing each other in the hallway area between the clerk's office and the entrance to the bailiff's office. Above the opposing bench is a framed text of "The Lawyer's Creed" along with photos of past Common Pleas judges.

The clerk's office is divided into three parts. On the east side is the official clerk's office, where all papers are filed and time-stamped. This is the busiest office in the building. People constantly pass in and out, signing out files, checking judgment entries, filing cases, motions, and moving mountains of paper. Three computer screens are available for public use to track the docket of each case. Above the computers are eleven photos, donated by Fred, of the courthouse in various seasons and light: silhouettes, fall colors, snow, summer, a wide-angle shot from directly below the entrance—very artistic, and it provided color to the room.

The second part of the clerk's office was located at the south end of the building and consisted of Denise Kaminski's office and the office of her chief deputy. The third part is on the west side of the building across the hall where another office is located, similar in size to the main clerk's office. Four women process papers; send out information to probation departments and correctional centers; process indictments, bonds, executions, sheriff sales; and make sure the files are kept current. The office is always busy, always understaffed, and always under-budgeted by the county commissioners. Unlike Ashtabula County to the northeast, which is only open half-days because of budget problems, Denise has kept the office open full time and run efficiently. Ashtabula's Common Pleas judges had to file a judgment entry that extended the statute of limitations dates until noon the day following the statutory date. The Supreme Court of Ohio has recognized the budget difficulty and issued a ruling permitting the extension.

Tim motioned Judy to the bench.

"Judy, you okay? How has this situation in the courthouse affected you or your job?"

"The place is in an uproar. We couldn't get into the building until after lunch. You can see: they still have that area blocked off."

Tim had noticed. Yellow tape was strung across the judge's chambers and the double doors providing access to the bailiff's office and the courtroom. "I see." He also saw the head of a deputy, through the windows, sitting in the bailiff's office. "What's the scoop? Do they have any idea who did it?"

"I don't know."

"What about gossip? There's got to be lots of gossip in the courthouse. There always is. What's the poop? Whose names have been thrown around?"

"What's your interest?"

"Fred's my friend. I'm going to help him out."

"Ahh, everyone knows he didn't do it. That's so much hype. Everyone knows it except the chief of police. Boy, he's an arrogant ass."

"Tell me about it." He smiled a knowing look.

"Oh yeah, he's your buddy, isn't he?" she said sarcastically.

"Yeah, he's my buddy." Tim faked spitting on the floor with a jerk of his head at the same time. "So what do you hear? Who are the suspects?"

"Tim, you've got to know, I don't know these people they are talking about, but I'll tell you their names. You get to figure it out for yourself."

"I'm going to go into the clerk's office to research some old files looking for people, but I thought it might be helpful to get the skinny from inside the courthouse first. So who are you hearing about?"

"Three names, Allan Schmucker, the judge put him in jail a couple of times; Mark Wellman—"

"Oh yeah, Mark. Who else?"

"Pastor Bob someone."

"Oh, down in Troy. That guy. But that was several years ago, wasn't it? I remember him. Ran a church school. His kid was playing around with the students."

"Yes, that's him. Those are the only three names that keep coming up. Although some people have said that Fred had an argument with Earl William a couple of weeks ago that was pretty ugly. And surprisingly, none of the cops have talked to anyone in the courthouse except EW's employees."

"Give them time. They are probably starting from the inside out. They'll get to everyone. But that's the scuttlebutt, huh? Just three names. He's got to have lots of enemies. He wasn't known as the nicest guy around. No other attorneys mentioned?"

Judy blushed instantly, but said, "Not that I've heard. Not that I know. No. I mean, there's a couple of attorneys he has greatly embarrassed, but that is normal. Not something you kill someone for. And those aren't *grudges*—you just don't like the guy. Several of them are female and they are not going to go out to kill the judge."

"No, I don't think this was a female thing. He was too heavy to move."

"I heard you were one of the first ones to see him?"

"Yeah, Linda came out screaming her head off. I guess I saw him next. Not a pretty sight."

"Was it really a baseball bat, like they say?"

"A little one. Like the Louisville Sluggers they give kids who go to the games at the Jake on a Saturday night. Not a big one!" Tim laughed. "Wouldn't that be something if a regular-sized bat was used. Whoa, a little pain in the ass there." He shook with quiet laughter.

"And his head in the toilet?"

"Yep. Dunking for toadstools."

"Tim." Judy slapped him on the arm. "Don't be irreverent. His people really liked him. Don't let anyone hear you say that stuff." Judy stood. "I've got to go and get dinner for the kids."

"How are they? How are you and hubby doing?"

"The kids are fine …" She let trail her statement, nothing about her husband.

"That bad, huh?"

"Let's just say things aren't working out all that well. We have our problems. We've grown apart somewhat."

"Well, Sis, it's none of my business, and I'm not going to stick my nose into it, but it doesn't help when you are putting a wedge into your marriage by trying to replace him before you are already divorced."

"Good-bye, Tim." She gave him the finger, quickly turned, and went down the stairs.

Tim knew she had been seeing Joe Parker on the side for some dinner dates. She wasn't brazen about it, but several people had told him they saw her and Joe at the Red Hawk Grill on Auburn Road in Concord. Joe and Earl William weren't the best of friends either. After that nasty campaign, Tim was surprised they ever talked to each other. *Ever.* One of the nastiest campaigns the county had ever seen.

\* \* \* \* \* \*

Tim met with Denise for ten minutes. By the time they were done, all of the clerk's employees had left. Denise showed Tim how to access the older files. She cautioned him that this was just some research he was doing for a paper and she was accommodating him. Nothing more, nothing to do with the murder of Earl William. She didn't want to get wrapped up in it, but as sure as she knows cotton was a monkey, Fred did not kill Earl William.

"Cotton was a monkey?" Tim smiled.

"It keeps me from swearing."

"I like it. And, hey, Denise, I got a couple of names. Let me run them by you. See if they mean anything to you. Just bounce them off you to see if they ring a bell. Schmucker?"

"I don't know that one."

"Pastor Bob?"

"Oh, I remember him. I think he threatened to kill the judge at one time. But that was several years ago. He's too wimpy for that, I think."

"Mark Wellman?"

"Everybody remembers him. He got disbarred for a while. I think Earl William did that, too. But to kill someone … I don't know. He's back now. I've seen him several times filing things. He's courteous, but there *is* something about him. Those bushy eyebrows. I think he never combs his hair. He gives me the creeps. I don't know. I wouldn't want to be on the other side of the courtroom from him. He seems like he can be downright mean."

"Anybody else you think I haven't covered? Anyone else I should look at in your files."

Denise hesitated. She sighed deeply, turned a shade pink, said, "I don't want to talk out of school, but if you're looking at cases, Joe Parker hasn't won a case with Earl William since he's been on the bench."

*Joe Parker,* Tim thought. *But murder?*

"I'll look at them. Think there was anything between them?"

"Not really, but maybe. How can I say it? That last campaign was really ugly. I ran unopposed in the same campaign, so I saw how they attacked each other. Earl William said things in the background. Really not-nice things."

"Like what?"

"You're not supposed to speak ill of the dead, you know. But, things like 'In the land of the blind, the one-eyed man would be king. And, we are not in the land of the blind.' Just to say that about a real one-eyed man was mean. You know the story of how he lost his eye, don't you?"

"No, actually, I don't. I heard rumors, but never really knew. What was it?"

"Apparently, when they were kids, middle school or something, Joe and Earl William's brother were the best of friends. They got to horsing around in one of their houses, like kids do, and Earl William's brother jabbed something in Joe's eye. He lost the eye altogether. It was hanging out, I think.

"Then, I guess they weren't best friends after that. Understandable, of course. But that's not the end of it. Those two ran against each other for class president in Cardinal High School their senior year. I was in the class behind them. Earl William's brother—his name was Robert—said the same very nasty things about Joe's eye: 'In the land of the blind, the one-eyed man would be king, but folks, we are not in the land of the blind. We would be the laughingstock of the county if we had a one-eyed president.'

"You mean the same exact thing Earl William said while campaigning against Joe, by the guy who poked his eye out?"

"Yeah, and that's not all. He would call Joe 'Mr. Verbosity,' because he was on the debating team and he could talk up a storm. It was really nasty. I heard some of the same things from Earl William in the campaign. Like he was dredging it all back up."

"But murder, Denise?"

"Oh, Tim, I'm not saying he committed murder; I'm just giving you some of the background you asked for."

"Sorry." He waved his hands palms out in apology. "What else?"

"Something very weird happened. About a month after graduation, maybe right before college of that same summer, Robert Kuhmer disappeared. Just gone. No one ever heard from him again."

"You know, I think I remember that. They never found the body, did they?"

"No. And Joe was questioned a number of times, but they never found anything."

Denise took a long breath, glanced down the hall to make sure no one was present. "I got the feeling, but I'm not sure, that Earl William thought Joe had something to do with his brother's disappearance. Or, even if he didn't have something to do with it, that he blamed Joe for it. It's all I can think of. I saw them on the campaign trail. They really hated each other's guts, but they were professional about it. You know, like attorneys after a case where they lie to each other, are nasty and mean, and then at the end of the case they are all smiles and congratulate one another. It was like that. But not quite—there was an undercurrent of real hate. 'Hey, I'm a professional; I'll say you're a nice guy to your face, but you are like a piece of cotton-was-a-monkey.'"

"Anyone else with a loss record like Joe's?"

"Not that I can think of. Boy, this really screws up the Maple Festival, doesn't it?"

"Yeah, it does, the snow doesn't help much either ... with the tent. And look at Fred, arrested at the Maple Festival. President, and he gets arrested. This is going to be one strange case." Tim paused, "Okay, let me look at these cases. I'll start with the names I have and then branch out. Do you have time, Denise? I have to be in the tent later for security. From what I saw out there, it will be up in the next hour."

"Take as long as you want, I have some other work to do. Good luck."

Tim turned to the bank of computer screens.

# CHAPTER 13

F red stood. It was 4:30 p.m., time to check the tent. He slipped on his rubbers—no reason to get his shoes wet. Placed his wide-brim rain hat on his head; a silver maple leaf pinned to it showed Maple Festival support. As soon as the door opened, the sounds of the festival assailed him: loud variations of music, screeching rides, a siren, a huge diesel generator, and people. Screams of joyous terror at the moment of maximum drop or swing of the rides. The cacophony of sounds was soothing to Fred. This was the sound of the community coming together for its annual spring rite.

The bright sun slanted low in the sky casting long shadows. The temperature, in the mid-forties, was balmy by all accounts. With the snow melting quickly, the roads and sidewalks were clear, and only a two-inch slushy layer of snow lay on the grass and mud. The tent was fully erected, and vendors were already parked at the ends reloading their wares. Traffic was congested. Vendors double-parked or just stopped in the street while their wives or children ran to and fro, taking supplies into the tent. East Park Street was stopped, with all the traffic channeled into one lane. Horns honked from angry drivers. Local residents trying to get home after a busy day at the office became quite frustrated with the festival: this was the germ of discontent with the event. It interfered with their orderly lives.

There were some Chardon residents who did not like the festival. As unbelievable as it sounded to Fred, they thought it was just one big *carnival*. They didn't come uptown for the maple stirs, didn't care about the syrup producers' contest or participants, didn't like the queen contest, didn't watch the bathtub race or the parades, and were negative in all aspects. When they looked at the square from the outside, it was only a cheesy carnival. If they would or could have viewed the festival from the inside, they would have seen a community celebration of the end of snow, the coming of green leaves and plants and shrubs, the flow of maple sap, the change from sap to syrup, the transition from winter to spring. They would have seen their neighbors walking their children uptown for a stir, for a turn on the Dragon Ride, telling their children to slow down; they could watch the high-school bands in the parade, see their friends and neighbors participating, enjoy the fun of it all. But they didn't open their eyes to all these things, because some silly vendor blocked their way on East Park Street and made them angry, and the anger spread inward, feeding a bias against the entire festival. They were the naysayers. They wrote letters to the editor complaining about the noise, the damage to the park, about anything. If the festival weren't there, some other facet of life that inconvenienced them would be the subject of their complaint, but fortunately for them, the festival provided a great outlet for their frustrated angst.

A few years ago, a past president had written an article to the local paper to be included as a guest editorial. He expressed thanks to all the local participants, to all the community groups that supplemented their budgets by helping at the Maple Festival. Here is that letter printed in *the Geauga Times Leader*:

> *Guest Editorial*
> *Festival Madness*
> *By Paul A. Newman*
>
> *It seems to go on endlessly, but I can't figure out why. For what reason do these Geaugans celebrate the Festival of the Maple Syrup—a sweetish substance, pleasant to the palate, and tacky to the touch. Big deal—why waste the time?*
> *The energy expended by the obviously numerous persons, for what appears to be (I guess I don't know). Why do they do it? Why do the Kiwanians sell the syrup for such a small gain to them? What motivates the Rotarians' mushkabob commitment? Does the Humane Society activate 85 people in four-hour shifts to sell tickets for the rides merely because the festival board contributes a small sum to the Society? (Maybe.) And who are those boys (good Scouts, I'm sure), and*

*parents picking up the trash constantly dropped during the festival (can the festival board adequately compensate them?). I can't believe the Chardon Jaycees clean up the park for that small sum of money! And you say the Jaycettes sell tickets for the Antique Show, Sheauga Quilters at the Quilt Show, and parishioners at the St. Mary's Art Show—but why? Is that the Welcome Wagon in the Information Booth?*

*What do they get for it?*

*I mean, why would all those units join the parade—those prizes aren't that great, are they?*

*I can't figure out all those businesses either—*The Times Leader, Weekly Mail, *and* News Herald—*why all that free advertising and free brochures. It can't sell newspapers! And the Republican Party giving their offices for a whole week, with their wonderful secretary (why is this done?)—it hasn't changed my politics—has it?)*

*Is there something I'm missing? It seems like the entire county activates itself for a sacrifice. All these pancakes sold by the Eagles, Pilgrim Christians, OAPSE, Crescendo Club, Masons, and Catholics—what energy! And those members work for what.?*

*And that crazy Chardon Board of Education allowing such use of their facilities—oh my, why everyone gets to use them. Is that right? So what if they are public facilities. What about all those parking lots donated by those businesses for those social groups to get money. Why do the Judges hold courthouse tours on Tappin' day?—a Sunday at that. Do you mean to tell me that the Geauga Lyric Theatre Guild is motivated by lucre—they don't even get paid. And between the Methodist Church and Chamber of Commerce putting on the old-timers dinner—well, I just don't know. Why does John Brindo holler "ham" until he is hoarse?*

*There exists something in this county that causes fear for apathy. So many people are doing so many services for which they receive little or no compensation. This community effort has culminated in the festival celebrating the maple syrup.*

> *This cataclysm of selfless sacrifice and energy by Geauga County Volunteers is, or so it overwhelmingly appears, what makes the Festival the community effort it is.*
> *Thanks.*

> *Editor's Note: Paul Newman was president of the Geauga County Maple Festival Board this year.*

But what about *this* year? What was happening at the festival? The courthouse was closed, and festival patrons were squeezing their vehicles into the parking lot. A pickup truck with a thirty-foot horse trailer was parked in the center of the lot, which interfered with access to the far end of the lot. The pony rides were erected at the southern edge of the parking lot on the asphalt surface. This saved wear and tear on the park. Straw was strewn on the ground to soak up the snow and slush.

A line had formed for the pony rides. Parents walked next to the ponies, holding their children for physical and psychological support. No one wanted their kid to fall off the little pony—a big horse to the little ones—and some kids were guardedly afraid of the little, but big-to-them, ponies. The ride operator was a short man, bow-legged, dressed in dungarees and denim jacket, scuffed and worn cowboy boots with a huge, tan cowboy hat. His features were grizzled and weather-worn. He was the typical cowboy. Year after year, he set up the pipe fence, installed the center post, hooked the ponies, saddled them, and provided rides for kiddies. Oftentimes, the parents enjoyed the ride more than the kids, taking photographs for posterity.

Fred removed his camera from his bag, took off the 18–55 mm zoom lens and replaced it with the Tamron 28–300 mm zoom. With the multiplication factor of 1.6 of the APS-sized sensor on his Canon Digital Rebel, it turned into a 44-450 mm lens. Fred could zoom right in on faces and expressions. He snapped several photos. He zoomed in on the cowboy; his face was in shade, so he zoomed closer to remove the exterior light. Fred caught parents in ecstasy with their children. These were good times for parents; they so enjoyed the joy and adventures of their children.

Fred checked his ISO reading. It was set at 100. He reset it to 400. Later in the evening, he would move it to 800 and then to 1600 for fast low-light photos. He kept the control at P for automatic program and auto focus. It was much easier with snapshots on P. Fred took fifteen shots of the kids, ponies, and parents, and then moved on.

He walked on the diagonal path from the courthouse toward Main Street, past the funhouse on the right where a grubby-looking man was taking tickets. *Grubby* was a genial adjective for the manner in which the man was dressed. A dirty baseball cap, greasy Carhartt tan jacket, greasy blue jeans, he looked like he had just changed the oil on a car and gotten caught in the oil. Fred made a point to have a talk with John Richardson, the ride owner, about the cleanliness of the ticket takers and ride operators. In accordance with the Ride Operator Contract, the employees were required to wear uniform shirts identifying themselves. This operator was completely identifiable by his filthy clothing, but nameless. Fred walked past the Italian pastry concession on the left selling cannolis and twenty other varieties of pastries. He intended to purchase some to take home to his wife later. The park was crowded. Fred was pleased.

Friday was one of the two *local* days. Thursday night was considered *suicide night*. The local kids dubbed it so, thinking they were the testers for the rides. And so they were, but only after rigorous inspection by the state inspectors. The Maple Festival, the first festival of the year in Ohio, was thoroughly inspected to be made doubly sure of the safety of the rides. It was more trouble for J & J Amusements, but it was safer all around. Fred did not complain when a ride failed to be approved. But he did complain if the ride sat throughout the entire festival without being repaired or used after it failed inspection. That had happened a time or two. The contract with the ride company allowed for a flux factor for the number of rides provided, but when a ride occupied space and was not being used, that was a loss of money for the ride operator and the festival. There were fifteen rides permitted, of which five had to be kiddie rides and five had to be major rides. The kiddie rides were located at the southeastern end of the park south of the log cabin. The major rides were interspersed throughout the park and located as much as possible on the edge of Main Street for ease of erection and to prevent the necessity for the use of expensive plywood to set a base for the ride in the muddy park.

All of the rides were required to use plywood when they were inserted. The plywood was supplied by J & J Amusements one year, by the festival the following year, alternating every other year. It was placed under the wheels of the tractor and trailer while being installed. A line of men picked up the plywood over which the ride had traveled, carried it forward and placed it in front of the tractor, and made a plywood floating road for insertion. It was the only way to keep the park from incurring deep ruts into its soft topsoil. There had been so much topsoil placed in the park by the festival cleanup committee over the years that it was the best soil in the county; however, it was soft, especially when wet after being dumped on with slushy snow. One year, a ride slid off the plywood to become embedded three-feet-deep in the topsoil. A much larger tractor had to be used to pull it out.

Gene Adams and Gary Dysert oversaw the installation of the rides and used a tractor, generously donated by Middlefield Farm and Garden some years and by Spear Tractor in other years. Ride installation occurred on Easter Sunday night after six o'clock. The square buzzed with activity. The mayor, village administrator, zoning inspector, and members of the council huddled around watching, keeping a close eye on the proceedings to make sure the plywood was used and no damage to the park occurred. They were the watchdogs for the naysayers to whom they often listened too closely. Ameliorating all sides was politic.

Fred walked past the four Dumpsters located at the west end of Short Court Street at the west entrance to the main tent. Two Dumpsters were placed on each side of the cement barrier separating the middle of Short Court Street. At the end of the evening, the Chardon Lions Club policed the area picking up debris and depositing it into the Dumpsters for the nightly pickup by Waste Management. By midnight, the park was clean. The Lions Club had cleaned the park for years. The compensation was fair, raised about every five years with the cost of everything else. The money raised by the Lions was used to support the Chardon Football League run by the Lions. They operated in the dark and very few people saw them operate, but the service they provided was invaluable. Without the cleanup, the naysayers would have an edge.

Vendors were parked in Main Street offloading their wares and ferrying them into the tent. A bustle of energy exuded in the pell-mell of people running in and out of the tent. Fred walked on Main Street, looked north toward Bank One, located at the north end of the square. People had emerged after the snowstorm and were lined up at the concessions. DiRusso's Sausage, cheese on a stick, apple fritters, steak sandwiches, breaded hot dogs on a stick, elephant ears, anything to satisfy the craving for junk food.

Fred turned and walked toward the stage. There wouldn't be activity until six p.m., when the band showed to provide live entertainment for the teenagers to dance wildly in the streets.

Parked in front of the stage was a television truck with its antennae stretched skyward sixty feet. A small crowd was gathered around a speaker talking to several teenagers, as a cameraman pointed a shoulder-mounted camera at them. Fred approached to hear the dialog. He positioned himself so he could see the TV celebrity, but he didn't know who she was. She was exquisitely beautiful, sharp features, perfectly coiffed blonde hair that fell to her shoulder and, with each slight nod of her head, sent an affirmation to the teenager who was speaking. Her lips were glossed with shiny dark lipstick that set off her brilliant, even white teeth when she smiled. She managed to pull off a professional yet seductive stance.

"I think he did it," said the young interviewee. "He's a lawyer, isn't he? They all can kill anybody. Why else would they arrest him?" The kid whipped his head in an effort to throw his long hair off his face. It fell instantly back and then slipped forward again, getting ready to be thrown back with a hand flick or a quick toss of his head. He was enjoying himself immensely in the limelight, smiling for the camera, throwing his hair back, showing off.

"But, sir, do you think that maybe you are prejudging this man accused of a crime before you even know all the facts? You don't know the man personally, do you?"

"Well, no." A shake of his head to throw the hair into place.

"And you really don't know any of the facts about the crime, do you?"

"Well, no, I guess not." A hand through his hair.

"So, if that is the case, why would you think he was guilty?"

"He's a lawyer, ain't he?" He laughed, and his friends laughed with him. The reporter smiled her beautiful smile. Fred was mesmerized by her even white teeth. How could they be so perfect? *What a mouth to kiss,* he thought. She caught sight of Fred's big hat, noticed that he was not the typical teenager, and quickly cut off hair-shake boy.

"Thank you, John, for your introspective analysis; we always appreciate the views of our young citizens." John put his hand through his hair as she walked past him toward Fred. "Here's a slightly older citizen."

Fred smiled but did not walk away. This could be fun.

"Good afternoon, sir."

"Good afternoon, ma'am." Fred tipped his finger to his hat in acknowledgment. He watched her mouth, so fine, the lips so perfectly formed, the teeth so white. He caught himself and looked into her eyes.

The camera was on him; she was standing close.

"Sir, are you aware of the situation on the square."

"I like to think I am."

"What's your opinion of what's going on?"

Fred knew she wanted to talk about Earl William, but he was going to have some fun.

"The festival is a great celebration of the community. The people get together in an annual rite of spring, celebrating the last snow, the flowing maple tree sap, the first get-together of the season." Fred saw the teenager who had previously spoken adjusting his hair with a toss of his head.

"No, no, no, I agree with you on the Maple Festival, but I was talking about the situation with the murder."

"Murder?" Fred looked quizzical. "You mean you don't want to talk about the tent falling down?"

"Surely you heard that Judge Kuhmer was murdered in the courthouse?"

"Oh that; yes, I heard."

"And that they arrested Fred Newman, a prominent local attorney and the president of the Maple Festival."

"Oh yes, I heard. It's all balderdash."

Her perfectly formed red lips formed a silent *O*. "What do you mean? Do you think the judge was not murdered?"

"Oh no, he was murdered, and that is a sad and terrible thing to happen to the judge and to happen to Chardon, especially during the Maple Festival. But they arrested Fred. I know Fred; there is no way in the world he would do such a thing. It's balderdash."

She put the mike back to her perfect lips and was, for a second, lost for words.

"You think he did not do it."

"I know he did not do it."

"The young man who spoke before you thought Mr. Newman *did* do it."

"Yes, I heard him say so. I was greatly impressed by the young man's attention to the United States Constitution, which provides for due process and a fair trial. His education is obviously complete. He used his prejudice against lawyers to convict the man without hearing any evidence of anything. I wish him luck when he gets arrested for a bad haircut and the jury looks at him and convicts him without any evidence." The crowd laughed. The young teenager's friends pointed their fingers at him. He blushed, pushed his hand through his hair, and smiled weakly.

"But sir, this Mr. Newman, he was a ranger in Vietnam. He apparently has the capacity to kill. He even got the Purple Heart—that meant he was in combat. Don't you think that is significant?"

Fred furrowed his brow, compressed his lips in a frown. "Okay, ma'am, so you are telling me that a man is sent to war by his country, serves his country in the best capacity he can, and that then his fellow citizens are going to use that service to his country against him? Pleeeeaase, give me a break. Rather than use it against him, why don't you use it *for* him? This man served his country; he deserves our support even more because of it. He doesn't deserve to be looked at as a killer because he served his country. Your view is askew. You have turned the tables upside down. Rather than put your arm around the guy and say 'thanks, good job,' you want to point the finger at him and say, 'bad boy, you served your country and killed the enemy of your country.' Ma'am, you have it back ass-wards, you truly do."

Fred could see she was uncomfortable with his answers. He knew she was going to cut him real short now. He saw her eyes searching the crowd for the next person to interview. He saw her perfect lips in a tight pout. This man was not your typical head-shake boy, the kind she liked to interview, the kind she could lead about with a suggestion, a pretty smile, a slight toss of the golden hair.

"Well, thank you sir, that is an interesting viewpoint. Now, let us get another view from this young lady here." She smiled with her perfect lips and whiter-than-white teeth, a false smile but yet so captivating, and turned from Fred.

The crowd surged past him to listen to the perfect teeth and the perfect lips surrounded by the golden, perfectly coiffed hair.

Someone tapped Fred on the shoulder; he turned.

"Great job, Fred. Guess she didn't know who you were."

A tall, bony Ichabod Crane–type man, whom Fred knew from the auditor's office, stood before him with a rabbit-fur cap covering his bald head, made all the more bald by a daily shaving of the sides.

"Say, Bob. No, I guess she didn't. Lucky for me. Of course, at this time, after all that has happened, I'm not sure I know who I am." He paused. "She sure had a nice smile, didn't she?"

"Yes, she did, along with her nice agenda," he added as he glanced over. She was still interviewing the young teenaged girl. Howls of laughter erupted from the people surrounding her.

"She's not here to talk about the festival, that is for sure," said Bob. "It's you she wants to talk about."

"Lucky me. It's good to see you up here. Getting ready to go home?"

"Yeah, thought I'd get some fries and a couple of sausage sandwiches to take home. I sure don't want to walk around in this slop." He pointed to the melting snow.

"Yes, I understand."

"Well, Fred. I'm not going to bother you. You have enough problems right now without me adding any on top. I'll see you when the festival is over. I have an idea you might like, about some photos. Good luck on your big problem."

"Thanks, Bob." Fred gave a weak wave as Bob walked to the fries booth.

Fred understood. People would shun him. Not intentionally, but they would avoid him when they could. No one knew how to deal with the stigma attached to him after the newspaper articles and TV depicting his arrest. They didn't know what to say to him. Avoidance was the easiest and maybe the best method to deal with Fred's problem. In that manner, they didn't offend, they didn't get involved, and they could later say, "I never believed he did it," or "I stayed away from him because I always thought he did it." Fred couldn't win, and they couldn't win. Better to just stay away from him.

Fred looked at the television newswoman. What a perfect face to place in front of a camera. Now, if they could just give her some depth of intelligence, she could be a perfect woman. He aimed his camera, zoomed in close, and turned the perfect teeth and the perfect smile into perfect pixels. He walked along Main Street. Lots of teenagers gathering for the street dance.

At Water Street, he made a left, passed the Richards Maple Products booth, passed the Gerry Tvergyack's historical maple production demonstration. Gerry was not demonstrating, maybe tomorrow. Gerry, brother of Mike Tvergyack, the groundsman for the festival, had a collection of historical sugar-making items. One structure was a hollowed log into which he would pour sap and then add red-hot rocks from a fire to set the sap boiling until it was reduced to syrup. It was primitive and it worked. Gerry demonstrated for fun, without fee, and without financial support, just to show people how the craft has progressed and because he liked it. Like his brother, Mike, he was a talker. He engaged anyone in conversation, and he did it with an attitude that was gentle, concerned, and understanding. People gathered to listen to him.

Melting snow covered his equipment. There was not a single footprint on the snow in the roped-off area. Fred took photos.

Fred walked to East Park Street and back to his office. He needed to contact the tent company now that it was erected. They had intimated that there might be a problem with costs.

# CHAPTER 14

Tim Snyder paged through the computer files and the hard-copy files; he found several leads.

Allan Schmucker—a deadbeat dad. Earl William had put him in jail for contempt of court charges for non-payment of child support on three separate occasions. Looked like he added extra time on the third imposition. Must have angered Earl William. Must talk to the bailiff about Schmucker. Tim remembered reading in the newspaper about Schmucker screaming in the courtroom that he was going to kill Earl William. It was big news at the time. Earl William was quoted as saying, "That's what happens to deadbeat dads." It got him votes for sure.

Mark Wellman, an attorney from Cleveland who had moved to Chesterland but practiced a lot in Geauga County. Tim knew Wellman, a Yale Law School graduate. He was a very short attorney, must be five-five at the tallest. He had wild, black, bushy eyebrows and piercing, little beady eyes. The eyebrows needed trimming. He still had black hair at age sixty with very little gray at the temples. He always wore a suit, never a sport coat. His tie was never unloosened. Always looked the part of the aggressive attorney he was. Too aggressive, according to Earl William.

Tim was aware that Wellman had been suspended from the practice of law as a result of a grievance filed by Earl William. But grievance procedures were confidential until the Supreme Court issued its opinion on the matter. Tim would have to look up the published opinion.

He found the divorce file on Wellman vs. Wellman. A three-inch thick file with much discovery, motions to compel, status reports, psychological reports. It appeared to be a major custody battle. The divorce occurred after the grievance. Wellman tried to get Earl William kicked off the case for bias, with a petition to the Supreme Court of Ohio. The Supreme

Court found no bias even though Earl William had personally filed a grievance against Wellman.

Tim read the final divorce-judgment entry. Mark did not fare well in the divorce. A 60–40 split of assets in favor of the wife, Jezebel. *If you marry someone by the name of Jezebel, I guess you get what's coming to you. Wonder what Mark thinks of Jezebel after this divorce?* Lost custody of his two kids. The court found that the best interests of the children mandated that the children reside with Jezebel, standard visitation to Mark. Now that would piss off anyone. Here you are asking for custody, you think you are a normal parent interested in your kids, and the court only gives you standard visitation. You get to see your children every other weekend from Friday night at six p.m. to Sunday night at six. Nothing in between. Alternating holidays and three continuous weeks in the summer. *What a slap in the face that was; no, on second thought, maybe it was a baseball bat up the wazoo.* No doubt, with the grievance and this custody case, Mark Wellman was a suspect.

But he seemed merely a suspect of anger, not murder.

Tim followed up on Denise's suggestion to look at Joe Parker. Joe had been an attorney in the area forever. Several years older than Tim, he had grown up in Middlefield, graduated from Cardinal High School, gone to Kent State and then to Ohio State University Law School. Joe was blind in one eye. Tim couldn't remember which eye, now that he thought about it.

Joe had run against Earl William for the position of judge. It was a nasty campaign. Tim had stayed away from candidate nights. He knew who he was voting for from the get-go: Joe Parker. With his visual disability, Joe had an element of compassion that was missing from Earl William. Earl William was mean. He disguised that meanness, but it was there underlying his talks.

According to the public record, Joe had lots of cases pending. He was a busy lawyer. His office was located on the second floor above the Lawyer's Title building on the corner of Main and Court Street. Joe's office had been above Lawyer's Title for fifteen years, ever since he began practicing on his own after leaving the largest law firm in town.

The building was beautifully refurbished several years ago, painted a golden color with a tan-brown trim. The skateboarders routinely hopped on the step leading into the building, making it smooth. The manager,

Aggie Sojka, married to attorney Mark Sperry, had devised some clever device to thwart the skateboarders. Merely going out to yell at them only brought jibes and gesticulations from the teenagers. Three of her patrons had slipped on the smooth surface of the step before she figured how to cause the skateboarders trouble. Aggie no longer had skateboarders ruining her step.

As Tim found each file of completed litigation Joe had before Earl William, he saw a pattern that looked like a straight line. Joe had lost each and every case he had in front of Judge Kuhmer. Six cases tried and lost. As Tim read the opinions of Earl William, he thought the cases could go either way, but they went against Joe each and every time. Each individual case would not reflect the relationship between the two, but all six cases that turned on a legal hair against Joe spoke loudly. Something was not copacetic between Joe and Earl William, but murder? Joe didn't seem the type to take it to that extreme.

The last case Tim paged through was a case in which Joe was the plaintiff. Fred Newman was his attorney. Joe had an adjoining property owner to an Amishman. Swine Creek traversed the front of Joe's property so that he had to gain access to his property by traveling over the Amishman's property. The Amishman's deed reserved an undefined easement over and across his property for the ingress and egress of the adjoining property, to wit, Joe's. The case was tried at the court for two days. Because it was a legal issue and not necessarily a factual issue, the court decided it rather than a jury.

There was no transcript in the file, so Tim read between the lines of Earl William's opinion. Joe testified that the easement in use for years traversed several hundred feet directly from the road and then made a left turn onto his property; that he used the easement several times a year and had spoken to the Amishman when the Amishman was building his house adjacent to the route of ingress Joe used; that the Amishman had built a barn directly over the easement preventing access. The Amishman testified that he didn't know about any easement; that no one told him about it even though it was a reservation on his deed, which he had never read; and that he never saw Joe on the property.

Earl William was clever. Tim knew in advance, based on the last six cases, that Joe was going to lose, but how to frame that loss with legal reasoning was the question.

Earl William guised his opinion on the basis of credibility. He acknowledged the existence of the easement as a reservation in the deed, but because the easement was undefined and the testimony on the location of the easement lacked credibility, he located the easement along the bed of Swine Creek.

Of course, this was a ludicrous location for an easement for ingress. When Swine Creek flooded, there would be no access at all. The Amishman won hands down. Earl William opined that Joe lacked credibility as a witness—that he was a liar.

Tim thought that would anger anyone. He pictured a car attempting to drive the creek bank with swollen waters pushing the vehicle forward. Earl William had made Joe's property worthless. There was clearly bad blood between the two of them if the outcome of these cases had any significance at all.

And Fred was Joe's attorney. Tim would have to talk to Fred about their relationship.

Tim glanced at his watch, 7:30 p.m. He had tent duty at eleven. Denise was still working in her office. Tim had five people he had to talk to: Schmucker, Pastor Bob, Wellman, and Joe Parker. And Fred. It was a start.

He reached for the phone, dialed 9 and then the number for Chardon Police. "Yes, this is Tim Snyder; could I talk to Lieutenant McKenna?"

Mike must have been standing right next to Dispatch, because he was on the phone in two seconds. "Yeah, Tim, what's up?"

"Did you find anything out on the key cards for the law library?"

"Why do you want to know?"

"Well, I know that every time someone enters the courthouse through the basement with a key card, that person's name shows on the computer at the station. So, in looking at this entire situation and seeing how the chief treated Fred at the arrest and in court, I thought I'd see if I could help Fred out on this one. I owe him, and I don't think he did this. I think the chief's got it in for him, so I thought I'd see if I could assist."

"I agree, but don't let the chief catch you. He doesn't like you at all, and Fred even less. But you know that. No way in the world would Fred do this, but man, the key cards don't work in his favor."

"Who came in when?"

"Okay, let's see," McKenna shuffled through a pile of papers. "At 10:06 p.m., Earl William enters the courthouse via the basement with his key card.

"At 10:34, Fred enters the courthouse, same entrance.

"At 1:19 a.m. the next morning, Fred exits the courthouse."

"No record of Earl William's key card leaving the courthouse?"

"That's where this gets a little confusing. At 11:02 p.m., the record shows Earl William's key card was used to open the door. We know Earl William didn't leave, but that's what it shows."

"So someone could have killed him, used his own key card to escape." Tim's mind was racing.

"Jenkins thinks Fred did it on purpose. Used the judge's key card to throw off the scent, stayed in the courthouse to show he was doing legal work. He knew his key card showed on the computer record, he couldn't get away from that, so he created a red herring by putting Earl William's key card showing an exit. He covered his tracks as best he could."

"Or someone else murdered Earl William," suggested Tim.

"Yeah, or someone else murdered Earl William, but no one else went into the courthouse."

"Maybe they went in *with* Earl William."

"Yeah, maybe. Fat chance."

"So are you guys doing fingerprints?" Snyder asked.

"All over the place. We don't have any results back yet, but they are everywhere. We did the exit door, all of Earl William's chambers, the bailiff's office, the hallway, the bathroom, everywhere. The place has been dusted clean now. The coroner hasn't given us the complete cause of death yet, but they think it was drowning."

"Oh man, drowned in a toilet. That's disgusting."

"Yeah, but he was hit in the head first. Looks like the baseball bat. You know which one I am talking about. That was the one used to hit him in the head, they think; then he was dragged to the bathroom. You know the rest."

"What did Earl William weigh?"

"I don't have that info, yet. But I'd guess over 300. He was a porker."

"I would think that should indicate the suspect was a male."

"Yeah, that's what we think, too." The lieutenant saw the chief through the window coming into the office. "Gotta go, Chief coming in." He placed the phone down.

# CHAPTER 15

F red's law partner, Tom Brice, looked in the doorway to Fred's office. Fred's look of incredulousness made him laugh.

"What do you mean, it's not covered?"

"Mr. Newman," said the voice in the speaker. "There is a specific exclusion in the policy under rental equipment. It reads under exclusions: 'Equipment owned by another for which a rental agreement for consideration is in effect.'"

"So, you are not going to cover the collapsed tent?"

"No sir."

"Why didn't they offer the stupid coverage to us when we paid for the policy? It cost $5,000 for four days' coverage."

"Mr. Newman, it is your obligation to read the policy and know your coverages. It is, after all, my understanding that you are an attorney. I mean you should know better, if anyone does."

Fred's face was a mixture of pain, anger, frustration, and guilt. He should have known, but … Yes, but.

"That policy is at least a hundred pages. Whoever reads those?"

"All the same, it is your obligation. The company will not cover the loss. Maybe you can get coverage for it next year."

"Yeah, and maybe I can get another company who will properly advise us on the risks and coverages, rather than just taking our premiums and bailing out when there is a claim. Good-bye!" He slammed his palm on the disconnect button.

Tom smiled broadly. "Your festival seems to be going along just fine this year!"

"Oh man," Fred shook his head, "no coverage for the tent. It must cost $20,000. Who the heck has money to pay for that? Not the Maple

Festival, that's for sure. I feel like Job in the Bible for what has happened the last two days."

"Not quite yet, but you are getting close. What else can happen? Tent collapsed, charged with murder, snow on your parade. What else, Fred?"

"You know, Tom, I just don't know. It's getting to me. People who know what is going on avoid me like the plague, or they come over and give me suspicious encouragement like they think, 'Maybe he did kill the judge, maybe not. But I know Fred, so I will go through the motions of saying good luck, just in case he's innocent.'"

"We ought to talk about it, don't you think?" Tom sat in one of the two, heavy, wooden captain's chairs in front of the desk. He pushed aside a pile of papers so he had a clear view of Fred. "We haven't had time yet. So tell me, what did happen?"

The office could have been a library. Books lined three walls: treatises on torts, contracts, wills, trusts, domestic relations, trial procedure, and practice. On one shelf, there sat Fred's worldwide collection of knick-knacks. Fred called them art, but to Tom they were items no office should display. A small statue of Buddha; another of Jesus Christ; a delicately carved sandalwood statue of Saraswati, the Hindu goddess of learning; a cobra in a bottle of liqueur from Vietnam; a stone-carved bison; a papier-mâché soldier holding an American flag; a Beetle Bailey jeep.

Fred's appreciation of art was eclectic. Although he was a photographer, he had no photographs in his office; instead, he had two oil paintings hanging. A picture of a young Vietnamese woman sitting on the side of a bed adjusting an earring; red drapes partly obscured the bedspread of the same pattern. Her dress of the same color made the picture complete. Fred had purchased the picture in Saigon at an art store that specialized in copying masters. A very nice copy, but the face was slightly askew, which Fred never noticed until oil painter/artist Gerry Rouge pointed to the discrepancies. Fred's appreciation of the piece then diminished slightly; he saw the flaws whenever he viewed the painting. But he liked the emotional impact of the courtesan politely putting on her earring, combined with the color red.

The other painting was the work of Glenn Jambor, a local painter. It was a painting of a jury trial, twelve men and women in a jury box. The top-left juror had a frying pan for a head, the bottom-right juror wore the glasses of a blind man. The remaining ten jurors had heads that appeared to be footballs and doubled as masks with no eyes. This, ostensibly, signified that the jurors were to enter the courtroom without any preconceived ideas about the case, without bias or prejudice. The attorney, presumably Fred, was depicted as a head on top of a geometric line drawing. The interpretation: a calculating attorney. The picture was fascinating. Clients wanted an immediate interpretation, but Fred always asked their opinion first before he told them his.

Tom Brice did not like Fred's choice of this particular painting hanging in his office. Tom's office artwork only related to baseball. Not Fred's choice at all. But these two attorneys had been together in practice for twenty years, accepting each other's foibles and preferences.

Fred rummaged through a pile of files on his credenza below the bookshelves. He located a file marked, GCMF Ins. He placed it on his desk, which was cluttered with multiple files, telephone messages, notes, and paper.

"Okay, Tom, here goes. Thursday night was the Queen Pageant at the Geauga Theatre. I always have to take photos of the queens at the end of the program. I went home about six o'clock to feed the cows and horses and then got back here about 6:45.

"I get all my camera gear and go to the theater. I get there between seven and eight p.m., watch the remainder of the show. There always seems to be a seat for me in the first row, on the right by the stage. The mayor and the ex-mayors are in the front row, and they always seem to save me a seat. It just happens like magic every year."

"Alright, alright, enough of the small stuff," said Tom, waving his hand in dismissal, "get to it."

"Oh wait, you'll like this. The three mayors were there: John Reid, Bob Eldridge, and the present mayor, John Park. They were sitting in a row, so I got them to pose in the see-no-evil, hear-no-evil, speak-no-evil pose, and I took their picture. A great photo. I'm trying to figure out what to do with it."

Fred saw Tom was getting antsy, so he continued. "At about 10:15, I am done taking all the queens' photos. I come back to the office, dump my camera gear, get the Anderson *vs* Anderson file, get my law-library key card, and go over to the law library to do some research. I have a brief due

Monday in Earl William's court, which I guess might not be due now, given the circumstances. I sure can't concentrate on it with all of this going on.

"The issue was on transubstantiation—what amount of the husband's property, which was premarital, became marital by his incorporating it into the marriage with his estate plan. There is some authority to show that merely planning for one's death and creating an estate plan does not convert the nonmarital property to marital property. And there is some authority to show that, depending on the extent of the incorporation into marital funds, it can be transubstantiated into a marital asset, and therefore, for the wife in this case, subject to property division. Fun issue. I found some good stuff. The brief was coming along.

"No one else was there. I unlocked the outside door with the key card and then the law library door with the keys that we have—and I leave it open. I go into the Ohio Room, turn on the lights, go to the copy room, make sure the copier is turned on—the warm-up time is forever—then I start the research. I was using a *Treatise on Domestic Relations Law* by Banks Baldwin, so I didn't need the computer room. I started writing the brief in longhand to be dictated later.

"I thought I heard the door open or close about eleven, but I couldn't be sure. Saw no one, heard no one except for the door, and I left about 1:15 in the morning. I was whipped. It was a long day.

"I went home, didn't even stop at the office, put my briefcase in the back of the van, and crashed. Woke up about six a.m. I slept in for once, fed the animals, did some light weightlifting, pushups, sit-ups, jumped rope for two minutes, showered, and then came to the office.

"First thing, I get here at the office, and Joe Parker is waiting to hire me for something. Gives me five thousand dollars as a retainer but won't tell me what the matter is about. This is all confidential. You're my attorney, I'm his attorney—double-extension confidence."

Tom tilts his head, raises an eyebrow. "You think?" His expression a knowing look. Was Parker already involved?

"I don't know, but it puts me as the *pickle in the middle*, that is for sure."

"Parker hires you to represent him on something he won't tell you about?"

"That's it. I had read about a similar case in one of the Perry Mason novels by Erle Stanley Gardner. A client hires an attorney but won't tell him what for. Same thing. That was a murder too."

"Okay, then what?"

"Parker leaves; I go out to check on the festival. It's snowing like crazy. I go to breakfast at the pancake tent. I see a bunch of cop cars at the courthouse, but I don't think anything about it. Figured some deadbeat was turning violent and they needed lots of security.

"Then Tim Snyder sits down with me for breakfast. He doesn't say a thing about the murder, so I don't even know it has happened. I ask Tim what's up at the courthouse. He tells me he can't tell me. What's that all about? Can't tell me. Big secret at the courthouse. Gee whiz. He says the chief instructed everyone to keep quiet.

"Then Chief Jenkins comes into the tent with Lieutenant McKenna. In comes the big chief himself puffing his big belly and red face, looking like an overstuffed balloon. He comes right up to our table. He starts by asking me if I was in the law library last night. I was, so I told him I was. Then he asks me what I know about Earl William. 'Judge Kuhmer,' he says. I say, 'I know a lot and that someone ought to shove a baseball bat up his ass.'

"He gets a look on his face like he is an infant who just pooped his pants. One of those slow, smarmy grins. Tim Snyder is bug-eyed. McKenna steps back. The chief demands that I say it again, so I say it very slowly so he can understand it. I don't think it's a big thing. I say, 'Someone ought to shove a baseball bat up his ass.'

"Then he goes crazy, grabs me, throws me on the table in front of all those people, handcuffs me, and takes me to the police station. I have no idea what's going on. I later learn that Earl William is dead and that a baseball bat was shoved up his ass."

Fred pauses, Tom looks at him.

"Nice move, Sherlock."

"Yeah, how coincidental is that? The rest, you know. Tim Snyder came over to tell you. I'd still be in jail if it weren't for you and Judge Craig."

"Yes, you probably would."

They sat in silence for two minutes, each wrapped in thought.

"They'll probably indict you next week when the grand jury meets. They're not going to want a preliminary hearing in Craig's court. I got a call from Tim Snyder; he says he's looking into it. He works for the Maple Festival, which I gather is somehow through the Village of Chardon, and every once in a while for Chardon part-time. He's not too keen on the chief, but he gets along with McKenna, so maybe he can get somewhere. Maybe he'll get some inside dope."

"I sure hope so."

# CHAPTER 16

After Tom left, Fred raised his feet on the pullout writing board of his desk, slid down in his chair slightly so his neck was supported, crossed his hands in front of him, closed his eyes, breathed deeply, repeatedly, and descended into a deep, meditative sleep. Ten minutes later, he slowly edged from the netherworld, opened his eyes, patiently waited a minute, got up, looked at the digital clock across the room, which read six p.m., and decided to make a tour of the festival.

Another half hour and the street dance would start. Fred put on his rubbers, coat, and hat. Slid the camera-bag strap over his shoulder and locked the door as he exited. The wind had picked up slightly, a nice fifty degrees, balmy; it would help melt the remaining snow. The sounds of the festival enveloped him as he left the porch.

The lights on the rides shone garishly. Fred walked on the east side of East Park Street, past the main tent. A few vendors were still loading equipment and wares, double-parked, running into and out of the tent. Horns honked. Fred crossed at the tent, stepped over a muddy spot by the concession trailer, and onto a piece of plywood that doubled as a sidewalk. The concession trailer was a loan from Paul Richards of Richards Maple Products. It was the headquarters for Gene Adams and Gary Dysert, the concession managers. Running concessions was the most difficult job of the festival. They had to coordinate each contract with each of the sixty vendors. A week before, on Easter Sunday night, Gene and Gary had had to direct the installation of all the rides. Each ride had to be placed precisely and inserted safely with plywood laid down for the ride and the tractor rig backing the ride into position. In this manner, the rain-soaked park remained rut-free. After the rides were inserted, Monday and Tuesday was devoted to their assembly.

On Monday, if the weather was dry, the tent was erected on Short Court Street in front of the courthouse. Mike Tvergyak and friends immediately began to build the interior superstructure to house and divide the sixty vendors inside the tent.

On Wednesday, Gene and Gary had used the tractor, graciously loaned from Middlefield Farm and Garden, to insert all the concession trailers. They'd had maps of the park area identified in pencil, where each and every vendor was located down to the inch. The insertion, although not scientific, was measured. The trailers inside the park were inserted first, followed by the outlying vendors, and then the trailers that lined Main Street and East Park Street. By Thursday noon, all the vendors were located. On Thursday noon, all the county office workers and businesses on the square streamed out of the buildings to get their gyros, sausage sandwiches, elephant ears, Chinese cooking, cheese on a stick, French fries with a sprinkle of salt and vinegar, steak-on-a-stick, corn dogs, and various "gourmet" lunches. Lunch on Thursday was a significant and traditional local social event for the employees on the square. Fred had made sure he was there to snap photos of assistant prosecutors shoving fries at their faces or the auditor, Tracy Jemison, bingeing on sausage sandwiches, or the treasurer, Chris Hitchcox, treating his son to a frozen banana covered with chocolate. Fred delighted in taking the photos. If they turned out, he would enlarge and print them to eventually send to the person in the photo.

By Friday, Gene and Gary were in skating mode. Most of the difficult work was complete. They were ready for a beer or maple cocktail. On Saturday and Sunday, the vendors who wished to return the following year would come to the concession trailer to sign contracts, submit their security deposit, chit-chat, have a beer or maple cocktail, and get back to work. The vendors were a tough, hardworking group, all trying to make a buck for themselves and their families. Some vendors operated for a supplemental income to their regular jobs, some for fun, and some because it appeared they must be masochists. Many trailers were operated by the entire family in shifts. Teenagers waiting on the teenagers, young kids getting Cokes, parents cooking and grilling, friends taking the pay and giving change. The first festival of the year was an exciting event for all the families.

Fred climbed the three steps to the trailer, stuck his head in the door, and was instantly hailed by Gary in a loud voice, smiling broadly.

"Here's the killer, Gene! Watch out, get the gun! He's come to get us. Put away the baseball bat. Maybe we can protect ourselves if we gang up on him. Hi, Fred, good to see you."

"Need a beer, Fred?" asked Gary.

"I sure do. Gary, you better sit as far away as possible, I'm in a baseball-swinging mood."

"Don't bend over, Gene, you heard him. He's trouble today."

Gene, from his sitting position, opened the refrigerator, stuck his arm in without looking, and handed Fred a beer. Fred put his camera bag on the counter and sat next to Gary at the small table that served as the dining room/kitchen table. Fred popped the top of an MGD and drank.

"Boy, I needed that."

"So, how are you holding up. Kind of scary, isn't it?" asked Gary. "Have you ever seen a more bizarre festival? I mean, this is crazy. When was the last time the tent fell?"

"We called Bob Eldridge to check it out for us. Here." Gary extended a newspaper article to Fred. "He dropped off a copy of a *Geauga Times Leader* article from 1974! That was the last time the tent fell. More than twenty-five years ago. A quarter of a century."

Fred looked at the article with a photo of the collapsed tent.

"But we've never had a judge killed at the festival before. That's a first. And then to have the president charged with the murder, that's a first, too." Gary turned serious. "You *are* innocent, aren't you?"

"Yes, Gary, I am innocent. But they just don't have anyone else to stick it on yet."

"They better hurry up. The festival can't wait."

"They really charged you with it? Why?" asked Gene.

"Well, I can't really go into details or talk about it, but suffice it to say, I said the wrong thing at the wrong time to the wrong person. When the chief came up to me in the pancake tent and asked me about the judge, I told him somebody oughta shove a baseball bat up his ass. Unfortunately, someone *had* shoved a baseball bat up his ass, and he died. They arrested me right then and there. Wrong thing, wrong person—Jenkins hates my guts, as you well know, because of this festival—wrong time. Pretty clear from their side of the fence. Pretty muddy from mine. So that's all I can say about it. I didn't do it, and that's that. Now I have to figure out how to deal with it."

"So let's see," mused Gary, "we can call you murder boy."

"Or bat boy," added Gene.

"Yeah, great," Fred laughed. "So, how's the tent?"

"Everyone's in," said Gene. "They seem okay with the problem. We're handling everything. A couple of vendors wanted a rebate on some of their money, but I showed them the clause in the contract that we are not responsible for weather problems. They weren't happy, but then neither are we. It's going okay."

"Things are humming now," added Gary. "No one lost any produce or equipment, so they are alright with it. They better be."

"Now that they are making some money, they are happy," said Gene. "The crowd is building out there. Looks like it will be a good night." He paused and then added, "That is, if you don't get arrested again."

Gene and Gary laughed and laughed. Fred stood up, put his empty beer can into the trash can, shook his head slowly, gave them each a raised middle finger, and moved toward the door, buttoning his coat.

"You guys—and I want you to know this and I say it with all sincerity— are assholes." He opened the door and exited to their laughter and shouts of "Go get 'em, bat boy!"

Although Fred knew he was going to be the butt of jokes in the future, he was warmed to the heart by the absolute acceptance of Gene and Gary that he had nothing to do with Earl William. They wouldn't have treated it so lightly otherwise. Now, if he could just get the legal tangle straightened out, he would be okay.

Fred walked across East Park Street to the festival office in the Keeney House, one of the oldest century homes on the square—century homes are those homes older than a century. The building was shared by the Maple Festival Board and the Chardon Chamber of Commerce. It was old and dilapidated. Owned by the Geauga County Public Library, of which Fred was on the board of trustees, it was leased for one dollar per year on a triple-net lease to the Chamber of Commerce with the proviso that they would do certain repairs and upkeep, but which they did not perform and the library board did nothing about. The chamber did not have enough money to make the repairs. The library board had other matters to deal with than being a property manager and never enforced the provision in the lease. The old house consumed cash with its demands for repair, leaving none for improvements.

The chamber office was rearranged for the festival. A large table was placed in the middle of the room so people could gather, eat, look at the old Maple Festival articles and photographs. Although Fred had been publishing a photo album for fifteen years, Bev Carver had been collecting articles from newspapers for twenty-five years. She collated and pasted albums by year. A meticulous, time-consuming job, performed wonderfully and with a passion.

Mary Tvergyak, sister of Mike, was monitoring the phone. She leaped from the chair when she saw Fred, issued a cry of welcome, and gave him a big long hug.

"How are you, Fred? Are you okay? I can't believe all this. It's crazy! You of all people. No way. Are you okay?" She finally paused for an intake of breath but still had Fred in a bear hug. He squeezed back and she released him.

"I'm okay. A little pressure, but doing fine."

"I just can't believe this. Earl William was such a neat guy. He had a great sense of humor. Just like yours. I can't believe he was killed. And I can't believe you got charged with the killing. I know you didn't do it … did you?" She laughed. "No, I'm just kidding. I know you didn't. You don't even have to answer that … So, are you okay? Can you even concentrate on the festival with all this other stuff?"

"I'm doing fine, Mary. Relax. We'll get over it. The real murderer will be found, I am sure. It just takes some time and good police work." He paused. "How are the calls? Getting questions?"

"Lots. People are so excited about the festival this year, what with the tent collapsing, and of course, your thing. I think they want to come up just to get a look at you. We've had a couple of nasty calls, too. People are so mean, such jerks."

"Like what?"

"Oh, just nasty calls. You wouldn't be interested."

"Mary, just tell me, I can handle it. Who is calling and what did they say?"

"Okay, but don't say I didn't warn you. One woman called. I got from her that you were her husband's attorney in her divorce. It was clear she didn't like you. Wouldn't give her name. And I was real nice to her too." Mary paused. "She said, 'That Fred Newman deserves to be hung by his b— from the biggest maple tree in Chardon.' Then she said, 'That would make it a real Maple *Ball* Festival.' Then she called you some names I won't repeat."

"No name?"

"Of course not. And we don't have caller ID here, so I couldn't get her number either. And I got a call right after that, so when I thought of star 69, it was too late. The woman was a real jerk."

"Any other calls?"

"Oh sure. We got a lot of calls on information for the festival. What's open, are the rides operating. Is the Old-Timers' Dinner still on at the church tomorrow? Just the usual festival questions, but more questions than usual.

"One guy just swore at me. No message, just swore. I should hook him up with the woman who wants you hung."

"You mean well-hung," added Fred. Mary laughed.

The phone rang.

"Hello," Mary said, "the Geauga County Maple Festival Office.... Yes, ma'am, we do.... Yes, ma'am, we are...." Mary listened for a full two minutes. She rolled her eyes at Fred in astonishment. "Yes, ma'am, I'll tell him. And thank you. He's going to need those words of encouragement. That's very nice.... Okay, thank you again. Good-bye." She hung up.

"See?" said Mary. "There's someone who likes you." She laughed her celebrated, booming laugh. "She's praying for you. She says you're a very nice man, that you came out to her house to sign some documents when she couldn't walk after an operation, and that you didn't even charge her for the extra time. She supports you all the way. I forgot to ask her name."

"I think I know who it is. She lives in a trailer park along Swine Creek Road in Middlefield or Parkman. I had to go next door to get a witness. The people thought I was nuts asking them to come over and be a witness. But she's a neat old lady. That was nice of her."

"There are more nice people than jerks; it's just that the jerks are jerks so they call and act jerky."

"Wow, Mary, can I quote you on that?"

"You're a jerk too." Again she laughed her loud, booming laugh. "How's the tent?"

"The vendors are in, people shuffling through. There's good attendance tonight. The weather is changing for the good. But what a day! I'm exhausted."

"I'll bet."

"I think I'll go home, feed the animals, and hit the hay."

Mary got up and gave Fred another huge, tight hug.

"Tomorrow will be a better day. Just like the song 'Tomorrow.'" She smiled at Fred and gave a small wave as he exited.

# CHAPTER 17

Fred pulled into the drive. Slush, water, snow, and repeated driving over the driveway had created large potholes. Fred maneuvered the van to miss the deepest of them. The brutal winter, combined with the snowplow guy, had deposited most of the stone from the drive onto areas of the lawn in huge piles. Fred did not look forward to hooking the blade to the tractor in the spring to retrieve the stone for the drive, scraping the drive repeatedly to fill in the potholes, and then raking the lawn by hand to be free of stone. It usually took him a week or two at half an hour each morning to retrieve his driveway. Hey, what are you doing today? Well, I'm retrieving my driveway. Huh? Similar to the festival, it was a rite of spring.

Fred's wife, Mary, greeted him at the door. She had been crying. The television news had played the murder as their prime story. Mary had even seen Fred's interview on the TV. No one on the TV group of people yet knew it was he talking. Fred explained his day to Mary. It took an hour. He was tired, he was hungry, the animals were hungry. There was nothing he could do at this point. He had to rely on Tim Snyder. Tomorrow would be a brutal day if it was anything like this one. Mary was not happy; she kept muttering, "Murder, charged with murder. Oh my God!"

Fred pulled on his knee-high boots, exited the basement entrance, walked to the barn, unhooked the chain on the malamute-collie mix, Bowser, to let him run, entered the barn, turned on the lights, and began the feeding process.

The cats got three scoops. Two of them were so wild, Fred had never petted them. But they kept the barn clean of rats and mice. Fred picked up two buckets, carried them to a huge oil drum converted to a feed-storage bin, opened the lid, and scooped three full scoops of Western Reserve Co-op 12-percent grain into each bucket. He went to the passageway in front of the two steers and poured them each a bucket of grain in the tray area in front of the stall. He petted them and spoke to each.

"Well, Complaint, well, Counterclaim, we are in the shit now. This has probably been the second-worst day of my life. The worst, you ask? Well, you don't remember, but I got hit by that booby trap in Vietnam, had to be medevacked. It was thirty years before you guys were born. But that was a bad day too. This one compares; it just doesn't have the physical pain. Only mental pain. And, it is a pain in the ass. Yes, you don't believe me. It's true."

Fred then moved the buckets to the three fifty-gallon plastic drums. He lined up three buckets, one for each of the horses. Unscrewed the lid on the big yellow drum, scooped one small scoop of barley into each bucket. Screwed the lid back on, went to the next big drum, orange this time, unscrewed the lid and scooped a trowel of oats into each bucket. Then to the next drum, from which he poured a small scoop of 12-percent sweet feed into two of the buckets, put two scoops into bucket number three for Ranger, the sixteen-hands-high Arabian.

Next, Fred crossed the aisle to a plastic box, which was originally sold as a tool box for the back of a pickup truck, but which worked wonderfully for two fifty-pound bags of bran. He scooped one small portion for Rosie, the twenty-five-year-old Appaloosa, and for Trial, the other high-strung but younger, nervous Arabian. This kept them free of colic and their bowels moving. Trial had a bout with colic so bad she collapsed in the yard and couldn't get up. Fred had been walking her to free up her innards. He finally had to call the vet who pumped soapy water and oil down her. After a shot of something, she got up and healed herself quickly. Ever since then, Fred had added bran to the mix, and it had worked. Not another incident of colic. The morale of the story: poop and ye will be free of colic.

Fred thought, maybe I need some bran for the day I've had today—the cleansing might be just what the doctor ordered. Then he dumped the contents of each bucket into the tray for each horse stall.

"Yeah, Rosie, did you hear what I was telling your stupid bovine friends over there? This has been a bad day. I'm sure you know all about it. As I was telling the steer boys, I've been charged with murder. Do you believe that, murder? That is deep doo-doo. The chief hates my guts. He doesn't care whether I did it or not; he wants to pin it on me. Of course, I said the wrong thing at the wrong time to the wrong person, but still …"

Fred piled the buckets by the horse feed, hooked up the hose to the water line, closed the hose-cock, and turned on the water. He pulled the hose to each of the horse stalls and filled the buckets. Ranger slurped up two bucketsful because he was so large. The buckets were all heated. There wasn't anything much worse than breaking ice in buckets. Wires ran from the buckets to extension cords of 14-gauge wire. Fred had to protect the wires from the inquisitive mouths of the horses, so he pounded boards to protect them where they came close to the horses' stalls. He opened the hose-cock at each bucket filling the bucket.

"So what do you think, Rosie? I'd ask Ranger or Trial, but as you know, they may be fast, but they really are dumb. Let's see if we can analyze this:

"I'm charged with murder.

"I was in the law library when the murder was committed.

"The murderer must have come out the basement door. I thought I had heard something, but I thought nothing of it at the time.

"Go ahead, Rosie, pipe in whenever you want.

"So what are they going to do? Obviously, dust for fingerprints. Where? All around where Earl William was found. His office. I was in his chambers last week for a pretrial. If no one cleaned the area, my prints are in there. But will the fingerprint guy be good enough to tell which prints overlay other prints? This isn't *CSI* here, this is Chardon. So, they will have my fingerprints. Not too good. But they shouldn't have my fingerprints around the scene of the crime.

"So, Rosie, we have opportunity. I was there in the building, my key card shows it clearly, can't deny it. There is evidence of my presence, at some time, in Earl William's chambers. What about motive? I am dead in the water on that one. But for murder. What's my motive, you ask? I really am enjoying this analysis, Rosie. You are asking the most perspicacious and pertinent questions.

"Motive. How about that argument I had with Earl William—what was it, a month ago? Remember, afterward at the pancake breakfast, when he was in line with his wife, he wouldn't even shake my hand. No bygones-be-bygones there. He was pissed, and still pissed a week after the argument. Oh, you don't remember the argument? Let me refresh your aging memory.

"It was right after we lost that trial representing Joe Parker. Man, we should not have lost that case. Joe got reamed. Unfortunately, Joe ran against Earl William for judge. That was a nasty campaign. Earl William doesn't forget a grudge—remember my handshake? I know, you are thinking, *Joe? Where does he fit in?* Yeah, he fits in with a five-thousand-dollar retainer this morning for a case I am to know nothing about. But we are not analyzing Joe at this point, Rosie, we are analyzing me; so let's stick to the subject.

"So, Rosie, you can hear me over this running water, can't you? Are you listening? Do you even care? I wouldn't blame you if you didn't, but keep in mind, I'm the one doing the feeding here."

Fred moved from bucket to bucket filling them with water.

"All right, the argument I had with Earl William. It was the first week of March. I remember, because the judge went to the pancake breakfast on the third week. You know, at Berkshire High School, the pancake breakfasts put on by the Burton-Middlefield Rotary Club. They have been doing it for fifty-two years. Only one week was it called off and that was when I was president in 1992. The weather was so cold, windy, and snowy, no one was coming anyway. We made up for it the week after."

Rosie snickered.

"Okay, okay, I'll get to it. Quit being so pushy."

Fred dragged the hose to the bovine buckets, turned the hose-cock to add water.

"So, Rosie, there I was, I had a trial scheduled in this divorce case in front of Earl William. Pat Bowers was the wife's attorney. We talk about the trial. There is so much farm equipment, Pat wants it appraised. I tell her my client knows the values of them. There are six pieces of real estate, only two of which have been appraised. She wants to know all of them. I tell her that is fine with me. Pat wants to continue the trial. I say go ahead. She says her client would get mad at her if she asks for the continuance, would I ask for it? I'm not ready for the trial anyway, so I say, sure, as a favor to you, I will go ahead and ask for a continuance. But, Pat, I said, you know Earl William is going to be very angry. You better stick up for me when he starts yelling. 'Sure, Fred, no problem.'

"Now Pat started practicing just a few years after me. She went to grade school with my younger sister, Phyllis. So we go way back, and I expect a certain amount of loyalty. Well, Rosie, I didn't get it. She didn't object to the continuance at all; in fact, she wanted it, but made me get to it."

Fred turned off the hose-cock, shut off the water, put the end of the hose down the drain, turned on the hose-cock to release the water in the hose, unhooked the hose from the water pipe to allow it to drain. In this manner, the water in the hose would drain and he would not have a frozen piece blocking the hose for the entire winter. There was no heat in the barn other than that provided by the animals and their bodily wastes, which generated lots of heat.

He walked over to Rosie, sat in a dusty white plastic chair, and continued his story.

"Rosie, this is good. I am purging myself here. I like the confidentiality of this discussion. Not a damn soul is listening other than you. The rest of these beasts don't care about anything but grain and water. Right, Ranger?"

Ranger ignored him.

"Okay, Rosie, So I file the motion for continuance on the Friday, the trial is scheduled the next Monday. The judge denies it within a half hour of my filing it. So I call the bailiff and whine. I tell her of the need for the appraisals, how Pat was going along with it, that the case is not ripe for an evidentiary hearing yet, that I am sure the judge would want all the evidence so he could make a learned decision, etc. She goes back to the judge twice. She comes back and says he is not happy, but that he will convert it to a pretrial, though he insists the clients be present.

"All right, we are happy. I call Pat, give her the good news, let the clients know. It's no big deal to us. Not like he was going to have to call off a jury or anything. Plus, it would give the judge more time to devote to other cases. He'd understand, he used to practice. He knew what it was like to be under the gun. Or so I thought.

"We show up on Monday, all bright and eager. We go into the back room on the north end of the courthouse, second-floor jury room. Pat and her client on one side, me and my client on the other side. We start going through the itemization of real and personal property that I had printed out, which was my trial sheet. I put another column on it for Pat's client's hoped-for values. We start arguing, negotiating, insulting, the usual bluster and points to make. We are making progress, when the bailiff comes in and says the judge wants to see the attorneys and the clients.

"Pat looks at me, her eyes wide open. Having the clients in on a pretrial does not bode well for us. What does he want the clients to know that we haven't already told them? But hey, Rosie, we're experienced attorneys, we can roll with the punches. I figured he should already be over his upset at the motion for continuance. After all, it was no big deal. My client is excited about meeting the judge. He says: 'About time we met the judge.'

"So in we go, Rosie. Are you listening to this stuff?"

Surprisingly, Rosie lifted her head from the bucket, nickered, shook her head up and down, and went back to the bucket.

"Great, you're a great listener. Besides, I really don't want to tell anyone else this stuff. If the chief knew, he'd pull my bail if he could."

Fred stretched out his feet, put his hands into his Carhartt jacket pocket, and leaned back.

"The judge gets formally introduced to the clients; Pat and her client sit on one side of the long table, we are on the other. Our table is perpendicular to the judge's desk. The judge sits at his desk facing all of us.

"He starts right in on the difficulties of operating the court with all the cases and how busy his schedule is, et cetera. That it is a disservice to the court, the community and the legal profession to take advantage of the courts and ask for continuances only days before a trial that has been scheduled for months.

"We say nothing. There is nothing to say, Rosie.

"The judge announces that there will be no more continuances. That the matter will go to trial on the scheduled date. He asks if the clients have any questions. Of course, my client does. My client asks if the judge is related to someone from Troy Township, and they get into a who-knows-who discussion. I can tell the judge is just being nice, but my client thinks *he* is scoring points. The judge is seething. What I can't figure out is why. What's the big deal? It's a continuance. We get continuances all the time. Ever since I represented Parker in that losing easement case, the judge has been acting squirrely toward me. You'd think he'd get over it.

"The judge finally dismisses us. We walk back toward the jury room and my client says: 'Boy, he sure reamed you, didn't he?' What was I supposed to say? So I said, 'Yeah, he sure did, felt good.' The client liked that, he laughed.

"We sit down to start negotiating again, then the bailiff comes in and says the judge wants to see the attorneys only this time.

"Pat and I exchange questioning glances. What does he want now? We hope his mad-on is over, but who knows. Maybe he wants the last lick in. So in we go, sit down. The judge is not smiling. His lips are quivering he is so angry. What for? I ask myself. It's just a stupid continuance. We ask for them all the time. He asked for them when he was in private practice.

"The judge starts in on us. He begins to berate attorneys who ask for continuances. His focus is on me, Rosie. It's on me, because I accommodated Pat and her client by doing the asking. Do you think Pat comes to my rescue? No. She just sits there prim and proper. Doesn't contribute anything, doesn't explain to the judge that I only asked for it because she didn't want to anger her client, but that she wanted it also. Not a word, Rosie.

"The judge must have talked for ten minutes. I was getting a little piqued. There was no real reason to be digging in like this. 'Waste the court's time.' Like the court is some third person on high who needs to be honored and has some great distinction. It's just him, not *The Court*. It drives me crazy when judges speak of the court as if it was some third party separate and distinct from them. As if it gives the office a greater power. The court will now take a recess, the court determines that you are of unsound mind, the court is not pleased with your performance. Well, Rosie, to hell with the court. It is just the judge, a human being just like me. A real animal, just like you. Not *the court*.

"I know, you are wondering where this conversation is going. You are such a good listener.

"So the judge now focuses his gaze on me and says in a nasty and mean tone: 'It is arrogance, that's what it is. Just pure arrogance.'

"I'm thinking, Rosie. *My arrogance? What the heck is he talking about?* My mind had slipped a little when he was ranting, I wasn't even listening. But then he started to say that I was the arrogant one. And there's Pat, just quiet as a church mouse during Sunday mass. Yeah, Rosie, quiet as a church mouse. I'd like to sic some of these crazy barn cats on her. She wouldn't be so quiet then. And he's calling me arrogant because I filed the motion. Enough was enough.

"The judge paused, Rosie. I turned and looked at him and said in a straightforward, direct, quiet, and controlled manner: 'My arrogance, or yours?'

"Well, Rosie, I don't know if you have ever seen those cartoons where something happens, and the cartoonist, in order to show how the atmosphere has changed, has a row of icicles form rapidly around the ceiling of a room. Well, that is what happened here. It was as if the room turned to frost, the icicles snapped into place along the ceiling, and the room was cold. The judge was stunned. Someone spoke back to him. The treachery of it all! Probably thinking, *the arrogance of it all.* And thankfully, Rosie, it was off the record. And, it *was* arrogant, no doubt. Okay, Rosie, I admit it, my comment was arrogant, but dammit, you have to have arrogance if you're going to be an advocate for your client. And who should have to take a verbal berating for doing someone a favor?

"Anyway, Rosie, there was more than a distinct chill pervading the chambers; it was freezing. Pat's eyes widened into globes, but she didn't look at the judge, and she looked away from me.

"The judge, and I've got to hand it to him, now handled himself in a very controlled manner. He was not happy. He was fuming. I saw his lips tremble. His face was flushed. He kept playing with a pen on his desk, tapping it, twisting it, tapping it twice, twisting it. I think he wanted to stab me with it. I bet two minutes passed before anything was said.

"The judge then went on as if I had not said anything. However, the ice in the room was not melting. And I had said something, Rosie. And he knew it and it stuck in his craw. I didn't fight in this man's army in Vietnam to come home and be spoken to like I was a fifth grader. Enough was enough. So the judge went on for about two more minutes. I didn't hear a thing he said. Then he dismissed us.

"We exited the chamber, and we were walking by the bailiff's office when Pat said: 'Oh my God, Fred. What did you do that for?' I answered her, loudly. I said: 'To hell with that judge." The bailiff looked up, I smiled at her. Then I said, 'And thanks a lot for your help in there, Pat.'

"And, Rosie, do you know, we went back in there with our clients and further negotiated the case for another hour and a half. We got through everything, but there were several pieces of farm equipment still not evaluated by Pat. And she wanted to have an appraiser look at a piece of real estate she missed. I figured we would eventually resolve it, but I didn't know if the judge would resolve his anger.

"Then, Rosie—and this is the clincher—two weeks later, at the Burton-Middlefield Rotary Pancake Breakfast at Berkshire High School, the judge is in line waiting to get served. I am in charge of the kitchen, as you well know, and have been for fifteen years. Brian Brockway, who does a wonderful job, and I have been co-captains in the kitchen forever. We work well together. So the judge is in line. I go up to shake his hand, figuring we will bury the hatchet like good attorneys, and say, 'Hi, Judge.'

"Do you know what happened, Rosie? He wouldn't even extend his hand to shake mine. He looks away. I am a mere bagatelle. Talk about a slap in the face. Here we are at a function for the community, raising money for events for the community, and he is harboring an ill will toward me for something that happened two weeks previously. I was astounded. I immediately think, 'Oh, I've got problems, don't I?' He's probably the judge in this county for life, and I now have a mortal enemy.

"The judge was obviously angry with me, Rosie. But I wasn't angry with him. I let it blow right by me. Big deal, we got into a dispute. Seems to be a power dispute, but it was only one-sided as far as I was concerned. But he harbored this anger toward me. What would that do to my practice down the road? I don't need to be on bad terms with the local judges. Look what it did for Parker with his cases. In fact, I'd rather be on good terms with the judges. I'm an easy-going guy, but I'm not going to be pushed over the cliff like some sheep or buffalo or some lemming.

"Well, Rosie, I was embarrassed. Extend my hand, and he won't take it. His wife was embarrassed, too, I could see. So I smiled and said: 'I hope you have a great breakfast. We make the best pancakes,' and I walked away. But I was troubled. I kept saying to myself, *What's the big deal?' It was just a continuance. Get over it. Be a professional.* But it was now blown out of all proportion. I'm thinking, *That judge and I had better have a talk.*

"The real problem, Rosie, was that this all occurred only four weeks ago and the judge has had a mad-on for me ever since. He hasn't decided any of my cases, but I've had several pre-trials before him. I can sense that his formal, stiff treatment of me bodes ill will toward me. I kept thinking during the pre-trials, *This, for the rest of my career. Give me a break.*

"Then he gets killed! If Jenkins finds out about this little dispute, which appears to be a big dispute from the judge's perspective, then he has the following against me, Rosie: motive, opportunity, and an ability to commit the crime. Premeditated, Rosie. Yeah, think about it. You get into a little dispute over arrogance, and it's premeditated murder. Gee, you sure wouldn't think so, would you?

# Chapter 18

F red walked the circuit of the Maple Festival early Saturday morning. The snow had melted, the temperature was up to fifty degrees, it looked to be a great day for the festival. Fred saw several early-morning walkers, took photographs of an empty Main Street with the early-morning light casting its golden glistening on the face of the eastward-facing buildings. He moved the flap from the main tent and walked into its shaded interior. Sitting in the middle was Tim Snyder, who stood and came toward Fred, not recognizing him.

"Oh, Fred, it's you. Didn't recognize you with the backlight, couldn't see your face."

"Long night, Tim?"

"Yeah, boring. A couple of teenagers got in, started necking. I surprised them. 'You got a permit to stick your tongue in her mouth?' The guy almost flipped out. I think he broke a tooth trying to untangle. The girl was crying. They won't be coming in again. Yep, real exciting night. Not like yesterday, though, huh?"

"I hope there's not ever another day like yesterday."

"For your sake, I hope so, too." Tim paused. "Hey, Fred, you know I was the first one on the scene. First policeman, that is."

"I didn't know that. Wish you would have told me about the baseball bat. Man, did I stick my foot in my mouth with that one."

Tim laughed heartily. "You sure did. Don't tell anyone, but I took photos of the scene. I'd rather not show them to you now; you might get too much information, which won't do you any good. But if you get down the road, I'll provide you a disc of them. I already made several discs. It might give your attorney some examination point."

"I hope it never gets there, but thanks."

"Also, the chief has ordered me to not do anything on this case. He has specifically told me that my only job with the Chardon Police Department is working for the Maple Festival. He's afraid I might solve the case. I know you didn't do it, so I am looking into it on my own."

"The chief is still pissed at you for showing him up on those burglaries? That was years ago."

"Yeah, but that doesn't make a difference. He developed a basic dislike for me, and it isn't going to change. But I need to ask you a couple of things about the timing."

"He developed a basic dislike for me, too. As you well-observed yesterday."

Fred explained his use of the law library, the research he was doing, the timing as best he could remember, and then the scene in the tent when he was arrested.

"I'm telling you, it scared the bejesus out of me. And here you are a police officer—I shouldn't even be talking to you. The cardinal rule of defense attorneys: don't talk to the police." Fred snickered.

"But you're talking to a police officer not on this case. Especially dismissed from it, per the chief." Tim snickered, too. "I was at the clerk's office yesterday," he said. "Denise let me stay after hours to look at some things. I have a couple of questions for you. Maybe you can tie up some things for me. I am looking for patterns, for reasons for people to want to kill Earl William. Legal reasons first. They lost a case, or cases; he put them in jail; he humiliated them, whatever. If I can find some kind of pattern in the cases, then maybe we can get additional suspects."

"Attorneys, too?"

"Yes. In fact, one attorney's name keeps popping up. Joe Parker. He lost a couple of cases. One case, you represented him."

"Yeah, I did. An easement case. Earl William shoved it up his wazoo. Wow, that's maybe a bad analogy, given this case.... Anyway, we tried the case, had the law and the facts. Earl William found against him. It was clear the Amishman lied. It seemed like a personal vendetta against Joe."

"Well, Fred, you know, Joe ran against him in the last election. That was a nasty campaign. Never saw such nasty stuff. Earl William circulated the rumor that 'In the land of the blind, the one-eyed man would be king, but this isn't the land of the blind.' What a terrible thing to say about a half-blind man. And Joe said some nasty things about Earl William, too. Might be something to look at."

"But hey, I still represent Joe, so I can't talk about him, really. Give you the basics on the case, but not much more. Can't give you any details about him. You'd have to find those out for yourself. Maybe ask your sister."

"Why would I ask my sister?" Tim wondered aloud.

"She's been going out with him, hasn't she?"

Tim stood a little straighter. His eyes opened a little wider, his head moved upright looking over Fred's head.

"She has?"

"For quite a while, I think. That's not something that's privileged, so I can tell you. Yeah, for quite a while."

"She's married! He's married! What the hell!" Tim slowly shook his head from side to side. "Yeah, I'll talk to my sister."

"Well, don't tell her I told you! I still have to do things in probate court. I don't want to get all messed up there because some clerk is pissed at me."

"Don't worry. I won't tell her where it came from. I can't believe it. I'll talk to her. I talked to her yesterday; she didn't say a word. My sister!" He pulled at the sides of his mustache. "Married. Going out with a married man. My nephews. Man oh man. What a goofy world. God save Ireland, Fred." Tim punched canvas covering a vendor's booth. It sounded with a whump.

"Alright, forget Joe Parker," Fred urged. "I'll get to him later. Damn. I got a couple of others … What about a guy named Pastor Bob? Do you know him?"

Fred thought a minute. "Pastor Bob. Now there's a minister to be afraid of. He came to me to represent his son. No way. The kid, about seventeen years old, had been doing weird things to the kids living under Pastor Bob's protection. He ran a boarding school of some sort with oversight by the Department of Human Services. Must have had thirty kids there. His son was getting blowjobs from boys *and* girls. And doing some other things to the girls and boys. Nasty kid.

"Good old Pastor Bob was more interested in getting his son off the charge than protecting his thirty wards. Didn't think the kids were harmed by what his son did. And this was a religious man. I couldn't represent his son. I was too offended. I didn't like his son. That doesn't happen often, but in this case it did. I have represented some pretty foul characters in some pretty nasty cases of rape and attempted murder, but the attitude of the father in this case was reprehensible: all the kids were liars; his son was right. He didn't care for the truth; he wanted his son off. I think he finally got the public defender to represent the son. Kid went to prison. He was tried as an adult and sent to prison. Good old Pastor Bob lost his license, as he should have. What a piece of work. I don't even know which judge had the case."

"Earl William." Tim informed him.

"Makes sense. I can't imagine Pastor Bob would have the guts to commit murder though. He's not a big guy. About five feet four inches. I don't think he *could* he have killed Earl William."

"I'm going to talk to him anyway. What about a guy named Allan Armstrong?"

"Never heard of him. What did he do?"

"Earl William put him in jail a number of times for child support. I'm going to check him out, too. How about Mark Wellman?"

"Yeah, I know Mark pretty well. I represented him in a grievance filed by Earl William. Mark got disbarred for six months. He and Earl did not see eye to eye, that is for sure. Earl seemed to have it in for Mark. He lost a custody case in front of Earl after the grievance problem. I don't know who represented him in that case. But he was not happy with Earl William."

"The grievance was public record," Fred continued. "It was published in the green book. One of the decisions of the Supreme Court. Mark had a medical malpractice case. Before the trial, the defense offered some money to Mark. Mark did not disclose the offer to his client. The jury came back with a defense verdict. Somehow, Earl William found out that Mark had not informed his client of the offer, and he filed a grievance against him. Mark wasn't too keen on cooperating with the grievance committee, and that caused some of his problems, but Earl William pushed hard. Mark got a year disbarred, with six months suspended. He's been back for a while."

"Capable of murder?" queried Tim.

"Oh, I don't know. I know he gets angry. He's a bitter man now. He tried to get EW kicked off the custody case, but the Supreme Court didn't think that EW filing a grievance would affect his judicial ability to be fair and open-minded. Mark got creamed. Only sees his kids on alternate weekends. The ex-wife even tries to prevent that. But murder? No, I don't think so. He's really a good attorney. A little loud, a lot abrasive, very obnoxious, and very pushy, but a good attorney. Knows the law and prepares his cases well. And his mind is sharp. I think he'd rather beat Earl William legally than physically. But who knows. Are you going to talk to him?"

"Yeah, I have to. Sounds rather personal, doesn't it?"

"Earl was not nice to him. Mark thinks it's because he's Jewish. But I think it was because he was Mark. Mark doesn't put up with anything. And when he gets pushed around, he pushes back. But he pushes legally. He's a legal attack dog. He'll file motions and discovery and bury the other attorney. But not murder. That's my opinion. But what do I know? Look where I'm at. Here I am, an ex-Army Ranger. The TV reporters say I have the ability to kill, that I served my country, therefore, I am a murderer. Yeah, they'll look at me before they'll look at Mark."

"Don't get maudlin on me here," Tim said, twirling the end of his mustache. "I'll talk to him. Make my own decisions. Anyone else you can think of who might have had it in for Earl William?"

"Not really. He could be an SOB on the bench. And he was, even to me. But not a killing offense. No doubt he had to make some hard decisions. Sending people to jail cannot be fun. Hearing families cry and having to make decisions that cut off people's kids, monies, properties, lives ... I'm sure he's made lots of enemies. But I don't know who they are. At least who would be capable of killing him because of his decisions. He's not like Craig Albert; that's for sure. Craig can put a guy in jail for six months and he still loves the judge. Craig listens to defendants, engages him or her in conversation, makes them feel as if they are someone. EW can let a guy *out* of jail, and the guy is hating EW. It's the way he does it. The lecture, the dehumanizing, the talking down to the defendant; he treats them like doo-doo.

"Tim, I sure wish you luck. I want you to find the killer more than anything else. It sets me free. 'The truth shall set you free.' Yeah, look what it did for me."

"Well, Fred, I'm looking. Hey, look at the time, I'm off duty! Eight-o-five a.m. I've got things to do, places to go, people to meet. God save Ireland. I'll keep you posted, Fred."

"Thanks."

# CHAPTER 19

D an Shipek, the Geauga County coroner's investigator, was perusing the papers on the Earl William case, when the receptionist buzzed him for Tim Snyder's call. "Yes, Tim, What can I do for you?"

"Earl William. Do you have a time of death for him?"

"What's your connection with the case, Tim?"

"Just trying to help out Fred Newman. No official capacity. Just don't think he did it, and I know Chief Jenkins will just push it through on Fred."

"Want to show up the chief, huh?" Dan was aware of Tim's ejection, albeit camouflaged, from the Chardon Police Department. Anyone connected with law enforcement in Geauga County knew the chief was jealous of Tim's celebrity status after solving the robberies in Chardon Village.

"Want to clear Fred, actually. The chief can go you know where."

"You know, Tim, I can't just toss out this information to anyone."

"Yes, I know you can't. That's why I called. It's me, Dan. Tim. Remember me? The guy who referred you to that wonderful job you got where you can sit in the catbird seat and tell guys you can't give information to them. You remember that, don't you, Dan?"

"Yeah, yeah, okay, you got me. Let's see …" Dan shuffled paper while he perched the phone between his shoulder and ear. The phone slipped, hit the desk, and landed on the floor.

"Sorry, dropped the phone. Here we go. Had to send it to the Cuyahoga County coroner. Just got the report half an hour ago." Dan scrolled his finger down the page, reading as he went. "'Several serious bruises to the head, one fractured skull, left frontal cranium, broken eardrum, left side … death by drowning.' Seems he was unconscious when the murderer stuck his head in the toilet. 'Water in his lungs, unable to aspirate.' Pretty nasty guy to stick someone's head in a toilet, don't you think?" said Dan.

"I'll say. The toilet must have been the *coup de grace*."

"Let's see, 'rigor mortis, degree of lividity'—that's the pull of gravity on the blood, kind of settles in the low parts when the body doesn't move for a long time. You remember that stuff, right?"

"Dan, just because I am in Burton doesn't mean I have stuck *my* head in a toilet. What else? Time of death?"

"Time of death. Looks like between 10:45 and 11:15. Tending more toward 10:45, I'd say. Fred was there, wasn't he?" asked Dan.

"In the law library, I believe. In the basement. Used his own key card to get in. If he was going to murder Earl William, I don't think he'd use his own key card."

"Maybe not, unless that was the red herring. Let's see. 'Baseball bat inserted into rectum eighteen inches.' Lot of force with that one. Lot of force. Had to be a man. Big strong man or little strong man to be able to shove that up there that distance. 'Big end' went in first. Wow. Ripped up his large intestine, broke it loose 'four inches from the first turn of the intestine. Tore right through, squashed the small intestine, went all the way to the wall of the left lung.' Nasty. Guy had to really dislike the judge for this one," added Dan.

"Dislike! Malevolent hatred, more like."

"Yeah, you're right. Hatred. Malice. Anger. A big strong man with a chip on his shoulder."

"Anything on the crime scene? Fingerprints?"

"Bunch of fingerprints. Let me get that sheet." Tim heard the shuffling of papers. Dan breathed closely into the phone. "Lots of fingerprints. Over fifty different prints in his chambers. The bathroom was pretty clear. Someone must have cleaned it. But his office, what a jumble. On chairs, desks, under desks, doors, pens. They are all over the place. We have matches already for thirty of them. But people come and go in that office. It's a turnstile of attorneys and insurance adjusters. Too many attorneys, if you ask me. They are a pain in the you know what."

Dan only realized at that moment that Tim was an attorney also. "Present company excluded, of course … Looks like there might be more areas of fingerprints coming in later. Took them at different areas of the courthouse, entrances to the courthouse, and down in the law library."

"'Present company,' yeah, of course, Dan. I just consider the source."

"Hee-hee," chuckled Dan with a false laugh. "Lots of attorneys on this list. Chardon Village has the list if you can get in there to see it."

"Let me give you a few names, see if they are on the list."

"Okay, shoot."

"Allan Armstrong?"

"No."

"Mark Wellman?"

"Yes. They are located. Right on the desk. Middle right. Looks like he got right in the judge's face. Whole palm and all five fingers, right hand only. He's that mean little shit, isn't he?"

"Some say so. I don't know him very well. I'm going to talk to him," said Tim.

"How about Fred?"

"Yep. On the table that faces the desk. Last three fingers on the right hand, perfect images. Good match. Also, left index finger on side of table, left side. Probably sitting on the chair, pushing away from the table. Who else?"

"Joe Parker?"

"Yeah, got several of his. Couple of them smeared, but there were enough points of similarity. On the table, side of the table, right side. Doorjamb. The doorknob was wiped clean. Table was attempted to be wiped clean, but unsuccessfully. A couple in the hallway. And two matches in the bathroom. Not on the toilet, but on the sink, left side, two fingers, index and middle. Anyone else?"

"Pastor Bob Pietsmeyer?"

"Oh, I remember him. Dirty little guy. Let his kid diddle those orphans. No. Nothing on him. No prints found. Doesn't mean he wasn't there, though.

"No prints on the baseball bat. Big surprise. Couldn't get any prints off any of the judge's hard surfaces, like his belt. He had a medallion on a chain that got broken and was in the bottom of the toilet. That murderer was one angry dude, that's for sure. He dragged the body, all 302 pounds of it, out of chambers, down the hall, up three steps, into the bathroom, and maneuvered it so that he could still shove the baseball bat up the judge's butt. Strong man. If it was a woman, she was an Amazon.

"'Scuff marks and abrasions on' Earl William's 'face, hands, knees, thighs, and stomach.' Rug burns, too. Must have used lots of force dragging him up those steps. Not a pretty vision when you try to imagine the scene as it happened. The marble floor in the main hall would have been smooth dragging, but the carpeted area by the bailiff's office and the hallway to the bathroom would have had a great friction factor. Hard to drag someone down there. But, if his adrenaline was flowing, as I am sure it was, that would give him the strength to drag him that distance." Dan paused. "So what else do you need, Sherlock?"

"I guess that's as good as it's going to get, huh?"

"Yep."

"Thanks, Dan. I'll let you know how I progress."

"No problem. Good luck. Tell Fred we're rooting for him."

"Will do, over and out."

# CHAPTER 20

For those weaned on maple syrup, it remains in their blood their entire lives. Age and time might thin the content, but its adherence to the tissues cemented maple as the passion for the Maple Festival. The noise and rides intruded on hearing aids, making sharp and painful sounds. Thoughts of one's youth enjoying the rides and gorging oneself on food and maple stirs remained, but the ability to continue to perform such activities was likened to a downward scale on a graph. Diminishing desire and ability. You can only eat so much of a maple stir when you are diabetic. You can step over the stall mats spread over the wires traversing the walkways only with great difficulty when using a cane or a walker. You can only be jostled by the crowds so much before you tumble to the earth.

The consequences of aging necessitated a different forum for old-timers. Loretta Holmes devised an Old-Timers Dinner. Anyone over sixty was invited. The event was held the Saturday of the festival between 11:00 a.m. and 1:30 p.m. at the Methodist Church on North Street. It was co-sponsored by the Chardon Chamber of Commerce. There was lots of parking, access to the building was handicapped-enabled, and it was away from the noise and bustle of the festival.

The chamber president was the master of ceremonies. The event opened in the church-proper after registration, with an invocation, a selected singing group—a barbershop quartet, the Sweet Adelines, or some other group that performed music of the era of the senior citizens. After the entertainment, the assemblage moved to the cafeteria where the ladies of the Methodist Church provided a delicious and wholesome lunch, with specific exceptions for dietary restrictions, for the attendees. Favors were placed on the tables in the form of some type of maple product—this year it was eight fluid ounces of maple syrup in small, jug containers with green ribbons tied in a bow at the handle.

Each year, Fred appeared to photograph whatever Loretta desired. He took photos of the entire group from the stage. Loretta assembled the over-ninety crowd, Fred photographed them and then sent 8 x 6 photos to Loretta to distribute to them. He did it immediately after the festival for the obvious reason that when one reached the chronological age of ninety, every day was a great event of surprise, amazement, and thanks—any delay and the enjoyment of the photo might not occur.

Loretta assembled the couples that had been married in excess of sixty years to the same person, and Fred photographed them. He also gave those photos to Loretta to distribute.

The Old-Timers Dinner was a nice, genial, gregarious, geriatric event. Loretta hosted a wonderful party that allowed the seniors to participate in the Maple Festival on a level more attuned to their status in life. Most of the seniors knew each other. This event allowed them to catch up with old acquaintances; it was old-home week.

This year, the Department on Aging got involved and created a category of Senior Maple Queen. They had a regular election, and there were a number of candidates. It was a fun venture to vote for the Senior Maple Queen. Ruth Armstrong was the winner. The Armstrongs had been maple producers for a hundred years. It was fitting for Ruth to be the first queen. She was so delighted with her tiara, she posed for Fred in multiple pictures. The Armstrongs had built a new sugar house this year and wanted Fred out to photograph it. He hadn't gotten out there yet.

After the initial invocation, John Elzroth, president of the Chamber of Commerce, introduced the key players. A round of applause was given for Loretta. Fred was introduced and was expected to make some comments. When he arrived in the church hallway, people either engaged him or moved away. The murder was the talk of the town. Not many wanted to mingle with a murderer. It was easy to believe the police were not wrong. After all, this was an aging crowd who believed in the power of the government and the honesty of the police. Their own comfort and security depended on their belief.

Fred noticed people avoiding him, the looks—the surprised looks that he had even appeared given the circumstances—and the not-so-subtle moving away from him. But others, those who knew Fred more intimately, came up to him, gave him hugs, wished him well, said they didn't believe all the hype the newspaper wrote, and generally supported him. Fred knew his introduction to this group had to be handled gently.

"Ladies and gentlemen," boomed Fred into the microphone.

"This year I have had the honor and privilege to be the Geauga County Maple Festival president. This year, the tent fell down from the snow. This year, a judge was murdered on the Friday of the festival, yesterday. I can tell you that the honor of being this year's president is … well … somewhat dubious.

"What I can also tell you, with certainty, is that I did not murder Judge Earl William Kuhmer! I know when I came in here, some of you were pointing your fingers at me. I know I have been arrested for the charge. But it is totally untrue. You will discover, in due time, that it is untrue. But in the meantime, I tell you, I did not commit that horrible crime.

"I will say no more on the subject to you. It is neither fitting nor appropriate. I am walking around with a cloud over my head this weekend, and it is not comfortable. However, I have duties as president of the Geauga County Maple Festival, and I will continue to fulfill those duties. As you are aware, the tent fell down yesterday morning. A replacement tent has already been put into place, and the festival is going full speed ahead. Regardless of the weather, the festival will go forward.

"I thank you for attending this event in this sloppy weather. I invite you to the parade to watch Ruth Armstrong show off her beauty and poise as Senior Queen. I offer my condolences to the family of Judge Kuhmer. And I wish you well."

Fred received a round of applause, little more than lukewarm, but sufficient to know that they had listened to him and were going to be courteous to him.

Loretta Holmes next addressed the assemblage.

# CHAPTER 21

Tim Snyder knew Court Street in Chardon from the days when he was employed in the town. He missed those days. The nostalgia for the job conflicted with his enmity toward the chief. From the center of the square, Court Street steeply descended west one-eighth of a mile downhill to Washington Street. Armstrong lived in the third house past Washington. He had the same name as the Armstrong's in the festival, but he was no relation—at least not as far as anyone can remember. He had easy access to one of two car washes and a Burger King. A look at the cars in the driveway—there was no garage—showed three cars that would benefit from the car wash, but a closer look clearly indicated that even a car wash could not help the appearance of those vehicles. No matter how much soap and power washing was applied to them, the rust would still show, the faded and peeled paint would still remain, and the plastic covering the right rear window secured by duct tape would be power-washed off.

Court Street dead-ended at the car washes, but a car could get through to Burger King on Water Street; a sharp turn was all it needed. Or, a car could go through the car wash drive and slip through to Center Street. Although not a regular thoroughfare, they were used as shortcuts, by those who knew them as a handy way around the increasing traffic congestion.

Tim was still in uniform from the night before. The patch on the right shoulder read "Burton Police • Where History Lives." He knocked on the door; there was no doorbell. The screen door had a rip in it along one corner and flapped loosely.

Tim was taken aback at the first sight of Allan Armstrong. He was five-foot-ten, medium build, slack muscles in his face and arms, brown hair, green eyes, goatee, Fu Manchu style, and answering the door in a tank top and shorts. *No icicles hanging from this dude.* Around age thirty-three, he had a tattoo on each arm. On the left arm, a black snake winding around a tree that went from his bicep to his wrist. On his right arm, a snake in reverse, a mirror image, winding down a tree. This one had red, blue, and green colors in it.

His hair was unkempt. Face unshaven. The ponytail was ragged, tied with a rubber band, with as much hair outside the band as within it. Armstrong kept brushing the hair from his face with his right hand, the multicolored snake arm.

Tim didn't ask to come in; he just stepped in when the door opened. Armstrong was not the type to extend hospitality—it wasn't in his upbringing. The smell hit Tim two seconds after entering. Stuffy, sweaty, armpit stuff, old socks, gymnasium, dirt, rotten food, old food, dog, cat urine—every olfactory sense became acute and pinged with pain on the nerve endings. Clothes were strewn about, looked like they had been strewn about for quite a while. Plates of food, half-eaten, on the floor, on the table, on the TV. Tim made his breathing shallow. *The smell, whew!*

"Armstrong? Allan Armstrong? I'm Sergeant Snyder from the police department. Mind if I talk to you a bit?"

Armstrong didn't respond, his head looking down, hair hanging in his face, an expression of suppressed disgust and fear, a smirk. He rubbed his goatee up and down, causing a more disheveled appearance than he'd had.

"Wha?" was all Armstrong responded.

"I thought you and I could talk some. This thing about Judge Earl William Kuhmer."

"That EW ain't worth a shit." Armstrong woke up, became energized, anger and dislike emanating. "A guy doesn't have a job, and he puts him in jail for nonsupport. *Impute minimum wage* when I got no job. Impute this, MF. We're going to pretend you're making this money because we think you *can* make this money. Then, when you don't pay your child support from this pretend money you're not making, we're going to put you in the real jail, Mr. Armstrong, not a pretend jail, Mr. Armstrong. That's what we're going to pretend to do for real, MF. Pretend this!" Armstrong extended his black tattooed arm holding up his middle finger within six inches of Tim's face.

A song popped into Tim's head—an instant memory: *Put another nickel in, In the nickelodeon.* The man had just started talking. Tim said one thing, and he started talking. Tim looked a little closer.

"I can't hold a job. Sometimes it's them, sometimes it's me. Take that job at Carlisle. I thought I was going to get cancer from the smell of all those chemicals—even the government says they have pollution in the ground from all those chemicals. What, I got to wait till my lungs paralyze before I quit that job? Oh yeah, pretend those chemicals don't smell.

"And Trusco, well, that one I can understand, ruined a whole load of huge trusses, must have been fifteen of them, thirty-five feet long, all broken, all had to be redone. They were nice about it, though, just thought I didn't have the skills necessary for the job. Even paid me for the day I screwed up.

"St. Gobain, well, those Frenchies were too clean. Not a speck of dust anywhere. And they watched you all the time. I couldn't take it after a while. I worked there a long time, man. At least a year and a half. That was pretty good. Paid support during that time. Didn't even have to pretend on that one!"

Tim watched him. The man kept talking. Not nervous, but jumpy. *Must be on something right now. Looks like speed or methamphetamine. Large black pupils.* He keeps talking, unprompted.

"Then I worked at Kraft Maid for a long time, too. *Everyone* smoked in the glue section, and I get caught. I think they set me up. 'No tolerance,' they said. Fired. I liked that job, just didn't like the assembly line. Same thing over and over. That glue never caught fire. Made you kinda high sometimes, goofy. I got unemployment after that job. Pretty neat. Didn't have to work for nine months. I pretended to work, man, pretended. Get it?" Armstrong laughed at his own joke.

"Ya know, I don't really like to work. I mean, I admit it. I got to sometimes to get some bread for food or weed, but it ain't fun. If it ain't fun, why do it?"

*What's with this guy?* thought Tim. *Telling me his life story. I think he doesn't even know Earl William is dead. Excuse me, but what an asshole.*

"That was the trouble in the Marines. Man, I was gung-ho that first week. But after all those stupid pushups, I kinda lost my interest. Man yelling at me all the time, spittin' in my face. Bullshit. I don't need that crap. All those other guys, just going along, 'Yes, Sergeant, no, Sergeant.' Just a bunch of bull. Just refused to do any more. They didn't know what to do with me. Shoved me in the pool a couple of times, got a blanket party one night, but hey, I got out of there, didn't I?

"Wish I coulda stayed in to get a pension or disability or something. Man, that would have been sweet.

"Drugs, sure I do drugs. Don't do no alcohol though. That drinking is bad shit. Weed, that's my gig. Toke up, pass the pipe. Just mellow. I do meth here and there. Not too often. Lose my head on that one. But I ain't got any on me, so you can't bust me, man.

"Must have been on meth when Brittany was born, because I sure don't remember having sex with her mother. Ugliest bitch on the planet, and I had sex with her. Sure glad I don't remember it. I must have been really zonked to plunk her. DNA says I did it though—99.9 percent positive. That's good enough for the court, but I tried to argue if it ain't 100 percent, it ain't true. Case got transferred from Juvenile Court to Common Pleas, to EW. But my kid's cute. Hard to believe that ugly bitch got a cute kid."

*Put another nickel in, In the nickelodeon. This is unreal.*

"Yeah, I visit pretty regular. She always has people there when I pick up the kid. They just stare at me, don't talk. Like I'm going to bite the kid. Weird. They think *I'm* weird. Brittany's four years old. What do you do with a four-year-old. Take her to McDonald's, eat some fries, then take her back home. I don't get overnight visitation until I have a regular place to stay without all these people around.

"Hey, these are okay guys. But it's okay, don't want a kid around when we are smokin' and jokin.' Probably not right. Then those meth days, nah, don't want the kid overnight anyway. Cute kid, though, from that ugly bitch.

"I never visit with Tressa, who is now ten. She doesn't like me, doesn't like the way I smell. Can you believe that? Doesn't like the way I smell. Like she's afraid of me. Her mother turned her against me. *Her* mother, now she was a sweet lay. We were regular for a month or so. Wow, what great times. She finally got married, good for her. Husband's a wimp. Skinny little dude from Cleveland, Ohio. Like the song. Works in some office somewhere. Heather is still good-looking. Wish she'd invite me in sometime. But she hates my guts. Turned that kid's head against me. You can hear it from the kid. 'How come you don't have a job?' 'Why are you driving this rusted-out old junker?' Where's a kid get a term like *rusted-out old junker*? From her mother, that's where. Finally, the kid said she wouldn't go with me anymore, says she don't like the way I smell. Smell this, MoFo. What am I going to do? Can't afford a lawyer to get my rights. They all want at least five hundred bucks down. Legal Aid won't help. They have a list, and it's six months long. Can't take a simple visitation case, because there are too many domestic violence cases that take precedence. I ought to beat Heather for turning that kid against me. Then maybe I can get Legal Aid to help me. A domestic violence case. Don't like the way I smell.

"And I still got to pay support for Tressa, even though I get no visitation. Actually, I don't want visitation with a brat that just gives me a hard time anyway. Says I stink. But Heather, oh well, dream on. That one is over."

*Put another nickel in, In the nickelodeon.* The melody kept pounding through Tim's head. The rhyme was just right. This guy *was* a nickelodeon.

"Allan," interrupted Tim, "what about EW, the judge?"

"Oh yeah, EW. That SOB. I told him I would kill him if he put me in jail again. I wasn't pretending, either. And then he did. Three times he's put me in jail in two years. For what? For not having a job. For not paying support from the pretend money I don't get. For digging into a vacuum pit and pulling out nothing. There's nothing there, how can I pay support? Boy, that was a scene! I screamed I would kill him. He didn't look too worried. I think he had a gun under his bench. Sheriff's deputy standing right there. I'm handcuffed in my bright orange suit. I pretended I was Mafia. Cool. Got me more jail time, I'm sure."

"He's dead," interrupted Tim.

""Wha?" Again, the *t* was lost. The word ended with Armstrong's mouth stuck wide open.

"He's dead. Was murdered Thursday night in the courthouse."

"Wha?" This time, even though the *t* was lost and his mouth stayed open, his eyes narrowed. A thought passed through his brain.

"Yeah. Dead. Murdered. In the courthouse." *Put another nickel in …*

"He's dead." Armstrong said flatly. "Well," he continued as if he had not been interrupted, "I don't wish him ill. I think he was just doing his job, but he didn't have to be so nasty about it. He's dead? Really?"

"Really."

"Oh man, now I'll get another judge who might be worse. That sucks ... Wait. They think I'm involved?" It slowly dawned on Armstrong that there was a cop in his house. The judge was dead. There might be some connection. He brushed his hair back and breathed deeply through his nostrils, which gave a wheezing, snorting sound.

"That's a laugh. When did it happen?"

"Thursday night."

"Hmm, Thursday night. What the f*** was I doing Thursday night? Maybe it happened on Thursday night—a meth night. I got out of jail on Tuesday. Thursday was a total meth day. I celebrated getting out of jail. I pretended to make some money and pretended to take some meth. I don't even remember what I did Thursday night. Kinda like the night with the ugly bitch. Hope I didn't get some broad pregnant again. Here I am telling you, a cop, I was on meth, taking an illegal substance." He stressed the illegal with a long pronunciation of each syllable: ill-leeee-gallll.

"Don't think I coulda killed EW, though. How would I do it? The last place in the world I wanted to be was in that courthouse. But I got no alibi, because I don't know what I did. I thought I was at my bedroom on Court Street, zonked out. Yeah, that was it. But no one can verify that, huh? Man, charged with murder. That would be too much. Yeah, I threatened to kill him, but how? Maybe Legal Aid could defend me now, got some domestic violence involved. Maybe get a real attorney, not some Legal Aid attorney."

Tim got up, walked to the door; Armstrong was still talking to the chair where Tim had been sitting. Tim left.

*Put another nickel in, in the nickelodeon.*

"God save Ireland," said Tim.

# CHAPTER 22

The Mom-and-Dad Calling contest was scheduled for one p.m., followed immediately by the Husband-Wife Calling contest.

Fred meandered to the fringe of the crowd at 1:20. The Old-Timers Dinner had been somewhat embarrassing, but he'd survived it. He was going to get that kind of treatment from now on, he knew that. Didn't like it particularly, but accepted it. People suspecting he was a murderer. Others embracing him, but wondering about it. No one really knows.

"Mom!" screeched a small girl dressed in blue jeans and a denim shirt. The loudspeaker boomed the lament of demand, order, plea, scream, and whine. The crowd applauded.

Tim Grau, master of ceremonies, spoke. "Well, Melissa, that was a nice scream. Now why don't you go stand with the rest of the screamers in the back while we hear the final two contestants. Okay, who's next, Michelle? Oh, Tanya. Okay, Tanya, who are you going to call, your mom or your dad?"

"My dad."

"How old are you, Tanya?"

"Fourteen." Tanya was a heavyset girl with blonde hair hanging to her waist. She wore blue jeans and a green jacket without a collar.

"Okay, Tanya, here's the microphone, let her rip."

Tanya gripped the wireless mike, walked to one side of the stage, performed a curtsey with a slight bend at the knees, holding her arms at a coquettish angle and tilting her head with a huge smile, walked to the other end of the stage, performed another curtsey, and then walked to the middle for the final. The crowd mildly applauded this display of panache. In contrast to the gentile setup, Tanya bellowed into the mike. *"DAD! DAD! GET IN HERE, THE DOG THREW UP. AAAAAGGGGGHHHHHH!"*

The crowd wildly responded in screaming applause.

Fred turned in response to a tapping on his shoulder. Tim Snyder stood there dressed in his Burton Police Department uniform.

"Hey, Fred."

"Hey, Tim. Did you hear that? Hate to be in her house when the dog throws up." He zoomed his 28–300 mm lens to the maximum and shot several photos.

"She'll make someone a nice prom date soon," said Tim.

"Oh boy," Fred answered. "So how are you doing? Making any progress?"

"I just talked to that guy, Allan Armstrong. Lives on Court Street."

"What did he have to say?"

"He was zonked out on meth. Guy was like one of those stuffed animals that talk when you pull the string. He started talking, and he continued talking, and talking, and talking. Didn't even know I was there. Gave me his whole life story. Didn't even know Earl William was dead. Said he was so zonked on meth Thursday night that he doesn't even remember what he did or where he was. He's still zonked."

"Should have busted him."

"Not my jurisdiction. They ejected me from this jurisdiction, remember?"

Fred smiled.

"Anyway, although he was screwed up, I think he had nothing to do with Earl William. No connection at all other than jail time from Earl William. He threatened to kill EW, but he doesn't have the capacity or know-how. What a druggie. I don't think he could get sober enough to commit a murder."

Fred said nothing.

The last contestant grabbed the microphone, smiled at the crowd, and yelled, "Mommy, Mommy, Mommy, Mommy!" It was a wail, a complaint, a cry for help. The girl was smiling, but the words spoke hurt and pain. The crowd applauded. Not as much as the dog-vomit contestant, but a nice round of applause.

Tim Grau then had all the contestants move to the front of the stage, leaving enough room for him to maneuver in front of them.

Fred took some more photos.

"That was wonderful, Amanda. Now we get to hear a one-word call from each contestant. Then, I will go to each contestant and hold my hand up, and depending on the applause of the crowd—the committee, that is the crowd and Michelle back there—raise your hand, Michelle."

Michelle Piscopo raised her hand. She wore a bright green vest with a long-sleeved white blouse and matching bright green pants. Very maple-festive. On her lapel was a large plastic maple leaf with her name carved into it and the word *Director* under her name. Fred purposely did not wear his badge, given the circumstances.

Tim Grau held the mike in front of each contestant as they each screamed the one word of *Mom* or *Dad* and the crowd just grinned. "Now we are going to determine the winner. It is up to you, the audience, to clap the loudest for the one you liked the best. They all deserve applause, don't forget that. But for the one you liked the best, that is when you let it all out. Are you ready?"

"Yes!" boomed the crowd.

Tim walked behind the contestants and held his hand over the first in line.

"Let's hear it for Bobby." Applause.

"Judy." More applause.

Fred took photos.

"Tanya." The crowd screamed and clapped their hands. Tanya would win hands down.

Finally Tim got to the end of the line.

"Okay, now I need to confer with Michelle. Just give me a minute, folks, and I will come right back and tell you who the winner is."

Tim Grau and Michelle huddled.

"So what's next?" Fred asked Tim Snyder.

"I'm going to see if I can connect with two other people today: Pastor Bob and Mark Wellman."

"You won't like Mark."

"From all I've heard, probably not."

"Hates Earl William's guts. But probably not a murderer, unless it was so clear-cut that he could get away with it. You'll find him interesting."

"Well, his fingerprints were in Earl William's chambers, so I have to see him."

"You got the fingerprint results?"

"Yes, I talked to Dan Shipek, coroner's assistant. Lots of fingerprints. But I am only checking on the people who look like they might have a pattern of hatred for Earl William. Several of them also have fingerprints that were found in Earl William's chambers. Let's see. You, of course."

"Yeah, I was there last week in a pretrial. Unless someone cleaned up."

"Mark Wellman, Joe Parker, no Pastor Bob, no Allan Armstrong. Over fifty sets of prints. I am sure the police will look at all the people whose prints were found. Maybe not, if they think you did it. Maybe they are done looking, but I think not. But, that's not my way. I'm looking for patterns, for reasons. Why kill Earl William? It's got to be the history of hate toward him."

"Okay, we have a winner!" The MC held aloft a large wooden maple leaf with a gold plaque proclaiming the first-place winner of the Mom-and -ad Calling contest. He walked from one end of the stage to the other and then back again. The kids were apprehensive whenever Mr. Grau passed them. Then he stopped at Tanya and handed her the plaque. The crowd erupted into hoots and hollers and applause. Tanya was jubilant, jumping up and down, screaming her delight. She re-performed her curtseys to more applause.

Fred took several photos and then clapped. He looked at Snyder, who stood there with a scowl on his face. Fred jabbed his elbow into the good cop's ribs—he couldn't reach much higher—and clapped harder trying to give Tim the message. Tim clapped lightly in response.

"Shipek say anything else?" asked Fred.

"Time of death, between 10:45 and 11:15, probably closer to 10:45. He talked lividity of blood, gravity, and a bunch of other stuff, but said that's about the best they could do on time." He watched the contestants exit the stage, walk down the steps to be greeted by their families and friends. Tanya joined four girls, and they all jumped up and down in reckless excitement. "You were there at that time, weren't you? At the law library, I mean?"

"Yes, I was. I had taken photos at the Queens Contest at the Geauga Lyric Theater Guild, then I went to the office about 10:15. Those young girls are beautiful. So young, so much to live for. So much promise. I don't think that I could have gotten up in front of a crowd in the twelfth grade to speak or put on a skit. They really are impressive young ladies. Youth is beauty when channeled in a positive manner."

"When did you leave?"

"I left about 1:10, 1:15 a.m., Friday morning. I was preparing for another ugly divorce I have, actually, had, next week. In front of Earl William. Don't suppose it will go forward now. I was working on the trial brief. An issue of transubstantiation." A look of puzzlement enveloped Tim's face. He had no idea what transubstantiation meant.

"That's the movement of nonmarital assets into marital assets by actions of one of the parties to the marriage. Did they intend to transfer to the spouse as a gift and thereby become marital property, or was it merely an accommodation for an estate plan? Husband, who I represent, had lots of assets before the marriage, but being the farmer he was, he had to borrow against the property each spring for seed, fertilizer, and other stuff for the farm. Since he was married, the banks required him to have his wife sign the financing documents. She wouldn't sign unless she was on the deeds. If she was going to be liable, she wanted the asset.

"It's a reasonable approach, but hubby should have looked at it with a jaundiced eye at that time. Of course, his big-head perspective was skewed by his little head. He puts all the property into joint and survivorship with wifey. Third wifey, at that. So, the question is, is the property marital or premarital? I say premarital. That way, hubby gets to keep it all and wifey can leave with half the actual marital. Which is, I must say, a much bigger chunk of change than she came into the marriage with. They have only been married five years, and she walks away with a cool hundred grand when she came in with a negative seventeen grand in credit card debt?" Fred had been speaking directly forward while watching Tim Grau move from the Mom-and-Dad–Calling contest to the Husband-Calling contest. He glanced at Tim Snyder. No interest or comprehension there.

"Not your cup of tea, huh?"

"Now I know why I don't do divorce work. Ugh."

"Actually, this is an interesting issue. At least they're not fighting over who gets the single champagne glass that they got one New Year's eve at some insignificant event. Or some ugly dog that's not even house-trained. Legally, it's fascinating. Factually, a little more difficult. This is the kind of case that you wonder why they didn't come to see you before they dove into the mess. But they don't. They create their own problems, then blame the lawyers for helping them to untangle them."

"Sounds like bullshit to me."

Fred laughed.

Tim Grau had assembled ten females on the stage. "Any other brave and strong ladies out there who want to let the world know how they call their husbands? Come right up." No one in the crowd moved.

"Go, Judy! Go, girl!" shouted a bystander to one of the participants, who raised her fist in salute.

"All right then, here we go." Tim Grau issued the ground rules for the contest.

"Anyway, Tim," said Fred, "when I was working in the law library, I thought for sure I heard something about 11:00. Thought I heard the door. But then no one came in. Just a figment of memory, but I remember thinking about it at the time. Who would be coming into the law library at 11:00 at night? I expected someone to come around the corner. Nada. So I went back to reading on transubstantiation. That is also, for your edification and deification, if you ever become a god, the exact moment when the unleavened host and the watered-down white wine become the body and blood of Jesus Christ in the Mass of the Catholic religion. Why they use white wine when the blood is red, and red wine is available, is unknown to me."

"More pedant bullshit!" said Tim.

"Oh, yeah. You learn something, and I'm the pedant. How else do I get information to the masses so they can make wise decisions." Fred chuckled.

"Okay, ladies, are we ready?" boomed Tim Grau. "I can see from the determined looks on your faces that we are in for some pretty impressive husband calling. If you husbands are out there ... well, I guess I pity you." The crowd hooted and booed.

"We'll go right down the line. Number one. What's your name, and where are you from?"

Judy Whitright and I'm from right here in Chardon, Ohio."

Fred took two photos of Judy.

"Okay, Judy, what's your husband's name?"

"Hank."

"Now you know the rules; you can call him for anything, any reason. But don't be nasty, okay?"

"No problem," Judy leered.

"Go, Judy, go, girl!"

The female bystander, pink hair sprouting from the front of her head flowing into a brilliant bleached blonde. Each hair, not more than two inches long, was spiked in pointed clumps with some kind of goo. As she turned her head to raise her right fist in support, Fred saw multiple pierced earrings on her left ear and several in her left eyebrow. He winced in sympathetic pain.

He zoomed in on the green-haired pincushion, filled the screen with her head, and waited until she turned to the left again and then took a photo.

"Okay, Judy, let 'er rip." Tim handed the microphone to Judy. Judy, in true thespian mode, spread her legs to make herself stable. At that instant the crowd erupted in noises of approval. Judy looked to her left, slowly, looked to her right, slowly. The old "step by step" routine of the Three Stooges. Then she let out a bellowing holler more unintelligible by its volume than its content.

"Henry!!! Dinner's on the table. Git. I said. Git, now!!! Git, Git, Git!!!"

The crowd rewarded Judy with thunderous applause. Judy's fist shot into the air in salute.

Fred's immediate response was a brief analysis of the statement and the mode in which it was uttered, which indicated a subservient woman cooking in the kitchen who had absolute control over her man in accordance with the politically correct concept of women's liberation and women's rights. A time-honored relationship between married couples. But the voice was a little too brassy. It would grate on one's auditory receptors in about three minutes.

"So, Tim, is that the way your wife calls you?" Fred said smiling.

"Yes, she does." Laughing and shaking his head. "And she gives me the black power salute, just like Judy did. But my wife says 'Git' to get me *out* of the house, not to come for dinner. God save Ireland." Then he added, "You didn't happen to use the computer while you were down there, did you?"

"Yes, I did. It was shortly after I heard the noise that I went into the computer room. Probably just a couple of minutes. I bet Susan, the law librarian, can figure out the time. It had to be just around eleven o'clock that I used the computers. Used them for about an hour. Time-wise, it doesn't seem that it would make much difference, though."

"Maybe, maybe not. I'll talk to her, see if she can pinpoint it anyway." Tim jerked his thumb toward the stage. "I've had enough of this stuff, Fred;, I'm out of here."

"What do you mean? This is great stuff. You're going to miss the mustache contest next." Fred took several more photos.

# CHAPTER 23

Fred moved along Main Street toward his office, taking photos of interesting people and activities. Mothers pushing baby carriages, some with doubles. Fathers with small children perched on their shoulders. Dogs, dogs, and dogs.

Year after year, the festival put notices in the newspapers, in brochures, and made radio announcements that dogs were not welcome at the festival. *Please don't bring dogs to the festival.* But people defied or ignored the requests. Dog clubs inculcated their members to bring dogs to the festival to socialize them. Big dogs, Great Danes, mountain dogs, little dogs, hound dogs, cute dogs, ugly dogs. Too many dogs. Fred took photos of dogs and the people who looked like their dogs. Only one dog bite was reported to the police last year. And it was just a nip. Poor kid in a stroller just happened to be the right height for the dog to take the hot dog right out of her mouth. The scratch along the child's lip was not too severe, only required two stitches. It was the scream of the mother that attracted most of the attention.

Ohio law provides strict liability on the dog owner for a dog bite unless the owner can show that the alleged victim was taunting the dog. The festival itself, with all the noise and garbage on the ground, was a delicious taunt to the dog. But people loved their dogs. Dogs were their children, their family, and by golly, you had better not interfere with them. If the dogs can handle the festival, they can handle any social situation. *My dog is a nice dog.* Fred took photos.

Fred framed the courthouse within the large, circular ride and snapped photos. He saw no one he knew or he would have placed them in the foreground and taken their photo. That is, if they would even acknowledge his presence. They would be surprised in a year when they got a 9 x 6 photo in the mail from an attorney. Fred sent hundreds of photos to people every year. Some thanked him, some did not. He didn't care. It was fun to send a nice picture of people in situations where they never would have photographed themselves.

As Fred walked through the courthouse parking lot, he heard the screeching, loud engines of the chainsaws in the Log Chopping and Sawing Event. Jim Freeman was the master of ceremonies; all of his sons participated in the events. Jim put on log-sawing-and-chopping shows all over the United States. Fred intended to photograph the show on Sunday.

He made his way to the office.

He put his photo gear on the desk, checked his email, opened a bottle of St. Emilion, poured a metal goblet half full, raised his feet to the pullout writing board of his desk and just contemplated life. The muffled noises of the festival reached him. The screaming chain saws were too noisy.

Life was not pleasant at present. Connections. Tim Snyder was helping him. Good cop. Good investigator. Bad relationship with the chief. But then Fred's relationship with the chief was not good. In fact, it was terrible. But Tim was in a good position to conduct an investigation. He had contacts with the department and police forces throughout the county.

Joe Parker and the five *K*. What was the case? The judge's murder? Could be. Probably had to be. It was too coincidental and strange. The judge had treated him shabbily. There were obviously more facts behind the scenes than even Fred knew. But how would that play into Fred being arrested for the killing? Fred, duty-bound to keep any information about his client confidential, risked his own conviction.

Couldn't imagine Wellman killing anyone. A mean and nasty attorney, but not a killer.

Pastor Bob: no idea.

A baseball bat. Wrong ditty to utter at the wrong time. What a *faux pas*. What a coincidence. *Would I have been arrested even if I hadn't made the statement?* Maybe so. That statement, though, will go down in history.

Time of death: the same time as when Fred got to the law library. Too convenient. What was that noise? Someone leaving? Did they see anything? Did they know they'd set him up? Was it a two-birds-with-one-stone kind of thing? *Who's got it in for me?*

Fred sipped wine. The festival noise continued.

# CHAPTER 24

The parade began at three o'clock. Fred usually walked the route where the parade set up along Washington Street and Fifth Avenue in order to take photos of people preparing for the parade—floats with all the participants, Queens, commissioners, fire trucks, car drivers, kids, signs—to present a pictorial approach to part of the fun and work of the festival. However, given his present status as a person arrested for murder of a popular judge in a small town, his mental paranoia had convinced him people were putting on an act around him or intentionally avoiding him. People obviously felt funny around him. They didn't know whether to hug him or run from him. He decided not to inflict his presence on the parade participants. He wasn't going to make people uncomfortable just to say hello to him. Why embarrass them? Actually, he decided not to inflict the pain on himself. He'd take photos of the parade, but not the setup. He would take his annual photos of the parade on his northeast corner of the square.

Fred loved the parade. *Everybody loves a parade.* It is a culmination of community spirit and participation and pride. The floats created by the Assembly of God Church, the Hambden Elementary School, the 4-H clubs, and a dozen others showed an unparalleled community spirit.

Fred and Tom, his partner, invited people to watch the parade from the porch at the office of Newman & Brice—a porch party. This year, the same invites went out.

The porch party was a gathering of the attorneys' friends and relatives. The office porch was the ideal site to watch the parade. If it rained, you were protected. If it was cold, you could go inside the house to get warm. If you were thirsty, there was pop, beer, wine, and maple cocktails. Bathrooms were available. Fred and Tom didn't provide food—the attendees could spend money at the festival. Repeat attendees brought gyros, hamburgers, corn dogs, bison burgers, popcorn, and any other item sold by the festival vendors. A picnic table on the porch provided a gathering place. Kids sat on the cement porch railings to watch the parade. The steps were always crowded with people sitting on them. The porch party was going to be slim this year.

It was not completely shunned, as Fred had expected, but people were hesitant to associate with *him*—it was completely understandable, albeit hurtful. After all, he had been charged with murder. They might believe he would not commit such a crime, but they weren't going to embrace a murderer before a jury determined guilt or innocence. They were cautious, timid, uncertain, and when they really thought about it, maybe Fred *did* murder the judge: He was a ranger in Vietnam. He certainly had the capacity to kill. He probably killed in Vietnam. And if he was convicted of murder and went to jail for life, people would remember who went to that last porch party and rubbed shoulders with a murderer. No, people were not going to put themselves in the position of supporting Fred until they knew for sure. Later on, if he was found innocent, they could always say that was what they'd thought, even if it weren't true. How do you ever know? And Fred would not miss them this year surely. Besides, there was that other appointment that just happened to be made for Saturday and Sunday afternoon. Just couldn't make it. So sorry. Would have loved to. Thanks for the invite anyway.

Fred was a pariah, a leper; he was sure of it. President of the Maple Festival and charged with murder. This was supposed to be a fun year, but it wasn't. Fred sipped his wine. He saw people gathering on the porch. Tom Brice came in with his wife.

The phone rang, Fred picked up the receiver, pressed the button to access the line.

"Fred Newman speaking."

"Fred, Gene. Got a problem at the T-shirt booth. The guy did his wiring wrong. Some lady with her kid got a shock, jumped out of the booth and broke her leg. Maybe you better get over here."

"On my way."

Fred gathered his camera bag, put the strap over his shoulder, and took one last sip of wine.

"Tom, you got the store. I've got an emergency over at the T-shirt booth. Some lady broke her leg. You can handle it, right."

"Right!"

\* \* \* \* \* \*

Fred hurried to the T-shirt booth. The streets were lined on both sides with parade watchers. The weather was perfect for the parade—fifty degrees, sun shining, people smiling. They brought their own chairs. Not many sat directly on the ground unless they had a tarp for protection. The melted snow made the ground too wet to sit.

When Fred arrived, the EMTs were loading a rather obese woman onto a gurney. Gene, who was president of the Chardon Fire Department board of trustees and an EMT himself, was directing the firemen. Fred sidled up to Gary.

"So what happened?"

"This woman was in the booth holding her kid, and the girl got a shock when she touched the counter. She was scared, so she handed her kid out to her grand-mother and then jumped off the trailer because she didn't want to step on the metal steps. Fell right into the mud. Looks like she broke her ankle."

"What is the problem with the electric?"

"Come on over here, I'll show you." Gary led Fred to the rear of the trailer and pointed to a grounding rod. "You better take a photo of this. It's grounded wrong. The whole place was electrified. I can't believe no one else noticed it for the last two days. This isn't the same electric that Billy Mitchell inspected. Someone changed it. Some asshole."

Fred took photos from three angles. Took photos of the booth from all sides to give perspective to the trailer's positioning at the festival.

The EMTs were pulling and pushing the gurney through the mud to the sidewalk in the middle of the park to get to the ambulance parked by the log cabin.

Fire-engine sirens blocked out all noise. The parade had started. The piercing sirens whooped, blared, and caused little children and seniors to cover their ears in pain.

"Let's talk to the owner," said Fred.

A boy about sixteen was the only person handling the store. Long greasy hair that hadn't been combed in a week was offset by a bright pink T-shirt that read "Floyd's the Boyd," whatever that meant.

"Where's the owner?" asked Fred.

"He's out for a bite to eat. Not here." The boy was sullen. Wouldn't look Fred in the eye. His long, black hair hung to his shoulders. Fred could see the dots of two earrings poking through his hair. A tattoo inked from his ear, under his chin, and into his shirt. Fred couldn't decipher what it was supposed to be.

"What's his name?"

"Nelson, Judd Nelson."

"It's his first year here," added Gary.

"Well, son, you're going to have to close up. Can't have people getting shocked because the wiring's wrong. Did you do anything with the wiring?"

"No, I don't know that stuff. How come I never got shocked?"

"I don't know," said Gary, "go ahead and touch that metal band on the counter there." Pointing to a slim metal band bordering the cashier's counter.

The boy touched it and immediately jerked away. Shocked.

"I guess there's a first time for everything, isn't there?" said Gary, laughing.

"So you're going to have to shut down. Gary, can you shut off the electric to this place?"

"Got it." Gary went into the trailer, making sure he didn't touch any metal. He put on a glove, opened the fuse box, and shut down the electric breaker to the trailer. The lights in the trailer extinguished. The illuminated signs on the exterior dimmed and shut off.

"Judd's not going to like this."

Gary colored. A kid telling him who is in charge, when he is in charge. "You tell Judd to come see me as soon as he gets back." He stressed the *me*. "I'm Gary, the concession manager. You tell him I don't like this. I don't like people messing with the electric after it has been inspected. You tell him that. You got it? And after you tell him that, then tell him that the lady who broke her leg will probably sue him."

Then he added, "And don't even think about doing business until Mr. Nelson talks to me. Any sign that you are doing business until this thing gets straightened out and I'll haul this trailer out of here right now. You got that?"

The boy didn't answer, just looked at Gary's boots.

Gary was angry. As they walked to the concession trailer, Gary said, "That little SOB—'Judd's not going to like this.' What the hell. Judd's not going to like what he gets from me, that's for sure."

"Well, no doubt, we'll get a lawsuit on this one, that's for sure. Make sure we have his insurance papers lined up so I can refer it on to our carrier. In fact, get a copy of it. I'll put it in my file with the police report when I get it."

Fred went back to the office. The porch party was not more than twenty people, instead of the usual fifty. His status as a murderer was directly proportional to his support from his acquaintances.

He went in, picked up his Norelco dictating machine, and dictated the incident of the T-shirt booth including a description of the tattooed clerk.

The parade had already progressed around the square. The floats were halfway past Fred's office. He decided to pass up photos of the parade today. He just didn't feel like it. A malaise had descended on him when he saw the low attendance at the porch party. He didn't want to do anything. He still had tomorrow's parade to take photos when Mark Sperry was to be in the parade. Sunday's was a better parade anyway. His depression increased; it was turning into an inverted gyro and he was being sucked into its vortex.

The wine glass was still half full, or was it half empty? Did he even care? Could he even have any optimism? He wondered. He picked up the glass and sipped. He could finish this bottle of wine before he had to go and suffer more indignities at the Hospitality location at Bank One.

# CHAPTER 25

The Bank One building was previously the Chardon Savings Bank building until Bank One paid a premium for the stock of Chardon Savings Bank and it was no more. The stockholders made lots of money and the community lost a locally owned and operated bank. But change, as ever, was inevitable. Chardon was overwhelmed with banks. There was Bank One, First Merit Bank, National City Bank, Huntington Bank, Middlefield Bank, Fifth Third Bank, Sky Bank, Northwest Bank, Geauga Savings Bank, and First National Bank. Banks meeting their demise in the last number of years were Chardon Savings Bank, Security Federal Bank, Women's Federal Bank, Metropolitan Bank, and First County Savings Bank,

Bank One, a generous community citizen to the Maple Festival, located on the northwest corner of the square, allowed the Boy Scouts to use their parking lot for a fundraiser to charge people to park close to the square. It also permitted the festival Sap Run committee to use the drive-through area, protected from the weather, to register runners on Sunday morning for the Sap Run. But its main concession was to allow the festival to use the hall on the third floor for Hospitality each day after the parade.

Hospitality was provided by a committee comprising Debbie and Larry Crow; they organized the food and invitees. The list of invitees was extensive starting with the queens—they hailed from Milan Melon Festival, Brunswick Old Fashioned Days, Dalton Holidays Festival, Holmes City Antique Festival, Barnesville Pumpkin Festival, Utica Old Fashioned Ice Cream Festival, Geneva Grape Jamboree, Dennison Railroad Festival, Ohio Hill Folk Festival, London Strawberry Festival, Lorain International Festival, Huntsburg Pumpkin Festival, Coshocton Canal Festival, Brennan Oil Derrick Days, Happy Apple Days Festival,

Berlin Heights Basket Festival, and the Deercreek Dam Days. Among the queens in these festivals were the families that drove them in the parade.

Longtime vendors were invited, provided they brought some eats along with them. Unless they were longtime vendors, they felt somewhat uncomfortable with all of the locals. It was okay to take their money, but to socialize with them, well, it was not as interesting.

The festival board and committee members were welcome unless they were on the job for the festival somewhere else. They continually cruised in, made a sandwich, sipped a maple cocktail, and cruised out.

The queens, the maple producers, the Maple Hall of Fame honorees, and the parade marshal, along with their drivers and families were all invited.

The local dignitaries, the county commissioners, the Chardon Village mayor and council, the village manager, and even the police chief were invited. Some attended, some did not. Fred hoped the police chief would be absent this year. He generally did not attend, something to do with his inbred personality defect, Fred surmised. Lieutenant McKenna generally did attend. He was a friend to the festival inasmuch as his position permitted him. People liked him and respected him. His boss, the chief, hadn't attended in five years.

The visiting queens and their entourages attended. At times the hall was crowded. A monitor was placed at the maple-cocktail bar to prevent minors from the temptation of the sweet nectar.

After the queens had traversed the entire perimeter of the square in the parade, they were deposited in front of Bank One to make their way, along with their escorts, back down Main Street to the grandstand for introductions along with all of the dignitaries and the festival officers. The master of ceremonies finalized the parade with the introductions, and then everyone again walked along Main Street to the Hospitality room.

Fred didn't want to be introduced this year given the facts of the weekend so far, but he felt obligated because of his presidential position. He did not look forward to this event. He walked to the grandstand, shooting photos along the way. The queens were lined up at the back of the stage as Mayor Park addressed the large crowd in front of the grandstand.

Tim Grau motioned Fred to center stage. Upon completion of the mayor's remarks, Tim introduced Fred as the Geauga County Maple Festival president. Very light clapping, some undercurrent of boos.

Fred took the microphone. "Welcome to the Geauga County Maple Festival. We have survived yesterday's storm. We have re-erected the tent. The parade was wonderful. And all of you have a good time."

"Murderer!" was shouted from the crowd. "Killer, murderer!"

Fred ignored the catcall, handed the microphone to Tim, and made his way off the grandstand. People moved away from the man who was yelling. He stood isolated in a ten-foot radius of people. Fred glanced at the man, whom he did not know. Fred would have liked to walk over and punch the stupid guy in the nose, but there was no reason to ruin the festival further by putting himself into a confrontation with someone and have the chief of police arrest him for disorderly conduct or assault. Even in a crowd such as this, Fred was feeling lonely. Before he stepped off the stage, he zoomed the camera lens and took a photo of the angry man. He would remember that face. Who knew when he would meet him again? Fred made his way toward the north end of the square to Hospitality.

\* \* \* \* \* \*

The weather had completed a one-eighty-degree turn for the better. Sun shining, sixty-eight degrees, young ladies tying their jackets at their waists. The place was hopping. Lines formed at each vendor. Root beer, lemonade, DiRusso's sausage sandwich, corn dogs, cheese on a stick, waffles, French fries, cotton candy, steak-on-a-stick, funnel cakes, tenderloin, fresh-baked pastries, Greek gyros, mushrooms, onion rings, elephant ears, egg rolls— they were doing a bumper-crop business.

Fred saw several people he knew. They casually, but intentionally, avoided him. Looked the other way, got into line at a vendor, bent over to talk to their child. They didn't know if he was a murderer or not. They didn't know him well enough to trust that he wasn't.

Fred pushed the elevator button and waited three minutes before it descended to open. This elevator was actually slower than the elevator in the courthouse! He was joined by four other people he did not know. The elevator slowly closed. A seven-second delay before it started its slow, jerky journey upward. It caught, jerked, caught, and kept ascending. An occasional gasp or moan escaped. It stopped. Another seven-second delay before the door opened. No one spoke. Fred, having been first in, was last out. As the visitors proceeded to the main entrance, Fred took the shortcut to the kitchen.

He deposited his jacket on the pile of jackets placed loosely on the counter by the committee members. It fell on the floor. He picked it up and tossed it to the center of the pile. Picked up his camera bag and moved to the kitchen.

Claudia Battaglia saw him and went to him, gave him a big hug, and asked how he was doing.

"Just fine, just fine."

"Tough weekend, huh?"

"Just fine. A usual festival weekend."

"You need a maple cocktail. I'll get you one." She scooted off. Fred removed his camera. The place was crowded. The doors to the veranda were open, people stood on the veranda overlooking the square. Good crowd at the festival.

Fred took photos of Debbie Crow placing sliced meats and cheese on a plate. She looked up at the flash, smiled.

Claudia handed Fred a Styrofoam cup filled to the brim with maple cocktail and ice.

"Thanks. Here's to you." He sipped the strong lemon-flavored sweet maple syrup drink of choice. There were years that this drink had made Fred sick, but he'd learned to modify his intake. One cup of this quality was enough. But today, maybe he would have two, or three.

Fred was hugged by well-wishers, shunned by those who were uncertain, and ignored by those who did not know him. He made himself a sandwich of sliced meats, cheeses, mustard, and mayonnaise. A second cup of maple cocktail went down easily.

"Are you ready to take pictures of the queens, Fred?" asked Claudia.

"Sure, let's have at them. You'll organize them, right?"

"Two minutes."

Fred got his tripod and made his way to the veranda. He put his camera bag against the window so no one would step on it, placed his camera on the tripod, and made all the necessary adjustments and settings required to photograph. Claudia got the women on the porch. They waited for instructions.

They all knew this was the guy who was charged with murdering the judge. Most were in high school and didn't know how to act in front of him. Think him guilty or think him not-guilty? He was charged, so he must be guilty. The police wouldn't charge someone if they were not guilty.

"Okay, ladies. First, I'll take a photo of all of you together, then the queen and her two runners-up. Then the queen, by herself. Then, if you want, I can take photos of each of you individually, with your boyfriend or with your family.

"Now some of you are looking at me funny. I just want you to know that although I am charged with the judge's murder, I had nothing to do with it. That's all I'll say on it. *Nothing*, you hear me. So we can put that stuff aside and do this session in a nice fashion without thinking about that other matter. I know you ladies don't know how to deal with me on that, so we won't deal with it at all. Just enjoy yourselves. And let's get some good photos. I can't remember a better bunch of queens at any festival."

Fred always told the queen and the committee they were the best-looking bunch, because that is what they wanted to hear. And they always were the best. This was a weekend for compliments. The girls were dressed in their best. They were *queens* this weekend, and Fred was going to help make this the best weekend of their lives.

He took photos with flash and without flash, focused just past the queens to get the appropriate depth-of-field to encompass the entire festival overview behind them. The crowd was fair-sized. Tomorrow would be better. The sun was shining, and Fred was photographing directly into the sun. He shaded his lens with his hat to keep the halos off the photos. He took close-ups of the girls. On several, he knew he would have to touch up a blemish or two in Photoshop, but no problem. They would look their best in the photos he would produce.

Several of the girls, the queen included, wanted photos with their families. Brothers, sisters, dads, and moms. Two fathers shook Fred's hand. One wished him well and told him the chief was an asshole and got the wrong guy. Totally unsolicited. Fred smiled.

Aggie Sojka brought Mark Sperry, her husband and tomorrow's parade marshal, out to be photographed.

"Well, young fellow," said Mark, "I see they got you up for a charge of murder. Well, I think they certainly got the wrong charge."

"Mark!" exclaimed Aggie. "Now's not the time. You can insult Fred later. Right now, we're going to get our pictures taken."

"Oh we are, are we? Well, in that case, let me light up a cigar." Mark slowly and deliberately selected a cigar, unwrapped it, put the paper in Aggie's hand, which she quickly put into her pocket, placed it in his mouth, pulled out another cigar, extended his hand, and offered it to Fred. Fred took it, put it into his shirt pocket.

"Thanks, Mark, I needed that."

"That's to show my good faith. To extend the peace pipe, as they say. Keep that in mind as the vultures fly around you pointing their ugly talons. It's all *bosch*."

"Over here, Mark." Aggie pulled him to the railing. Mark puffed the cigar.

"Turn a little to the left, Mark." The smoke from the cigar wafted in front of their faces.

"Actually, switch places. That way the smoke won't interfere with the photo. The wind is making it go right in front of Aggie."

"The haze will give her a glow!" said Mark.

People watching, smiled. Mark was a character. Also an attorney, he had been in practice in excess of fifty years. His full mane of white hair flowed gently over his brow. He had married Aggie, twenty-five years his junior, which was no surprise to anyone since they had been dating for years. Fred photographed their wedding on a New Year's Day ten years ago at their home with only ten people in attendance. Family and a few friends. They were married by Judge Craig Albert with Don Farinacci holding a Civil War musket aimed at Mark. It was a great photograph.

When Fred jogged around the block of his home, an eight and two-tenths-mile jaunt, he would sometimes stop in at the Sperry residence on Woodin Road to get a drink of water. He walked right in, was always welcome, and if no one was home, he got his drink of water and moved on. Mark would regale him with historical facts and tidbits about the people of Geauga County. He was a true historian with a breadth of knowledge unparalleled and the ability to tell a story that equaled Mark Twain's.

"A little to the right, Mark. Aggie, put your hand on his … you know what."

"Oh, you go to hell."

Fred took photos, close-ups, short depth-of-field, great depth-of-field, with flash, without flash, full body, faces only, puffing of cigar, blowing of smoke, and grins.

"That's it. I wasted too many pixels on you guys already."

"Fred, sit down and have a drink with us," said Mark.

"Yes, do, Fred," added Aggie.

"I'll do that. It will be nice to sit with friends. Let me get a refill of my drink—a couple more photos, and I'm done here.

"Anyone else want their photos taken?" Fred looked at the people standing at the rail. Claudia nodded to him. Fred waited while she gathered her family, Bob Eldridge, Sara Brougher, Cindy Martin, Keith Eldridge, and herself. Fred photographed, flashed, unflashed, and kept them smiling.

Fred refilled his Styrofoam cup with maple cocktail, unhitched his camera bag and set it on the floor, put his camera on the table, and sat to enjoy a relaxing moment with Mark Sperry. Aggie was entertaining a crowd by the food, hugging some virile young men.

"So," said Mark, "you've been having a little trouble, have you?"

"A little, I guess."

"You're not the kind of guy to shove a baseball bat up Earl William's butt, but I can see you in a duel to the death on the square."

Fred smiled.

"Somebody needed to shove a baseball bat up there, but they didn't need to kill him at the same time." Mark blew a huge cloud of cigar smoke upward. "Somebody's angry. I know you can get angry, but not that kind of angry. Somebody with a real chip. Somebody like Parker."

Fred heard, but he wasn't paying attention. Then it penetrated: *Parker. Parker, "that kind of angry." What did Mark know?* Fred focused.

Mark was still talking. "Or maybe Clancy in Chesterland; he's an angry young fellow. Someone had to be really angry at Earl William to add that insult to injury."

"Why is Parker angry?" Fred queried, as if he didn't know.

"Parker? It's obvious. Didn't they grow up in the same town, Burton or Middlefield? Didn't Earl William's brother put Parker's eye out? Didn't Parker run against Earl William for judge? Wasn't that one of the nastiest races for judge that you have ever seen? There wasn't any love lost there, no siree. Pure hate between those two. And, isn't it Parker diddling Joannie at Lawyer's Title?"

"Where the hell do you get all this stuff? I didn't know that. Earl William's brother put Parker's eye out? How, when? I didn't know Earl William even had a brother."

"Oh yes, they went to the Cardinal schools, I believe. Way back when, when they were kids, just fooling around. Seems Robert Parker and Robert Kuhmer, Earl William's brother, were best buddies. Something happened, Parker lost an eye. Then they weren't friends. You never heard this story?"

"No!" Fred admitted.

"Then, a couple of years later, Robert Kuhmer turns up missing. Just graduated from high school. Ready for college. Had his whole life before him, and he's gone. They searched for him everywhere. The police thought Parker did it. Did an investigation on Parker and a bunch of other kids. Nothing. Just never heard from Robert Kuhmer again.

"Angry. Yep, that's what he is. Angry. Angry about his eye. Angry about the nasty election. Who knows what else he is angry about. After office hours, he sneaks down from his office into Lawyer's Title, has his little trysts with Joannie in the big safe they have there. It used to be a bank at one time on that site. Must be interesting to do it in a safe. Quite a while they been doing that. Yep, someone angry like that. That's the type of person who sticks a baseball bat up someone's butt after he kills him. Angry."

*Parker, my client,* thought Fred. Now there's an imbroglio. I'm charged with the crime, and maybe my own client is the culprit. A client whose information I cannot disclose as long as he is my client. Actually, forever. I can't disclose it at all, whatever it is. He exhaled deeply, sipped the maple cocktail.

"How does he sneak into Lawyer's Title? Can't he just walk through the front door?"

"Oh my, he wouldn't do that. Someone might see him. There is a stairway. His office is above Lawyer's Title; he goes down the secret stairway after hours. Of course, Joannie has extra work to do. Then they go into the huge vault and do their thing. Oh, quite secret. No one knows about it. Least of all, not me. The last time they were there, oh yes, it was Thursday, about six in the evening. Active, big fellow he is.

"But, my young alleged murdering fellow, more interesting is the baseball bat," Mark continued, "Why a baseball bat? Handy or intentional? Why not a statue of Lady Justice? She's blind, *kind of.* You have to ask yourself: what was the significance of the baseball bat? And why the toilet?"

"Think it's a piece of shit or something."

"That's it. Think Earl William was a piece of cow dung and he belongs in a toilet. That's the anger. That's the little extra that makes it a crime of passion. Who knows, maybe Earl William deserved it, maybe he belongs in a toilet. I'm not saying either way. And he is dead, so I won't speak too ill of the dead, but maybe. The murderer was very angry.

"And you, Fred. You're not that angry. Maybe you got your anger out in the war. Maybe all those Purple Hearts and Bronze Stars drained the anger out of you. Or maybe Earl William just didn't bring it out in you. But, from my position—that is, my position on high here—you didn't, or don't, have that angry feeling toward Earl William. Therefore, you're not the killer."

"Can you testify at my trial?"

"Oh no, Fred. It won't get that far. I'd say 'trust me,' but I'm a lawyer, and lawyers learn to never say 'trust me.' It's the lawyer who says 'Trust me' that you can't trust. But keep it in mind; it won't get that far. Something will bust. The police will find something or someone."

"Tim Snyder's on it, too."

"Oh yes, burglary boy. He did a fine job on that crime spree. Cost him his job in the long run, you know. Too much competition for the chief. Can't show up your boss like that, you know. You get squeezed out. Council was too stupid on that one, but then, what can you expect from a committee of elected officials? Nothing productive is what I say."

# CHAPTER 26

Tim searched in the dark for the address on Old State Road, Route 608, just north of Middlefield. His headlights shone on the mailboxes for too short a time. He slowed. So many mailboxes without readable addresses. Wasn't there some federal regulation about having visible addresses? Why hadn't the fire department or sheriff's department made these people get the luminous green number signs along this road? *Kiwanis or Rotary ought to make this one of their community projects. It just isn't safe. And, more importantly, I can't find where the heck I am going.*

He came upon an Amish horse-and-buggy on the road, small blinking lights framing a square sign on its backside. The slow-moving-vehicle sign reflected his headlights. Once past the buggy, he saw the address, but if he stopped now the horse would run into his car. He passed the address, drove to Middlefield Cheese Factory, turned around in the parking lot, and headed south. A right turn into the driveway of Joe Parker's home. Lights were on, someone must be home. Two cars in the driveway, garage doors open. *Maybe I should have called before coming. Oh well, too late now. He might have said no.*

An old house, had to be a century home, had a porch that stretched on two sides of the house. Nice. Tim rapped the tarnished brass knocker between the screen and the door. He heard the yell through the door.

"Christine, get the front door." Then a pause. "I don't know who it is, I don't have x-ray vision. Just answer it."

The door opened. A girl, about fourteen with long, blonde hair falling over her shoulders, just looked at him.

"Hi, I'm Tim Snyder. I wonder if I might talk to Joe. Joe Parker, your dad. Just for a moment?"

She didn't answer him, merely turned her head and yelled. "Dad! Somebody here to see you. It's a cop." She walked away toward an adjoining room where a television was flickering. She didn't invite him in but left the door open.

A moment later, Joe came to the door, saw Tim and looked puzzled. Tim was in his Burton Police Department uniform; at first glance, it would appear to be an official visit.

"Evening, Joe. I wonder if I could talk to you for a few minutes?"

"Oh, Tim, it's you. Yeah, sure. Why not." Joe opened the screen door for Tim. "Come into the den." Joe led the way through the living room. Christine stared vacantly at the television, didn't even glance at Tim as he walked through the room. *Active teenager,* thought Tim sarcastically.

Joe motioned Tim to a seat across from a desk. Joe closed the door and sat behind the desk.

"What's up, Tim?"

"You know this thing with Judge Earl William Kuhmer? Well, I'm kinda looking into it for Fred Newman. He's in a pickle, and I don't think he did it. The chief has him picked out as the prime suspect, but I think the chief has blinders on because he hates Fred's guts. So I'm just trying to nose around, see if I can get some background stuff. Figure out where Earl William was coming from."

"Yeah, what's that got to do with me?" Joe frowned. He intertwined the fingers of his hands and slowly rotated his thumbs around each other. "The police already tried to talk to me, but I wouldn't talk to them. I know you're trying to help Fred, so I'll talk to you. After all, you know, Fred's my attorney."

"I'm sure this doesn't have a whole lot to do with you, Joe. But I was checking the courthouse records in the clerk's office. Looks like you haven't had much luck in Earl William's court."

"No luck at all. Absolutely none."

"That's what I discovered. But I wondered, how come?"

Joe said nothing.

"What I mean is, did the fact that you guys had an ugly campaign for judge make him your enemy?"

"I think he was my enemy long before that. But he was the meanest son of a bitch during the campaign. He did nasty things during that campaign."

"Why was he an enemy before the campaign?"

"Not so much an enemy, but we kept our distance. It was his brother who put my eye out."

"What?"

"Yeah, his brother. When we were kids, about the ninth grade. We were fooling around, and he shoved a stick in my eye. I lost my sight. Ruined my ability to participate in sports. Ruined a lot of things, but those are past. So, ever since, Earl William and I just kind of stayed away from each other. Not that we disliked each other, just that we kept our distance. Not the kind of guy I would go fishing with. It was mutual."

"Except he won the election for judge."

"Yeah, he won. He was a Republican in a Republican county. He was dirty about it too. Went around saying: 'In the land of the blind, the one-eyed man would be king. But this isn't the land of the blind. Is it?' Now you tell me, is that fair? A man who wants to be judge attacks someone for a physical disability caused by his brother? He wants to judge fairness on proceedings before him? Yeah, fat chance. Like the fairness he has imposed on my cases."

"I see you haven't won any in front of him."

"Yeah, go figure. I'm zero and six; the SOB had it in for me. I even had Fred represent me. Fred got along with him, was a fair guy, a straight shooter. I figured that would balance the scales a little. Didn't do any good. Earl William just shoved it to me."

Tim heard the statement. He didn't move, not a flinch. 'Shoved it to me.' Tit for tat? Maybe.

"What did Fred think of it?" asked Tim.

"Fred couldn't figure it out. That last case, I had an easement recorded. I had used the easement for the last ten years. Then the Amishman starts to build a house right on where I exercised the easement. The judge let him do it. Made my easement go alongside the creek. It would get washed out every year. What kind of easement is that? Makes the property totally worthless. Yeah, did he stick it to me? I guess he did. Is he my friend? I guess not!

"So, whoever killed him, he's got my thanks, that's for sure. Might not be the right thing to say under the circumstances, but that's the way I feel. That Earl William was a mean and nasty SOB, as far as I'm concerned."

"Any idea who would want him killed?"

"No, but it sure isn't Fred. That's a crazy notion. He gets along with everybody, but yet he is assertive. A good attorney." Joe paused, thinking. "That's strange, they arrested him."

"Yes, it is, but he was in the courthouse when it happened. Chief Jenkins thinks he did it. Went crazy on him actually. So, Joe, excuse me, but I have to ask you, what were you doing Thursday evening?"

"Oh boy, I'm a suspect, too, huh?" Joe smiled. "Thursday. I was in the office quite late. Ate a quick dinner, then got some more work done. Went home about nine, nine thirty. Even called my wife before I came home. I was still hungry. Other than that, nothing. Saw the festival going full blast in terrible weather. Not many people there. Didn't even fill up the parking lot behind the office. That's unusual for a Thursday night. The locals usually park all over the place. Not that night."

"Okay, Joe. If you get any ideas for me to help out Fred, I'd sure appreciate it."

"Yeah. I'd help if I could, that's for sure."

# CHAPTER 27

The Stir Booth at the Geauga County Maple Festival is a ramshackle affair. It is a cross between a log cabin, a clapboard shanty, and a sugar house. It is the sugar house for the festival, and it fulfills all the functions of a regular sugar house. On a side porch, there is a five-hundred-gallon holding tank for the sap drained from the local maple trees. The sugar house is located at the south end of the park on the square.

Bob Freeman has a transport tank on a trailer attached to a tractor. He and his wife, Sue, and sometimes friends or other people who just want the experience of collecting sap run from tree to tree with a five-gallon pail tipping the sap buckets. When the pail is full, the sap is poured into the holding tank on the trailer. No one actually waits for the pail to be full, because five gallons of syrup weigh more that fifty-five pounds. When the route is complete, or when the tank is full, it is drained into the holding tank on the porch of the sugar house.

From the sugar house tank, the sap is filtered and then piped into the pan. The pan is a flatbed four feet by eight feet made of stainless steel with channels that begin where the sap enters the pan and ends where the syrup exits the pan. As the liquid sap courses through the channel, up one side, then down the other, then up, then down, then up, then down, then once again, it becomes heated. Below the pan is an oil-furnace blower that heats the sap. It used to be done with wood, but that took too much energy and time. Plus, with all the people coming through the sugar house to watch the process, it created a danger to continue to open the firebox. Bob Freeman now devotes his time instructing the patrons on syrup making instead of feeding the firebox.

As the sap is heated to 219 degrees, the water evaporates into steam. At the roof of the sugar house is a cupola opening, which allows the steam to escape. One of the more romantic and nostalgic vistas in Geauga County for longtime residents is viewed when approaching Chardon from the south on Route 44, stopping at the light on the square, and watching the steam billowing from the sugar house blanketing the square in the direction with the wind.

The building itself is rectangular. On the north end is the porch with the holding tank. In the middle is the pan. Next to the pan is a rail to prevent festival attendees from getting too close to the super-heated pan. Everyone wants to touch everything. You can put up signs, you can tell people, you can show pictures of burns, but they will still touch the pan: "Oh, it can't be that hot. Ouch!" They get burned.

Bob Freeman stands behind the rail or in front of it. To the west end of the building is a table where Sue Freeman sells syrup products made onsite. This is the one perquisite they obtain by demonstrating the syrup process at the festival. She also sells candies, made elsewhere, of course.

On the south side of the building is the maple-stir section. Gary Thrasher was the previous operator; he turned it over to Dale Deimer. Dale assembles a great collection of volunteers to sell maple stirs. A maple stir is syrup heated to 234 degrees and then poured into a small paper saucer. Paper must be used because of the temperature of the syrup; Styrofoam melts, twists, and breaks. The saucer of syrup is sold for a dollar. Along with the saucer of syrup, the patron is given a small, flat stick to stir the syrup. As the stirred syrup cools, it hardens into a maple spread. Then as it cools more and is stirred more, it hardens into candy.

A maple stir is an absolute must for anyone attending the festival. Locals come to the parade, get a stir, and go home. They have done the festival.

Dale Deimer has his volunteers organized into shifts. The different shifts all have different personalities. Some sing, some insult patrons, some are just kindly and happy, and they all enjoy the fun and human contact. On Thursday and Friday, the local nights at the festival, the volunteers see all their friends and neighbors and force the sale of a stir by cajoling or embarrassing the patron. All in good fun.

There is a steady stream of festival-goers that pass through the sugar house watching the sugar-making process, buying syrup and stirs, and talking, showing their kids the maple syrup heritage of Geauga County, the Maple Capital of Ohio.

On occasion, a disruption occurs. Whenever people congregate, whenever people negotiate, whenever people are people, there comes a time when there is a blip in the radar, a disruption.

On Saturday evening, precisely at 8:15 p.m., such an event occurred at the Stir Booth.

FG walked into the sugar house to buy a stir. The initials F. G. stand for Freda Gale. Everyone who knows Freda thinks it stands for fat girl. Freda weighs in excess of 260 pounds on a five-foot, six-inch frame. Freda is a ton of fun. When she is in a good mood, she is lively, witty, cracks jokes at her own expense, and has a friendly smile, wide and broad. But when she is not in a good mood or when she gets angry, she goes off the deep end. She talks loudly, shouts. She swears. She throws things around. She has no self-control, and she does not hesitate to create a scene.

Dale Deimer knew FG. She had been getting maple stirs for years. She loved maple stirs. She hung around the sugar house many times; it was warm and jovial. She had never created a scene in the sugar house before, but Dale was aware of her reputation for occasional disturbances.

Saturday night was a hopping night for the festival. The tent was newly re-erected. Vendors were selling, the temperature was right, people were antsy, the sugar house was crowded with people buying stirs and observing the sugar-making process.

"Hey, FG, a stir?"

"You betcha."

FG stirred with the thin popsicle stick and blew on the stir to cool it quicker. She listened to Bob Freeman describe the flow of sap across the pan, the purpose of the channels, and the end result.

"Gimme another stir," said FG, sliding a dollar across the counter.

"Don't overdose on that sugar, FG. That's potent stuff."

"Nada. I can handle. You don't think I got this big eating vegetables, do you? I got to maintain my cellulite."

Dale laughed. FG laughed raucously. People turned to look at the source of the noise.

The crowd slowly moved through the sugar house. In the entrance, out the exit. A flow-through pattern that assisted crowd control. FG stood by the rail stirring her syrup to candy, intermittently tasting it to find the right texture, the right smoothness, the right graininess, the perfect stir. She finished her second stir and moved toward the line of stirs on the counter ready for sale.

"I get my third one for free." She reached for a stir.

"FG, what are you doing?" said Dale.

"I get my third one for free. I bought two of them already. I get my third one for free."

"You know we don't do that. We have never done that. I can't give you any for free. You have to pay. One dollar, please."

FG had picked up a stir. She turned away from Dale, ignoring him. Dale reached over the counter, grabbed the stir, bumped FG's hand, the stir fell to the edge of the counter and bounced onto the floor, face down.

FG immediately became enraged. She stomped on the fallen stir. Hot maple syrup squirted across the floor. She turned toward Dale, face flushed red.

"You motherfucker!" she screamed at the top of her lungs. Everyone in the sugar house turned to look.

"You cock-sucking, dick-licking, corn-holing, scumbag asshole, shitface, motherfucker!" FG swung her arm across the counter, sweeping fourteen maple stirs onto the floor behind the counter, in front of the counter, and three of them sticking and slowly dripping off her dirty, gray sweatshirt hoodie.

She stood in one spot and raised her head and howled an ear-piercing scream of rage and frustration. The crowd moved away from her as fast as they could. No one wanted maple syrup spilled on them. No one wanted to be close to a crazy person.

FG then moved to get behind the counter. Dale tried to prevent her. Dale yelled to call the cops. Bob Freeman got his arms around FG from the back and tried to hold her. She screamed and kicked. At 260 pounds, she was not easy to control. The sugar house was suddenly empty except for Bob, Sue, Dale, and two workers behind the counter who could not get past FG and Dale. Bob held her screaming and kicking. The foul swear words FG assembled in one sentence were truly amazing. Her knowledge and ability to string such unassociated words together was unparalleled.

In addition, it was quite disturbing to the patrons in the sugar house, especially parents with small children and the elderly. Several teenagers, hearing the racket, gathered outside the sugar house to watch the fun.

Bob and FG fell to the ground. Dale grabbed FG's legs to keep her from kicking wildly. FG continued to scream in rage and frustration. Bob yelled at her ear to "Shut the fuck up!" She ignored him or couldn't hear him or was insane.

If Fred were there, he would have taken photos, but alack, alas, he was not. This would have been one of those historical events at the Maple Festival that he liked to document. But Fred was not feeling too Maple Festivally at this time.

FG was bleeding from her mouth. During one of her screams, as she stuck her tongue out to fully effect a scream, the piercing on her tongue, a huge bulbous silver-mirrored object, got caught on her tooth and pulled so that it bled. She looked and sounded like a raging bull, or at least at what could be described as one.

Bob was getting tired of holding her. He could smell the beer odor from her breath, mixed with the sugary smell of the maple stir. Bob liked both beer and maple, but he revolted at the combination emanating from FG. He gagged twice and held his face in a different direction so he would not have to smell that odor.

FG began muttering. She relaxed. She cried. Blood dripped alongside her cheek.

"Let me up. Let me up. I'm okay."

"You done? You're not going to hit anybody. You sure?" said Bob.

"Yeah, I'm done. Just let me up. This hurts."

"You going to wait for the cops? You're not going anywhere, right?"

"Yeah, yeah, okay. I'll wait. Just let me up."

"Dale, you okay with it? We let her up? Sue, get that chair, put it by the rail. We'll let her sit there till the cops come." Slowly Bob and Dale disentangled themselves and let FG get up. She got on her hands and knees, looked around suspiciously.

"FG, don't even think about it," warned Bob. "We got you covered. Enough is enough. You got that?"

FG did not answer. She got to her feet and sat on the chair. Bob positioned himself two feet from her to dissuade her thought of escape. Dale stood at the other side to prevent her escape through the exit.

Two cops ran in. Mike McKenna and Randy Long.

"Hi, Mike," said FG, "about time you got here. These assholes have been beating me up. I want them arrested."

# CHAPTER 28

T im Snyder entered the Chardon Police Station through the back door to the Municipal Center. As he entered the second passageway, he saw FG sitting at a desk.

"FG, what are you doing here?"

FG smiled broadly. "Hey, Tim. I thought they fired you?"

"Cute, FG. What did you do now? Who were you screaming at? You got blood on your blouse."

FG laughed. "Those motherfuckers in the sugar house attacked me. Beat the shit out of me. I'm going to sue their pants off."

"What did you do now?"

"I'm telling you, they beat me up."

"She threw a fit," said Lt. Mike McKenna coming into the room. "Spilled maple stirs all over the place. Screaming like a banshee."

"Bullshit!" laughed FG.

Tim Snyder glanced at the counter where he was required to sign in for Maple Festival duty. He saw an overturned purse with its contents strewn in an orderly fashion across the counter.

"What's this stuff? Yours, FG?"

"Yeah, mine. Look what they do, throw it all over the place."

"What are you doing with a law-library key card?"

"What the hell are you talking about?"

Tim pointed to a slim card the size of a credit card with no writing but a squiggly pattern etched across the front. "That one. It's a library card. Where'd you get it?"

"Fuck you, guys, I ain't talking. Think I'd say a thing to McKenna? I'll talk to you, Tim, you've been good to me. But screw *him*."

Snyder glanced at McKenna, raised his eyebrows, tilted his head toward the door indicating McKenna should leave.

"Is that what I think it is?" asked McKenna. "The law library over there?" Pointing his finger in the direction of the courthouse.

Tim nodded.

"FG," said McKenna, "I'll let you talk to tall Tim here. But you give him any trouble and I'll charge you with resisting arrest too. Got me?"

"Screw you, Lieutenant McKenna. You're so tall the thin air must be getting to you. Get the hell out of here so I can talk with my buddy."

McKenna walked out of the room shaking his head. There was no reasoning with a person who had no reason.

Tim sat on the other side of the desk facing FG.

"FG, you can't go around talking to people like that all the time. They won't like you. You get more flies with honey than with sh**, you know."

"I just like to piss them off. They're such jerks."

"But those jerks are in control." He exhaled deeply. "So, what is this stuff? How did you get this card?" Tim brushed the card onto an index card with another index card, being careful to not touch it. He examined one side, which showed a pattern of squiggly lines. He turned it over with the index cards; it was completely white without any pattern side. There was writing in one corner with a magic marker, the initials *LL*. It looked like a credit card without the enhanced writing and without the magnetic strip. There was a magnetic strip, but it was bonded within the plastic. The card was waved in front of a sensor on either side of the courthouse basement door. When the green light illuminated, the door opened without an alarm sounding. The activity unlocked the door. If a person left from the interior of the courthouse without the key card, an alarm would sound in the police station.

"What is it?" asked FG.

"I think it is a key card to get into the basement door to the courthouse when the courthouse is closed."

Tim pulled out his wallet, fished out his law-library card, and compared.

"See, it is the same. That means it is a key card to get into the courthouse. Question is, what are you doing with it? You realize, FG, there was a murder in the courthouse Thursday."

"I didn't murder anybody. I can't stand going into that courthouse. Those judges suck."

Tim poked through FG's purse. He used the end of a pencil to hold up a small Baggy with a substance resembling tobacco in it.

"Oh, FG, for shame." He looked at the Baggy and then around the room, spotting the camera. At the angle he was at, the camera pointed to FG. He looked at FG, held the Baggy close to his chest, and spoke softly. "A deal, gone…?"

FG might be stupid, but she was also savvy. McKenna hadn't seen the Baggy yet. Discovery would put her back in jail. She might go to jail anyway, but she didn't need to go back for marijuana possession again. She was still on probation for the last one. It was a deal. She'd tell Tim all about the stupid little card she found, but no marijuana possession, hallelujah.

FG compressed her lips, lowered her eyelids, and then uttered grudgingly, "Yeah."

He put the Baggy into his shirt pocket. Tim continued to shuffle through the purse as if nothing had happened, napkins, makeup stuff, coins, a wallet, flashlight, and a ring of keys on the table.

"So, where did you get this thing?" Pointing to the key card.

"Dumpster-diving."

"Oh great, where?"

"Right there by the courthouse."

"FG, this is the Maple Festival. There are Dumpsters all over the place. Which one?"

"The one by the end of the big tent. There's a couple of Dumpsters there."

"Which end, East Park Street or Main Street?"

"Main Street. By the trailers where you buy food."

"Why don't you tell me how you got it? In your own words."

"You don't think I murdered anybody, do you?"

"FG, of course not. You might yell at someone so they die, but murder, no, I don't think so." He paused. "Go ahead."

"Okay. I was looking for something to eat." She saw the controlled expression of revulsion on Tim's face. "Hey, if you can't afford some of that stuff and they throw away a perfectly good sandwich, why not?"

Tim waved his hands in front of him in apology. "You're right. Who am I to say what's right? So when was it?"

"Thursday night. Probably about eleven fifteen. The festival was closing up. Actually, there was no one around. It was an ugly day with the tent falling down and stuff. The ground was all muddy. Ugh.... So I look around, no one around, the lights on the trailers were going off. The Dumpster was full. It was the one on the side of the barrier closest to the courthouse. Right on top, there was three-quarters of an elephant ear. In good shape, I could see it. So I grabbed it and this card fell on the ground. I heard it fall. I just picked it up and put it in my purse. Thought it might be a credit card. Wasn't going to use it, of course. But I could turn it in ... Don't look at me like that. I mighta turned it in." She raised her pierced eyebrow and winked.

"Sure, FG. That doesn't matter. Go on."

"So I looked at the elephant ear. It was good. I ate it. That's it. There wasn't much else on top to look at. Just trash.

"I haven't looked at that thing since I stuck it in my purse."

"You didn't see anyone throw it in the Dumpster, did you?"

"No, I checked around to see if anyone was looking. I'm not going to Dumpster-dive when people are looking."

"But you didn't see anyone throw anything into that particular Dumpster, did you?"

"No, not at all. There was no one around."

"What time was it, can you be precise?"

"No, I can't be *preee-cise*. It was after all the lights were going out on all the trailers. Right after eleven o'clock. About ten, fifteen minutes after."

"You didn't like Earl William, did you?"

"I'm telling you, Tim, I didn't do nothing." Panic spread across her pierced features.

"I know, I know, I'm just trying to get the whole picture here. I need the information to eliminate you as a suspect. After all, you were found with a key to open the courthouse door two days after he was found murdered."

"Hey, I was Dumpster-diving, that's all! I thought it was someone's credit card. I don't know nothing about that son of a bitch, Earl William."

"He was, wasn't he?"

"Yeah, he put me in jail for six months. Thought he was being nice letting me out ten days early. He didn't like me at all. Chewed me out. *Paraphernalia.* Big deal! A bong, a toot, put me in jail for six months. Everyone smokes out there. I get caught, I go to jail. He's a prick, that's what he is. A motherfuckin' dick-lickin' prick."

"Okay, go easy. I knew you didn't like him, but don't get worked up on me."

"He ain't like Judge Albert. Now there's a buddy. Like you, Tim. He puts me in jail for sixty days, and I still like him. Why is that? I'll tell you why, he treats me like a human being. He talks to me. He listens to me. He doesn't just chew me out and treat me like the scum of the earth. That's what Earl William did. He looked at you like you was scum, the bottom-of-the-Dumpster scum. Then he insulted you, made fun of you in front of all the people in the courtroom. Just because he has all those high-falutin' degrees and education and stuff, he thinks he is better than everybody. He ain't shit. And someone else thought so too. That's why he's dead. I'm glad he's dead. The son of a—"

"Okay, okay, I get the picture." Tim put his hand up, palms forward in defense. "You don't need to string a whole series of swear words together to get your point across. I understand."

"So screw him, I didn't kill him, but I'm glad someone else did. Good riddance."

# CHAPTER 29

"If the chief catches me telling you any of this stuff, it's my ass, you know?" said McKenna.

Tim Snyder was stretching his shoulders, extending his arms over his head, clasping his hands, and turning slowly to the left and then to the right.

"Yeah, yeah, I know. The chief hates my guts. He'd rather see a crime go unpunished than to have me get any information that might help find the murderer. That's why he's the chief. My presence here is legit. I'm checking in for my shift, early."

"That was good, what you did with FG," McKenna observed. "I watched on the TV. She's a piece of work, isn't she?

"Some people are not blessed with intelligence. Poor FG is one of them. What did she finish, the ninth grade? She just can't make it. Sorry to say, she's stupid, probably bipolar or some other personality dysfunction too. Can't think, can't reason, can't speak the queen's English, and now she's Dumpster-diving. Poor slob. But look, Mike. I know you're having domestic problems at home. I can fix you up with FG, if you want?"

"Screw you." McKenna laughed.

"So, what have you got so far? You tell me what you have, I'll tell you what I have."

"It's a deal, but if the chief comes waltzing in—it's a Saturday night, I don't expect him to come in, but if he does—you're just checking in. Move on."

"No problem," Tim agreed.

"We ran the prints on the judge's chambers, the bathroom, and the door to the law library. The outside door and the two inside doors. Fred's prints were all over the outside door, and the one inside door."

"Sure, he was in the library. Says he was."

"Okay, it could be a cover-up, but probably not. Fred's not the type to murder. He could kill. I think his ranger stuff in Vietnam shows that. Two Purple Hearts. Something went on. But I don't think Fred murdered him. His prints showed up in the chambers, but they were smeared as if they were made a while ago.

"Also on the library basement outside door were Earl William's prints, the law librarian's prints ..." McKenna looked at a sheet of paper before he continued. "The maintenance man, George, a guy named Mark Wellman; Joe Parker had three prints on the inside of the door, some disabled guy, that's the disabled entrance, you know. Name of Peter O'Leary, and of course, Fred. Oh, and a guy named Armstrong."

"Would that be Allan Armstrong?"

McKenna checked the sheet. "Yeah, that's him. Just on the outside of the door. Why, You know him?"

"I talked to him this morning. I had checked the clerk's office records and saw Earl William had put Armstrong in jail. Armstrong didn't even know the judge was dead. He was strung out on methamphetamine. He talked a mile a minute. Didn't like EW, but I wonder how his prints got on the door."

"I think they huddle back there when they want a joint or something. Who knows. You don't think he was involved, though?"

"No, I don't. But I'm sure you guys will talk to him. Good luck. What else?"

"That's it for the outside basement door. Pretty clean, actually. I think they had just cleaned it the week before. Maybe Armstrong took his meth in the alcove by the basement door. That would make sense.

"Let's see. On the inside library door—law librarian Susan, Fred, Mark Wellman ... there's a list of about twenty-two people. In chambers, lots. Lots of attorneys, insurance adjusters, secretaries, people from the clerk's office. Too many to isolate anyone."

"Any of the same that were on the outside door?"

"Fred, of course. Joe Parker, Mark Wellman. Interestingly, the table was wiped clean. Someone, after they offed the judge, wiped the table clean. That's where the murder was committed. Well, maybe not. There was a tussle in the chambers. Looks like, according to the crime lab, and we don't have their full report yet, but looks like EW was hit with a small baseball bat twice in the left arm, then twice in the head. You know, one of those bats they give away at the Indians' games for souvenirs, probably the same one stuck up his wazoo. So there was a fight in chambers. Then the body was dragged to the bathroom and the head was shoved into the toilet. He actually died from drowning. Water in his lungs. He must have been unconscious.

"I always thought there was some autonomic nervous system that shut down your esophagus when water tried to enter, but I guess not. Shows what I know about physiology. His lungs were not totally full of water, but enough so he couldn't get any oxygen."

"So," said Tim, "he died of drowning on the second floor of the highest building in the county on the highest geographical point in the five-county area 1,400 feet above sea level."

"I think it's 1,350 feet, and there is a place in Hambden or Montville that might be higher."

"Oh, excuse me, Mr. Prissy."

"More like *screw you*."

"Okay, what else? I saw the body with the baseball bat. Any prints on that?"

"They were too smeared. At least the ones in the body. There were none on the part outside the body. Wiped off. The whole area was wiped clean. No prints on anything central. Some prints, incidental, on different areas in the bathroom. But they appear to have been there awhile."

"Any of the same prints as on the outside door?"

"None. His left arm was broken by one of the hits on it. Think the murderer was right-handed. Left arm hit twice, then the head hit on the left side. Strong swing. Someone was angry or awfully strong.

"It appears that it was the judge's own baseball bat. He had it on a little holder on a credenza at the side of his office."

"What about fingerprints on the belt or buckle?" Tim asked.

"Nothing. I guess the killer unbuckled him, pulled his pants down, shoved the ball bat up there with great force, then wiped the buckle and belt clean when he wiped the bat. Looks like he might have kicked the ball bat some. There were some scuff marks on the end of the bat. Hard to push it up there that far without some extra force. Twenty-four inch bat with sixteen inches buried up the judge's wazoo. Crime lab thinks he, the murderer, kicked the bat up there after he got it in initially. Guy must have been angry."

"Guy?"

"Had to be a guy. Too strong. Drag that fat EW all the way down the hall, up those three steps, shove that bat in there, had to be a guy."

"If it wasn't so gruesome, it would be a comedy."

"Gruesome it was. What do you tell your kids? Daddy died with a baseball bat up his wazoo. Or Daddy drowned in a toilet. No, I feel sorry for the family. Even though EW was a mean SOB, his family didn't deserve this."

Tim was silent.

"So," asked McKenna, "what do you have?"

"Wait a minute, you're not done. What about time of death? What about key-card use?"

"Oh yeah." McKenna paged through the report. "Here it is. Time of death, between 10:40 p.m. and 11:00 p.m. Pretty narrow time. Bunch of stuff here on lividity, rigor mortis, can't make heads or tails out of it."

"That's just about the time Fred said he heard something. About 11:00. Maybe someone leaving."

"We'll leave that open for a while. Here's the law-library use: 'At 10:06, EW enters law library through basement door with his key card.'"

"Ten thirty-four p.m., Fred enters law library with his key card. Ten fifty-six p.m., EW's card shows his exit from the law library. Someone used it, obviously. One nineteen a.m., Fred exits law library. So if Fred did it, he stayed there for a couple of hours afterward. Cover his tracks? Use the judge's key card? Clever. But then why throw it in the closest Dumpster to the courthouse? Doesn't make sense."

"We don't know it's EW's card yet, but assuming it is, that's not the way to Fred's office either," added Tim.

"Unless he wants it to be found."

"Who but FG would have ever found that key card in the Dumpster? That Dumpster was dumped in the middle of the night. It would have been gone without a trace. You think anybody is going to go sift through Waste Management's dumpsite for anything? I don't think so, Lieutenant. In fact, I think the killer, whoever it was, used that key card, tossed it in the Dumpster thinking that was perfect disposal. FG was pure luck. Pure disgusting luck. That's one of the main reasons Fred didn't do it. If Fred did it, he would want that card found. Leave it somewhere to show someone used it. And, think about it: How does the card get found by FG at 11:15 when Fred is still in the law library until 1:19 in the morning? He can't scoot out, throw it in the Dumpster, and then scoot back in without using his card to show re-entry."

"But the computer showed its use anyway," McKenna pondered, "so it doesn't have any real impact, does it?"

"If that is EW's card, then from a timing standpoint, I think that clears Fred. I sure hope there's a print or two on it. That would be interesting. How long will that take?"

"Maybe by tomorrow morning or afternoon. Wouldn't that be something." McKenna stood. "Okay, what do you have? Probably nothing. And get rid of FG's stuff. I was overlooking it, but I like the way you did it."

Tim ignored the statement. "*Nothing* is what narrows the scope of the investigation, doesn't it? I did a check of the clerk's office records. Spent hours up there. I picked out about four people who appeared to have a grudge against Earl William. Armstrong was one. He threatened to kill the judge at one time. But was so zonked out on meth, he was worthless. He wouldn't even know about a key card. How would he get in the courthouse? Earl William's not going to let him in. Earl William probably let someone in, though. Who would he be friendly enough with to let them into the courthouse with him? It surely wouldn't be Armstrong. He's off the list.

"Then I talked to Joe Parker. His records show he has lost six cases in a row in front of Earl William. Looks like Earl William had a grudge against Parker. He lost the last case, and he should have won it easily. Earl William had to jump through hoops to make Parker lose. Fred represented Parker in that case. Even Fred was amazed at what Earl William did on the bench. Parker's got a history with Earl William. Ran against him for Common Pleas judge. Everyone says it: 'nasty campaign. One of the ugliest.' I talked to Parker before I came here tonight. He hated Earl William's guts. It was Earl William's brother who put Parker's eye out! Get that? Put his eye out. Would Parker have it in for Earl William? Probably not. Question is, did Earl William have it in for Parker? Okay, so then Earl William's brother,

Robert, disappears right after graduation from high school and is never heard from again. The eye-gouging incident occurred when Parker and Earl William's brother were in the ninth grade at Berkshire High School. Earl William was three years younger than Robert Kuhmer. It was three years after this incident that Robert Kuhmer disappears.

"Did Earl William blame Parker? Who knows? Long time to hold a grudge. Why didn't Parker win a single case in Earl William's court? Maybe only over the campaign issues. Maybe something deeper, *payback*. That was one of the nastiest campaigns we have seen in a long time. Maybe a bat up the ass in return for the nasty campaign."

"Geez!" said McKenna, "Parker. One-eyed Parker. 'In the land of the blind, the one-eyed man is king.' I heard Earl William say that. So what did you think when you talked to Parker?"

"He seemed on the up and up. Freely admits Earl William is on the bottom of his list of friends. Said they had a mutual dislike ever since he got his eye put out, or that was his feeling. They kept their distance. He acknowledged that Earl William had it in for him on every case. That was why he hired Fred to represent him. Maybe get him out of it a little. But it didn't work. He thought Fred was friends with Earl William and that would balance the scales.

"Said he worked in the office till about nine or nine thirty, then went home. But he's still on the list. I haven't ruled him out, just can't pinpoint him."

"What irony!" said McKenna,. "And here's Fred, charged with the murder. I think someone tried to talk to Parker; he wouldn't even see him."

"So, I also got the names of Mark Wellman; the judge filed a grievance against him. I'm going to talk to him tomorrow. And a Bob Pietsmeyer. They call him Pastor Bob. Earl William put his son away. The guy was diddling kids at Pastor Bob's religious school. Pastor Bob was not happy with Earl William. I'm going to talk to him tomorrow, too."

"Anyone else?"

"Nada."

# CHAPTER 30

F red set up his tripod on Main Street for several time-exposure shots of the rides with the courthouse in the background. He varied the aperture settings to automatically increase the length of time of the exposure; in this manner, the moving rides formed a blur in the photograph with other aspects of the photos in sharp detail. A very effective visual of movement. People took note of him, but passed him by. Fred identified a number of people he knew, but he also knew they would avoid him if they could, and they did. He would just deal with it. If he could extricate himself from this morass, then he could again be the proud president of the Maple Festival. But right now, he was the proud president of the Maple Festival accused of murdering a common-pleas judge. He was an obvious taint on this year's Maple Festival.

So he took his photos and immersed himself in his avocation of photography. He shot from the west side of the square, moving up and down Main Street; he shot from the sidewalk leading to the courthouse; he shot from East Park Street; and he shot from South Street. People ignored him, and he enjoyed himself for a short period of time. Some exposures were three minutes and longer.

Fred watched people as he waited for the exposure. They purchased stirs and gathered at the grandstand to listen to Alex Bevan, singer and songwriter, bellow his Lake Erie Islands songs. Long lines formed for the string of vendors on Main Street, and adolescents rode the same scary rides over and over again, emitting squeals of joy and terror. Kids yelled at one another to communicate even though they were only two feet away from each other.

This was teenager night at the festival. It was not advertised as such, but the teenagers came out in force on Saturday night at the festival. Look cool, hang with friends, show off tattoos and body piercings, flick your hair back, cruise the chicks, and cruise the hunks.

Fred heard about FG's acting-out tantrum. FG, that poor, misguided, ignorant, borderline-personality-disorder, overweight, fun girl just lost it. Say no and she cannot deal with it. One more item to list for this year's festival of fun. *Lots of fun,* Fred thought, sarcastically. This event will go down in history as the Fun Festival: murder, tent collapse, snow-bound on Thursday, electrocution-induced broken leg, FG going crazy, what's next?

A group of eight teenagers walked past Fred as he positioned his camera toward the square from South Street.

"Hey, mister, take our picture!" said one of them, a tall skinny blonde with straight hair down to her waist.

"Okay, let's do it," said Fred.

They stopped, looked at each other quizzically and started to form up in a group.

"Hey, you from the newspaper?"

"No."

"What are you taking pictures for?"

"For the Maple Festival. I'm the official photographer. Your picture will be in the history album for the festival."

"Cool, neat, way cool!"

"Okay, tighten up a little." Fred pointed to a tall girl on the end. "Can you move behind the short guy there? Hey, you make a nice couple." Several of them laughed in derision. The short guy frowned and said, "Eat shit."

"Nice talk," said Fred, "do you eat with that mouth?" Several more laughed.

Fred attached his large Speedlite flash, checked the settings, put it on automatic, and took a shot. The flash exploded with light.

"Whoa, I wasn't ready! Do it again. Let us know when you're going to take the picture."

"Okay, we'll do it again, but first you have to tell me your names. It can be your real name or what you want people to call you."

"Hey, cool, way cool."

Fred pointed to the short guy. "What's your name?"

"Dale."

Fred pointed to the next guy, a hefty, smiling young man with heavy glasses.

"Call me Tubby." Everyone laughed loudly at this one.

Fred continued to point.

"Brenda Boobs!" Hilarious laughter.

"Linda Legs!"

"Macho Man!"

"Ooowww," mocked the group.

"Bonnie Bigger-than-Brenda Boobs!"

"Oooowww," laughed the crowd; they were into it now.

"Fartman!"

"That's for sure," piped in another.

"Bogey Boy!"

"More like Bugger Boy," said another.

"Okay, you ready for the photo? One, two, three." Fred squeezed the shutter. The flash lit the group. Fred checked the histogram on the camera, good exposure.

"One more, one more, my eyes were closed."

"Okay, one more. Ready, this is the last one." Fred squeezed off the shot. Good exposure.

"Hey, kids, thanks, I enjoyed that."

"Be cool, man," and they were off to the festival.

\* \* \* \* \* \*

In every volunteer-based organization, there needs to be an internal celebration of the event among the volunteers. The committee forms a bond while preparing for and working at an event such as the Geauga County Maple Festival. Tempers flare, stress is apparent, red tape is shredded, friendships are formed, and the workers meet new people they like or don't like. After months of preparation, meetings monthly—sometimes weekly—since September, thousands of telephone calls to vendors, parade participants, and entertainment performers, the entire event culminates in four days of fun. Fun for the attendees who get to walk around, buy a sausage sandwich or cheese on a stick, look at the craft show, let the kiddies ride the rides, get a maple stir, compare the light through the winning syrups, and watch the entertainment. It is a little less fun and more work for the directors of the festival, twenty-five strong, and the innumerable stream of committee people. Because they get a little less fun, they must make some time solely devoted to fun. That fun is concentrated on Saturday night.

*Fun* is a word that is difficult to define. It is personally formed and appreciated by the individual. Fun can be watching a grandchild play with a ball or dog in the backyard. Fun can be a rollicking good time at a country-western bar half-looped while doing a perfect line dance. And fun can be a gathering of people who have all put in a tremendous effort to see a project come to fruition celebrating and enjoying each other's company. That is the nature of the fun that is concentrated on Saturday night at the Maple Festival in the sugar house after the festival is closed.

The sugar-house party was a formally informal affair. People were told about it, or they just appeared. Their volunteer or paid jobs completed for the evening, they sauntered to the sugar house, slid open the door, and walked into a crowd. With the syrup season completed, there was no reason to have the pan fired up, so the water sat, still simmering from the day's boiling. Alcohol and liquor were not permitted on the square, so clearly, *no one* brought any alcoholic libations; there was not a keg in the corner behind the sap pan; there was not a gallon of maple cocktail below the counter, no bottle of wine, already uncorked and re-corked, in Fred's pocket as he walked into the sugar house at twelve a.m., Sunday morning.

Fred entered to a round of applause, participated in by thirty of the forty people in attendance. *Not all,* Fred noticed. He had become acutely aware of people not paying attention to him by this time. Still, he participated with a sense of humor in the toast to "Mr. President" and "Bat Boy" and "Batman." He poured his nonexistent wine into a twenty-ounce plastic cup, raised the cup, acknowledged the toast, smiled, and sipped.

Sara—no *h*—Brougher, vice president of the festival, came up to him and planted a kiss on his lips. "That's just for good measure." Sara was feeling no pain, and Fred liked the touch of her lips, very nice, a little maple cocktaily, but nice.

Michelle Piscopo, entertainment director, not to be outdone, holding a cup of *nonexistent* beer, pushed in between Fred and Sara, put her cup down, and planted a kiss and hug on Fred twice as long as Sara's. *Also very nice,* thought Fred.

Maybe they were going to line up.

"That's another one just for good measure," smiled Michelle.

"Hey, you can't do one longer than mine!" said Sara, as she pushed Michelle aside. Fred laughed, they laughed, and everyone sipped their nonexistent drinks.

"Maybe we can do a threesome?" asked Fred.

"Now you're pushing it," said Michelle.

"So how are you doing?" asked Sara.

"Okay, and by the way, thanks for taking the parade. I didn't even get to take photos with that lady breaking her leg."

"Oh yeah, I heard about that. And I heard about that asshole at the bandstand. What a jerk."

"Goes with the territory. Next year it's your baby, Madame Vice President."

"There is no festival that will ever be as bad as this one."

"Amen," said Michelle and raised her nonexistent drink. They all sipped to that one.

"We made some money today. Did you see that crowd out there all afternoon?" asked Sara.

"They might have made up for Thursday and Friday; those were zeroes," said Michelle, "Let's hope tomorrow is as good as today, so we can at least break even."

"We'll be in deep doo-doo if we don't have a good day tomorrow," said Sara.

"Except," said Fred as he raised his cup, "for good old generous Ed Soubusta. Don't forget him."

"I know he left the festival some money in his will, but what else did he do? I heard he gave some money elsewhere too." said Michelle.

"He sure did," said Fred. "He gave us 10 percent of his estate; that was a hundred grand. He gave his two brothers ten thousand each. He wasn't too happy with them. I had to videotape the will signing because he wasn't giving much to his family. When and if there was a will contest, I wanted my ducks in line that the guy just didn't want to give to his family. I wanted him to set forth his reasons why they didn't deserve any money. And he was intelligent about it. Said they were older than he was and they were going to die and then what would they do with it? And he gets a phone call in the middle of the signing from his stockbroker and he's negotiating with the guy. Oxygen tanks with tubes going up his nose, and he's talking to his stockbroker. It was great. Showed he was competent. It couldn't have happened at a more opportune time.

"Only one problem that I saw. I don't know if you guys knew Tom Hummel. Well, Tom did *everything* for old Ed. He made syrup with him for twenty, maybe thirty, years, helped him when he needed, was like a son to him. Helped him when he had to go to the hospital or for rehabilitation, for everything. And if you know Ed, he was a slob. Never married, so no one harassed him to clean anything up, and he didn't. His backyard was a junk pile. Put this there, and it stayed for twenty years. I'm surprised the zoning or health-department officials didn't cite him for solid waste violations. I saw it and even asked Ed, 'What's all this junk?' He said it wasn't junk, he was going to need it someday."

"Okay, okay, you're boring me to tears, Fred, get to the point," said Sara.

"Hey, leave him alone, he's doing fine. I never heard this before," replied Michelle.

Fred raised his cup. "To Sara, may her body bring her much pleasure." He sipped.

"Hear, hear!" Sara sipped.

"Okay, that's done. So now, back to my story. Ed goes into the hospital. After his surgery for something, he has to go to Heather Hill for rehabilitation for several weeks. During this time, Hummel cleans up his backyard, thinking he would surprise Ed when he came back. Thinks he's doing a good thing, helping out his buddy. Ed comes back from Heather Hill, and he goes nuts over his backyard being cleaned. Disowns Tom Hummel, the guy who has been his buddy for thirty years, just like that. The guy who brings him home from Heather Hill. Ed kicks him off the place.

"I tried and tried to get him to leave something to Tom Hummel, but he was too mad. It was crazy—you don't let one little thing in life, a misunderstanding at that, no malice, overshadow all the good things the guy has done. Ed wouldn't hear of it. Cut him right out. What am I going to do? I can't write the guy's will for him; it's his money. But I sure tried. No way. He didn't like his junk moved.

"When I was there, in his living room, he had piles of newspapers. *The Wall Street Journal* piled everywhere. Place smelled like dogs. His dogs had the free roam of the house at night—what a smell! You wanted to breathe real shallow when you were in Ed's house, because you were afraid of the residue it would leave on your lungs. I didn't move any newspapers."

"What an old curmudgeon! Old people are weird," said Michelle.

"They are and they aren't," answered Fred. "I have seen elderly people give all their assets to the long-lost nephew who comes around the last year of their lives. 'He's the best nephew I ever had, he is so caring.' That nephew is just there for the money, it is so obvious, but you can't say anything against the person helping them. They then cut out the person who has been helping them for twenty years for this money-grubbing nephew. Happens all the time. Too bad, but it is their money; they get to make bad decisions with it. And they do.

"And I've seen them ignore their longtime caretakers and give it to a nephew or niece they have never seen. Family rules, regardless of what that family thinks of him. It doesn't make sense."

"I had an aunt who did that," said Michelle. "I never even knew who she was, and I get a three-thousand-dollar check in the mail. Weird. And then she was dead, and I didn't even get to say thank you."

"I wish I had an aunt like that," added Sara.

"Me too," agreed Fred. "And, hey, I know I am boring you, Sara, no *h*, but I have seen people cut out their family members for some slight thirty years earlier. Got along for the last thirty years, but they still remember that slight. It festered for thirty years, vengeance was theirs in the end, I guess.

"So, Sara, how much are you going to leave the festival in your will?"

"Oops, my glass is empty, gotta go get a refill."

* * * * * *

For the most part, Fred was among friends. People asked how he was doing, skirted the subject of murder by not asking him directly what was going on, and were pleasant. Copious amounts of liquids were consumed.

Scott Mihalic wanted to go out to ride some rides that weren't operating, but he said he knew how to turn them on. A snowball fight just happened to occur as hands dipped into the piles of wet slush on a darkened square. Mike Rear got a nasty bruise from one of the mud-filled snowballs, but he laughed it off, at least until the morning when he would be able to feel it. Dot Dysert and Kathy Dufur talked about the parade and tomorrow's parade, about no-shows and show-ups who had not registered. Their husbands, Gene and Gary, discussed the vendor with improper electric grounding and the subsequent broken leg—a lawsuit was sure to be forthcoming. Fred took photographs: groups, individuals, signs on the walls, and, as the evening progressed, individual parts of clothing, or an eye, or a mouth, just practicing with his zoom. The crowd was noisy but not rowdy, convivial but not romantic, and inebriated, but also tired.

At one a.m., Fred decided it was time to leave. As he made his way to the door, Mike McKenna slid the door open and entered. Cups disappeared. "Hey, Mike!" greeted him from all sides. He smiled sheepishly, declined any liquid refreshment, plucked a breaded vegetable from the tray of veggies provided by one of the vendors, and munched away while leaning on the Stir Booth counter. Mike motioned Fred over with a waggle of his finger.

"Yo, Fred, got some good news for you."

"That is exactly what I need, good news. What is it?"

Mike waved his hand to Fred to come closer, bent over so he could get more on Fred's level.

"Found EW's key card in the Dumpster. FG had it."

"You're kidding me? How did FG get it?"

"She got it out of the Dumpster at eleven p.m. Thursday night. That's going to clear you, I think."

"Holy——! You're not kidding. So if you got the key while I was still in the courthouse, I'm clean!"

"Maybe. You could have had an accomplice." Mike smiled, knowing he was stringing Fred along.

"Yeah, sure. I needed an accomplice to write that brief. Man, that is good news. What did the chief say?"

"He doesn't know yet. Nor, I may add, do you."

"Of course not. But you are the bearer of good news."

"I've got better, I think."

After an discernible pause affected to make Fred prompt him, Fred said, "Well, what is it?"

"We think we got a print on it. Don't know for sure, but we dusted it. There are several prints on it. If FG didn't finger it too much, we just might get a *good* print from it. Then we'll know for sure, won't we?"

"I guess. I sure hope so. Man, that is good news. You have made my night. Good thing I don't know anything about it."

"Make sure you don't."

\* \* \* \* \* \*

Fred stopped at the big tent to inform Tim Snyder of the recent development. As soon as he opened the flap, a voice boomed at him. "Halt, who goes there?"

"Hey, Tim, it's me, Fred."

The flashlight was redirected from Fred's face, and he squinted in the dark trying to get his vision back.

"That's a bright light."

"If I blind them first, then I don't have to shoot them."

"Makes sense," said Fred. "I just came from the sugar-house party, ran into Mike McKenna there. He told me something I thought you ought to know."

"I probably already know it."

"The key card?"

"Yep, I saw it on the counter with FG's purse. Asked where she got it. She got it Dumpster-diving," he laughed, "Dumpster-diving saves the day! They are sending the prints from it to determine whose they are. If there are prints on it, it would narrow the search tremendously. And if not, then it still helps you. Puts someone with the key card outside the courthouse while you were still in it."

"I'll say it helps. How you doing here? Kinda bleak, standing around in the dark."

"I get used to it. Helps me think things through. Like FG, for example. She throws a fit in the sugar house, then is nice as pie at the jail. Why? I figure she's got some mental problem ... I have been trying to figure out your case, too. Tomorrow, I talk to Wellman and Pastor Bob. Today I talked to Armstrong—I already told you about him, and Parker. Parker seems clean. Went home about nine p.m. on Thursday night, he said."

"Parker, my client. Mark Sperry told me he's been bonking Joannie at Lawyer's Title. You know her?"

"She the blonde with the big hooters?"

"Yes. A very nice-looking woman. Mark says that Joe sneaks down a back staircase after hours and that they do it in the big safe that is there. Apparently, the building was a bank at one time and there is a huge vault in it. How's that for a safe-and-secure affair?"

"Guy gets around. He didn't tell me that. I wonder why? Hey, what about client confidentiality?"

"Didn't get that from my client, got it from Mark Sperry, who knows absolutely everything. I won't tell you the other things he said, though. Well, Tim, I just stopped to tell you that stuff before I went home. You running tomorrow?"

"Bright and early; see you at the Sap Run."

"I won't be too fast tomorrow."

# CHAPTER 31

The Sap Run, not just for saps, is actually two runs, a one- and a five-mile run starting in front of the Chardon Library on East Park Street. Roger Sweet, who was a track coach at Chardon High School, was the first organizer back in 1978. He conducted it for several years and passed it off to Fred, who ran it for ten years. Since then, Steve Novak, in conjunction with the Northeast Ohio Running Club, has been operating the event. They conduct a number of runs in Northeast Ohio and have all the equipment necessary to organize an excellent race: tapes, loudspeakers, traffic cones, mileage signs, volunteers, and electronic timers that read the bar code on the runner's tag to identify him or her crossing the finish line.

The members who have not volunteered to coordinate the race run in it. Lean, mean, thin, wiry, fast runners. Sometimes they dress up—or down, if your eye is jaundiced—in costumes, such as Dr. Seuss's Cat in the Hat or Disney's Goofy. Watching Darth Vader run five miles in his black outfit on an unseasonably hot April day can be excruciating.

The weather this morning was perfect; fifty-four degrees, scattered clouds, slightly humid. Fred was feeling the effect of his consumption of the night before. A slight hangover, more like a lethargic malaise. His energy level was on low. His attitude wasn't much better. Maybe after mile one he would perk up, wake up, and snap to. His mind felt much better, though, ever since his discussion with Lieutenant McKenna. His mind felt really good. There was a light at the end of the tunnel. Question was, when would he arrive at the light? Rolling around in this tunnel with suspicious looks cast at him by doubters was unsettling.

Fred pulled into the parking lot of his office from North Hambden Street. A man approached him from the East Park Street entrance until he recognized him. Chardon Rotary and the Chardon Chamber of Commerce shared the manning of the parking lot. They charged for parking and made some money for their eleemosynary endeavors. Fred allowed them to operate the parking lot without cost; it protected the property from vendors who wanted to park all day and don't help traffic move to and from the festival.

He put his change of clothes on his desk and then walked to the registration desk located under the drive-through at Bank One across the square. Steve Novak had four tables lined up. Registration was at one table, preregistration at another, and two tables were used for handing out the numbers, pins, and long-sleeved T-shirts. Next to the shirts were boxes of water and crates of oranges to hand out at the finish line. Twenty-five people milled around, stood in line, tried on their T-shirts, and chatted. Families, moms, dads, kids, racers, teenagers, runners, joggers, overweight people—a cross-section of society—were entered in the race. Fred took several photographs. One of the ladies behind the desk had a baseball cap with her ponytail sticking out the back. Fred made sure he got the profile. She was cute, too. Then he went to the preregistration table, gave his name, and was handed a packet and told to move to the T-shirt table, where he received a very suspicious glare.

The T-shirt, bright yellow, strong yellow, screaming yellow with black writing covering the front, the back, and the sleeves with advertisers and sponsors. There was Lakeland Community College, Alltel Phone Company, Quality Buick, Oldsmobile, and GMC Truck, Chardon Oil Company, Bass Lake Tavern, McDonald's, Fredebaugh Well Drilling Company, The Miscellaneous Barn, The Cavs, The Indians, WBKC 1460 AM, and Geauga Cablevision Channel 51, better known as GTV or Dave's TV. There was even room for Geauga County Maple Festival and the Sap Runs overlaid on a green maple leaf showing two runners, along with the year the shirt was issued. This was a shirt Fred would wear often—no, probably not. Maybe around the yard when he cleaned up leaves or dug his tomato garden. But the kids milling around registration were proud of their free shirts, which went along with the registration fee. It was a badge of accomplishment. It meant they'd done the run. Well, they hadn't done it yet, but they *would* do it, and they would wear the shirt, albeit sweaty, proudly all day. They wore the shirt proudly now.

Fred offered to take a photo of a family that intended to run together. They smiled broadly in their matching shirts.

Steve Novak drove up in a pickup truck with four guys in the back. They jumped out and began to load cases of water for the water spots along the route. There were two water spots, at mile 1.5 and mile 2.5. The course was an out-and-back route, so there were actually three water spots, because the runners could stop at mile 4 on the way back and pick up a cup of water. Steve waved to Fred, but he was in a hurry and kept going.

Fred was early, so he walked along Main Street and took photos. The sun was low in the east and cast long shadows from the rides in the square across the street to the buildings on Main Street. A lovely picture. Fred snapped as he walked.

He walked along Main to Short Court Street and then turned toward the courthouse front steps and walked the middle sidewalk of the square through the closed, quiet festival. The vendors were shuttered. A few were beginning to move around. They lifted the awnings on the trailers, hooked them up, and looked like they were going to open for business. Several people walked toward the pancake tent, which opened at eight a.m., same time as the start of the one-mile run. Fred had a half hour to burn. He snapped photos; the early morning light was stunning. Laurie Deimer, sister of Dale Deimer, the man who had wrestled with FG, was walking toward him taking photos herself.

"Isn't the light great?" asked Laurie.

"The best. Try Main Street yet?"

"No, that's next."

Laurie was an x-ray technician who loved photography. She had attended the Rocky Mountain School of Photography and was a talented amateur ready to turn professional. But, unless you were Ansel Adams, photography was hard to sell. In this age of digital, everyone thought they could capture the same photo you were trying to sell. They couldn't, but they thought they could, so they didn't buy your photos. Photography, unlike painting, exactly depicted the scene photographed. There was room for interpretation, but it was a personal interpretation.

People did occasionally buy photographs of pictures with which they identified: they had been at that same spot, they saw the same thing, they had a good experience at that location, it was a nice memory. But they didn't spend the same quantities of money that they would for a watercolor or an oil or acrylic painting. At least not locally, they didn't. Laurie had shown hers at the local park system, Meyer Center, West Woods, Penitentiary Glen, and at a number of galleries. But photography was a hard sell.

Fred approached it differently, he just took photos because he liked to. If he captured an image that was stunning, he would enlarge and print it. His back bedroom had hundreds of framed prints that he had replaced on his walls with new photographs. Fred gave photos away. If he took a picture of someone doing an activity that normally wasn't a photographic moment, he would print the photo to a six-by-eight-inch size and send it to the person, *gratis*. Sometimes they called and thanked him or sent a note. Sometimes he never heard from them again. But he didn't really care; it was just fun to send a photo of a person doing something they do normally every day but which is never captured as an image. And those who did thank him, told him how they'd had it framed and where it hung, and how happy they were with it.

Fred took photos of people everywhere, laying brick walls, at work, at play, in sports, wrestling matches, golf league, at the festival, at the fair, everywhere. He only sent photos if they complimented the person. There was no reason to send a bad photograph. Of course, the recipient didn't always think the photo complimented them. "I always take such bad photographs." If you would stop frowning and trying to avoid the camera, throw out that nice smile that is hidden in there, we could get an excellent shot. But Fred didn't say that, just thought it. In India, when a person gets his photograph taken, he always says thank you. He is thanking the photographer for thinking he is a fit subject to photograph. It is such a nice gesture. Fred was overwhelmed when he got repeated thank-yous on his trip to India. The same did not occur in Chardon.

On occasion, Fred would send a bad photograph to someone. Not that the photo was bad; it was a good photo, but it reflected the person in a bad or less-than-exemplary position. There was the time he submitted a photo to the Great Geauga County Fair of John Hiscox and Ray Gilbert, Rotarians both, where they were talking to one another, both holding a drink in their hand closest to the photographer. It was at a time of their lives when they were comfortable, so comfortable that they let the muscles on their stomachs relax a little too much and the muscles of their elbows and jaws exercise too much. The paunches of both extended to such a degree that they were only an inch apart as they talked to one another with their faces at a comfortable distance such that they did not invade each other's space. Except for the dress and the faces, it was a mirror image. Fred did not win a prize for that photo, but John and Ray received multiple favorable comments from their friends and acquaintances about their anatomical abdominal display. They were great sports about it. Fred could only do that sort of thing with a friend, and they were friends.

On average, Fred sent three hundred photos a year. Sometimes, after he enlarged a photo, he didn't know the name of the person, so he had to ask around. Most times, he got the name, but he had a pile of photos in his basement at home of people he had no idea how to contact or identify. He paged through the photos occasionally to remember the people, and then if he ran into them somewhere, he would ask for their address. Then, they were suspicious. What do you want my address for? After he explained, they were pleasant and when they got the photo, they were happy. Fred had even sent Laurie Deimer a photo of herself taking photos. That would be a shot not duplicated.

"Okay, Fred, it's your turn." Laurie turned her camera toward Fred.

"Want the tip of the courthouse in it?" Fred moved to the edge of the sidewalk.

"Oh sure, that's great. What great light."

"You'll get lots of pictures today."

"I already have lots."

"Did you get the collapsed tent?"

"I wasn't here; I missed it."

"Congratulations on your photography award, nice picture," said Fred. Laurie had entered a photo of the gathering of maple sap during a brightly lit snow scene. It took second place in the Maple Festival Photo Contest. The photos were on display in storefronts on Main Street. JR Blanchard had run the photo contest for the last ten years. He now got over 150 entries annually in three categories: Maple, Animal, and Scenic. Van's Photo and Fred's law firm were sponsors. Fred directed his award of $250 for the winner in the Maple category. Fred loved photography and utilized it in many ways. He took photos everywhere with his pocket camera as unobtrusively as possible.

"Are you going to be at the award ceremony for your photo?" asked Fred.

"Wouldn't miss it. You?"

"Of course! I'm giving one of the awards. Well, it's my money that is the award, but I'm not giving it. This is not the year for me to be getting up in public and making speeches."

Laurie, obviously uncomfortable with the shift of conversation, said, "I understand."

"Well, I'm moving along. Don't forget to get the start of the Sap Run, about twenty minutes at the library." Fred pointed east toward the Chardon Library.

\* \* \* \* \* \*

The one-mile Sap Run was two and one-quarter laps around the square and then into the chute at the finish line on the north end of the square in front of Midland Title, attorney Ron Hanus's office, and Dr. Bernabie's office. The run started in front of Chardon Library on East Park Street. Steve Novak had a chalk line painted across the road for a starting line. With his portable loudspeaker, he announced the rules.

"Runners, listen up. This is the race for one-milers only. If you aren't registered for the one-mile race, make sure you do not go through the finish line chute. You will mess up the clock, which can only read the tags on the one-mile tags.

"You will run around the square twice, then at the north end of the square, you will go through the chute.

"The awards ceremony will be at the stage at noon. The stage is right across the park." Steve pointed with his loudspeaker across the square. "I will start the race in three minutes. I will say 'Runners set. Go.'"

Fred saw several attorneys he knew across the street, walked over, and told them to line up for a photo. "Let's get this legal photo together. There are a lot of attorneys who'll be running. You aren't doing the one-mile, are you?" Like Fred, they were all five-milers.

Six attorneys: Dennis Pilawa, insurance defense out of Solon, who lived in Munson; Hans Kuenzi, general practitioner from Lake County; Dave Furhy, magistrate in Chardon Municipal Court; and three more.

Fred positioned himself a hundred yards from the starting line so he could get photos of the runners starting and breezing past him. Runners were kids, old folks, racers from the five-mile who were warming up for that race, families, fathers and sons, mothers and daughters, two wheelchair entries, a nice crowd of a hundred runners.

"Runners, line up on the start line," shouted Steve Novak. He waited ten seconds.

"Runners, on your mark. Go!"

And they were off. The winners were already strides ahead before those in the back had even started to move. Fred snapped shots on automatic. Nine continuous shots as the runners streamed past.

Fred then walked to the west side of the square to take photos of the runners racing around the square. Because of the low rising of the sun, half of the street was in the shade. Fred opened his shutter a full stop, increased the ISO to 800, and shot the runners as they raced by. He got kids panting, sweating, in obvious distress. Teenage girls quick as an elk. Several walkers.

As he was taking the last of the runners, the winners had caught up to them and were passing them. Fred wouldn't get them at the finish line, they were too fast for him. By the time Fred walked to the finish line, twenty runners had already passed through, but he got good photos of the kids gasping for breath. Fred positioned himself to take photos with kids bursting with last bits of energy to kick into the finish chute. The crowd cheered. "Go, Sonny!" "Just a little farther, Bobby!" "Go girl, kick ass!" "You did it, you did it!"

The chief of police was holding up traffic on North Hambden. This had to be distressing to Jenkins, thought Fred. Holding up traffic for a Maple Festival event had to drive him crazy. Fred had run the New York Marathon, twenty-six miles through countless boroughs, bands on every corner, crowds cheering the 27,000 runners through the city, and completed the run in four hours and seventeen minutes. It was after this run that he had assumed the job for the Sap Run. In dealing with the chief, the same chief who arrested him, Fred learned that Jenkins's main complaint with the Sap Run was that it would hold up traffic on two state routes, Route 6 and Route 44. His job was safety and he didn't like the idea of holding up traffic on state routes. Fred had patiently explained the ability of the New York Police to hold up traffic for five hours in the most populous city in the United States over a twenty-six-mile course winding through the city, but it had no effect on the Chardon police chief. His were deaf ears to anything that might enhance the Maple Festival, or Fred, or make things easier for the festival. If it involved any disruption of the ordinary work of the police, he was against it. If it came from Fred, he was against it.

The chief did not look toward Fred the entire time. He wasn't happy Fred was free, he wasn't happy he had to stop traffic for the festival, he just wasn't a happy man. Fred took a photo of his back as he directed traffic.

\* \* \* \* \* \*

Fred deposited his big camera in the office, put his small camera in his jacket pocket, took off his long pants, and got ready for the five-mile run. He stretched his calves, touched his toes, stretched his calves again, locked his office, and walked toward the starting line. Fred wore Air Nike shoes, short Nike socks, red tricot shorts, a blue-and-white jacket over a lemon yellow T-shirt top, and a fluorescent green baseball cap. The other runners were dressed even more garishly. Fred positioned himself to get a photo of the start of the race, and then he would join in with the runners for the five-mile challenge.

Fred spotted Tim Snyder's tall head above the crowd of runners. As a result of the turn in the weather, a large crowd of runners had signed up at the last minute. It looked to be more than three hundred runners. A good number for the Sap Run.

"Runners. Get Ready, Set, Go!"

Fred got three photos as the herd thundered past. He joined in. Tim Snyder, who had seen Fred, joined him.

"Hey, Tim, get any sleep last night?"

"Not with that sugar house party going on till four o'clock in the morning. Those guys were drunk. They got a couple of the kiddie rides going and were having fun. They stayed away from the tent though."

They turned right at the corner, heading downhill on North Hambden Street, past Fred's office on the corner.

They passed, albeit slowly, about a seven-minute-per-mile pace, slower runners. They passed a tall man wearing a Burger King costume. It looked hot. Hot temperature, not *hot,* hot.

"Want to know some developments?" asked Tim.

"Yeah, duh, isn't that why we're running together?"

Tim laughed. "I met with a guy named Armstrong yesterday, as I told you. He had threatened to kill EW in a court hearing. But he's not a suspect. He's a stoner, zonked out on methamphetamines. I think he didn't even know I was there. Guy kept talking even when I moved out his line of vision. Weird. And I met with Joe Parker yesterday evening."

Fred glanced up quickly at Tim, nothing. They turned left at Maple Avenue toward Maple Elementary and Chardon High School. They were passing more people, as the novices were out of breath for starting too quickly. Fred was trying to breathe evenly. He knew he was slowing Tim down, and although he was exceeding his regular pace, he couldn't go much faster or he wouldn't be able to breathe.

"What's Joe say?"

"Not much. He worked at the office, went home about nine, nine thirty. Sounded credible to me. His daughter doesn't have much in the way of social graces. I got to the house and asked for Joe and she screamed at the top of her lungs for him. Won't she be fun to be married to! Won't have to get hearing aids when you get older, if you can stay with her that long."

Neither runner looked at each other, they just breathed deeply, measuring the jogging with the talking and breathing. You can carry on a conversation in a race, but not at the same pace as a normal conversation. It must be timed with your ability to provide oxygen to your blood. Respiration must be deep and thorough. Talking interfered with the normal breathing process. So the runners didn't speak in full, flowing sentences but in short, halting bursts that didn't interfere with the oxygen intake.

They crossed Chardon Avenue, Chardon High School on the left, Maple Elementary on the right.

"You didn't see Joe's wife?"

"No, should I have?" Tim inquired casually.

"Only because she is absolutely gorgeous. What a looker!" Fred breathed deeply. "I never heard her scream though. Might like to under the right circumstances, though."

"Oww, dirty old man."

"Aren't we all?"

"Yeah, but don't tell anybody. I've got it hidden pretty well. Look at that, up front, in the green."

Fred looked. A petite woman, long, blonde hair tied in a ponytail reaching to the middle of her back with four bands of a fluffy green texture that matched her bright, lime-green tights, black shoes that matched her black halter top and black headband. Slim, perfectly shaped, a smooth runner. Slight pronation with the right foot, but that just added to her attractiveness.

"Just lovely," commented Fred.

"You can look, but you can't touch."

"Just like a candy store. Joe tell you he wouldn't talk to the cops?"

"Found that out. Guess he doesn't like cops. Why'd he talk to me?" Tim wondered aloud.

"Brother attorney. Fraternity of the legal eagles. He knows you won't lie about things. Or push him around. Who knows? I obviously don't know anything anymore."

"He's your client, Fred."

Past the Chardon Recreation Board swimming pool on the right as Maple Street turned into Canfield Drive and gently curved to the west. Past the Keith Eldridge home on the right, the Tom Brice home on the left. Fred got a great view of the runners stretched out before him on the slight decline and incline. He stopped and took a photo and then ran to catch up to Tim and continue the conversation.

"Which, I might add, is why I can't say much about him."

"Looks like Earl William had it in for Joe."

"From a conservative position, after representing Joe in front of Earl William, I would say that is a fair statement."

Past the new Jim and Kathy Gillette home. Jim sat on a backhoe tractor watching the runners stream past. Landscaping for fun and pleasure on your own property saved a lot of money.

The road dipped and then started to climb toward Ravenna Road. They were steadily passing people now. Fred was lagging a bit behind Tim, so Tim slowed a little. Fred could tell he didn't want to, but he needed to finish the conversation before he split off.

"There's no doubt that Joe hated EW's guts. With that election and all the nastiness, it's pretty clear why. And looking at the cases, it's clear EW hated Joe's guts."

"But, *why* is the question."

"Yes, why. That's what I'm working on. By the way, they found a key card for the library door. You know that girl, FG. She found it Dumpster-diving."

Fred nodded. "McKenna told me last night at the sugar house. I told you about it. He said it was EW's card."

"Oh. I knew it was a key card, I didn't know it was EW's. That's even better. Better for you, that is."

"You're not kidding," Fred smiled. "Apparently FG found it while I was still in the courthouse. Kind of hard to be in two places at the same time."

They turned the corner at Ravenna Road. Tim and Fred waved to Deputy Larry Hunt who had stopped traffic and was encouraging the runners. Dorothy Sabula's house on the left. The Chardon Methodist Church on the left with its architecturally modern and beautiful cross. Pastor Henry Woodruff led his mission with a beneficent and genial attitude. He looked like a kind and gentle Santa Claus with his snowy white beard and cherubic smile.

At the crest of the hill before Wintergreen Road, Fred ran to the left side of the road, took a quick photo of the runners descending and ascending the hill, and then ran back.

"Playing devil's advocate: unless you had an accomplice."

"I would have had the accomplice finish the brief I was working on, if I'd had an accomplice."

"I tell ya, Fred, that should exculpate you from this charge."

"Keep in mind, we're dealing with Chief Jenkins. Shoulda, woulda, coulda!"

"Oh yes, my good buddy, the chief."

"*Our* good buddy."

Past Wintergreen Road, with a small but attractive waterfall on the property of Hal Henderson. The waterfall was four feet seven inches in height. Fred had only seen it dry twice as he drove along Ravenna Road. Unlike Lake County, Geauga County was not blessed with great waterfalls. Several cascades of lengths in excess of fifty feet, but few waterfalls higher than ten feet. At the higher elevation of Geauga County, compared to the surrounding counties, the waters did not have enough erosion power to carve hollows and caves and great valleys. By the time the waters left Geauga and reached Lake, Ashtabula, Trumbull, Portage, and Cuyahoga, they had enough erosion power to create wonderful waterfalls. Geauga County was the headwaters for four watersheds: Grand River Watershed starting in Parkman Township, Chagrin River Watershed starting in Munson Township, Cuyahoga River Watershed starting in Montville Township, and the Mahoning River Watershed starting in Troy Township.

At Wintergreen, the real hills began. Fred and Tim were passing walkers now. People who had not paced themselves, went out too fast, dressed too warmly for the temperature, or just weren't in shape. Walkers tied their jackets and sweatshirts around their waists. Shouts of encouragement from an occasional jogger to a walker jarred the air.

A slapper started to pace Fred and Tim. Each step of the jogger behind them was a slap on the pavement of the sole of the jogger's shoe. Slap, slap, slap, slap. It was rhythmic but disconcerting. Just slightly out of sync with the pace of Fred and Tim. They either had to quicken their pace or slow it to escape the slap, slap, slap.

"I'm going to talk to Pastor Bob and Mark Wellman today. You know Wellman; I saw you represented him in his grievance. Pastor Bob is the guy whose son was playing around with the kids in his school. Seems they both might have an axe to grind with EW."

"You probably won't like Wellman, but he is a good attorney. Aggressive, smart, and maybe a little too mean sometimes."

"With his meanness and EW's meanness, good battle."

"He got the shaft on his grievance. I can't really discuss it: I represented him throughout the proceedings. But suffice it to say, his attitude is what did him in. What he did for the grievance was reasonable given the circumstances, but his response was not conducive to good relationships. It pissed off the committee."

"I'll see if he'll talk about it. Maybe not. At least I'll get a feel for his relationship with EW."

"Bitter, bitter, bitter." Fred gasped for breath. They had sped up to get away from the slapper, and it was just a bit too much for Fred's breathing. He could sense that he was holding Tim back. "Tim, you go on ahead. I've got to slow down a little. You're killing me."

"Okay, I need to stretch out a little anyway. I'll talk to you later, after I meet with Wellman and Pastor Bob. Let you know how it went."

"Got it. Take off."

Tim stretched his long legs, sprinted forward, took the turn at Woodin Road, waved to Deputy Tom Dewey holding traffic, and disappeared. Fred slowed to a normal pace so he could breathe. He took out his camera, stopped in the middle of the road and shot photos of the runners returning at a very fast pace. This allowed him to catch his breath. Four photos, ten seconds of regular breathing. He adjusted his hat to get the sweat dripping down his cheeks. Woodin Road was downhill; five hundred feet from Robinson Road was the turnaround water station. Then Woodin Road was uphill on the return. Fred turned the corner, got a cup of water, squeezed the lip of the cup tightly so it wouldn't spill while he jogged, sipped, and resumed jogging. He checked his time, 17:33, way too fast. The return trip would be slower, for sure. He let Snyder pull him too fast. The slapper passed him.

\* \* \* \* \* \*

Woodin to Ravenna to Canfield to Maple to North Hambden. Except for several dips in the roads, it was all uphill. Chardon is on top of the hill, hence, the high school's mascot name, *Hilltopper*. Fred had slowed considerably. The last stretch up North Hambden Street was grueling. Fred could walk faster than he was jogging, but he kept up the jogging. He was going to be fagged all day. He couldn't concentrate on anything but the pain in his thighs, the need for oxygen in his lungs, the sweat dripping over his headband onto his glasses. There was nothing to wipe them off with that wasn't sweaty. Better to leave them as is.

Finally, the finish chute. Fred glanced at the huge timer, 41:35. His pace had slowed considerably from past years. It was soon going to be Tylenol time.

"Good run," said Steve Novak as he ripped the bottom tab from the runner's number pinned to Fred's front shirt. Fred couldn't respond. Fred got a bottle of water handed to him by one of the helpers. He picked an orange off the table. Fred bent slightly over, sweating, breathing deeply, trying to cool off. The temperature was sixty degrees; it was going to be a glorious day for the festival.

Once his body stopped discharging, Fred took out his camera and photographed runners being greeted by their families, couples embracing, kids at the finish line, anyone but the chief still detaining traffic at the corner.

# CHAPTER 32

Tim Snyder, in uniform, knocked on Mark Wellman's front door. He had a difficult time locating the house on Chillicothe Road in Chester Township; the mailbox had been knocked over and propped up with a two-by-four. The box itself had been squashed or bent back into a haphazard condition for a mailbox, but the numbers were unreadable; two of them were knocked off completely.

The house was a century home, white with green shutters, nicely maintained, unlike the mailbox. The drive was gravel; Tim avoided the deeper winter potholes and parked at the loop by the detached garage. Two huge maple trees lined the drive, leaves budding in a light green with the spring sunshine, the ground littered with fallen branches and twigs. Today would be a great day to pick up the yard debris.

A boy about twelve, short with bushy black hair, answered the door.

"May I help you, sir?"

"I'm here to see Mark Wellman."

"Just a moment, sir." He disappeared, leaving Tim on the porch staring at the screen door.

A moment later, Mark Wellman came to the door. Five-foot-five, wild, black, bushy eyebrows that needed trimming, black hair neatly combed and parted, looked to be in good physical shape, wore a button-down white shirt with blue jeans and penny loafers with no socks.

"You're Snyder, right?"

"Yes, and you're Mark Wellman. We spoke on the phone."

"Yes, come on in." He turned toward the inside of the house, letting Snyder open the screen door to let himself in. Tim's first thought was that graciousness was not his strong point.

Tim was led to a room off the central hallway. A large, menorah sat on a pedestal in the hallway; it was dusty. They entered the library. Two walls were covered with shelves filled with books. Books stacked on top of books, vertical, horizontal, piled on the desk, on the floor, and squeezed on top of the books in the shelves. A desk with a chair and two lounge chairs invited them. Wellman indicated one of the lounge chairs to Tim. The coffee table next to the chair Tim sat in was piled with magazines and books and two empty coffee cups—already used with dried coffee marks solidified in the bottom.

Wellman was obviously a reader. But then he should be; he was a graduate of Yale University and Yale Law School, *summa cum laude*. Fourth in his class, he was educated, bright, and smart. He had been the *Law Review* editor-in-chief, a very high honor in law school.

"I know you're here about Kuhmer, right?"

"Yes, Judge Kuhmer."

"Judge my ass. He didn't deserve that appellation. If there's a fitting title for him, even if he is dead, it was Prick Nazi Kuhmer."

A dead silence ensued, ten seconds, fifteen seconds. Tim was caught off guard with the instant vitriol, the intense anger, and clear hatred.

"Okay, that's a good start. I guess you two didn't get along."

"You got that right. Okay, Snyder, tell me what you want to know. I'll tell you the straight dope. I am not going to screw around with you. I know you're helping Fred. I called him after you called last night. He says you're okay. That you're helping him. Well, if Fred says you're okay, I'll go with it. Let's get me off your list of suspects. The sooner the better."

Tim took a deep breath. The intensity of the man. So short, but so much energy, so much anger, so much gloomy exuberance.

"It was Thursday night, right?"

"Yes, Mark, may I call you Mark?"

"Sure, go ahead, I don't care what you call me. I've been called worse. Just don't call me Jewboy."

"I won't!" Tim said, "Okay, Mark, the murder was Thursday night about eleven p.m. Where were you?"

"At eleven, I was driving home after dropping the kids off at the bitch's house in Bainbridge on Taylor-May Road, just past the YMCA Centerville

Mills Camp. Check with her, I'll give you her number. Hopefully she won't lie like she always does in court."

A thought zipped by Tim; if she always lied, even if she gave him an alibi, would it be a lie? What gives here?

"I took Isaiah and Abraham, my two kids, ages eleven and twelve, to the Maple Festival. Got there about 8:30 p.m. It was cold, nasty weather. Not many people there. Kids rode two rides. Tickets are too expensive. They ought to let the kids ride for free in that weather. Got a maple stir, ate some cannoli, kids ate frozen chocolate bananas. Can you imagine that, frozen bananas on a night like that?

"Had one problem. I had to pee, so I told the kids to wait for me. I went to the Port-a-Potties across East Park Street. Three of them were locked, shut down. I had to wait for two women. Are they ever slow. I get back, the kids are gone. I go nuts looking all over for them. Finally find them at the police station. Can you believe that? Got them out of there at about ten p.m., and took them home to whatshername. She who cannot be named.

"Cops told you I was there, didn't they?"

"Actually, no. They haven't said a thing. Maybe the timing was off for the time of death. It was about eleven p.m., and you're talking an hour before, so maybe, nothing."

"Yeah, good. Nothing. I want nothing to do with Prick Nazi Kuhmer. You want to talk to the kids?"

"Not yet. Tell me about your relationship with Kuhmer?"

"We had no relationship. None at all.

"Last year, February, I divorced my wife of sixteen years. She divorced me. We had a custody battle. I represented myself. What the hell. Yeah, I know, a lawyer who represents himself has a fool for a client. Maybe I did, but I got the shaft. I had the law, the facts, the psychologists, everything that could go my way in a court of law did, except for the judge. It was Kuhmer. He gave custody of two boys to that cheating whore. Why? Because he and I never saw eye to eye. He hates Jews, and I won't put up with his shit. I object where I am supposed to object, but he lets the evidence in anyway. Continuously. Court of Appeals: 'oh, it was not prejudicial, it was only harmless error.' Think they ever want to reverse a custody case? No way, José.

"We have a three-day trial. I lose. Then to top it all, he gives me *standard* visitation. Now the psychologists said I was better for the kids, but he only gives me standard visitation. I don't even get to see them during the week. Every other weekend. What kind of shit is that? Family values, huh? Yeah, that's what Kuhmer touted at the election, *family values*. And he gives me every other weekend. Yeah, you can sure develop a relationship with your kids two out of every fourteen days. He did it to spite me. He was one mean, nasty, Jew-hating bigot.

"Then he has the gall to say that her 'outside dalliances,' as he called them, were not relevant since he was going to find us incompatible. Says it didn't happen in front of the kids, so it has no effect on her ability to be custodian. Who do you think lives with her now, without the benefit of marriage? Yeah, great family values. I tell you, Snyder, I hate that man. I am glad he is dead. Really, not the best thing to say to a cop who is investigating you for a murder, but I really hate that man."

"Yeah, that's pretty obvious."

"You know, I wouldn't be talking to you if I hadn't talked to Fred first. He said you were okay. I sure hope so."

"Yeah, me too."

"So that's reason number one and two. One, he hates Jews. Two, he goes against the evidence in my custody case because he hates me. The third is that he gets me disbarred for six months.

"I represented an old couple in a personal injury case. The insurance company was being tight-assed with their money. Liability was somewhat shaky: it could go either way. I had long conversations with my clients on the value of the case. I thought that, at a minimum, it was worth $25,000, even with the limited liability. If we hit, it would be a $150,000 case. So the day of the trial, defense counsel offers me $10,000. I flatly reject it. My clients had authorized me in accordance with our previous discussions to reject any offers under $25,000. So I did.

"So that Jew-hating Kuhmer sees the whole thing. He doesn't say a thing. We are in his chambers. I tell them 'No.' He's setting me up. Defense counsel says, 'Aren't you going to at least present it to your client?' I tell him, 'No. What part of no don't you understand.' I was angry at them for offering so little. These old folks were in their late seventies. 'Give them some money! You've had record profits for the last five years. These people are hurting. Look at these bills. Your offer doesn't cover a third of them.' Then we try the case. Defense verdict. That's what I get for trying a jury trial in Geauga County. The most conservative jury verdicts for personal injuries in the state of Ohio. These rich folks in Geauga County just can't feel anyone's pain but their own. Pain and suffering, oh, balderdash! What's that? Come on, old folks, get up and move, do some exercise. Why are you always blaming someone else?

"Tim, this was a rear-ender, for God's sake. Defense claimed pre-existing injuries. Yeah, they are in their seventies. Their whole body is a pre-existing injury. The jury gave nothing." Wellman shook his head, took a breath that looked like resignation.

"I'm giving Fred my PI cases from now on if they go to trial. I can't take these juries. If the case is one over real estate, big bucks pass. If it's personal injury, *nada*. Sometimes I think people are just mean. Like Kuhmer. I won't even call him judge—he is so mean he doesn't deserve the title. And, because he is such a bigot, he doesn't deserve the title." Wellman straightened the items on his desk. Lined up a pen and pencil, shifted papers, getting a grip on himself.

"Anyway, back to my story. Appeal time passes, Kuhmer files a grievance against me with the Bar Association. He signs the affidavit personally. Says I failed to live up to the standards of conduct set down by the Supreme Court by failing to convey to my client a bona fide offer. The committee bought it. We tried the case in front of the committee. Fred represented me. He did everything right. All the evidence came in that could come in. My clients couldn't testify—one was in the hospital, and the other had developed dementia by the time of the hearing. So where was I? Up shit creek without a paddle, of course. And the fact that *Kuhmer* testified against me carried the day. Even the three Jews on the twelve-man committee went along with it. Boy, talk about being sandbagged!"

Tim took notes, keeping his face as neutral as he could muster. He did feel he was getting the whole story, that's for sure.

"They recommended a year's suspension. The Supreme Court reduced it to six months. I just got back in two months ago. Had to take a bunch of Continuing Legal Education courses, extra hours of ethics and substance abuse. How many old drunks can you listen to? 'Don't do what I did. I was weak and drank too much. You don't have to. Just say no.' Bunch of horseshit. If you're going to be an alkie, attending a substance-abuse seminar is not going to turn the tide for you."

"They found your prints in EW's chambers," said Tim.

"Yeah, I hope so. I had a pretrial last Tuesday. I asked him to recuse himself. 'What for?' he says. 'I have nothing against you, Mark. I just think you need to comply with the disciplinary rules.' Real pontifical he is. Supercilious. I'm-better-than-you attitude. He's got that smarmy, shit-eating grin on his face. I know what he's really saying. He's saying 'Mess with me again and I will do it to you again. You'd better bow down and genuflect in front of me. I am your God.' I wanted to reach across the table and punch him in his fat face.' Sometimes, and I wax philosophical here for a moment, sometimes, life just ain't fair."

"God save Ireland for sure this time."

# CHAPTER 33

Tim Snyder, on a spur-of-the-moment gut feeling, decided to stop at Armstrong's house again before going to interview Pastor Bob.

He knocked on the screen door. The wooden door was wide open. Someone yelled, "Come in!" The smell of old clothes still permeated the air. And some other smell, unidentifiable. Not pleasant. Old clothes and vinegar.

"Allan, are you here?"

Tim observed someone sleeping on the couch. It looked like a woman with long hair falling over the edge of the couch. He then realized it was Armstrong without the ponytail rubber band. Someone walked in from the kitchen dressed in blue jeans, no shoes or socks, no shirt, skinny, about twenty years old, shaved head, tattoos over his entire chest and arms. He saw Tim's uniform. A look of scared shock crossed his face. He averted his enlarged-pupil eyes.

"What? Man. What?"

"Just here to see Armstrong. He's sleeping pretty heavy."

"Yeah, he had a long night. See if you can wake him." He quickly turned back to the kitchen without another word.

Tim shook Armstrong. He mumbled. Tim shook him harder. The smell was atrocious. Armstrong turned over, slightly opened his eyes.

"Hey man, what?"

"Allan, wake up. Allan, I need to talk to you."

Armstrong slowly moved his feet off the couch to the floor and then sat up partially. He rubbed his face with the palms of his hands, threw back his hair with a shake of his head, not altogether successfully, so he tried two more times before his hair fell along his back. The hair had snarls. It looked as if a thistle had caught in one area above his ear. How a thistle got there at this time of the year, who knew. But Armstrong liked his hair, liked throwing his mane around.

"Allan, you awake? Can you talk?"

"Yeah, man. Oh geesh, man, was I dreaming. Dreaming hard. Can't remember what I was dreaming, but it was deep, man. Geesh!" He continued to rub his face with his palms, using his fingers to massage his eye sockets.

"Hey, man, didn't we talk yesterday? I remember something."

"Yes, we did. But I have one more thing to ask you. You awake? You sober?"

"Yeah, man. Too sober. Maybe that's why I was sleeping so hard. So, what, man? What you want with me?" He brushed his hair back, felt the thistle. "What the …" He used two hands to work it free and then flicked it on the floor. He then smoothed his hair until he felt pretty again. "Okay, man, what?"

"Let me get right to the point, Allan. Your fingerprints were found at the back door of the courthouse. Any idea how they got there?"

"What? What do you mean? What fingerprints?"

"Remember when I was here yesterday? Judge Kuhmer was murdered. Remember? You told me about your kids and girlfriends. Remember?"

"No man, I really don't. Kuhmer, that SOB died? Man, geesh!

"You lookin' at me for it? No way! I hated that SOB, but murder, naaahh, not me."

"Well, Allan, that's why I'm asking you about your fingerprints at the back of the courthouse. How did they get there?"

The shirtless man-boy from the kitchen stuck his head out. "Hey, Allan, you ain't got to say shit to him." Then he ducked back in.

Allan looked confused.

"Look, Allan. He's right, you ain't got to say shit to me. But how did your fingerprints get on the door to the courthouse? That's all I got to know from you."

"That's all?"

"Yes, that's all."

"You mean the door by the air-conditioning thing? Where the disabled people go into the courthouse?

"Yes, absolutely. How did your fingerprints get on that door?"

"That's where we do our stuff, man. You know, take some meth. That's a great hiding place, no cameras there.

"I never went in that door. I never went out that door. I don't even know where it goes. But you got those brick walls on both sides, no one can see you. We do meth there. Sometimes smoke a joint. The door is always locked. We check it. Just in case, you know what I mean."

"Just in case you can get in? Maybe there would be something to take home?"

"Hey man, I ain't no thief. A little meth, but I ain't no thief."

"Allan, I didn't imply that you were. So you hang out there by the courthouse sometimes. When were you there last?"

"Last …" Allan was deep in thought. He bent over and his hair fell in front of his face, which then gave him an opportunity to throw back his head in a grand gesture with his hair slipping behind him. "Last, oh man, last week, I think."

"Do you know what day?"

"What day is today, man?"

"Sunday."

"Sunday, really? Oh man. Sunday. Where does the time go?"

Tim watched him. *Where does the time go? Probably to some drug-induced time-altering world.* There is no time when your neurons are chemically titillated.

"I can't remember, man. There was a bunch of us. Just did a little meth last time there … I think."

The one thing Tim was sure he did not do was think.

"But we never got in the courthouse in that door, man. Never."

"Oh, God save Ireland, a little bit this time."

# CHAPTER 34

The Bathtub Race is a raucous affair. On a beautiful day such as this Sunday at the Maple Festival, the crowds lined both sides of Main Street. Fred estimated seven hundred spectators. And dogs. Fred counted twelve dogs. All were on leashes, but still, dogs at the Maple Festival. Dogs and crowds don't mix well. The festival had had a number of dog-human interactions the prior year. There had been rumors of a municipal ordinance to prohibit dogs at the festival, but it had not been passed by Village Council yet. So the dogs were present.

Geauga TV had scaffolding set up with power hookups to Sebastian's Restaurant directly across from the stage. Chris Grau was behind the huge camera, eight feet off the ground.

The race was initially promoted years ago as an event at the festival by then-president Doris Cook. She got the committee together, and it has been an event for more than twenty years. The present committee chair was Dan McCaskey. He issued the entries, took the money, organized the races according to make and style of tub and entries.

Tim Grau and Scott Mihalic were the MCs. They entertained, and they were the primary the voices behind the mobile microphones that blasted over this section of the square. The repartee between Tim and Scott was humorous, inane, and legendary. The loudspeakers at the north end of the square were silenced until noon because the Assembly of God Church was still conducting services. Years ago, the festival board had capitulated to the local pastors for quiet time during church services. Complaints were made to the board, and, after several heated meetings, it was agreed to observe silence in front of the two churches on the square until noon on Sunday. Since then, the churches and the festival have worked well together.

The Tim and Scott Show tossed jibes at the racers, the tubs, the festival directors, and at themselves. All in good fun.

The racers are required to have two people pushing the bathtub, one person steering it. All of the bathtubs had been modified to have a steering mechanism and wheels. The steering mechanisms varied: a long pole bent around the lip of the tub, a steering wheel connected to a pole inserted through a hole in the tub to the front wheel, a single front wheel, or two wheels close together, or two wheels far apart with steering rods connecting them so they turned at the same time. The simpler model was one wheel on a sprocket that turned with the turn of the stick, but when the tub had to turn 180 degrees halfway through the run, these tubs tended to fall over.

The push bar was a welded piece of pipe connected to perpendicular pipes attached to the tub or the frame supporting the wheels. This allowed the pushers to run behind the tub at top speed and control the tub at the turn by pulling and pushing at the same time. One held the tub back while the rider turned the front wheel and the outside pusher pushed. This method prevented the untimely spill of the tub and all its human cargo.

The teams came from everywhere. Fire departments who thought they were the cat's meow sent teams from southern Ohio. Politicians such as Tim Grendell, state representative, and Tracy Jemison, county auditor, teamed up and pushed a tub themselves. But only during election years. Still, in the years they were not running for election, they sponsored a team. Of course, time and gravity have their effect, and these elected officials were no longer spring chickens. The exertion of pushing an extremely heavy bathtub after the age of fifty was good cause for an aneurysm, so no one faulted them for exercising wise restraint and heartily cheering on their team of young bucks. They received great publicity with the their team members and fans sporting T-shirts with their political names emblazoned on the front and back.

Only two tubs could race at a time. Tim and Scott alternated starting them. The racers pushed the tubs as fast as they could 300 feet along Main Street. At the far end were two traffic cones around which the tubs had to maneuver before they raced back to the finish line. At the finish line, Tim or Scott called the winner. At the same time, these hosts yelled into their microphones for the pushers to hold onto their tubs and not let them loose. Loose, heavy tubs crashing into spectators cause injuries—experience has shown this to be true. Police tape wrapped around the traffic barrels lining Main Street kept the spectators sufficiently distant from the racers to prevent tub–human collisions. The racers moved down the street, and necks craned to keep them in sight. As a consequence, the barrels inched forward by the crowd pressure, decreasing the racers' space but allowing a better view by the spectators. Police were employed to keep the crowd under control, to push the barrels back, and to allow them a better view than anyone else.

In the staging area, only festival board directors and racers and tubs were permitted. That was a loosely controlled regulation, but it was repeatedly stressed by Tim and Scott to prevent the finish-line loose tub from cascading into unsuspecting bystanders. Fred wore his luminescent green Maple Festival cap and his maple leaf identification badge so he could gain entry to the restricted area and take photos.

"Coming up next is Chardon Toastmasters versus McCaskey Landscape and Design. So let's see, folks. That's the old dudes versus the young, aggressive, healthy, and good-looking dudes," announced Scott.

The crowd laughed appreciatively.

"Tim, what *is* a Chardon Toastmaster?"

"I think they make toast!"

"So they are master toasters. Does that mean they are toaster boasters? I mean, Tim, really, how hard is it to make toast? You plink it in the toaster, push the button down, and when it is done, it pops up. You mean to tell me you can become a master at that? Unbelievable!"

"Scott, here's John Elzroth, he's the Chamber of Commerce president. Maybe he can tell us what a toastmaster is."

"Hey, John!" hollered Scott, "can you tell us what a Chardon Toastmaster is?"

"Yes, Scott, I can. Contrary to your statements, it has nothing to do with toasted bread. The Chardon Toastmasters is a group of people who are dedicated to improving their speaking skills. They meet weekly at the Chamber of Commerce office. There are table topics; there are speeches prepared in advance; there are strict timetables and a structure for the giving of speeches, and everyone has a grand time. Everyone is welcome! There are about twenty members presently. Several members have ranked in the district and state competitions. It is a wonderful program to learn how to speak in public. I recommend it for anyone, even you, Scott. Even you, Tim!"

Scott feigned umbrage. "Okay, folks, John thinks I need lessons in public speaking. Are the racers ready yet?" Scott sidetracked. "No, okay, you heard John say he thinks I need to learn how to speak publicly and that I should join the Chardon Toastmasters. All those who think I need lessons in public speaking, give me a cheer."

The crowd resounded with ear-splitting cheers and applause.

"Well, that's what I needed, your vote of confidence. John, I'm going to join next week. What day did you say they meet? Thursday, folks, at seven p.m. at the Chardon Chamber of Commerce office? I'll be there, I'll be square, and I'll see many of you there." Scott showed John to a graceful exit and turned back to the crowd. "Okay, thank you, John. Are our racers ready? Okay, Tim, start them off!"

The Maple Queen and her court stood in between the two tubs and took turns waving the start flag to the racers while Tim bellowed into the mike. "Bring the tubs to the line! Jim McCaskey, line up that tub. Not over the line! Back it up a little. You're on the committee, we're not going to let you cheat! Okay ... on your mark!"

The runners tensed.

"Get set."

The runners lowered themselves to the maximum pushing position.

"Go!"

The Maple Queen dropped the flag. The runners pushed. The crowed hollered. The barrels edged forward into the street at the far end of the route as the spectators craned for a better a view. Cameras were raised.

Fred had positioned himself behind the racers to get the backsides of them as they started and raced down the street. He zoomed his 300 mm Tamron lens as they raced down the street. At the turn, McCaskey was ahead of Toastmasters. Scott kept up his stream of talking, shouting, encouraging, joking.

"And here they come! It's McCaskey by a landslide! I guess those old dudes at the Chardon Toastmasters are spending too much time talking and not enough time exercising. Hey, what do you think, folks?"

Applause followed McCaskey's tub past the finish line. The racers held onto the heavy tub and slowed it to a stop thirty feet past the finish line.

"McCaskey moves up to the next challenge. But we'll let them take a rest first. Next on the line is Auburn Township Fire Department versus

Pohl Plumbing. Oh, we have a battle here, folks! There is no one in better shape than firefighters. These guys and gals are in superb shape. Look out, Pohl Plumbing, the fire-eaters are coming after you! Fire-eaters, isn't that the name of those demons in the Harry Potter books? Yeah, I'm sure it is, *fire-eaters*. Those fiends that fly around and suck your breath out."

"Scott, no one cares, move on!" interrupted Tim.

"What, no one cares? I don't believe that. Okay, Tim, watch this. How many people have read at least one Harry Potter book? Raise your hand and say 'Yeah.'"

A quarter of the crowd cheered and raised their hands.

"See Tim, this is a literary crowd. Wasn't I right about the fire-eaters?"

The crowd cheered.

"Oh, Tim, look at these guys! They are huge. They *are* fire-eaters! Hey guys, take a bow. Come on, take a bow. Look at the size of these guys, can you believe it? They look like Arnold Schwarzenegger! They must not have very many fires in Auburn Township. These guys have too much time on their hands. They must be lifting weights all day, every day, and nighttime too. Wow!"

"Go easy, Scott. Okay, they are in good shape, but don't get mushy over them. Maybe you can talk to them after the race if they interest you that much."

"Whoa, Tim. What are you thinking? Gee, folks, I commend someone on their physical shape and look what happens. What's he accusing me of? Can you believe it?"

"We believe it," someone shouted from the audience.

Scott hung his head in mock shame.

"I confess folks. Those guys just look too good."

"Stop right there, Scott. We have a race to run. None of these true confessions now."

"You're right, Tim. Later folks. Okay, here we have the beefy Auburn Township Fire Department—like that description better, folks?—versus the able-bodied Pohl Plumbing. Pohl Plumbing, right here in Chardon, Ohio. They will fix all your leaks. Look at that tub. Now that's a tub. Leave it to a plumber to design a tub like that. See those racing lines? Wow! Okay, Tim, start them off."

"Racers, pull up to the line. Perfect. On your mark! Queen, are you ready? Get set! Go!"

And they were off!. Pohl Plumbing kept up with the massive fire-eaters until the turn. Pohl Plumbing failed to make the turn, and the tub went crashing into the crowd at the far end. A large groan, gasp, and grunt from the crowd accompanied the collision.

Fred had his 300 mm lens maxed out, shooting in continuous mode. He knew there would be trouble from this. The policeman at the end tried to stop the tub and was tossed into the air, landing face first on the tub driver. The two pushers tried to stop the tub, but the policeman's foot crashed into the face of the right-sided pusher, forcing him to let go. The tub careened slightly right, through the police tape into a woman sitting on a lawn chair, knocking her over.

Fred, shooting photographs, groaned. Another fiasco. What a festival.

Auburn Township fire-eaters stopped their tub before the finish line and ran back to the accident scene. The crowd around the accident momentarily spread out. The policeman disentangled himself from the tub driver and tub. He didn't appear injured yet.

The firefighters surrounded the woman on the ground. Already a siren was heard from the Chardon Fire Department less than five hundred feet away. With all the police and fire at the scene, someone had already called the ambulance. The force of the collision was apparent; it had to have caused an injury.

*Another lawsuit,* thought Fred. The tent, the murder, the electrocution, the tub. What next?

Scott was calming the crowd, asking them to move aside to allow the ambulance entrance. Room was made for the ambulance to pull in. The barrels were moved, the tape retracted.

With the crowd around the injured woman, no one could see what was happening. A stretcher was brought out. From a glimpse, she didn't appear conscious. There was no movement from her. The ambulance drove away. Scott and Tim warned the crowd about the dangers related to the event and resumed the bathtub race. The police moved the spectators away from the turning area in the event another turn failed.

Fred moved away toward the Log Chopping and Sawing Contest at the north end of the square. Another issue to deal with after the dust settled.

# CHAPTER 35

Tim walked into the small church of the Auburn Christian Believers. He had changed from his uniform into slacks and a sweater. Sunday services appeared halfway completed. Attendance was sparse, ten people. Three couples, two children, and two old ladies were sitting in the first three rows. Tim sat in the second-to-last row.

The church was simple. A center aisle between twenty rows of pews. No kneeling pads at the pews. The windows allowed light into the church through long narrow strips of colored glass that cast a shadowy appearance. A crucifix stood upright in the center of the altar. To the left of the altar was the sermon podium, elevated slightly, with intricate carvings on three sides. Lit candles were assembled in groups of five on both sides of the altar. A single candle on a huge candlestick stood six feet in height at the right side of the altar; Tim surmised it was the Paschal Candle—a candle providing for the passion of Christ.

There was no choir. Pastor Bob—Tim figured the person doing the officiating was Pastor Bob—broke into a halting melody of "Jesus, Our Savior." Tim had never heard the hymn before. It was a plaintive cry of adoration expressed in a haunting plea; it produced a feeling in Tim of pain mingled with sacrifice. The maudlin tone made chills crawl up and down his spine.

This was a dying church. The parishioners knew it, the pastor knew it, and Tim felt it strongly. Pastor Bob made several announcements about current affairs, meetings of several committees of the parish, whom he had visited during the past week, requests for prayers for the sick and dying, and wished the congregation all a good Christian week.

Pastor Bob led the way to the church entrance and spoke with each of the parishioners as they left. Tim was last. "Welcome, sir, I am glad that you came to our humble church." Pastor Bob extended his hand to shake Tim's.

Tim shook his hand.

"Reverend Pietsmeyer, I am Tim Snyder. I'm a policeman, and I wondered if I might have a few minutes of your time to talk about something."

Pastor Bob's face sagged immediately. He recovered, took a deep breath, and said, "Yes, young man, please. Come into my home, and we can talk over a cup of coffee."

Pastor Bob closed the church doors. He did not lock them, merely closed them quietly. Tim saw his hands shaking. Tim followed him to the house next door, a small Cape Cod–style home with a glassed-in porch and fifties'-style aluminum siding. The steps were covered with indoor/outdoor bright green carpeting. Pastor Bob directed Tim to sit on the porch. The sun shining onto the porch had warmed it nicely. Tim sat.

"I'll just be a minute. Cream or sugar in your coffee?"

"Just black, thank you."

Tim felt sorry for the old man. He wasn't that old, maybe sixty. He was short, five feet eight inches, balding, hair gray around the edges, a little too long over the shoulders. Teeth a little too yellow, but clean overall. His paunch protruded a little too much. The house, or rather, the porch, was clean and neat.

Pastor Bob came out and sat down. "The coffee will be just a minute. We had to make a new pot," said Pastor Bob. "So, young man, what did you say your name was?"

"Tim Snyder."

"Yes, Tim," said Pastor Bob genially, "what would you like to talk about?"

"Well, sir," started Tim when he was immediately interrupted.

"No, please, call me Bob. Or Pastor Bob if it makes you feel better."

"Well, Bob, or Pastor Bob. I wanted to ask you a few questions about Judge Kuhmer."

Pastor Bob interrupted Tim again. "Oh, that poor man, I heard about his death. How tragic, how sad for his family."

"Yes, I am sure it was and is. But maybe I can cut this short. You weren't by chance at the Maple Festival Thursday night, were you?"

"Yes, my wife and I went up to the Maple Festival. We are trying to keep things as normal as we can, so we went up for our annual maple stir. I see they raised the price this year. We always get a stir, walk around, then sometimes get something to take back and eat later."

"What time were you there?"

"Oh, let's see. We left about nine thirty, ten o'clock. We didn't stay too long; it was cold and windy and snowy. But we like to keep our routine, so we went to get our annual stir."

Mrs. Pastor Bob Pietsmeyer brought in two cups of coffee on a tray, set it on the table, smiled at Tim, and said, "There you are, dearie."

"Thank you."

"Mr. Snyder, this is my wife, Gerta. Gerta, Mr. Snyder. He is asking about Thursday night at the Maple Festival. That is when Judge Kuhmer met his untimely demise."

Gerta burst into tears and fled the room.

"Sorry," said Tim.

"Oh no, don't you worry about it. This whole affair has her so upset."

"Whole affair? You don't mean Judge Kuhmer's death, do you?"

"No, just the whole thing. I'm sure that's why you came here. The whole thing with my son, Jonah. That is why you are here, right?"

"Well, I did look at the old records and your name, or your son's name, came up as someone connected in an unfavorable way with Judge Kuhmer. So yes, that is why I am here."

"Oh, so sad. It is so sad."

"What is?" Tim wasn't certain if he was talking about EW or his son or what.

"The whole affair. My son, the judge, our life, our church, our school. The whole thing."

"Pastor Bob, you want to just tell me about it rather than me asking all these intrusive questions? If it will make it any easier? I looked up the case against your son. I see he is in the state penitentiary for six years. That he was tried as an adult even though he was a minor. And that it was Judge Kuhmer who sentenced him."

"Judge Kuhmer was not a nice man." Pastor Bob took a deep breath as if trying to hold back tears. "What he did to my son was in violation of everything the Lord stands for. He was a Satan. Let me start at the beginning." Pastor Bob wrung his hands as if he were warming them from the now-cooling coffee cup.

"We moved here eight years ago from Massachusetts. My family has a long history of service to the Lord. We are descended from the original pilgrims, and we take our covenant with the Lord personally and very seriously. I had the calling from the Lord to set up a church and a school for wayward children.

"I received all the necessary permits from the state and the Department of Human Services. I had the inspections from the social workers and the Health Department. They did a background check on me to make sure I was who I said I was. We started the church, and people started to join. It was a good congregation. We had fifty families and were still growing when it all happened. We had started the school. The county would place the children with us, or if some individual family were having trouble with one of their children, then that child would be placed with us. We had contracts drawn up; everything was legal. We made sure that all the families, and especially the social workers, understood that we would use corporal punishment as a means of discipline. 'Spare the rod and spoil the child' is not just an idle saying. It is true. I, myself, was raised in that fashion, maybe a little too severely based on the scars on my back, but I learned my lessons. I learned respect. I learned to honor my parents." The preacher took a sip of his coffee and then mopped his whole face with a small napkin.

"My son, Jonah, was raised with the Bible. He knew it backwards and forwards. I had him teaching Bible studies to the children. We had twenty-four children enrolled in the school. Fourteen of them were residential. We have a dormitory out back where the children's rooms were. There were no more than three children to a room. Social Services checked on the rooms and gave us an okay. We were a clean, God-loving community.

"Things were going along famously. Children were progressing through our school. They learned to deal with one another, they learned to pray, and they learned the Bible. Children would leave the school and ask to stay. They loved it here. Then, a year ago, two of the girls in the school—they bunked together and were friends—they conspired to harm my son, Jonah. They accused Jonah of making them do things to him to avoid corporal punishment. Corporal punishment was always imposed by me, not by Jonah. Jonah was only permitted to paddle with one swat when the circumstances warranted."

Tim shifted in his seat, feigned dropping his notebook pencil, thinking, *What in the world were you thinking, old man, to let a seventeen-year-old spank fourteen-year-olds?*

"Jonah was very mature for his age. He had just turned seventeen. He was a good boy. He taught Bible classes to the children on Sundays, Tuesdays, and Thursdays. On Sundays, the classes were after church. On Tuesdays and Thursdays, the classes were in the evenings for the residential students only.

"The school had been in operation for over five years. These two girls, one thirteen, one fourteen, accused Jonah of these indiscretions. Jonah denied it. The Social Services came down on us like the wrath of God. The Health Department all of a sudden found problems with the facilities that they had previously approved. Jonah was indicted as an adult. A hearing was held in juvenile court to have him determined to be tried as an adult. We found an attorney, but we couldn't afford him. We had to get the public defender. The case was transferred to Judge Kuhmer in the Court of Common Pleas. That was a bad day for us. Judge Kuhmer was not a nice man. Not a Christian in any sense of the word."

"In what way?" asked Tim, hoping to tease out the father's antagonism toward the judge.

"Hear me out!" snapped the pastor, but Tim didn't react and the preacher collected himself and resumed immediately. "The public defender advised us to not take a polygraph test. The prosecutor wanted us to do it, but we were advised against it: they are so unreliable. And with a child taking it, it could give us bad results."

Tim nodded sympathetically, but thought, *The reason you didn't take it was because you were probably assured he would fail. Then it could be used against him in accordance with the agreement to be bound by the results. Take off those rose-colored glasses, old man.*

"So those two girls testified to such horrible things. They said Jonah did those things to them. That Jonah made them do those things to him. How can you defend against such lies? None of the other kids supported the two girls. Just their say-so. Jonah denied it, but Judge Kuhmer didn't believe a single word Jonah said. Not a single word."

*Why*, Tim thought? *What facts did the judge have that made him believe the two girls?* "Why do you suppose that was?" he fished.

"Praise the Lord, God only knows. Anyway, Jonah was convicted. All of the parents who had put children in our school removed them. Social Services withdrew our permits. We were out of business. I was unable to perform the Lord's calling. This is my sacrifice for the Lord, my pain on earth! I pray I may enter the Kingdom with a clean slate." A tear rolled down Pastor Bob's right cheek. He let it drop.

This was a defeated old man, thought Tim, believing his perspective was sincere, if misguided, and it had aged him beyond his years. Old in spirit. A spirit worn and smashed. A life destroyed by the mere impetus of life itself.

"The parishioners were initially supportive, but after Jonah was convicted, they just started to drift away. You saw what we were left with. We have six families left. We are broke. The bank is foreclosing on our house and church. I don't know what to do. I pray to God every day for Jonah. May he persevere. May the Lord bless him and preserve him to do the Lord's duty.

"We have visited Jonah at the jail. It is horrible. I can see the change in him. He has been corrupted by those with whom he is forced to live. This must be God's test for him. God is a loving God, so this must be his way of showing us how he loves us. It must be."

"Was that your only contact with Judge Kuhmer?" asked Tim.

"Oh no. We had more contact with him. That attorney, the one who is charged with murder, what's his name?"

"Fred Newman?"

"Yes! That's it. *He sued us.* He represented the families of the two girls. He also is not a nice man. I think he is a Satan as well. We have nothing, but he sued us. Then he somehow finagled to get our homeowner's insurance company into the case. I didn't want to give him the policy, but Judge Kuhmer threatened to throw me in jail for contempt of court if I didn't give it to *Attorney* Newman. So I gave it to him. There was a rider on the policy for teachers. *Attorney* Newman somehow latched onto that and extorted money from the insurance company. He got lots of money from them. Hundreds of thousands of dollars. It was highway robbery.

He got money for something that never occurred. Our legal system is so crooked, so crooked.

"He took my deposition and Jonah's deposition. He had nothing, no facts, and the insurance company paid all that money. 'Post-traumatic stress syndrome': he kept repeating it. Like I was supposed to be an expert on it. There was nothing wrong with those kids that a good spanking wouldn't cure. And Attorney Newman was nasty about the whole thing. He is not a nice man.

"I don't know why he killed Judge Kuhmer, but I can see he is the type of attorney who *would* do such a thing. He has that killer spirit in him. He used it against my family. I know the Lord says 'Love thy neighbor,' but I have a very difficult time expressing any positive feelings for Attorney Newman or Judge Kuhmer. I hate them to their very cores. I pray to God to get over this hate for these two human beings, but I have been unable to do so. They deserve hatred. Now that Judge Kuhmer is dead, he will meet his Maker and his sins will be paraded before him. He will get the just deserts he deserves. The Lord knows all. The Lord knows how evil he has been to our family. I pray the Lord exercises the justice and vengeance against Judge Kuhmer that Judge Kuhmer exercised during his lifetime against my son, Jonah."

Tim listened. The man was delusional. Insurance companies don't pay money based on no facts. There obviously were facts. *Your son did it, old man. Face up to it.*

"I pray for vengeance."

*Great, pray for bad things. That, I guess, is the power of love that you preach from your pulpit. It is not the church I am going to join at any time soon. Oh, pray to God to save Ireland.*

# CHAPTER 36

S lowly ambling from the bathtub race to the Log Chopping and Sawing Contest on the north lawn of the courthouse, Fred took multiple photographs. The sun was bright and the shaded areas would be too dark. It was worthless to take a photo of a person's face if he or she were wearing a baseball cap that shaded the face. It would be black. The contrast between the bright sunlit skin and the shaded area was too great to capture on either film or digital media.

How many more fiascos could this year's festival withstand? Fred thought, *It's not even an adventure, more like a laughable tragedy, a travesty.* A death, a tent collapsing, an electrocution, an FG spectacle, a bathtub bobble. Maybe, just maybe, he'd better not go over to the log sawing and chopping; someone might get an arm or leg cut off. Maybe he was the jinx.

He photographed teenagers dressed like ghouls, fat men with messages on their T-shirts, fat women stuffing their faces with sausage sandwiches or fried dough, eating over garbage cans so they didn't drip on the ground or themselves. Four large women surrounded a yellow garbage can. *How fitting,* thought Fred. *Bobbing for garbage.* Fred took a photo and then a second. He moved away.

He made his way through the tent, exited at the middle, walked toward the courthouse, past the pony rides, around the courthouse to the screaming noise of several high-powered gasoline chainsaws. An area approximately fifty feet by forty feet was staked with police tape connecting the stakes to isolate the contest area. Jim Freeman, father of Bob in the sugar house, Ken at the log chopping, and Matt, a contestant, was speaking into the microphone.

The chainsaws were being warmed up for the next event. When they shut off, it was dead quiet for a few seconds. Fred noticed that the participants were all wearing earplugs. Fred did not have earplugs. His bilateral hearing loss from his wartime years would not help him to listen to the screaming chainsaws, but he needed some photos.

A squared-off log, twelve inches by twelve inches by eight feet, was bolted by chains to two sawhorses. The log protruded on both ends. Ken Freeman marked the log at several spots on both ends. The two contestants were required to place their chainsaws on the ground by the ends of the log, place their hands on the log, and wait for the starter to start. When the starter said go, they picked up their chainsaws, pulled a rope start, and applied the chainsaw to the log, cutting down, cutting up, and then cutting down again, making three slices one and one-half inches wide.

These chainsaws were souped-up affairs. A two-cycle Honda motor of 200 cc starts at the single pull of a rope and buzzes through the wood as if it were butter.

Jim Freeman spoke to the crowd, "On your mark, set, go!"

The contestants wore huge goggles, Kevlar chaps, steel-toed boots, blue jeans, checkered shirts of red and blue. One was thin and wiry, the other big and muscular. They let go of the log, bent to their saws, pulled the cords in unison; both machines screamed simultaneously, down, up, down. They shut off the machines.

The quiet was golden.

"The winner is Harry Finder with 3.25 seconds. Good job, Joe. Next up is Bill Rygert versus Bob Basalt."

Fred took photos of the spectators with his 28–300 mm lens attached. He got up close and personal. He took photos of the families of the contestants who sat on the bed of the pickup trucks backed up to the saw area. The trucks transported the saws, the axes for the axe-throwing contest, and other tools of avocations. These were the modern-day Paul Bunyans.

Fred couldn't stand the noise—too painful; he moved away and headed back toward the stage. It was time for the Syrup Auction.

This time Fred took the long route, up the center of the square, through the middle of the long tent, toward the pancake tent, past the sugar house, around the south end of the square to Main Street to the stage. The festival was getting crowded as he wove his way between people moving in the opposite direction.

Scott Mihalic was on the stage. All remnants of the bathtub race were gone. The festival queen and her court were lined up at the back of the stage. One pretty member of the court—and they were all pretty—stood next to Scott holding a quart jar of syrup. Fred moved in close to get a shot of her. He attached his flash unit. The stage faced the west and the sun, at one p.m., was angled slightly toward the tent over the stage. The shadows under the tent would come out black without a flash because the sunlight was so harsh outside.

Fred moved in closer to the stage, tilted his camera upward so his viewfinder included the syrup jar she was holding and her face. Lovely. He turned the camera on Scott, zoomed in, took several shots with the microphone blocking Scott's face.

The syrup auction brought out the syrup producers. Fred looked in the crowd. He saw JR Blanchard, a former winner; Jim Cermak, a former winner; the Rhodes sisters, former winners; Marilyn Anderson and her husband, Dick; and Nancy Kothera with a gathering of family around them. Paul Richards, who operated Richards Maple Products. James Miller, an Amishman who had won several times. Chuck Lausin and his wife, former winners and big buyers at the auction. Burton Armstrong and his entire family, this year's winner.

Many festival board members were in the audience: Sara Brougher and her husband, Ed, who every year bid on the painted sap bucket; Gene Adams and Gary Dysert, concession managers; Mike Martin, a director; Claudia Battaglia, a director; Charline Heiden, treasurer; Kelly Bolan, a director, and her husband, Joe; and Bob Eldridge, a director.

Politicians aplenty were in attendance also: Neil Hofstetter, a county commissioner, and Lillian, his wife; Tim Grendell, state senator, and his wife, the Honorable Diane Grendell, Eleventh Appellate District judge, who perennially tried to bid on the winning syrup until it got too expensive, and then they settled for the runner-up; Tracy Jemison, county auditor, and his wife, Bonnie; and Chris Hitchcox, county treasurer, and his son.

The syrup auction was the pinnacle of the festival. The price of the winning syrup dictated the feeling of success of the festival to those connected with it. To Fred, this year would be a loss financially with the *uninsured* collapse of the tent, and the snow days, but if the syrup went for a goodly amount, then the feeling of goodwill permeated those involved with syrup production. Maple syrup was the be-all and end-all of the festival. It was created to promote the syrup industry, to celebrate the rite of spring sap flowing up into the trees, to welcome a new season, and to have the community gather after hiding in their homes during the deep winter months.

Fred saw his acquaintances, but he did not go over to talk to them. Fred was an anathema, a pariah, a *persona non grata*, an inimical person to society, a baneful, corrupt, deplorable, diabolic, notorious fiend. No one really wanted to associate with him. They hoped he wasn't the murderer, but they weren't sure. They didn't want to identify or associate with him, especially if they relied on votes from their constituents. They could just imagine the headlines: "Politician Endorses Murderer." Fred knew this, he felt it in his bones, in his psyche, and in the reaction to everyone with whom he spoke. He was not going to insult their credibility by forcing himself on them, forcing them to issue false platitudes of support. Fred was embarrassed enough by the situation, but he still had the responsibilities of the festival to contend with. He still had to perform certain acts. He still had to take photos of the various activities of the festival.

"Okay, folks," said Scott, "this is a blue-ribbon syrup from the Cermak Farm out on Route 528. You know which one that is, folks, that's the big barn with the Ohio Bicentennial logo on it. You can go into the big tent and buy this same syrup for a very small amount of money from the Cermaks themselves. They have a very nice display. You've seen it, very nice. But this particular jar, this is *the* blue-ribbon syrup. This is the syrup that Jim Cermak himself selected and filtered and made sure it was the best syrup he could make to enter into the contest.

"Look at the clarity of this syrup. Here, Bonnie, hold that up for all to see. Okay, folks, once again this is a blue-ribbon syrup. Who'll give me a hundred dollars? Hundred dollars. Hey biddee: one hundred. Gimme two hundred. Two hundred dollars. Hey biddee one hundred dollars. Gimme two hundred, two hundred fifty. We're way under here!"

Scott spied a hand raised. "Okay, we're at forty dollars here. Hey biddee, forty dollars, gimme fifty, hey biddee forty dollars, gimme fifty, fifty dollars, fifty-five! Don't forget, this is the blue-ribbon syrup, not some run-of-the-mill cloudy syrup—blue ribbon, it's worth ten times this amount.

Scott pointed to Diane Grendell. "Diane, are you ready to start bidding? Hey, folks, that's Diane Grendell over there, everybody knows her. She is the Eleventh District Court of Appeals judge. That covers five counties, folks; that's an important job, and here she is supporting the Maple Festival. How about it Diane—forty-five dollars?"

Diane gave a big smile and a nod that Fred captured with his camera.

"Okay, folks, we're at forty-five, who'll give me fifty dollars? Fifty dollars here. Hey biddee fifty, gimme fifty-five, hey biddee fifty, gimme fifty-five, sixty dollars! Okay, I got fifty dollars from Keith. Diane?"

She nodded.

"Fifty-five, Keith?" Scott pointed his index finger at Keith with an intense look.

He raised his arm to his shoulder with his index finger pointed skyward. Fred took a photo, zoomed in on Keith's face.

Scott, with the same finger, now pointed at Diane with the same intensity. No smiling now, this was serious business.

"Okay, I got fifty-five dollars. Diane? How about it, go sixty. Sixty bucks. It's a great jar of syrup, one of the best."

She nodded. The crowd looked to Diane, then to Keith, then to Scott, back to Diane. It was now getting interesting. A quart of syrup normally sells for thirteen dollars, now up to sixty. The crowd was having fun.

"It's only sixty bucks, Diane. On that great salary the taxpayers pay you, this is a pittance."

Diane nodded.

"Okay, Keith, sixty-five dollars. Who'll give me seventy? Seventy dollars here! Hey biddee seventy dollars, gimme seventy-five; hey biddee seventy, gimme seventy-five, eighty dollars!"

Diane nodded. Scott back to Keith.

"Okay at seventy, Keith?"

Keith raised his finger.

"Diane, seventy dollars, only seventy dollars, will you go seventy-five?"

Diane nodded. She turned to talk to her husband, State Senator Timothy Grendell; he laughed.

"Seventy-five, Keith, it's nothing for you, this is a great bottle of syrup. Look at it. Who'll give me eighty? Seventy-five dollars here, Hey biddee seventy-five, gimme eighty dollars, hey biddee seventy-seven, gimme eighty, eight-five dollars. What do you say, Keith, eighty dollars?"

Keith raised the finger." His sister, Sara, punched him in the arm.

"Okay, folks, we're nickel-and-diming here. Five bucks a jump isn't enough for this syrup. What's your bottom line, Diane? How much is this syrup worth to you?

Diane turned and whispered to her husband. He said something back. The crowd murmured. Bonnie of the Queens Court was still holding the jar of syrup, still looking pretty and smiling. A veritable Vanna White.

"I'll go a hundred dollars, Scott!" shouted Diane.

"You heard that, folks, one hundred dollars. Judge Diane Grendell will pay a hundred dollars for this syrup. Okay, Keith, a hundred dollars, who'll give me one oh five? Hey biddee, a hundred dollar, one hundred here, gimme a hundred five; hey biddee hundred dollar, gimme one oh five, one hundred ten. What do you say, Keith, a hundred five?" Scott pointed the dreaded finger at him, intense. The crowd murmuring increased.

"Keith?"

Keith raised his finger, the crowd applauded.

"C'mon, Diane, one oh five. Oh you can't let it go for only five dollars. Come on Diane, only a hundred and five He's running out of gas. Will you go a hundred ten, Diane."

She shakes her head from side to side.

"How about a hundred seven dollars and fifty cents? Will that do it, Diane? Only two fifty more. That's half a sausage sandwich. Who'll give me a hundred ten? A hundred five dollars here. Hey biddee a hundred ten; hey biddee one oh five, gimme a hundred ten dollars please, one oh seven fifty?"

Diane nodded. The crowd laughed.

"Okay, Keith, I'm at a hundred seven dollars and fifty cents! Will you go a hundred ten"

Keith raised the finger.

"Are you crazy, Keith?" says Sara.

"Diane, a hundred ten; what do you say, will you go a hundred fifteen? Who'll give me a hundred fifteen? Hey biddee one ten, gimme one fifteen; hey biddee a hundred ten; gimme one fifteen, a hundred twenty dollar!

What do you say, Diane, a hundred twelve dollars and fifty cents? How about it, Diane?"

Diane shook her head no, vigorously. No, no, no.

Scott, having been in the auction business for years knew when a sale had reached its peak. He was acutely attuned to the reactions of the crowds.

"Okay, going once at a hundred ten, going twice, sold to Keith Eldridge for a hundred and ten dollars! Good purchase, Keith. And the Maple Festival thanks you. Let's give Keith Eldridge a round of applause, folks. He's been a great supporter of the Geauga County Maple Festival for years.

"Okay, next up is another blue-ribbon syrup, folks. This one is from the Rhodes Sisters Farm. You all know where that is, out there on Clay Street and … what's the name of the cross street, Nancy?"

Scott directed his question to Nancy Kothera, one of the Rhodes sisters.

"Huntley Road!" shouted Nancy.

"That's it, folks, Clay Street and Huntley Road. You've all been there to buy your Christmas trees. You even get to chop them down yourselves, and they wrap them up for you and tie them to your car or pickup truck or motorcycle or whatever you're driving. Great place, folks. So, here's a blue-ribbon syrup from the Rhodes sisters. Now you know this is good syrup because they have been the triple-crown winners twice before. You ask, 'What is a triple-crown winner?' Well, let me tell you. That is the greatest prize for Geauga County Maple Syrup: you win the Geauga County Maple Festival Syrup Contest; you win the Great Geauga County Fair Syrup Contest; and you win the Ohio State Fair Syrup Contest all in one year. Think about it! Different judges from all over the state of Ohio think your syrup is the best in the state. Triple-crown winner, folks. You know this is a great syrup. And they have won it twice. What do you think of that?"

Fred kept shooting photos of the queens, the crowd, the sausage vendor watching the auction, people dressed in strange clothing, kids rolling around on the ground in front of the stage.

"So if you have a jar of syrup from the farm that has twice won the Triple Crown, then you know they know how to make great syrup. Who'll give five hundred dollars? Gimme six hundred, seven hundred dollars!"

Fred had taken enough photos of the auction; he walked behind the stage, through the mud, past the area where the Boy Scouts set up tents for their overnights. They did not stay overnight on Friday with all the snow, but they slept in their pup tents on Saturday night. The ground was muddy; Fred watched where he stepped.

# CHAPTER 37

The Sunday parade starts at three p.m. The crowds begin to position themselves between one and two o'clock. By two, the outside of Main Street and both sides of East Park Street are lined with people in chairs, sitting on the backs of pickup trucks, blankets, ponchos, anything to keep the wet ground off of them. During the parade, traffic in uptown Chardon is completely halted. The parade lines up on Fifth Avenue and on North Street, so traffic has to be directed south to skirt the village and continue. If the traffic is on Route 6 heading east, then it is shuttled to Park Avenue by the cemetery, to Moffitt Avenue, to South Hambden Street, then to Grant Street and back onto Route 6. If traffic is heading north on Route 44, then it is directed to the west on Park Avenue to Wilson Mills and then back to Route 44 north, which is Center Street. Very little traffic is processed during the parade. It is gridlock. Large trucks sit on Route 44; they can't get around the turns on the side streets.

Chardon Village had several opportunities to purchase rights of way to alleviate the traffic, but it didn't occur. Now the village bears the brunt of gridlock because it did not take the leadership steps when it had the opportunity. Whoever thought the village and the surrounding environs would grow so quickly? There was never enough money to purchase the rights of way. The people didn't want them. A casual survey was taken by the village administrator at the time, and it was negative. There were and are so many reasons why something wasn't done when it should have been. So, Chardon Village Square has stayed on everyone's traffic route to the frustration and angst of everyone. The increase in stoplights throughout the town has been exponential. It appears there is a traffic light at every intersection. There isn't, but it sure seems so when you accelerate from a stoplight to be immediately stopped by another.

From the top of the square heading north on North Street until Allynd Boulevard, families have gatherings and reunions. Both sides of the streets on the tree lawns are lined with chairs and people. The fire departments line up on Allynd Boulevard; the Chardon High School Band and cheerleaders line up on North Street north of Fifth Avenue. Along Fifth Avenue, this year's parade marshal, Larry Morrow, the festival officers, political dignitaries, the queens, visiting queens, maple-syrup producer of the year, and numerous other individual units line up. Beginning at the intersection of Washington Street and Fifth Avenue, the floats, Boy Scout and Girl Scout groups, and any group that wants to enter the parade line up along Washington Street. The parking lots of Chardon Rubber and Rimes Trucking are full of groups practicing their routines, dogs lying in the dirt or jumping for their master's attention, children petting the horses, which are stamping and eager to move.

Generally Fred would walk the parade route, taking photos and talking to everyone. Not this year. He told Michelle to take his place in the Maple Festival Officers golf cart. He wasn't going to subject himself and everyone else to the uncomfortable feeling of uncertainty: *Did he or didn't he?* Or to get some heckler like the guy yesterday at the grandstand. It was just not necessary or desirable. Fred would just stand on the corner across the street from Newman & Brice Law Firm building and take photos and drink wine from a to-go coffee cup. He had taken photos from that location for fifteen years; he was an institution on that corner during the parade. And that's just the way it was going to be. Damn, he wished Tim Snyder would get moving on this thing. It was getting on his nerves. His wife wouldn't even come up to the festival because she was so embarrassed.

The Snyder Family held a Snyder Family mini-reunion at the Sunday Maple Festival Parade every year. For twenty-five years, ever since they were kids and their parents brought them to the festival, they had secured their spot to watch the parade. They were there when it was sunny, cloudy, or rainy. The spot was located in front of Farinacci Auto Body and Sales. A minimum of twelve chairs was needed for the adults, Tim and his wife, Carolyn, brothers Troy and Daniel and their wives, sister Judy and her husband, Henry, and their parents, who still loved to come to the parade. Two extra chairs were brought for kids. If more kids wanted to sit, they had to bring their own chairs.

Troy had chair duty this year. Chair duty involved getting the chairs to the square along with their parents. He had to get there by one, or the traffic would be locked up and he wouldn't be able to unload the furniture and his parents. Troy made his son, Chad, and his wife, Barbara, help. As they stopped at the red light on South Street at the square, it was like a Chinese fire drill. All the doors opened, Chad unloaded all the chairs, Mr. and Mrs. Snyder slowly exited the vehicle with the help of Barbara, and stood by the pile of chairs at the side of the street while Chad finished unloading. The light was so long, there was no difficulty in unloading, getting everything to the side of the road, closing the doors, and waving to Troy. Troy then went to park wherever he could find a place. This was the most difficult time to find a space, because everyone was coming to the parade.

Chad moved six chairs at a time to the spot. Grandpa went with him on the first load and then would sit in a chair and make sure no one else was going to invade their spot. Grandma would come with the second load. Grandma had to hold onto Chad, actually, one of the chairs that he was holding, and Barbara on the other hand. The progress across the street was slow, but the light was so long, there was no problem. Grandma and Grandpa sat in the middle chairs and the kids sat all around them. The grandchildren came and went. Some were in the parade in some float or group or band.

Chad put the first six chairs at the spot immediately in front of a tiny house set on a trailer. The sign read "Burton-Middlefield Rotary Victorian Cottage." It was a quaint little cottage, more like a fancy outdoor shed for tools. The spot would impede the view from the Victorian Cottage, but it was too far back in the Farinacci parking area to consider. There would be many people in front of it, not just the Snyder family. The initial spot had to provide for traffic coming from Water Street and turning right to the south on South Street. So the chairs were set by the street, but not in the street. As the time for the parade got closer, the chairs would be inched forward so that at all times the moving spot was the premier view of the parade and no one settled in front of them.

Chad went back for the second group of chairs. Grandpa went to look at the Victorian Cottage. He abandoned the chairs for a short while.

Someone may sit in them, but Grandpa wasn't worried about getting them back with his three big boys in attendance.

Chad escorted the chairs and Grandma to the spot. Grandma immediately sat. Barbara wrapped a blanket around her, tucked it behind her legs, and asked if she were okay.

"Just peachy, Barbara. Just peachy. Where's Grandpa?"

Chad looked around, spotted Grandpa. "He's back there by that little house. Looks like he's buying raffle tickets." Chad silently laughed. Grandpa would buy tickets for anything. Especially if it was for a cause, any cause, good or bad. He would always say it was for a good cause and buy a ticket. He just liked buying tickets, Chad thought.

The Snyder family assembled over the next two hours. Daniel and his wife arrived at two. Their children, three of them, were on a 4-H float in the parade. Judy arrived without Henry; her son was one of the pooper-scoopers behind the horses—kids who dressed up to be unidentifiable and who cleaned up when one of the horses left a deposit on the street. This was designed so that marchers in the parade were not subject to dancing around road apples or ruining their shoes. The pooper-scoopers, three of them, one boy driving an all-terrain four-wheeler with a trailer behind it, the other two running around picking up poop or acting like nuts. Their dress was outrageous. It was a combination of clown, ghoul, farmer, and state trooper. Whatever was in the closet. They had fun.

Tim and Carolyn arrived at ten to three. They had no idea where their boys were. One was somewhere in the parade. The other had a girlfriend—that explained his absence.

Tim sat next to Grandpa. "How are you, Dad?"

"Just great, son. Just great. Look. I got these tickets. See that house back there on that trailer?"

Tim turned and looked at the Victorian Cottage. "Yes, what about it?"

"I just bought twenty tickets, I'm going to win that thing."

"What is it for?"

"Rotary. What is it, Burton-Middlefield Rotary. They built it. It's a tool shed or a playhouse or something. They did a really nice job on it. Great construction. Oak floors, oak trim. Really a wonderful building."

"What's it for?"

"Oh, that. They are raising money for defibrillators for the sheriffs' cars. Twenty-three of them. They want to raise $70,000. Put a defibrillator in each and every sheriff car in the county. And if they get more money, they'll put them in the local police cars. Pretty nice deal, huh?"

"So, how much did you spend?"

"Twenty tickets. I'm going to win, I'm sure."

"How much was a ticket?"

"Five bucks, cheap. Good deal."

"Aww, Dad." Tim, like Chad, chuckled. Dad was a sucker for a gamble.

"They're not allowed to sell those tickets at the festival, so they have to sell them over here. I guess you can't have raffles at the festival. But the festival doesn't have control of the Farinacci parking lot, so they can sell them here. I wonder why they don't let them have raffle tickets at the festival. Do you know, Tim?"

"Maybe everybody and his brother would have a raffle for a hundred good causes. It might drive everybody nuts. Sounds like a good rule to me. You'd be pestered everywhere you went."

"Yeah, maybe."

"Did you get your maple stir yet?"

"Chad got them for us. They were as good as usual."

Judy arrived without Henry. In response to Mom's open-palmed, double-handed gesture and a slight jerky tilt of her head demonstrating inquiry, Judy said, "Oh, he says he's got some things to do around the house, and this was the first good day of weather to do it. I think he just didn't want to come."

"Can't imagine wanting to miss the parade," said Mom Snyder.

Tim had been waiting for Judy. He wanted to talk to her about what he had heard about Parker. Judy must have known Tim wanted to talk to her—she looked extremely nervous.

"Hey, Judy," said brother Tim, "how about we have a little chat?" Tim pointed toward the Geauga Theatre. Judy followed him, dodging chairs, people sitting on the ground, the crowd gathering for the parade.

"I've been wanting to talk to you, too," said Judy. "I've got a problem."

"Yeah, so do I. What's this I hear about you and Parker? For God's sake, Judy, you're married. You've got kids. You're going to throw it all away. What the hell are you doing? And why do I have to hear about it from someone else?"

Judy twisted her hands together. Extremely uncomfortable, a tear rolled down her right cheek. "I've got a problem, Tim. I don't need your recriminations; I need your advice, your help, maybe."

Tim softened. "Sorry, it's just that I don't want to see you compromised. Your job is so public. It'll get all over town if it hasn't already."

"I know." Hands twisting faster.

"Okay, what is it? I'll switch gears from cop to priest. Well, maybe not. It might be the cop part I need. Oh-oh? Okay, go ahead."

"First of all, my private life is none of your business."

"Bullshit!"

"Second of all, what I am going to tell you *is* your business. I have seen Parker, only one time though. We went to dinner at the Red Hawk Grille, up by Quail Hollow, Route 90 and 44.

He's nice. At least he talks to me more than Henry does. And you don't know about my situation. Henry has his own little dalliance going on, so don't look so smug, Mr. Big Cop. Life isn't always fair. And it isn't being fair to me now. Just like you aren't being fair."

"Alright, alright! I'll back off. So you met Parker one time, okay, big deal."

"It is a big deal. It was Thursday night. You know, *the* Thursday night."

"Okay … Thursday night. Then what?"

"We met at about seven, had a nice dinner. Then at nine thirty, he said he had to go. He had an appointment with EW."

"Thursday night?"

"Yes. That's what I'm telling you. After he left me, he went to have an appointment with EW. That's the night EW was killed. He called me the next day and asked me to be sure I didn't tell anyone that he'd had the appointment. He said he didn't make it, that he got a flat tire and it took him an hour and a half at the gas station, so he blew it off. He said that if the police even knew he had an appointment, he'd be in deep doo-doo, so better to not say anything since he didn't make the appointment anyway.

"But I don't know what to think. I haven't spoken to him since. I'm afraid to. What if he did it? What if he murdered EW?"

"Okay, calm down. There's nothing you can do about it now. In the meantime, don't say anything to anyone about this. I'll handle it."

"What's there to handle? I just don't know what to do. Should I tell the police?"

"Uhh, excuse me? You just did! Thank you very much. In case you didn't know it, I am investigating on behalf of Fred. I know he didn't do it. It's just the chief who wants Fred to be the murderer. As usual, he looks to the conclusion before he looks at the facts leading to the conclusion."

Both Tim and his sister looked around, making sure no one was eavesdropping on them, looked at their feet, pretending they were just waiting for the parade.

"But this little tidbit puts another twist on it. It adds one little fact that we didn't have before. I talked to Parker. He said he was in the office until nine, nine thirty on Thursday, then went home. Said he even called his wife that he was coming home. Nothing about a flat tire, nothing about dinner with you. Two lies there. It is getting interesting." The more excited Tim got, the more ashen Judy looked. "Of course, you're my sister. I wouldn't expect him to tell me about you. And in his own house. Who knows who's listening? Could get him in more trouble than ever."

Tim stared at the huge circle ride with the courthouse framed behind it and mumbled, "Motive, timing, appointment—"

"What?"

"Oh, nothing. Let's go back to the family."

# CHAPTER 38

"Everybody loves a parade" is how the saying goes. As Fred looked from his office porch, the saying must be true. People lined East Park Street on both sides. Some brought chairs, some sat on the curb, some had ponchos or pieces of plastic or garbage bags to sit on.

The sunny weather immediately following miserable weather had brought out the crowds. People were everywhere. Fred's photo spot across the street from his office was still open. The rounded curb was filled with kids and adults, but the first vehicle next to the curb was a pickup truck. Fred liked that because the bumper on the pickup truck was flat; he could put his coffee mug filled with wine on the bumper rather than on the ground as he had to in previous years. It was going to be a fine parade.

The porch party, or at least what passed as the porch party, was in full progress. Only about twenty people showed for it. A little maple cocktail, a little beer, a little wine. Fred declined to provide any eats; they could buy them at the festival. That was part of the lure for the porch party: spend money at the festival. The people who did attend the porch party were very nice about Fred's situation. They ignored it or just said "Good luck." That was fine with Fred. He would love to ignore it, but it was like his shadow on a sunny day; he couldn't escape it unless he climbed into a dark area by himself. Fred was hoping he could avoid having to do that. The dark area was in his mind. That was difficult to escape.

Fred knew he was shirking many of his presidential duties, but everyone was glad that he was. His presence made everyone very uncomfortable. No one knew what to say to him. Suspected murderer. Charged with the murder. Yet, he couldn't bury himself in self-pity. He had to put on a good face. He had to confront it. He knew he was innocent. But, thanks to the chief, no one else did.

Fred got his camera with the 28–300 mm lens, tripod, and a full mug of Pinot Noir hidden in a Millstone Coffee mug. The porch party attendees would be relieved to have Fred across the street. Then they could talk about him, how pitiable the situation was, their support of him, or their suspicions. It was all great gossip, and everyone loved it.

Sixty-five degrees, sunny, what wonderful weather for a parade! The fire engine sirens were screaming. The parade was heading south on North Street. Fred loved the parade, but this year, he knew he would merely be the photographer. He wouldn't be able to address the participants jocularly, make fun of those he knew in the parade, compliment those he did not, offer a drink of wine to Dewey Locher's wife, Lois—an annual tradition for both of them. The fun would not be in this parade as in year's past.

*Just the photographs, ma'am. Just the photographs.*

Chardon Village's motorcycle unit zoomed around North Street past Fred, making sure the way was clear. He circled back and paused by Deputy Larry Hunt who was stopping traffic coming up the hill on North Hambden Street heading east. The sirens were screaming, whooping, wailing, piercing, hurting.

Slowly around the corner marched the Chardon VFW and Chardon American Legion carrying the American flag, POW flag, VFW and American Legion flags. In line, trying to keep in step, clean crisp white shirts, aging veterans in support of their nation.

## The Parade

Division I

1. Chardon VFW and Chardon American Legion
2. Scouts Post 6519
3. American Legion jeep
4. Ohio Army National Guard Humvee
5. Bicentennial Bell (The bell is set up on John Deere tractor driven by George, the county groundskeeper. Bari Stith, the county archivist, walks alongside ringing the bell.)
6. Chardon police car (without the chief of course. Mike McKenna gave a small wave to Fred.)
7. Ohio State Patrol car

8. Geauga County Sheriff (The sheriff waved to Fred.)
9. Geauga Park Ranger vehicle
10. Chardon Fire Department (three screaming, honking, whooping vehicles—shiny, clean, sparkling)
11. Hambden Fire Department
12. Munson Fire Department
13. Chesterland Fire Department
14. Bainbridge Fire Department
15. Concord Fire Department
16. Russell Fire Department
17. Burton Fire Department
18. Montville Fire Department
19. Middlefield Fire Department
20. Troy Fire Department
21. Newbury Fire Department
22. Maple Festival Board (without Fred, in two golf carts with banners stretched across the front)
23. Grand Marshal Larry Morrow (in convertible provided by Junction Auto)
24. Maple Festival Queen and her Court (seven convertibles provided by Junction Auto)
25. Senior Queen and her Court (three cars and the Geauga County Transit Bus)
26. Maple Festival Prince and Princess (car provided by Junction Auto)
27. Chardon Village Council (In two vehicles, the riders acknowledged Fred *slightly.*)
28. Diane Grendell & Tim Grendell (11th District Court of Appeals judge and state senator for Senate District)
29. Matthew Dolan (State Representative)
30. Judge Mark Hassett (Chardon municipal judge)
31. Denise Kaminski and Ed Kaminski (Clerk of Courts, Common Pleas Court, and Hambden Township trustee)
32. Mary Margaret McBride (Geauga county recorder, walking behind a little red convertible driven by Dr. John Bonk, podiatrist and boyfriend)

33. Commissioner Bill Young (Geauga Board of County Commissioners)
34. Steven Borawski (Chardon Township trustee)
35. Mary Briggs (Claridon Township trustee)
36. Chardon Chamber of Commerce
37. Chardon Square Association
38. Visiting Queens
39. Pumpkin
40. Grape
41. Watermelon
42. Etc.
43. Maple Hall of Fame Inductee Debbie Richards
44. First Place Syrup Producer
45. First Place Hobbyist Maple Syrup
46. Al Koran Shriners (The Maple Festival is the Shriners first parade of the year and they go all out to make it one of their best. They bring as many as twenty units.)
47. Boats
48. Cars
49. Cycles
50. Clowns
51. Etc.


Division II

46. Geauga Amvets Post 1968
47. Sons of the American Revolution
48. Matt Sheehe (Jeep)
49. Geauga Aeries Float (Eagles)
50. Rudy Schumer (In a 1978 Oldsmobile Toronado, the "Birdman" whistles and makes sounds.)
51. Jim Willis (1959 Oldsmobile, 98)
52. Heinen's
53. Emerald City Twirlers
54. Geauga YMCA Adventure Guides
55. Chardon Community Day Care Center Float

56. Senior Clown
57. Munson Cub Scout Pack 91
58. Boy Scout Tiger Cubs 191
59. Middlefield Girl Scouts Troop 1333
60. Cub Scouts Pack 93 Float
61. Grass Gobblers Float
62. Cub Pack 96 Float
63. Kenston Sparklettes
64. Johnathan Torre (1929 Model A pickup)
65. Tony Torre (1931 US Postal truck)
66. Mike Skolaris (1947 Studebaker truck)
67. John Balch (1964 Studebaker)
68. Huntington Bank (vehicle and walkers)
69. A Time to Dance (flatbed with dancers)
70. Sunnyside Chevrolet (two vehicles)
71. Champs (walkers)
72. Twilight Twirlers
73. Hambden Alliance Church Float
74. Geauga County Dog Shelter
75. University Hospitals Health System Geauga Regional Hospital Float
76. Hambden Elementary Float
77. Geauga Park District Float
78. Hambden Grange #2482 Float
79. Preston Superstore (new-car dealer, one vehicle)
80. Remax (real-estate company truck)
81. Irish Wolfhounds
82. Junior Fair Board Float
83. DeBord Plumbing and Heating
84. Michele Horvat (van)
85. Munson CoOp Float
86. The Ghoul (take-off of Goulardi, thirty years previously on television)
87. St. Mary School Float
88. Ronald McDonald
89. Realty One (Greg Pernus, Hummer)

90. Warthogs (motorcycle group)
91. Bathtub Race Winners
92. WKKY Radio Van
93. Carey Masci (Go Go bus)

Division III

94. American Legion Post 459 (Burton)
95. Legion Vehicles (Jeep and ammo carrier)
96. Highlanders (pipe band led by Tom Dewey)
97. Geauga County Sheriff Department Jeep
98. Big Browns Bag
99. Glenn Warner (1952 Henry J)
100. Boob Hood (1961 Chrysler Barracuda)
101. Honey Bees
102. GWRRA—Chapter D & Z
103. Dawn Hewett (1961 Chevy Impala)
104. Dewey Locher (1957 Cadillac [Dewey's wife insisted he stop so she could get a sip of wine from Fred. She motioned Fred close to give him a hug and a kiss and wish him good luck.])
105. Thompson Kart Raceway
106. Judi Faidiga
107. Waffle House
108. Mr. Formal Limo
109. PT Cruise Car Club (seventeen PT Cruisers decorated and shiny)
110. Geauga Sheriff Department Mounted Unit (four horses with riders)
111. Riders & Wranglers 4H Club (eight horses and riders)
112. Rising Sun Farm Miniature Horses (six horses, no riders)
113. Ohio Horsemen's Council (four horses)
114. Pooper Scoopers (One of the pooper-scoopers scooped up a shovel full of poop and brought it over to Fred for a photograph.)
115. Scott Nobel Tractor
116. Karen & Thom Michel (real estate brokers)
117. Geauga County Library Bookmobile
118. Joe Knautz (1961 John Deere tractor)

119. Patterson Fruit Farm
120. Chester Auto Wash
121. Scheid's Truck 'N' RV
122. Smylie One Heating
123. Eco Water/Servisoft
124. DeBord Plumbing Truck
125. Western Reserve Campers (two units)
126. Northeastern Kitchen & Bath (large van)
127. Mapledale Farms (large truck)
128. Bill Spear Tractor
129. Auburn Heating
130. DT Custom Landscapes
131. Wolcott Septic Cleaning
132. O'Reilly Equipment
133. Bob's Trucking
134. Xtreme Towing
135. The Great Geauga County Fair Band

One note about the band: The Great Geauga County Fair Band had always been the final entry in the parade ever since the Rube Band went out of existence about ten years ago. The Rube Band had been the final entry since the parade began. A new tradition commenced with the Great Geauga County Fair Band. The band was on a flatbed redesigned to accommodate them and pulled by a tractor driven by Larry Heiden and his lovely wife, Sonya. To show how small this town is, Larry's mother and aunt were members of the Fair Band, and Sonya's mother was one of the Rhodes sisters, famous for their maple syrup.

# CHAPTER 39

W*hat a great parade,* thought Fred. The weather cooperated. No one yelled bad jibes at him, just let him alone to take photographs. The sun was shining, and everything was grand for the grand marshal and the grand parade.

Following the Great Geauga County Fair Band, people closed ranks. The streets filled with people carrying chairs and blankets, people ready to get their gyro or sausage sandwich. It was time to eat.

Fred entered his office. Tom was entertaining the porch party with a baseball story. Fred changed the lens on his camera from the Tamron 28–300 mm to the Canon 18–55 mm. His next stop was Hospitality, and this was the correct lens for portraits.

The mood at Hospitality was 50 percent better than the day before. Larry Morrow, the parade marshal, had a dozen people surrounding him. He was experiencing his first maple cocktail.

Fred plopped his coat on the table by the kitchen, picked up a Styrofoam cup, and filled it with ice and maple cocktail. He didn't use the little paper cups, because they didn't hold enough liquid and the cocktail made them soft after one drink. Sunday at the festival, the parade complete, things winding down, it was time to have a healthy drink or two or three.

Fred went onto the deck overlooking the festival. The budding trees made the maples look red. Main Street was packed with thousands of people. Fred watched. Financial salvation. People spending money. Have to make up for Thursday and Friday. Spend, spend, spend.

Fred photographed his office with the courthouse in the frame; the crowd of people on Main Street, again with the courthouse, framed both horizontally and vertically; and the Assembly of God Church with the crowd of people on the square. He went inside and photographed the visiting queens and families, the festival committee members, the food, the maple cocktail punch bowl, Larry Morrow. Fred, even as the president, was invisible. The taint of anathema still clung to him like gasoline spilled on his pants—it wouldn't go away.

He meandered over to Larry Morrow and introduced himself.

"The man charged with murder?" said Larry.

"Not guilty, Your Honor."

"How can you stand it? Isn't everybody looking at you?"

"Not guilty, Your Honor."

"It's got to ruin your festival, eh?"

"You wouldn't believe. This has been a tough festival," said Fred, "but I want to thank you for volunteering to be the parade marshal. It was delightful. I am sorry you got such a difficult festival to be the marshal in, but thanks. I really appreciate it, and I hope you had a good time."

"It's the best. I'm telling you, Fred. It's the best. I love this festival. I was the parade marshal about twenty years ago, and it was the best then too. The people. The people are so friendly. And this cocktail," raising his little paper cup, "is wonderful."

"Don't drink too much," Fred cautioned. "It sneaks up on you very quickly."

"Oh don't worry about me. Three's my limit. And they are so little, like a shot glass. A paper shot glass."

"That's why I use the coffee cups." Fred raised his eight-ounce cup, shaking the ice mixture.

"Too big. I have to drive home yet."

Debbie Crow and Brenda Brcak came up on both sides of Larry, put their arms around his waist, and demanded that Fred take their photo.

Fred snapped off three quick shots and moved on. Conversation was too difficult. Everyone wanted to ask him why he did it? Did he really do it? And on and on, but were afraid to ask.

Some more photos and he would walk Main Street to get the crowd, the kids, the dogs, the families.

# CHAPTER 40

Tim Snyder was both sad and happy. He was sad about his sister being in the formative stages of an affair with a man who might be a murderer. Tim understood that relationships go bad, but it shouldn't have to happen in his family. Parker lied to him about his activities on Thursday night. What else had he lied about?

His colleague, Fred, was implicated in the murder of a judge whose murder might just have been committed by his own client.

Tim looked for McKenna; it was time for another talk. Time to exchange some information.

McKenna was directing traffic in front of Bank One. The yellow-orange barrels blocked off Main Street, so all traffic from North Hambden was directed west on Center Street. People were lined on the third floor balcony of Bank One overlooking the festival.

"Hey, Mike," said Snyder.

"Hey, Tim," responded McKenna, furiously waving a slow moving van to speed up. "Gee, these people are slow," he said, "all they do is gawk. It's a festival, been here for years, drive on, will you please?"

"Got some information to exchange," said Snyder.

"Yeah, me too. What do you have?"

"You first."

"Bullshit, you first!"

"Hey, I found you that key card," Tim reminded him.

"Hey, I found you that job in Burton."

"Oh man, going way back now, aren't you?"

"Yep, what you got?"

"Parker."

"I'm listening."

"Parker."

"I heard you. I'm still listening. What about him?"

"Thursday night. When I went to visit him yesterday, he told me he went home about nine p.m. It doesn't seem to be the case. Said he was working in the office. That wasn't the case."

"Okay, okay, what *was* the case?"

"Here's what I pieced together. Parker was having an affair with Joannie who works at Lawyer's Title. I don't know whether he met her Thursday after work, but they have been exercising their tryst in the safe room at Lawyer's Title after closing hours. He says he was working in the office. Then, at about eight o'clock, he meets my sister, Judy, at the Red Hawk Grille for dinner."

"Judy? Judy from probate court? Your *sister*? Whoowee!"

"Yeah, my sister. I'm not too happy about it, but that's what it is. Meets her for dinner. They are together for an hour, hour and a half. He tells her that he has a meeting with the judge at ten o'clock. Bingo!"

"Oh my goodness. Your sister. She's married, isn't she?"

"Yes, forget my sister for a moment. Go back to Parker. Got all the times, got the places, got it tied up."

"One more thing ties up too: we got a partial print of Parker on the FG's key card. That old girl must not have handled it too much. But how does Parker's print get on the key card unless he had it or was Dumpster-diving himself?"

"It's on the way to his office, too—just toss it in the Dumpster. Whoever would have thought it would have been found? Fortuitous."

"So Parker's our man. We have been holding off talking to him about the key card unless we got something else. The print didn't have enough points to make it hold up in court, but it is sufficient for us for probable cause. And with your information from your sister. Your sister really went out with Parker?"

"Screw you. She had a hard time telling me."

McKenna laughed. "We'll have to talk to her, you know."

"I told her that. That way, the chief can take all the credit."

"Well, everyone knows he did all the work on this case. He preserved the evidence, he found the key card, he discovered your sister. Of course he's going to take the credit. But at least, we'll feel better knowing we got the killer. It really is unbelievable. Parker! One-eyed Parker. In the land of the blind, the one-eyed man is king." McKenna yelled at a driver, "Move it! Move it!" waving his right arm in a circular motion. "After I talk to your sister, then we'll figure out how to approach Parker. This should make Fred feel a little better."

"I told him about the key card; that makes him feel a little better already."

McKenna stepped forward to a man in a Corvette with the window sliding down. A question, directions, pointing.

Snyder walked along Main Street.

# CHAPTER 41

From the Bank One balcony, Fred recognized Lieutenant McKenna talking to Tim Snyder and directing traffic at the same time. McKenna was vigorously waving his arm in a circular motion and then rapidly waving it in the direction he wanted a particular car to go. Main Street was still blocked off by orange reflective barrels and would remain so until six p.m., at which time the vendors were permitted to access the area with their vehicles to begin the unloading and packing-up process.

Fred wondered what the two were hatching. Snyder was helping to exculpate him and McKenna wasn't keen on the chief. That worked in Fred's favor. It wouldn't be a good idea for Fred to be seen speaking with McKenna in public, but talking to Snyder, who was not in uniform, might be a good idea. Find out what had happened since he told Fred about the key card.

\* \* \* \* \* \*

Fred took the awfully slow elevator with its clunking and scraping that made one fear a fall of three stories. Three people were in the elevator with him; they knew who he was, but they did not speak. Fred saw the exchange of glances. The silent verbal exchange: "We're riding the elevator with a murderer."

The passengers hastened away when the slow door finally opened. Fred caught up to Snyder by Short Court Street where all the motorcycles were parked. Main Street was packed with people—with mothers and fathers pushing baby carts, with dogs on leashes sniffing every passerby and scaring or fascinating children. The garbage cans, fifty-gallon drums of steel painted yellow, overflowed with garbage. People tossed their wrappers toward the drums, because they were full and trash lay all around them. *The Lions Club and their friends will have a tough time cleaning up tonight.*

"Fred, just the man I was looking for," said Snyder.

"Ditto. What do you have?"

"Looks like Parker. I know you represent him, but it looks like him."

"Can you tell me?" Fred asked.

"Sure, why not, I'm not on anybody's payroll for this. Especially not Chardon's."

"Bitter, bitter!"

"You're darn right. Alright, here it is. The key card that FG found, it's got a partial print of Parker's on it. It was found in the Dumpster on the way to Parker's office. Very convenient to just toss it in and have it get lost with the rest of the garbage. I had talked to Parker yesterday—he said he worked late, to about nine or nine thirty on Thursday; then he went home. Well, it so happens that wasn't quite the case. Seems he went out to dinner at the Red Hawk Grille with my sister, Judy."

"Judy, probate?"

"Yep. I'm not too happy about it. Anyway, he lied to me. And according to Judy, he had an appointment with EW that night. Thursday night, after nine thirty, when he left the Red Hawk Grille. He even asked Judy not to say anything about their meeting that night. Judy wasn't comfortable with that since she knew he had an appointment with EW."

"So that's it. Once McKenna coordinates with the chief, they talk to Judy to confirm the story; it's probably indictment time for Parker. Sorry, Fred. Actually, it's good and bad for you."

The descending sun cast a shadow over Fred and Snyder. They edged into the sunlight.

# CHAPTER 42

Six p.m. and the barriers at the end of Main Street were moved to allow the vendors to drive their vehicles to their trailers or at the end of the tent to begin moving their wares from the tent to their vehicles. Double-parked, triple-parked, odd angles, no angles. Dollies piled with boxes rolled from the tent. The quicker the vendor could transfer the goods to his vehicle, the quicker he could get out of there. The scene was one of organized pandemonium.

At the East Park Street side of the tent, only one lane was open. Vendors clogged the lane closest to the park. The street had been reopened to traffic after the parade, but attempting to traverse it was hopeless. Horns honked, arms gesticulated, voices shouted, but traffic moved very slowly. Vendors cruised, looking for a spot to stop to load their vehicles. Did the location where they stopped impede traffic? "Maybe, who cares, I got to get my stuff out of there. I'm not driving around the square again. They can wait, I can't. Why doesn't the Maple Festival committee make it so we can get our stuff and get out of here?"

Fred was feeling fine. He was almost off the hook. No one but he and Tim Snyder knew it, but the fact that he knew it gave him such a feeling of relief that he was awash with a complacency and feeling of well-being that he hadn't experienced for three days. He could endure the stares, frowns, and shunning for another day or week or month, so long as he knew he would be out of the legal pickle his improvident statement had caused. Ahh, life was good—sometimes.

He took photographs of vendors wheeling their wares to their vehicles, young children carrying boxes for their parents to their cars, and vehicles parked at absurd angles causing traffic flow to dwindle to a trickle. The festival was winding down. Teenagers roamed the grounds in groups. The festival was a hustle-bustle of frenetic unloading and loading, transferring, dollying, carrying, shouting, moving, and happy quitting. The vendors were pleased to get in two days of great weather after the tent fiasco. They still made a profit. They still signed a contract for next year. As risky as the Maple Festival was for weather, when the weather was good, the profits were high. The first festival of the year brought out the best and the worst of the weather, the people, and this year, the crimes.

The rides had stopped operating. The noise level dropped hundreds of decibels and was produced by cars and vans and trucks and people. No screeching metal, no booming music, or what passed for music; the only irritant was the continuing noise from the generator. It would run until the carnies no longer needed power.

# CHAPTER 43

Once again ensconced in his office, Fred dialed the number for Joe Parker. Six rings later, Joe picked up.

"Joe, Fred Newman here."

"Hey, Fred, how are you doing?"

"Okay, okay, I survived the weekend. But I think we got a little problem. Not something I can talk to you over the phone about, but I think we need to meet and talk in person. Like maybe tomorrow morning, eight o'clock? That okay with you?"

"What gives?"

"I've been hearing some things about you. Doesn't sound good, Joe. I don't want you talking to anyone. You understand? Anyone. Things are closing in, Joe. We need to figure out the next *several* legal steps. I mean it, Joe: speak to no one. You already spoke to Tim Snyder and that got you into some hot water, some contradictions. Let's keep mum, okay?"

"Yeah, guess so. Eight, huh?"

"Eight o'clock."

"Alright." The despondency in Joe's voice was palpable.

# CHAPTER 44

At 7:30 Monday morning, Fred was in a good mood. He would be cleared of this legal morass hanging over his head. The sun was shining brightly as he pulled into the parking lot at his office from the North Hambden Street drive. With his camera, he walked the park. All the rides save one had been removed; all the trailers, except those in the middle of the park, had been removed.

Mike Tvergyak and crew were noisily disassembling the interior structure in the big tent. Not much trash littered the ground—the Lions Club had done a wonderful cleanup job. Fred shot photos. One huge rut obviously caused by the removal of a ride would have to be dealt with. Under the contract with J&J Amusements, the festival board was entitled to fifty dollars for each rut so created. It was never enforced, but it was in the contract. With the wet ground from the snow, ruts were to be expected in the haste of the ride operators to vacate the premises.

Traffic on Main Street was back to normal, backed up. Cones were placed in front of the grandstand so the tent company would have access to remove the tent later on in the day. Mike's crew would switch to the grandstand for disassembly after the big tent.

After the grandstand, the sugar house would be next in line for teardown. The structure, fully apart, was stored at the Cleveland Electric Illuminating Company. They graciously permitted storage without cost. Fred shot photos of every aspect of the park, the curb areas where the village had plowed snow over the winter and left a residue of black gravel, the ruts, the packed straw into the grass areas, the clean streets, everything.

Fred meandered toward his office and the meeting with Joe Parker.

# CHAPTER 45

Fred wasn't looking forward to this meeting with Joe. He was going to have to get off this case, return the retainer. He did not like to return retainers. It was money in the bank, and he had to take it out and give it back. Mentally, it was already spent. Physically, the Supreme Court disallowed any expenditure of it until the fee was earned. Only quandaries presented themselves.

Joe was sitting in the reception area as Fred entered.

"Come in, Joe," Fred beckoned, opening the door immediately to his left. He hung his jacket on the hook behind the door.

"Coffee?"

"Sure, just a little cream, please."

Fred went out the door to the rear of the office into the paralegal's office, who was not in today, to the kitchen area. When the parsonage was built in 1837, the paralegal's office was the kitchen. The present kitchen was a cupboard area. Fred put a little powdered Cremora into one cup and poured coffee into two cups. He picked up the two cups and went to the secretarial area.

"No interruptions, please."

"Okay, sir."

Fred placed the two cups on the table, shut the door to the reception area and the door to the paralegal's office and sat down.

"Joe, we've got a problem. A real big problem."

Joe nodded his head slowly, gritted his teeth so his lips parted slightly showing the movement. His jawbones moved slowly. "Okay. Let's have it." He set his mug down on his side of Fred's desk and leans back in his chair.

"Tim Snyder's been looking into this murder. The chief wants me to be guilty of it. We both know that isn't the case, but the chief has blinders on because he hates my guts. It appears that FG—you know her, the fat girl who goes all over town, has the episodes of screaming and stuff. Crazy lady. She went Dumpster-diving on Thursday night about eleven o'clock. Got herself three-quarters of an elephant ear and a law-library card. She put the card in her purse. She got arrested Saturday night at the log cabin for creating a scene. Snyder spotted the key card, brought it to the attention of Lieutenant McKenna, who promptly had it examined for fingerprints.

Joe tensed, sat up straighter, and opened his mouth to speak.

Fred raised his palm to stop him. "No, don't say anything yet; let me finish. They got a partial print on the key card. Your print. Might not be sufficient enough for forensic purposes—you know, all the points that make a print admissible—but probably sufficient for an indictment."

Joe sat frozen, barely breathing, while his coffee steamed into the air.

Fred continued, "Snyder puts two and two together. I was in the courthouse law library at the time that FG found the key card, so that pretty much eliminates me as the suspect. I can't be at two places at one time and the police station would have had a record if I had kept the door open for any considerable period of time so as to run out with the card, throw it in the Dumpster, and then run back. It didn't happen. Something else did."

Fred tested his coffee. Cool enough to drink. He took a sip as Joe looked at him, waiting. "Thursday night. You told Snyder when he talked to you …" Fred hesitated again, looked sternly at Joe, "How many damn times do I have to tell clients not to talk to the cops? You can't out-clever them. But here you are, a defense attorney yourself, and you go ahead and talk to the cops. A private cop, but nonetheless a cop. So you tell Snyder that you went home about nine o'clock from the office after working late."

Fred paused. "Duh! You were on a date, a dinner date with Snyder's sister? Oh, give me a break. Did you think she wouldn't talk to him? Did you think she wouldn't tell him that you asked her not to tell him about the date? Alarm bells? Siren? What more did you need to tell her that inculpated you?"

Joe put his head into his hands. Eager to say something.

Fred put his hands up again. "Not yet. Give me a minute or two more." Fred inhaled deeply, already exhausted, getting angry, frustrated, and at the same time relieved. Joe's guilt was Fred's innocence. Fred felt the tear of the obligation to the client versus the obligation to himself. He took another drink of his coffee. "They found your fingerprints in several more places in the courthouse. Probably understandable. They have your history with EW. Snyder went through the court cases with the clerk of court's help. Not hard to find them, you know! Losses in front of EW. The campaign against EW. Everyone knew EW had a bad case against you."

Fred paused almost a full minute. He pressed his hands together in a praying motion, brought the fingertips to his mouth, compressed his lips, and rocked his head slightly forward and back. "You're in deep shit, Joe. They are going to hang your balls. Do you want to say something now?"

"Yeah, I guess it's about time I got this stuff off my chest. Attorney-client privilege and all that crap. I knew I screwed up when I asked Judy to say nothing about Thursday night, but what could I do? She knew I was going to meet EW after I left her. It was going to come out one way or the other. I think I knew that."

Joe inhaled deeply, put his hands firmly on the arms of the chair, crossed his legs, and began. "It started a long time ago. It was in the ninth grade at Cardinal High School. Robert Kuhmer and I were best friends. Robert—you didn't know him—was EW's brother. We did everything together."

Joe glanced at Fred and then looked out the window. He began to speak in a monotone, staring out the window. "Life has not been fair to me. I was big enough to play football but prevented from doing so because I was blind in one eye. And it wasn't my fault. That damned Robert Kuhmer put my eye out with a stick back in the ninth grade. I think he did it on purpose. We were just messing around in his basement, watching TV, wrestling, and he gets pissed off, grabs the stick, and shoves it in my face! Man, we were best friends, why did he do that? My eye popped out and was pierced. No way the doctors could fix it. I was rushed to Geauga Hospital, then to Metro in Cleveland. In the hospital for seventeen days. I couldn't believe it. Blind in one eye in the ninth grade. What the hell was that going to do for me to play any sports? I couldn't. Couldn't play football, couldn't play basketball, couldn't play baseball. And I was good at all of them."

Joe compressed his lips, breathed rapidly and deeply through his nose, dilating his nostrils, getting angry just remembering it all. "At first Robert was apologetic. I'm not sure I believed him. It sounded hollow. Then he wouldn't even come around anymore. Didn't want to hang around a 'one-eye.' That glass eye they gave me seemed to go all over the place. I could see people trying to focus on me, but my eye was looking elsewhere and not seeing anything. They were uncomfortable, and I was uncomfortable. I could see them avoiding my eye. Then Robert started saying bad things about me. I ask why? He was the one who did it. It just wasn't fair. My life was in the pits."

He noticed his coffee then, not steaming anymore in front of him. Took a sip of it. Still warm enough. "Then when we were seniors, he beat me for class president. I was the better debater. I was a fantastic debater. Won third place in state. Can't be much better than that. But those people in Cardinal High School, so juvenile. Didn't want a *one-eyed* president. Robert capitalized on that one, didn't he? Not for long though," Parker chuckled, staring into the past.

"He won the presidency, two to one. I overheard him telling some students: 'You know that in the land of the blind, the one-eyed man is king. But folks, we aren't in the land of the blind. You don't want a one-eyed president. We will be the laughingstock of all the Geauga County high schools.' Boy, did that piss me off. He makes me blind, then he says that because of what he did, I shouldn't be class president. Well, I swore he'd get his someday." Suddenly he looked up, his gaze meeting Fred's.

"And that day came. And a good day it was. Two weeks before college started, I saw him at Swine Creek Park. I was much bigger than him by then. I had a baseball bat in the car and got it. Thought I'd rough him up a little. Then I followed him down the trail for about half a mile. It was around the big pond, then around the big field, but the field was high with grass and wildflowers. Those orange things, hawkweed or something, and Queen Anne's lace stuff. Pretty but useless flowers. Yeah, something you might like, Fred. Good things to photograph."

Fred wanted to shrug, grimace, something, but he kept his face blank.

"So, anyway, I caught up to him, said, 'Hey, Robert, long time no see.' He looked at me funny. Like why was I here, and what was that baseball bat doing in my hand? He was suspicious, that was for sure. But he didn't know what to do, so he answered. 'Hey, Joe, yeah, long time no see.'

"I knew I was going to do something, just didn't know what. Whack him with the bat a time or two to let him know he couldn't put my eye out and get away with it. I said, 'I've been meaning to have a talk with you. You said some real nasty things about me when we were running for president. Why? What the fuck did I ever do to you?'

"His response caught me completely off guard. I thought he might be somewhat apologetic, but no. He says 'Hey, no one wants a one-eyed president!' And he said it in a very nasty tone. I lost it. I swung the bat right then and there. He saw it coming and blocked it with his arm, but I heard his arm break. Oh, that was a sweet sound. He was stunned. And I was so angry. Anger that I had held in for three years. I knew he was in pain, and I didn't care. He couldn't move, but I could. He didn't say a thing. Maybe a whimper or two. Or maybe I wasn't listening. Then I swung it again, this time at his head. He couldn't lift the arm this time, it was broken. I caught him turning away, but it smashed right across his nose and eyes. He turned the wrong way. It was a hard swing, knocked his block off, I did. He collapsed. I could hear him gurgling. I just stood there. I was pumped. Adrenaline was coursing through me. Then I looked around, nothing. Shit, was he still alive? I moved closer. He wasn't. No breathing, just some leaking from his nose and mouth. His eyeball sockets were smashed. I had taken a good swing. Good, the SOB. deserved it. Look what he did to me. And I wasn't sorry then."

Joe wanted to take a slug of his coffee, now cold, but his hands were shaking and he couldn't navigate it. He set it back down on Fred's desk instead.

"But hell, it was three o'clock in the afternoon. What do I do now? How do I get rid of him? Just leave him there? I was panicking. So I dragged him into the weeds about forty feet and laid him down. I was so pumped up, it was like nothing. I had killed him! The SOB. Then I took my bearings, so I figure, I'll get the body later. I left the baseball bat with the body. A pretty stupid move when I think about it now. My prints all over the bat, and I leave it with the body. Duh? Then it hit me. Holy shit, I killed somebody!"

Fred shifted in his seat, feeling a little sick to his stomach, but Joe didn't seem to notice and just kept talking, his one eye intense, wild, looking into what Fred figured was his own dark hole.

"That passed real quickly. I thought that, well, if anybody deserved it, he did. And, I was glad. He had made my life miserable. And now I had made his life miserable. Or as the case was, terminal. I looked around. No one around, no one saw me. I hotfooted it out of there. Then I went looking for a place to put him. What was I going to do with the body? I drove down to Parkman, saw the cemetery on 168 and said, 'Hey, bury the body where it is obvious. So obvious, no one will find it.' I drove through the cemetery. There was a fresh grave, I could see it. I got out and walked around as if I was a spectator looking for my grandfather or something. There it was. Someone was already buried there. A fresh grave. They bury them pretty deep. So maybe I could dig down and put Robert's body right on top of the casket. No one would ever look there for him. A fresh grave already used would not be dug up. Fantastic. Now, I just had to get him from Swine Creek to the graveyard.

"That night I got some industrial garbage bags and gloves. Swine Creek closes at eleven p.m., so I had time, so long as no one saw me. At nine, I went out there. Put the bags and gloves in a small backpack. Kept a watch out for rangers. 'Just on an evening hike in the woods.' Got a small flashlight. I wasn't planning on using it too much, because it might cause attention. I hiked out to the body; I finally found it. I had to turn on the flashlight to find where I had tramped down the weeds. It was gruesome shoving the bags over the body. He was already stiff. And heavy. Like a deer road-kill. I put him in a four-bag thickness. I didn't want him leaking or something. I put gloves on so there would be no fingerprints. He bent somewhat after I put him on my shoulder, but right then I knew what rigor mortis was. The body really gets hard and stiff." Joe was standing, almost acting it out. Fred was transfixed.

"I looked around. There were still two cars in the parking lot, but it was dark where I parked and I didn't see anyone, so I put him in the back of my pickup truck. I wiped the bat with the gloves to remove any fingerprints and drove to Parkman. I parked at a driveway two up from the cemetery. I didn't want to park at the cemetery; it would be too suspicious. But where I parked, there was no house and the truck was hidden off the road.

"But first, I stopped at the cemetery. No one was around, so I dropped off the body and the shovel. The bags were black, so no one could see them.

I put him behind a tree. Then I went and parked the car, came back and started to re-dig the new grave. I was so nervous. I kept looking around. It was noisy, too. I thought everyone in the world could hear me digging and throwing the dirt. I kept my gloves on in case I had to scoot out of there quickly. I didn't want any fingerprints around. It took me an hour to dig down to the cement thing, the vault that holds the casket. I'm glad I didn't have to touch the casket itself. Man, it was grueling, I was working fast. I kept thinking of the Edgar Allan Poe story where the lady was buried alive. I kept waiting for a sound from the grave.

"Finally, I dumped the body on the cement vault. I still dream about that. The sound of that body hitting the vault. Thump. It keeps coming back to me. I don't know why I would think of that, but that's the one thing that keeps coming back to me. I break out in sweats in the middle of the day. Just like I am right now."

Joe was staring out the window and sweating profusely. He wiped his forehead with a handkerchief. The whole picture made Fred feel nauseated. *This is the guy who was going to let me take the rap.*

"Then I piled all the dirt back in. I'm glad the dirt was already broken up. I don't think I could have dug through that clay in an entire night. Then I left. I threw the shovel into a ditch coming into Burton. I didn't want any comparison of the dirt on the shovel. I washed my shoes when I got home and threw the gloves out. All my clothes I put into the washing machine.

"I was exhausted. But I had done it. I got even with Robert for what he did to my eye. He deserved it. I felt bad, but not too bad. Life hadn't been easy with only one eye. It bothered me for a while. I had actually killed someone! The cops came and talked to me the day before I went to college at Kent about Robert being missing. All I said was that he made me blind, and we were not friends after that. I said I hadn't done anything with Robert since the ninth grade. I think the one deputy sheriff didn't believe me, but they couldn't connect me with anything. The perfect crime. Almost. Except I still have dreams about it.

"I didn't go to any of the memorial services they had for Robert at Christmastime. By then, they figured foul play had done something to him. I drove by the Parkman Cemetery and the grave was all covered with grass. I wasn't even sure which grave it was anymore—they all looked the same." Joe paused. Took a sip of his cold coffee. Looked across the desk at Fred. "And that's what started it with Earl William." He pronounced the name almost with a sneer, hateful, slow, deliberate, like it made him sick to think of it.

"You actually killed two people from the same family," Fred said, more as a statement than a question. "Jesus!"

"Yeah. Bizarre, isn't it? I mean really, bizarre." Joe wiped the sweat from his face, took off his sport coat, and laid it on the adjoining chair.

"So then what?"

"So then I went to college. Still only had one eye. Couldn't play football, basketball, or any ball sports. I was a debater. The master debater! I was good. Then to law school at Case Western Reserve University, then out here to practice. Been in the business a long time. I've been a good lawyer. Got some real scumbags off some real serious charges. Practice went along well. Until EW came along."

"Want to tell me about that?"

"Yeah, I guess so. You're my attorney. Might as well hear it all. It's all confidential. I got a job in Chardon at the Bostwick firm right out of law school. They were old-timers then. I stayed with them for four years until I had enough experience under my belt and went out on my own. Been on my own ever since.

"I ran into Earl William Kuhmer a number of times professionally. He was the younger brother of Robert. I never had much contact with him when we were growing up—he was three years younger than we were. But he must have known his brother and I had fallen out, because our relationship was cordial, professional but not friendly.

"We had about six or seven cases against each other during the years. No big deal about them. We argued our positions, tried one case; he lost. He mostly worked for the prosecutor's office in zoning, so I didn't have that much contact with him. Professionally, we were cordial, that's all I can say. Mutual tolerance.

"Then when the position of judge opened up with the retirement of Judge Stevens, things got dicey. Our relationship, or whatever relationship we had, turned sour. He did and said the same things his brother Robert did and said in the class president election! I couldn't believe it. He focused on my eye. Said nasty things about me professionally. Unfortunately, he was supported by the Republican Party. What that means in Geauga County is an 80 percent chance of winning. And he did win, but not by much. People told me what he was saying. That I couldn't do the research because I only had one eye. And that he actually repeated, 'In the land of the blind, the one-eyed man is king. But we aren't in the land of the blind, are we?' Aside from being totally false, it was just mean and nasty. It was a bitter campaign on both sides. EW was just a mean and nasty guy.

"Then, after he gets on the bench, we're not very cordial anymore, just professional. I make my case to him, and he rejects it. I have to ask for a jury trial anymore on every case, just in case it gets in front of him. I lost every debatable-evidence point. If there is any reason to deny a motion, he denies it. I cannot represent my clients effectively in front of him. *He* is still bitter about the campaign! Why? I had dared to run against him. Or who knows, maybe he suspected me in his brother's disappearance. All I know was he was going to wreak his vengeance on me.

"Luckily, no one knew this situation. A couple of attorneys I opposed were shocked at some of his rulings against me, but they just think it is because of their stellar performances and persuasive attitudes. That's all bullshit. He is just punishing *me*. He has a vendetta against *me. Personally.* I cost him money, and now it's going to cost me money. I wondered if I would ever win another case again in his court. Well, not now, because he is dead! And do you know what? I am glad he is dead. As terrible as that sounds, it's true.

"I hated losing cases I shouldn't have lost. He was impacting my livelihood. Then, when I had that trial last August where you represented me and we lost, I couldn't believe it. How can you lose an easement case? That's when you became aware of Earl's hostility toward me. Even you couldn't believe it. The Amishman was obviously lying about the easement, but Earl William found in his favor anyway. Now, if I want to exercise the easement, I have to put a road in alongside the creek. It will flood annually. It will cost a fortune. And it is all because of Earl William's meanness. That SOB cut into my pocket personally and professionally. Bad enough I lose cases in which I represent clients; it is altogether something else for me to lose my own case when I shouldn't have.

"Then he rules against me on a motion for summary judgment in a slip-and-fall case. Case dismissed. It was a good case. Now I have to go to the court of appeals to get him reversed, then come back down and redo the case. That will cost me a lot of time and money. I just wanted him to treat me fairly, like he is supposed to do as a judge. Not be a mean prick because of an election, and his brother, about which he knew nothing.

"At the last pretrial I had with him on Thursday, I suggested maybe we talk about our personal issues. It was *his* idea to meet late in the evening. He said he had some research to do anyway, he would meet me at the courthouse at ten p.m. Man, that was weird, pretty late to have a meeting at the courthouse, but what was I going to do? I had to meet with him. We had to hash this problem out. Ten at night—I think he was again punishing me. Make sure it was inconvenient for me. Well, at least no one would hear us talking. Maybe we can clear the air. I can't go on practicing like this, losing every case. It wasn't fair. We're either going to make up or be enemies forever. And losing my own case, even with you representing me, what a surprise that was. I guess his hatred of me surpasses his duty of fairness and attorney competence. You had the law on your side and the facts, and I lost because of Earl William. Fucking Earl William.

"Well, that night was interesting. I was as nervous as a two-peckered billy goat. My wife—you know Miriam—she asked where I was going. Luckily, I didn't tell her I was meeting the judge. I didn't tell anyone except Judy. I met her for dinner at the Red Hawk Grille up in Concord. I told her I had to stop at the office for some documents. That I had to take to take them to Trumbull County in the morning—there was no reason to go to the office in the morning with Maple Festival madness going on and try to get a parking spot, so I'd get the documents tonight, bring them home, and go to Trumbull in the morning. Easy as pie. Unfortunately, I also told her that I had an appointment with Earl William.

"I was somewhat cheating on Miriam. I had been seeing Judy from probate court, Tim Snyder's sister. We had never got past the dating stage, but she had marital problems and I had marital problems. We seemed to click. Got along nicely. I told her I had a meeting with the judge; she was the only one who knew. I hoped she liked me enough to say nothing at this point. What am I going to do about that? Deny that it occurred? Just say it was cancelled, never happened?"

"And what about Joannie?" interrupted Fred.

Joe looked at him quizzically and then smiled. "Oh my, you know about that, too, huh? Yeah, she and I were an item. What a number she is! That was just sex between us. We got along, but neither of us ever wanted any meaningful relationship. Just sex. After office hours, we'd go into that safe in Lawyer's Title and have a grand time. Man, is she energetic, and such nice skin."

*This guy,* thought Fred, starting to get impatient. He interrupted. "What about Thursday night, though?"

"Yeah, I met her before I went to Red Hawk to meet Judy. We spent about an hour at Lawyer's Title. Worked up a good appetite."

"Okay, so then what?"

"Judy and I had a nice, quiet dinner. Things were moving along for us. We were compatible. We had the same problems. We tried to make it a point to not talk about our domestic issues even though they were the same. My wife was distant, doing other things in life, not really interested in me or our family. Judy had the same issues; her husband was having an affair somewhere and was never home. She needed a companion, and I was there. But we never got past having dinner together."

"She did you in, you know?" Fred said nonchalantly.

"Yeah, what are you going to do? The weakest link. I never thought anything was going to happen at EW's chambers. This wasn't premeditated! Otherwise I wouldn't have said anything—"

"Okay, moving along."

"So I drove back to Chardon, parked behind my office, walked over to the basement of the courthouse. I had my key card out for the library door, and the judge was right in front of me. I didn't even need to use my card. As you know, the card reader identifies the person entering the courthouse after hours, so the police know exactly who is in there. The closed-circuit TV isn't working at night and isn't hooked up to the Chardon police station, but the entrance codes are. So when the judge appeared at the back entrance, I just went in with him. We used his card. Fortuitous. Except for what I had told Judy.

"No one was in the law library when we got there, but when I left, the lights were on and the doors were open; someone was in there. But I slipped out without them seeing me. Lucky for me. So Earl William passes his card over the reader to the first floor, and we go up the stairs to the second floor.

Never had to use my card. First thing he says, 'Well, what do you want to talk about?' As if he didn't know. As if things between us were as normal as ever. I said, 'Judge, you and I seem to be having a problem. At least from my point of view. Ever since the election, I have not won a single case in your courtroom.' He said: 'Maybe your cases aren't worth a shit!' He said it so … acerbically. As if it were *true*, even though it wasn't. So I said, 'Judge, maybe one or two of them, but all of them?' And I'm talking in a normal tone, almost apologetically, placating really. I mean, if we're going to get along, nastiness wouldn't do, but he was being nasty. So I continued, 'And that last one, where I was the plaintiff on the easement case: I never should have lost that case. Fred did a wonderful job, and I still lost.'

"He said, 'I didn't believe your testimony. In fact, I can't believe anything you say. Ever.' And then there was quiet. I was stunned. He can't believe anything I say. More like he *won't* believe anything I say. He was being downright mean. He didn't want to heal any rift. He was going to maintain this attitude toward me forever. This discussion was going nowhere. Absolutely nowhere. 'What do you mean?' I said. He says, 'I can't believe anything you say. I think you are a liar. I think you had something to do with Robert's disappearance. That's what I think.'

"*Oh shit*, I thought. *This is worse than I even imagined.* He was right, but I wasn't going to admit it to him. Now what the hell was I to do? He held the grudge. There was no way I was going to shake him from that.

"'You're serious, aren't you?' I asked. I was incredulous. He says, 'You bet. And what's more, Parker, you'd better go practice somewhere else, because you're never going to win a single case in my court for the rest of your life. I hate your fucking guts. It's the only way I can avenge Robert's life. What did you do with him?' He was shouting by now! "I didn't know *what* to say. He edged closer to me. His rage was palpable. His face red, flushed with anger or hatred. And I was angry. He was in my face. My entire life, screwed by this family. All because his brother put my eye out for no reason. *And I have to live with this?* I stood up. I was dizzy. I was becoming more enraged. My whole life in the Dumpster because of this man. Okay, he won the election, not necessarily fair and square, but he won. I can deal with that. But to harbor this hate against me. To ruin my life, totally. It was unacceptable.

275

"I was taller than EW. I stood up fully, and he's right there in my face. Spittle on his lips. I said, as evenly as I could. 'You fucking prick.' We stared at each other for a minute. The rage building. The anger festered to boiling. I pushed him. He did not expect that. A physical confrontation. He wasn't prepared for a physical confrontation. He thought his position as judge made him immune to real human reactions. He was sacrosanct. So superior. Well, not to me. The SOB, I pushed him again.

"He says, 'Keep your filthy hands off me, Parker. I'll have you jailed tonight if you touch me one more time.'

"I was pissed. Then I saw the little Louisville Slugger baseball bat. *How ironic,* I thought. *Another baseball bat. A family of baseball bats.* The judge picked up his letter opener. He was going to defend himself. He crouched slightly. I could see he was scared, but game. He was the judge, he had control of the court, and I was *in* the court. 'Get out, Parker, and don't you ever come back ever. I'll have you disbarred, you son of a bitch.'

"I picked up the bat. I said, 'Disbarred my ass. You're just a mean fat prick.' I swung the bat one-handed. It was a small bat. One of those samples they hand out at Friday night games at the Indians' Jacobs Field. Just handy enough to be a club. He put his left arm up, just like his brother did. I didn't hear a crack this time, but I knew it hurt. He's no athlete this guy. He can't handle it. He backed up toward the telephone. Then he lunged for it. I whacked him a hard one on the shoulder from the back. He fell against the desk. The phone went sprawling onto the floor. Then he pleaded, 'Don't!' he cried, 'please don't!' I hit the front of his head very hard. I heard the bonk. He collapsed on the floor. I was angry, pumped, adrenaline flowing. I was so pissed off. I had energy overflowing. I hit him again for good measure.

"Then I watched him. He was still breathing. What the hell am I going to do now? Holy shit. Two brothers with baseball bats. Man, I got to get out of here. I'll get disbarred for this for sure. And for a moment, I was thinking logically. Here I have just hit a judge with a baseball bat. A judge who threatened to have me disbarred. He will certainly follow through on his threat. I knew what had to be done, but I had to think about it for a minute or two: *I can't let him live. It is him or me in this life. If he lives, he is going to ruin my life. If I live, I am going to ruin his life. I have absolutely no leverage to ruin his life if he lives, but he has all the leverage in the world*

276

*to ruin my life if he lives.* The answer was there; it was obvious, and it was inescapable. *Think. What to do now."*

Parker was in a trance. Fred could see how pumped he was. It was like a black rage, and Fred saw his anger, the energy, the frustration. All of it.

"First of all, what to do with him? I'll show him. Then I thought, *Okay, EW, buddy, good honest judge, talk to me dirty, I'll put you where you belong, in the dirty toilet.* So I dragged his fat ass down the hall, up the three stairs to the bathroom at the north end of the second floor. I opened the bathroom door, lifted the toilet seat, and propped his body so his head hung in the toilet. He was praying to the porcelain goddess. Yes, we have all been there, throwing up usually. This is a different kind of praying. He was heavy to drag, but I had so much energy, no problem.

"I wrapped his arms around the bowl. His head was immersed in the water. I held his head in the water for two minutes. He stopped breathing. No convulsions at all. I was surprised at that.

"Then I thought, *now what? The baseball bat. Yeah, that'll do it.* He was going to shove it up my ass for the rest of my life. I'll shove it up his ass for the end of his life. I had a difficult time undoing his belt and pulling his pants down. It felt dirty doing this. But my anger flowed. I was still so damn angry. I was pissed off to the max. I don't ever remember being this angry in my life. I took some tissue and wiped the bat clean of my fingerprints and every other surface I think I touched in the bathroom. Then I took the small end of the bat and pushed it up his ass. It was difficult. I had to kick it to get it in. There wasn't much room in the bathroom to get an angle to kick it properly. But in it went. I shoved it in about halfway up the bat. 'There, you son of a bitch. Shove that up your ass!'

"Now I had to think. I had to get out of here. I can't use my card to get out, I need his admittance card. I looked for his wallet. Here he was perched over the toilet and here I am right behind him fishing in his pockets for his wallet. What a perverse picture. Of course, the murder itself was perverse, wasn't it? I got his wallet. I touched it, so I would have to take it so there would be no fingerprints available to the cops. I got the key card, put the wallet in my pocket, and retraced my steps to his chambers.

"I used the card to exit the first floor to the basement. The lights were on in the law library. *Oh shit, I can't let anyone see me.* It was 10:45 p.m. I was there a long time. Didn't seem that long. I slowly stepped by the lighted door to the law library. I saw a figure with a pile of books spread out before him. It was you, Fred. I thought, *What the hell's he doing here on a Thursday night?* He's president of the Maple Festival. How does he have time to do legal work during this week? Must have a hearing or something. I stepped cautiously past. You didn't see me. Sorry, Fred, I caused you a world of shit.

"So, I quickly walked by Susan Proboski's office, the law librarian, to the exit. Used Earl William's dead key card."

Joe chuckled. "It's not like a legal power of attorney that expires upon death as a matter of law; the key card continues to work until notification. It clicked green. I went out the door. The door made a noise, no doubt about it, but I was out of there. Now I hoped I had erased all of my fingerprints from any surface I touched in chambers or in the bathroom.

"I thought about you, Fred. I thought that Fred's going to have a real problem over this. His key card will show he was here at the same time as the judge. Oh man, I was fortunate to come in with Earl William. I thought, and sorry to say this. Fred, I thought, *Good luck. Fred. Don't call on me to represent you. I think I might have a slight conflict of interest.* Funny, huh?"

"Yeah, Joe, that's real funny."

"Hey, Fred, what the fuck. In for a penny, in for a pound. Imagine, I had killed two brothers, and both with baseball bats. And the weird thing was I didn't feel like a murderer. I felt like an avenger. They both did me wrong. Terrible wrongs. First my eye, then to gloat over it and hold it over me as a reason not to elect me class president? Then Earl William doing the same thing? Then taking it out on me on all the cases I was losing. Then to make me lose the easement case with one of the best lawyers around representing me? Yeah, Fred, even though I knew I was putting you in the shit, I still think you're one of the best attorneys around. At least in this town. But talk about abusing your judicial position! He abused it! Abuse it and lose it. He lost it. I just don't feel sorry about it. EW deserved it, is all I can say."

"So what now, Joe? They have your number. Judy told Tim, her brother, that you were going to see EW. FG found the key card, and it has one of your prints on it. By the way, what did you do with the wallet?"

"I threw it in the Dumpster along with the key card. Guess FG didn't find it. Or, if she did, she took the money and threw the rest away. I didn't even go through the wallet. Why?"

"Maybe as a souvenir," said Fred sarcastically.

Joe laughed. "Yeah, trouble is, someone would have found it eventually. Bad stroke of luck with FG digging into the Dumpster. God, that's disgusting."

"Joe, back up a second." Fred paused. "Don't you think, and keep an open mind for a second, that what you did with the baseball bat was disgusting?"

Joe hesitated and then said. "Yeah, you're right. It is. It's downright brutal and nasty. And that's just what it was. Brutal and nasty. Man, was I in a rage! I was so angry. I bet I could have lifted ten EWs. Just thinking about it makes me angry."

They sat there for a minute in silence. Fred studying Joe. Joe looking at his hands.

"So what now?" asked Fred. "I mean, what do you plan on doing now? It sounds like they have you cold with the fingerprint on the key card. I am still your attorney; what do you want me to do now? Maybe voluntary manslaughter. They might charge you with a death specification, but I don't think they would be successful. Regardless, it looks like twenty-five years in jail. You'll be eighty-five before you get out."

"What would you do, Fred?" Joe wondered.

"Man, I'd bolt. Or shoot myself. I sure wouldn't want to sit in prison for twenty-five years. What kind of life is that? We see so many movies of what happens in prison, you know they are true. You get beat up and beat down. You get raped, orally and anally. You get diseases. And you have to get along with all that stuff. No. I don't think I'd want to do that. Now I sure as hell am not telling you to bolt, but you asked what I would do."

Fred leaned back in his executive chair. Finished his coffee without taking his eyes off his colleague and friend and betrayer. "You know, Joe, as soon as they arrest you, they won't give you bail. Or it will be so high, you won't be able to afford it. You'll sit in jail until the trial—if there is one—unless we can plead to something less. Then you'll sit in prison until parole time. If you last long enough without dying of some disease or hopelessness."

Joe sat. Finally waking up to reality. "Fuck."

279

# CHAPTER 46

A noise in the lobby caused Fred and Joe to exchange glances. A booming voice, obviously that of the chief of police, announced to the secretary that he was here to arrest Joseph Parker, where was he? The response was inaudible.

Fred rose, opened the back door to his office to exit and walk around to the front where the secretaries worked. At the same time, the front door swung fully open, slamming into a chair against the wall with a huge bang. Fred turned around in the doorway to see Joe standing, his back to Fred and his hand in his pocket, the chief filling the front doorway. Another bang and a bullet ripped through Joe's pocket right into the chief's stomach.

Immediately behind the chief in the doorway was Tim Snyder, pulling his pistol. The chief was down holding his stomach, lying curled into a ball, groaning. Tim yelled, "Enough! Put the gun down, now! You hear me. Now. Put the gun down."

Joe pointed the gun at his face.

"What the hell are you doing, Joe?" screamed Fred.

"Just what you said you'd do, Fred," Joe said quietly. He moved the gun under his chin.

Fred stared, wide-eyed. The first thought that passed through his mind was how was he going to get his carpets cleaned of all this blood? The second thought was *suicide?* Yes, that's probably what he would do if he were in Joe's situation. How could he live with prison for years?

Tim Snyder didn't hesitate. Parker didn't hesitate. The shot banged through the office. Joe's head jerked back, exploded, and he crumpled to the ground. Momentarily, there was silence. Blood dripped down the window. Then McKenna jerked his radio off his belt and called for emergency rescue. "Newman & Brice's office. Fast. The chief's been shot."

The front door opened with a rush, slamming into the chief's shoulder, who was lying on the floor in the foyer, and two more officers with guns drawn charged in, almost stepping on the chief's head. Jenkins was groaning.

Fred walked around the desk to see Joe crumpled in a heap between two chairs, leaking blood. His head leaned on one of chair legs. The gun lay on the floor.

McKenna looked at Fred. Fred looked at McKenna. Fred looked at Snyder.

"What am I going to do except fire when the bastard is going to kill himself? God, for now, save Ireland," explained Tim Snyder.

Fred pursed his lips and slowly shook his head from side to side. Went back to his desk and sat down.

# CHAPTER 47

"Did I call that one, or what, young fellow?" queried Mark Sperry to Fred in Mark's rustic living room. The room had bare wood floors partially covered with several small area rugs. Adorning the mantel, walls, and hanging from the ceiling were guns, photos, antiques, and miscellaneous knick-knacks acquired throughout his world travels. In his running shorts and tank top, Fred drank a glass of well water, dripping sweat on Mark's floor.

"Yep, you sure did. He was the culprit?" He wiped the sweat from his face so it wouldn't drip on the floor.

"Took a while for the information to get out, why was that?"

"I wouldn't talk to the police until I got a release from the executrix of Joe's estate. Last thing I needed at that point was violation of the attorney-client privilege. Once his wife was appointed, she gave me a release, and I sang like a bird."

"What a sad affair," said Mark as he puffed on his cigar. The ash falling on the floor after hitting his pant leg. "Two brothers killed in the same manner by the same man thirty years apart. And, maybe, both deserving it. Only God knows the answer to that one. The final arbiter. Judge EW will get to plead his own case before the big Judge in the sky. Well, I bet you feel a lot better, now that you are off the hot seat."

"Yes I do. Those two days were something. I am amazed at the number of people who avoided me, thought I really did it, and just stayed away from me. Gives me some insight into the human reaction."

"Well, don't judge them too harshly, Fred. You *could* have done it." Mark smiled, puffed once, twice, and then continued. "Your timing was off, and you had a history with EW. Not quite the history Joe had, but a history nonetheless. And you have the capability. Maybe not the desire or the will to do it, but the capability. You've been there before. Not many people in this world have ever taken a life. And those who have will always be suspected of doing it again. So how's the chief doing? Got his right in the belly!" He laughed, blowing a stream of smoke toward Fred, who waved it away.

"Chief will do fine. I think he's out of the hospital already. He was in surgery for several hours. Bullet lodged in his liver, and they had to cut some of it out, but he'll be okay. I think he is going to retire. That will be good for me, for the police department, and for Chardon. In my opinion, of course."

"Of course, of course." Puff, puff. "Well, Fred, you're polluting my carpet. I think you'd better get the hell out of here and run home." Puff, puff.

Fred laughed. "I'm out of here, Mark. Thanks for the drink."

Fred slowly jogged the four and two-tenths miles home along Woodin, Old State, and Pearl Roads.

23181631R10178

Made in the USA
San Bernardino, CA
08 August 2015